GEORGE BARNWELL,

THE CITY APPRENTICE,

OR

LONDON LIFE IN THE LAST CENTURY.

PROLOGUE.

THE TWO WORLDS.

THERE are two worlds.

Each is distinct and different from the other.

One abounds with flowery paths leading to dismal cells and caves of horror.

The other is marked by rugged and toilsome ways which conduct to blissful bowers and charming prospects.

The name of the first world is VICE.

The name of the second world is VIRTUE.

It is for man to choose which of these worlds he will inhabit. There is but one period in his life when the selection can be made.

That period is youth.

The world of Vice, at the first glance, contains

1

much more to allure the eye and enchain the heart. There are no rigid restrictions to interfere with the pursuit of pleasure. Each one is allowed to follow the bent of his own inclinations, even to the commission of crime. The eye is dazzled by the glare of brilliant gems and tempting treasures; the ear is assailed by flattery and the hoarse bacchanalian sounds of revelry; the taste is invited to the participation of luxuries, and may indulge to excess. There is no barrier but satiety—nothing to interfere with enjoyment, but the incapacity longer to enjoy. So passes the first portion of the pilgrimage through this seductive region. But there is one peculiarity in this journey, the traveller cannot retrace his steps. However much he may wish to avoid pursuing the track, he can never return; once having commenced his progress, he must still onward, until his destination is reached. He may see the luxurious groves of dissipation left far behind, and their fresh and verdant hues changed to a pale and sickly yellow, but still he cannot return. He may behold frightful chasms surrounded with untold horrors, waiting to receive him, but still he cannot return. His goal must be reached, and what there awaits him? Terrors innumerable. Despair—destruction—DEATH! There are two ways in which this is accomplished. One is by the avenging angel of the other world, and this is Retribution! The other is by a scorpion that twines itself round the very heartstrings, and eats the vital marrow, till the victim dies in the most loathsome agony. This is the pang of an evil conscience. None who have ever voluntarily passed through this world have escaped one or other of these dreadful dooms. There is one way, however, of procuring an alleviation of these sufferings, and that is, by sincere repentance. Too often, alas! for the benefit of those in this world, the mediator arrives too late.

How different is the world of Virtue! Though the pilgrim may find the journey weary, and the roads tedious and uninviting at first, the prospect, as he proceeds, becomes brighter and more alluring. He finds the air fresh and balmy,—voiced with the songs of a thousand choristers, each eternally hymning the praises of truth and justice. He is rewarded at the termination of his task by future years of uninterrupted happiness. Reproaches and recriminations are never felt; the heart expands into communion with all mankind, and the intellect as it extends is strengthened by the assurance of true felicity. This is Virtue:—to woo is to win. Her smile is light—her frown darkness.

But there is a Fiend ever striving to hurl mortals from the pleasant eminences of virtue, down the awful precipices of vice. To avoid him, you must know the appellation by which he is recognised. Listen

The name of this arch-fiend is TEMPTATION.

But for him the world of vice would be untenanted—avoid him; he is a hideous skeleton sugared over with deceit—avoid him; a fiend of beauty that lures you to the verge of destruction, and then changing to a harpy, terrifies too late—AVOID HIM.

Would you learn in what insidious guise he makes his approach?

Read, and may the moral strike deep into thy heart!

CHAPTER I.

THE DEPARTURE FOR LONDON.

MARIA.—Barnwell! Ah, what of Barnwell?
　　　　Speak!
TUREMAN.—Listen, and you shall hear.
　　　LILLO'S TRAGEDY OF "GEORGE BARNWELL."

Come all ye gentles, now draw near,
　And listen to the tale I tell:
Of Barnwell's history you shall hear,
　And what strange fortunes him befell.

The "True and affecting Ballad of the
　LONDON APPRENTICE." 1735.

" And wilt thou prove constant to me, George?"
" Constant! aye, verily, as the bee is to the flower, the sun to the earth, or the battered coin transfixed by a rusty nail to one of these same merchant's counters that you've heard me speak of."

" And thou wilt not forsake me when you return to London, for one of its fair daughters, that are said to dazzle the eyes of all beholders with their beauty, and make no light comparison with us poor country maids?"

" Never!" replied the other : " trust me, dearest, ere I forget thee I shall forget myself, and all I hold most dear; thine image, wherever I may roam, will still be here;"—and, as the youth addressed these words to his fair companion, he placed one hand with energy on his heart, and with the other pressed the yielding form of her he spoke to nearer to his own.

The charms, indeed, of the maiden thus addressed might have extorted constancy from one more prone to change than he to whom she spoke. There was a softness of expression in her countenance that gave warrant for believing her mind to be as pure as her features were lovely.

Barnwell—for he was the speaker whom we have introduced to the reader—was, at the time of which we write, upon the verge of nineteen, and had the advantage of one year's seniority over his female companion. His person and appearance were rather prepossessing; his figure over than under the middle size; and his features such as betokened considerable abilities on the part of their possessor : but with all this a physiognomist might have detected those lines in the upper portion of the face, said, by those skilled in Lavater's art, to mark the owner's want of firmness.

As if impressed with a sense of the importance of the dialogue, some portion of which we have given above, the lovers walked on for some time in silence, gazing with feelings of admiration akin to awe upon the beauteous prospect that the rising eminence now opened to them. They had been hitherto wending their way through narrow green lanes overhung with branching elm trees, that seemed to curtain out the very light of day, and had now arrived at the summit of a hill, that repaid them with a view that few counties besides Staffordshire could exhibit; whilst, as the setting sun threw its refulgent rays upon the scene, lighting up each spire and turret, and throwing the smaller objects into darker shadow, both the young wanderers felt the influence of the time and season, and yielded to the impressions that the place conveyed.

"Dearest Alice," murmured Barnwell, "thy looks are sadder than they were wont to be, thine eyes are dimmed with tears, and thy steps falter: why this dejection? Are my vows once more thought false, or has some new idea filled thy breast, to make thee seem thus sorrowful?"

"Nay, George," answered the other, "if I appear sadder than my wont, it was to think that on this gorgeous scene of Nature's painting we look, perhaps, for the last time."

"Tush, girl! away with these idle fears: I shall soon return from town, rich and happy, to claim thee as my bride; and then—"

"Ah! would to heaven it might prove so; but I have a foreboding, a presentiment—call it what you will—that from this day we shall ne'er meet again. You smile, and deem my weakness credulous folly; but, trust me, 'tis an omen worth regarding."

"Nay," answered her lover, with a laugh; "if thou lettest thy tongue run on in this fashion, Alice, I shall think that thou hast caught somewhat of the spirit of Dame Hanson here of Lichfield, who sees an augury in every flight of crows, and prophesies the downfall of an empire for every upsetting of the salt-cellar. Come! these October nights feel somewhat chilly; we will descend, —the *last* time! Marry! if 'the fell sergeant Death' were as far off as *that*, we should live a goodly time, I reckon."

Endeavouring to disperse her fears by badinage such as this, Barnwell led his fair companion to the spot at which they had arrived when our narrative commenced. And here crossing into that wild but beautiful region, then known as now by the appellation of Stow Fields, they proceeded towards the church-yard, where the bright green grass, that waved over the tombs that were thickly scattered around them, formed a melancholy contrast, in its verdant freshness, to the remnants of frail humanity that were crumbling into dust beneath.

Singling out one upon which the corroding hand of Time had been apparently less busy than on the rest, Barnwell paused, and pointing to the inscription that appeared below, read as follows:—

SACRED
To the Memory of GEORGE BARNWELL,
Late of this City
Who Died June 25th, 1697,
Aged 70.

"Here, Alice," he at length exclaimed, whilst the tribute of a tear to his parent's memory bedewed his cheek, "do I plight my vows of constancy to thee. On my father's tomb do I swear that I am wholly and only thine; and as he, who rests beneath, while living breathed nought but truth, so,

when dead, may his avenging spirit punish my falsehood with his vengeance, if I prove false to thee!"

The enthusiasm with which this was said may be imagined, but cannot be described. Alice ceased to feel, or at least to express, those doubts that had before environed her; whilst Barnwell, rising from the devotional attitude he had assumed, progressed onwards with his fair companion; and here, leaving them to retrace their steps back again to the city, we shall give some account of the hero of our story.

George Barnwell was born of a good family in Staffordshire. His father, who died, as above stated, some years antecedent to our narrative, gave him the best education that the time and his means afforded, with a view of intending him for the Church; but dying before his wishes could be carried into effect, the widow determined upon sending him to a merchant's establishment in London, where a relative of his, an uncle by his father's side, was already residing. He had been there for some time, when from the high opinion Mr. Thorogood—the merchant just mentioned—entertained of his conduct, and five years of his apprenticeship having already expired, permission had been given him to revisit for a month the place of his birth; and the time having on that day expired, his departure was regarded with much regret, his affectionate disposition, and amiable qualities endearing him to everybody.

One of Barnwell's earliest and most favoured associates was Alice Travers, the only daughter of Colonel Travers, a descendant from one of those high-spirited adherents to Charles, who had in that very city kept the Parliamentary forces at bay during the long and turbulent period of the civil wars. The friendship that in childhood subsisted between them had now ripened into love; and the time was anxiously looked forward to by all parties when a happy union might unite them for ever.

Whilst these events were going on, at her own cottage sat Mrs. Rachel Barnwell, a once handsome and still good-looking woman, of about forty. Around her were gathered a few friends, whose presence had been by her deemed needful upon the occasion.

"Where can George be loitering all this while?" at length exclaimed his mother; "the flying waggon sets off at nine within a moment, and there is but an hour now wanting for it to take its departure."

Two loud knocks here interrupted the speaker.

"Here's George at last!" exclaimed a dozen voices at once, as the owners of each pressed forward to greet the new-comer with a hearty salutation.

"Ah! and Alice too," continued the mother; "now, then, can the delay be accounted for in good sooth."

"Nay, mother, thy jest is somewhat misplaced here: Alice and I did but linger on the brow of yonder hill to take a parting glance at the spires of our old-fashioned city—a scene I shall not see again, perhaps, for some time—when Alice, forsooth, must ascribe some mystic power to it, and make that view our last!"

The clear, blue eyes of Alice became for a moment filled with tears, as she gazed reproachfully upon her lover; but it was only for a moment; the glance that followed restored her previously assumed cheerfulness.

It were but of small advantage to the reader to

describe, in detail, all the minute circumstances attending Barnwell's departure. Let it suffice to say that the time having been chiefly taken up with parting admonitions and remembered oversights, it appeared as if the anxiety of the last few days had been concentrated into the one last moment,

The low, rumbling sound of the waggon was now heard, slowly increasing in loudness as the heavy wheels, rolling down the High-street, approached the cottage

"Farewell, George! May Heaven bless and prosper you in all your undertakings!" exclaimed his mother, as for the hundredth time the affectionate parent, with tears in her eyes, flung her arms round her son's neck, and impressed a dozen kisses on his lips.

"You will write, George, as often as you promised you would!" faltered Alice, as Barnwell was crossing the threshold.

The youth addressed caught her in his arms once more, and imprinted a kiss upon her brow as he made a faint reply.

Barnwell hastily stepped into the lumbering vehicle that was now waiting to receive him, and when, at a little distance, he turned back to take a last lingering look of his native home, he beheld, or fancied he beheld, a handkerchief of smaller size than the rest waved amongst others at the cottage door. "Heaven bless her!" he ejaculated, and in a faltering voice inwardly commended Alice to his mother's protection.

It was a fine clear night ; the moon was at the full, and flung down its pale white radiance o'er the earth with two-fold lustre. The town had by this time been left some miles behind, and the open country was now gained. The world seemed hushed to sleep, and all was quiet, save the creaking of the wheels as they jolted along over some frost-hardened rut, and the harsh jingling of the bells affixed to the head of the fore-horse. Occasionally the stealthy steps of the waggoner were heard, mingled with the suppressed bark of the dogs that accompanied him : but, with the exception of these sounds, there was nought to disturb the reverie into which Barnwell, almost immediately upon his entrance into the vehicle, had fallen. They were now winding round an eminence to the right. Below, appeared to Barnwell his native city wrapped in slumber. The lofty towers of the cathedral stood out in bold relief against the horizon, seeming even at that distance to veil their summits in the clouds. At intervals, a glimmering red light was seen peering from the windows of such of the houses whose inhabitants had not yet retired to rest, whilst beyond, light gossamer clouds flitted athwart the sky, seeming to the eyes of the imaginative like fairy cars wafted by the breath of heaven over the earth, and conveying the disembodied spirits of the departed to their final destination. The closely-matted boughs that now spread across the road entirely shut out the moonlit prospect, and so darkened the way that it was only with difficulty the guide preserved his path in a forward direction ; they soon, however emerged from here to the open heath, where the bleak wind that rushed across its surface threatened every instant to overturn the crazy vehicle in which our adventurer was seated. The rustling of the leaves as a startled hare or rabbit rose in tremor at the sound, and darted across the waste to nestle in some less exposed spot, served only to mark more strongly the loneliness of the road on which they were travelling; and Barnwell, tired of imagining evils that had no real existence, yielded at length his senses to repose, and sank into a feverish and unrefreshing slumber.

CHAPTER II.

THE ARRIVAL.

Waggoner.—How goes the enemy ?
Allspice.————Marry, 'tis nearly five.
    The sun has now been working at his trade
    For full an hour: and yet the sons of earth
    Have not so much as thought of their day's labour.
Waggoner.— What trade's the sun ?
Allspice.—Marry, a carver and gilder!
    For he carves his way first, and gilds it afterwards.

                           OLD PLAY.

WHILST our hero is thus forgetting his cares in sleep, let us turn the reader's attention for a moment to the state of travelling in England at that time. It must be recollected that no other communication existed, at the period we write of from one end of England to the other, than by waggon. The merchant to gather in his accounts ; the lover to unite himself with his mistress ; the soldier to join his regiment ; and the mariner to reach his vessel ; found no other mode of travelling open to them than by throwing themselves upon the tender mercies of a country waggoner, whose clumsy machine was equally well adapted for the carriage of goods and the conveyance of their owners The daring highwaymen by whom London and its high roads were infested at this time, rendered travelling to the capital an expedition of an equally important and dangerous nature. " Flying waggons," as they were termed, set out from Liverpool, then a comparatively obscure town compared with its present state of affluence, with the expectation of never reaching London under ten or eleven days after their departure, at the soonest— an assertion that may perhaps create a smile, when the present " coach travelling to Liverpool in four-and-twenty hours" is taken into consideration. But we must proceed to take charge of our hero's fortunes, from the period when we left him dozing away at the conclusion of the last chapter.

The morning's dawn awoke Barnwell to a sense of his situation. The jolting motion he had endured throughout the night, combined with the confined position in which he had slept, had caused the blood to stagnate within him; and now, taking advantage of the stoppage of the waggon for the purpose of changing horses, he gazed around to look at his fellow-passengers previous to invigorating his cramped frame by a brisk walk up the hill that was before them. The first person that his eyes encountered was a tall, stalwart personage, of the Quaker persuasion, who, with his eyes apparently fixed upon vacancy, and with clasped hands supported by his chest, seemed awaiting what scrutiny Barnwell was pleased to bestow upon his attenuated form. Turning from this corner to the opposite, a strange contrast presented itself in the person of a man attired in a military coat. This was no other than Major Mullins, of the Tamworth Militia, who, having been on the previous night in a most decided state of intoxication, had been taking his rest during the morning with his legs carefully perched upon a large hamper at one end of the waggon, whilst his face at the other was smothered under a heavy weight of straw.

As Barnwell now rose with the intention of pursuing his original determination, of walking a short distance, for the double purpose of giving a stimulus to the circulation of his blood, and relieving the jaded horses of a portion of their burden, he felt his garment plucked forcibly from behind, and, turning round, saw the Quaker endeavouring with all possible speed to follow his example. From the little conversation that passed between them, he learned that his companion was one Aminadab Cotton, a hosier in Cheapside, who had been to Liverpool and Manchester, for the purpose of procuring some winter goods, and that he then had in his possession a vast amount of money, received on his journey from some of his customers: a circumstance that gave rise to several quaintly-expressed fears lest, owing to the then dangerous state of the roads, he should be deprived of the hard-earned profits of his tour.

" Yea," continued the alarmist, " these sturdy rogues care not whom they pilfer, so they obtain a booty. Not longer ago than Thursday week a cousin of mine, a reverend prebendary, was waylaid on the Bath road by two men, who left him not even a Queen Anne's farthing to bless himself withal, or pursue his journey with. Thou must surely have heard, friend, of the exploits of these daring ruffians ?"

" Every one of course must have heard of such deeds as those you speak of," replied Barnwell; " but I have been happily not as yet an eye-witness to any of them. Here," added our hero, " would be a somewhat fitting place for such an exploit as that you have but now related."

" And what wouldst thou do in such an emergency ?" inquired the Quaker.

" Do !" echoed Barnwell; " why, guard what little I have to lose to the death."

" Indeed !" energetically exclaimed the other; " then put thy courage to the test now. Come, your money, or you die !" and suiting the action to the word, the self-styled Quaker plucked from his sable suit a blunderbuss of formidable dimensions, and grasped the astonished youth by the collar, who, astounded by the suddenness of the attack, was incapable of giving the slightest resistance. " Come !" impatiently cried the robber, changing his hitherto peaceable demeanour and whining tone for the bold bearing of a Turpin and the voice of a Stentor; " no parleying—your purse !" Hesitate for one moment, and the next brings with it your destruction !"

" Never !" cried Barnwell, endeavouring to release himself from the tight hold maintained by his opponent; " never will I tamely submit to an outrage like this !"

" Nay, then," thundered the other, " this must decide."

A struggle brief but desperate immediately ensued; but it required little powers of discrimination to prophesy which would be the victor. The slight though muscular form of Barnwell was no match for the powerful grasp of his adversary, and the contest, unequal as it was, would soon have been decided, had not the foot of the robber slipped as they approached a ditch by the road-side, and left him prostrate at Barnwell's feet—and thus entirely at his mercy.

" I spare your life," said Barnwell, seeing that his foe had fully prepared himself for receiving in his head the contents of the blunderbuss that had been wrested from his hand ! " but I will keep your weapon as a remembrance of the contest."

" Well, you are a brave-hearted fellow;" replied the footpad rising, " and you shall find that I am not ungrateful. The time may come when I may be of service to you ; when it does, ask for Jack Meggott, at the Almonry in Westminster, and you will find that he will keep his word. Of what is past, let not a word be said ; although my attack upon you was more in jest than earnest, egad ! it was likely to turn out no child's play. Your hand, young man ; we are now, I trust, friends : be cautious, and be silent." As the last words were uttered, the low-covered top of the waggon was seen rising over the brow of the hill, and as it approached, Meggott waved his hand to Barnwell, and disappeared behind the hedge that skirted the road they were now pursuing.

Our hero, not sorry to be rid of his late companion, now joined the waggoner, who was carefully guiding his team up the declivity, and again took up his station in the vehicle. Slowly and heavily the old waggon pursued its path, now jolting over the stones that marked the High Street of Nottingham, and anon wending its way through oak-sheltered lanes and marshy thoroughfares. The second evening at length began to draw its crimson curtains over the earth, and as the night advanced, the propriety of putting up the waggon was decided on. In the morning, however, they were again in motion, and passing through the beautiful antique town of St. Alban's and stealing a peep occasionally at its noble abbey with its ivy-crowned turrets and mullioned windows, the travellers found themselves by nightfall not far from their destination.

As they travelled onwards, lights could be perceived glimmering afar off, which as they approached, gave warrant that the metropolis was at hand. The " Angel," a low and dirty public-house, standing upon the site of the inn at present known by that name, was at length reached ; and here the journey was said to have terminated. As Barnwell, elated with the pleasure he experienced in finding himself once more in town, was descending from the waggon, and preparing to defray the expenses of the journey, a figure, clad in a long, dark cloak, that effectually preserved its wearer from observation, darted behind him, and uttered his name in a voice that might have belonged for its tone to a tenant of the tomb. Startled at the circumstance, Barnwell hastily turned round ; but before he could trace the figure of the speaker, the mysterious visitor had been enabled by the darkness of the night to elude the vigilance of those around him.

Leaving ample directions with the carrier for the transmission of his luggage, Barnwell alighted from the waggon, and turning down one of the bye streets, proceeded towards the city, leaving Major Mullins anxiously searching for his purse, which Barnwell imagined, and with some truth, that Meggott had ingeniously contrived to convey away with him. Crossing by Shoreditch church, then just erected, and leaving Aldersgate-street to the right, our hero pursued his path in a forward direction for some time, until turning into " the noble square of Finsburie," and by that means getting into Cheapside, he paused before a house, the extent and splendour of which betokened the master to be a merchant of some trade and opulence. Gently raising the knocker, and administering a few successive taps to the street-door, a light appeared soon after through the fan-light above, and the withdrawal of a bolt proved but a prelude to the appearance of a smartly dressed young damsel, who, opening the door in some trepidation, greeted Barnwell most warmly on his return. Preceding him up stairs to his apartment, and revealing to his view a room, the neatness and order of which proved evidently to him that he had been expected, Barnwell betook himself to rest, and, if the reader be curious respecting the nature of his dreams, we can enlighten him, by stating that they formed a curious combination of contrasted images in which waggons, Quakers, footpads, and the slight form of Alice Travers were all blended together into one heterogeneous mass.

The worthy merchant, whose name was singularly corroborative of the goodness of his character, received Barnwell on the following day with every expression of kindness and good feeling, His friend, Trueman, who had long maintained a high position in Mr. Thorogood's office, for his blandness of manner and sincerity of disposition, returned Barnwell's warm pressure of the hand with a cordiality which showed that the only rivalry existing between them was in who should endeavour to be foremost in their employer's service. Clara Thorogood, the merchant's daughter, had long engrossed Trueman's attention, but, fearful that an open avowal of his passion might displease her father, he preferred crushing the feeling altogether, rather than allow it to exist with the disapprobation of her parent. True it was, that if the returned pressure of the hand, and glance of the eye, might be taken as a criterion, the heart of Clara glowed with a love as ardent and as pure as his own; and it was also true that he had not even hinted to him the possibility of such an attachment existing, for, aware that her father had designed her for the bride of a wealthy peer, and knowing that he had little to bring her for a dower besides a fond heart and willing pair of hands, he, with a resolution worthy of a hero, determined to stifle the passion in its birth, ere it had attained the mastery over his reason.

With this view he sedulously avoided all further intercourse than was absolutely necessary, with the object of his adoration; and aware that the shafts of Cupid are as dangerous as those tipped, according to the Indian tradition, with the poison of the rattle-snake, he devoted the whole of his attention to business, and was thus enabled, by his assiduity, to make Barnwell's temporary absence a matter of less moment to his employer than it otherwise would have been.

CHAPTER III.

THE ASTROLOGER.

I know a cunning man who reads the stars,
And tells from them what things will come to pass;
His counsail will we seek in this sore strait.

　　　　　　　Fayre Mayde of Lamby the, 1673.

Here never shines the sun—here nothing breeds,
Except the night-owl and the fatal raven.
And when they showed me this accursed place,
They told me here at dead-time of the night
A thousand fiends, a thousand hissing snakes,
Ten thousand swelling toads and gibbering urchins,
Would make such fearful and confused cries,
That any mortal body hearing them
Would straight fall mad, or else die suddenly.

　　　　　　　Titus Andronicus.

SUCH was the position of affairs when Barnwell returned. Clara he had not seen before, as it was during his visit to Lichfield she had returned to London, from a convent at Paris, where, as was customary at that period, she had been sent for the purpose of completing her education. His first interview with her, however, convinced him that the enthusiastic description he had received from his friend Trueman had not been over-charged. Clara was one of those *sunny* beauties (if we may be allowed what seems to us the only expression capable of conveying our meaning,) whose charms make an impression on the hearts even of those who are least sensible of the power of female attractions. Her long residence in France had imparted to her that grace and freedom of motion which harmonises so exquisitely with the female form; and her features, when either animated by conversation or softened by repose, were equally remarkable for their faultless symmetry and expressive regularity.

"Of a verity," exclaimed Barnwell, the day after his first interview, "thou art a happy fellow, Ned, to monopolise the love of a girl like Clara. Your portraiture was as exact as if you had been a limner by profession."

"Nay, George," answered Trueman, "a truce to your jesting—Clara is no fit subject for me. That I love her, madly love her, I cannot disguise from myself; but, rather than cause her father one pang of uneasiness by my conduct, I would resign her for ever: aye, even though with her departs my happiness for ever."

"Psha!" retorted Barnwell, "what have you to fear in at once declaring yourself? Are not you, in preference to the rest of us, her father's special favourite? If any business of importance has to be transacted, to whom is it entrusted but to Trueman? In short, should our worthy master perchance require in his old age a partner in his profits and his toils, who would be the one selected but my very modest and diffident friend here, Ned Trueman?"

"Aye, but you know not, George," responded the other, "how dearly he prizes—and well he may—his daughter Clara! She is his only child—the sole object he has cherished through life, to be the solace of his declining days. I should indeed be unworthy of the confidence reposed in me were I, by winning the affections of his daughter, to repay with unkindness and treachery the favours I have at his hand received."

"But why not endeavour," inquired Barnwell, "to fathom his intentions upon the point of his daughter's marriage?"

" It would be useless," answered Trueman ; " I know them too well already. The entertainment that takes place here to-morrow evening, and to which all the young peers and wealthy citizens who have honoured our worthy master with their intimacy have been invited, is one given for the purpose of enabling Clara to choose, in accordance with her father's wish, a husband from the list of suitors, who have already proffered her their hand and fortunes."

" And will she so ?" eagerly inquired Barnwell.

" Would to Heaven that I knew," exclaimed the other ; " of Clara's constancy, and open, generous spirit, I entertain not a doubt. The gewgaws of wealth and splendour possess but little interest in her eyes when compared with the hours of wretchedness and misery by which they are often too dearly purchased ; but an anxious wish to obey her father's behest may, alas ! induce her to wed another, and thus blight my hopes of happiness for ever. I have but little faith in the astrologer's art, or I would now seek to dive into futurity, and learn from thence whether she may yet be mine."

" Would you accompany me now, if the means were found ?" asked Barnwell.

" Willingly !"

" Then listen," he continued. " In Lambythe Marsh lives one Fuller, an astrologer, whose fame can surely be no stranger to you. We will go thither this evening ; it is already nearly dusk, and in a few hours he will be accessible, for his avocation is one only to be carried on when the stars are above the horizon. What say you ?"

" I join you with pleasure," cried Trueman. " I have a little commission to execute for Mr. Thorogood in Southwark, which we will take on our road ; and thus will our absence be accounted for, and business executed at the same time."

" 'Tis well !" cried Barnwell : " we will start at once. I have a question or two myself I would gladly have answered, and would not willingly let this opportunity escape ; but I must to the 'Change, to meet our employer : he now expects me there ; and I have tarried somewhat beyond the wonted hour. Wait here, for my return."

Replying in the affirmative, Trueman resumed the task he was engaged on when Barnwell entered, and was soon lost, or seemed so to be, in the arithmetical intricacies that his employment presented, whilst Barnwell, hastily crossing the threshold of the door, was soon blended with the mass of people that, hurrying to and fro, might have been deemed, from their haste, bent upon matters of life and death.

Time flew fast, as time always does when its progress is unmarked, until the hour had at last arrived fixed upon for their visit to the astrologer. Crossing from Cheapside into Friday Street, and so on through Thames Street, described in the *London Guide* of that date as " a most noble street of exceeding width and grandeur, and garnished on each side with handsome mansions," they ultimately reached Queenhithe, at that period a place of some notoriety as a ferry station for the Middlesex shore.

" What, ho ! sculls ahoy !" shouted Barnwell, as he approached the wharf.

" Now, then, sculls to Southwark," echoed a voice in front. " Do you hear Bill ?"

" Aye, aye !" replied the party addressed, rising with a kind of unwieldly motion from the barge, which had hitherto rendered him invisible. " Sculls to Southwark, gentlemen ? Here they are !"

As if to establish the truth of an assertion like this, the waterman proceeded to transfer the implements in question from the bottom of the boat to the water's edge, when, allowing them to rest upon the surface, he proceeded to replenish a short pipe, which he had hitherto held between his lips, and adjusting a capacious pea-jacket about his person, signified to the speakers who had taken their seats in the wherry, that he was prepared to be again in motion. The heavy plunge that succeeded this intimation gave warrant that the warning was not ill-timed. Slowly and heavily at first the boat pursued its path ; but, merging into deeper water, the motion became less vibratory, and the passengers had now time to look around them.

A view from the river after night-fall is a scene always replete with objects of interest ; but it was more especially so at the period of which we write. Then, the successful speculation of Mr. Winsor shed no light upon the streets and alleys of our mighty Babylon, throwing its broad glare of light into the heavens, and making our thoroughfares as light as if illuminated by some nocturnal sun. Then, robberies on the river were as numerous as those on land. Dark forms might have been often seen in boats gliding noiselessly down the Thames, and, without landing, returning with *one passenger less.* Murders were of nightly occurrence ; and as the secrecy with which they were committed prevented the murderer becoming known, and screened him from the hands of justice, crime became bolder by the impunity that attended its commission, and more atrocious by the frequency of its going unpunished.

Whether thoughts similar to these flashed across Barnwell's mind at this period, we can only conjecture ; but the prospect that met his gaze on turning round was certainly not one calculated to dispel the dismal fancies his imagination had created. A thick mist that had for some time overshadowed the river was now beginning to dissolve in rain, and as the dark, black tide that rolled sluggishly on beneath, mirrored only the leaden colour of the heavens on its surface, the scene appeared dismal indeed when contrasted with the cheerful fire and carpeted parlour they had so recently quitted. The red lights that glimmered at intervals on the opposite shore seemed to make the surrounding darkness still more apparent, in the same way as the loud plashing of the sculls falling together into the water, and scattering a thousand ripples on each side, served only to make the intervening silence that prevailed more impressive. Still the boat proceeded onwards. The waterman taking but little interest in the feelings of his passengers, continued to smoke with the most imperturbable gravity until reaching their destination, when without exchanging a word he received his fare, and soon afterwards was seen returning in the same manner to the spot whence they had started.

The place at which they had landed was known at that time by the name of Dyot's Wharf, and stood upon the same spot of ground as that now occupied by the first arch on the Surrey side of Southwark bridge. Quickening his steps up the declivity, and beckoning Barnwell to follow, Trueman chose the path leading to the right, and after traversing numerous courts and alleys, the intricacies of which seemed perfectly familiar to him, they finally emerged through an open gateway into what was then termed the High Street since called the Southwark Bridge Road. Striking now to the right, and continuing for some time in a forward direction along "The Acre," our adventurers at last found themselves before a house, which, propped up by some slanted beams from the opposite side, had been pointed out to them as the residence of the astrologer they were in search of. The door was ajar, in order the more readily to admit persons who, under cover of the night, might wish, without being observed, to consult the reader of the planets; and as Trueman, half repenting his temerity, and yet anxious to proceed, pressed forward to ascend the dilapidated staircase that was before him, he saw, or it might have been he fancied that he saw, the shadows of two persons concealed behind the door, retreating as he entered. Disregarding the earnest admonitions of Barnwell, who exhorted him not to risk his safety by proceeding, Trueman hastily threw the door back with such violence as to shatter into atoms the frail bars that kept it together, and the whole coming lumbering down with no slight force, startled the originator of the disturbance as much as the cause of it, real or imaginary, had done.

A footstep was now heard upon the stairs, and shortly afterwards the faint glimmer of a rushlight was seen, apparently endeavouring to make itself visible over the bannisters.

"Who is there," inquired a feeble voice, "that makes so loud a noise at hours so unseemly?"

"Two who would speak with the learned doctor here!" said Trueman.

The light was withdrawn, and the retreating sound of footsteps heard, as if the interrogator, satisfied with the answer given, had retired for the purpose of consulting with another person above. Shortly, however, the noise of footsteps was again heard, and the tall bony figure of a man leaning over the banister was seen beckoning the visitors upstairs.

Following their gaunt conductor to the summit of the house, Trueman and Barnwell waited outside whilst he intimated to his master the presence of those whom he had conducted to the threshold of his room. Their suspense was of short duration as the door was speedily opened, and the two newcomers ushered into the presence of the astrologer.

The appearance of the room that now received them was one calculated to impress the mind of a stranger with an imposing idea of the learning and extensive qualifications of its owner. Neatly, without being elegantly furnished, its chief attractions consisted in the number of mathematical and astronomical instruments scattered about the apartment. Sextants, quadrants, telescopes and optical instruments of every description, most of them then unknown to the common people, caught the eye at every turn, whilst in the centre, seated before a large table, and intent in the perusal of a ponderous folio printed in black letter, sat Edmund Fuller the astrologer, with the snows of some sixty winters on his head, and with a brow furrowed by wrinkles that seemed the blended consequence of age and study.

Without raising his eyes from the book that he was reading, the old man mildly inquired the purport of their visit, which having been communicated by Trueman, a pause ensued, during which time a breathless silence was preserved by the three present, their conductor having departed almost immediately on their entrance.

"You would learn, young man," at length ex-claimed the astrologer, "what success will attend your endeavours in the court of Cupid? Well! 'tis to me no novel application. Youth are ever prone to dream away their golden days in fruitless searches after happiness, and only differ in the road they take to find her. You have chosen love—the most uncertain path of all. It is an *ignis fatuus* that betrays where it should guide, and is most remote when we believe it nearest. To dally with a woman when fame can be acquired is to grapple with the shade and lose the substance. He who builds his hopes on woman's truth, may compare them to the rainbow's gaudy hues—brilliant but transient—though created by sunny smiles they dissolve in tears."

"But Clara—" interrupted Trueman.

"Is one," continued the other, "whose charms are, by report, well known to me. There are few, indeed, who have not heard of the rich merchant's fair daughter, and many have been the gallants who, ere now, in this very room, have ruffled a brace of swords' points to win her. Nay, start not. You well know that you are not the only suitor for her hand—can it excite then surprise that two should quarrel for a prize like this? Where is your boasted stoicism now? Oh, man, man! how canst thou assume for thy reason the dominion of the world, when a mere look or glance from a pair of bright eyes maddens thy brain with haste or ecstasy!"

"Can thine heart, potent as it is, prognosticate the name of him who shall be Clara's husband?" asked Trueman,

"Aye," continued the seer; "but it must not be named to-night. Here is a packet; open it when thou requirest aid and advice; instructions how to act will be therein contained—but break not the seal till thy necessities command it; then act promptly and speedily. Farewell"

"Stay!" cried Barnwell, seeing that the astrologer was about to order his attendant to show them to the door; "I would have my nativity cast before I leave; here is the hour and minute of my birth; tell me, shall I ever be wealthy or renowned?"

"Thou wilt be both," answered the seer; "but it will be wealth granted but for a moment, and unlawfully acquired—renown lasting through ages, but unhappily conferred. The aspect of Venus and Mercury show that a woman of somewhat questionable character is interested in your career. The trine before me of Jove, Saturn, and Mars, threatens misfortune, evil deeds, nay, perchance, a violent and premature death; whilst the conjunction of Mars and Saturn, in an evil aspect, hint at what I dare not mention. The planets have exercised their malign influence at your birth; pray heaven they do not at your death!"

"Strange man," cried Barnwell; "although I would fain become a sceptic to thy doctrines, yet unfold me one thing further. Will—"

"The planets are not to be trifled with," interrupted the other; "the time has already expired some minutes. Godfrey, the door."

Without returning the salutation given by either at parting, the astrologer once more returned to his study; whilst piloted by the meagre individual who had been styled Godfrey, our adventurers retraced their steps to the entrance which, to their surprise, they discovered to be a different one to that they saw on their arrival, and were still more astonished to find that they had

travelled under-ground nearly as far as Cupar's Gardens, a place of amusement then open, standing on the site of the present Astley's theatre.

"We have mistaken the road," at length remarked Trueman, who, wrapped in thought, had hitherto paid but little attention to the path they were taking; "it is too late to call now upon the Southwark merchant: I shall defer my visit till to-morrow evening, when —— Stay, we are watched!"

"By whom?" inquired Barnwell.

"By those two figures yonder in cloaks—they have dogged our path from Southwark here, and seem intent upon committing some mischief. Are you content to sell your life dearly, if required?"

"Aye, or defend yours at the hazard of my own," replied George.

With this, Trueman, followed by Barnwell, led the way across the street to where the mysterious followers had been last seen. On arriving there, they found, however, that the robbers, if such they were, had eluded their vigilance by escaping up one of those gloomy turnings with which Lambeth at that time abounded: so, desisting from a chace as dangerous as it would have been useless, they turned their steps towards London bridge, crossing which they at last again arrived in Cheapside. And here, leaving them for the present, we shall beg to introduce, in our next chapter, a few new characters to the public, in addition to one who

has already made his appearance. under rather peculiar circumstances, on this the stage of our eventful history.

CHAPTER IV.

THE LONE HOUSE IN LAMBETH MARSH.

Come, fill your glasses ! Let each brim be crowned
With sparkling diadems of pearls and rubies,
Dug from the o'erflowing mines of generous wine,
That, springing from the vast abyss below,
Mount to the top, and prove their value there.
                    BONDUCA. A Tragedy (1714).

IN the parlour of a low public house, situated in the midst of that gloomy and desolate region in which the astrologer resided, might have been seen, on the evening when the events just detailed took place, a motley group of personages collected round a long deal table, covered with sundry half-emptied horn cups and tumblers, the oft-repeated calls for replenishing which afforded tolerable evidence of the bibulous propensities of those present.   At the further end sat one who apparently officiated as chairman; an occupation which in those days, much the same as at present, consisted in knocking a diminutive hammer most vigorously upon the table, and calling out "order" most lustily afterwards.

"Come, my coves," at length exclaimed the chairman, with rather more force than elegance in his appeal, "can't yer stow your chaffing for a while, and let a body speak? If a crib's to be cracked, surely it can be talked about to-morrow. Business is business," continued the speaker, with the air of a man laying down some novel and startling truth; "but remember, pleasure is pleasure also."

"Hang me. if Tom ain't right after all!" muttered one at his side.

"Whether he is or no, your hanging invitation will be accepted one day or other," chimed in a personage in a slouched hat who had hitherto seemed buried in meditation

"What's that Mark the scholar come to life again?" uttered a third; "let's have another song! Mark, what a blessin' 'tis to know readin' and writin' in the way you do."

The party addressed had indeed more reason to think quite the reverse.   Mark Haydon, at the time we introduce him to the reader, was a young man of seven-and-twenty, with a pale, sallow countenance, marked with the effects of dissipation. and a brow prematurely wrinkled by care. Descended from one of the first families in Lincolnshire, he had at an early period of his life come up to town. The money with which he had been most liberally supplied by his father, was now found to be inadequate to defray the nightly expenses of his follies and debaucheries. Afraid to ask for more, and receive it with the reproaches of his father, he forged upon him to an enormous amount. The crime carried with it its own punishment. The intelligence of his son's dishonesty contributed to hasten the old man's death, and Mark Haydon became, soon after, the inmate of a madhouse. On his recovery he plunged still deeper into dissipation to drown the remembrance of his conduct; and thieves, burglars, and women of questionable character, henceforward became his nightly companions. As a last resource he had lived for some time by planning and devising robberies for others to execute, receiving from them a share of the plunder. Homeless and characterless, with a mind vitiated by association, and a body emaciated by disease, the grave seemed almost yawning to receive its prey; but with all this, his spirits failed him not.

"Come, Mark, another song! Let's have one of your own," requested one at the table.

"Anything to drown the damning recollection of the past!" answered Haydon; "here's a song then." And swallowing at one long draught the contents of a cup of brandy that had been placed at his side, he commenced the following in a voice remarkable for the fulness and clearness of the tone:

Come fill up the goblet ! Though sages of old
Brimmed the red wine of Crete in pure goblets of gold,
We'll adopt a new plan, and our cup shall to win
Take its value without from the liquor within.
Ere we leave for a moment the joys that it brings,
Time shall moult every feather from off of his wings ;
And our toast shall be this inclination to sway—
He who drinks till to-morrow drowns care for to-day.

The Emperor sits on his canopied throne,
And commands this or that to be done or undone,
Whilst wrapped in his robes, midst his jewels so rare,
He fancies no mortal with him can compare ;
But we much better know, as we sit round the bowl,
And quaff the bright current that gladdens the soul,
That draughts such as these will to fancy lend wings,
And in one hour more make each one of us kings.

The Lover delights in soft accents and sighs,
And fond homage pays to his mistress's eyes ;
But excuse him we might, if they sparkled as clear,
Or equalled in lustre the brilliancy here.
Then fill up the goblet ; for Time's feathered wings
Should be damped with the source whence forgetfulness
    springs.
And with this for our maxim, all topers we sway—
He who drinks till to-morrow drowns care for the day.

The uproar attendant on the repetition of the last two lines as a chorus had scarcely subsided, when a loud knock was heard at the door, which, being opened, discovered two persons shrouded in cloaks, whose appearance seemed the signal for a general congratulation.

"What! honest Jack Meggott and Allen here?" said the chairman, as the two new-comers, divesting themselves of their outer garments, advanced to the middle of the room: "by the mass, lads, I'm glad to see you. Here, drawer! another stoup of canary for our new visitors; and mind ye draw it good. Why, what brought you here?" he continued, again addressing his conversation to those who had just entered.

"Part pleasure, part profit," replied Meggott, carelessly throwing himself into a chair placed between the last speaker and Mark Haydon: "the country trip turned out flat and unprofitable; and, as the Lancashire air did'nt exactly suit my complaint. I have returned to town. This said complaint being—"

"A crick i' the neck!" suggested Haydon.

A loud laugh followed this sally.

"Aye, lads, laugh away," continued Meggott; "he laughs who wins ; and, for mine own part, I care not to travel off the stones again. For a young man like myself, of talent, industry, and ingenuity, London is the place."

"Why, what new game's a-foot now?" pursued the first speaker. "Is some fair citizen's daughter to be cheated of her heart, or a father of his fortune? neither comes amiss, we know, to gallant Jack Meggott."

The only reply was a somewhat expressive glance, vouchsafed by Meggott in return, as he absorbed the contents of the tumbler placed before him.

The conversation now became more general.

"Did my information stand you in stead?" asked Haydon in an under tone to Meggott; "was it correct?"

"To the letter," rejoined the other; "I and Allen dogged him from the Bridge to the Marsh here; but his visit to Southwark, I overheard him say, would be deferred until to-morrow evening. The stripling that accompanied him is, if I mistake not, no stranger to me, and may be won over to my own purpose ere long. To-morrow will be made the grand attack."

"But why not to-night, when so many opportunities must have presented themselves?" inquired Haydon.

"The bird was not fledged, Mark," answered Meggott: "would you have had me, for the sake of a few paltry crowns, risk the loss of what booty may in four and-twenty hours' time be obtained? We must await his return from the Southwark merchant, and then—"

"Hush!" interrupted Haydon; "our companions may suspect us: if our designs be anticipated, all is lost."

Changing the topic to the one then under discussion by the rest, the speaker above alluded to allowed the conversation to merge into one general channel, which as it would not, in our humble opinion, tend to edify or interest the reader by relating, we pass over in silence, convinced that the crank phrases and slang terms by which it was distinguished would render its perusal a task of less pleasure than difficulty.

The following morning was one of considerable interest to the inhabitants of the merchant's house. Preparations on a scale of no ordinary splendour were being made for the entertainment of the night; and the mansion presented a scene of activity in each of its apartments, rarely to have been observed in the domicile of a London citizen at that period. In her own room was Clara, meditating upon the change in her prospects that a few hours might perchance open to her. Convinced that her father would not oppose her happiness, she yet feared to disclose to him the state of her affections towards Trueman; for, without deeming riches and a title indispensable qualifications in a suitor, he yet had cherished the hope of seeing his daughter united to a peer, not so much for his own aggrandizement as for the honour which he considered the union would confer upon the name of a London merchant. Amongst the many who had sought her hand, none had been more persevering in his attentions than the young and gallant Sir Robert Otway. Possessing, in addition to a handsome exterior, all those pleasing accomplishments calculated to win the heart of woman, his success might have been thought indubitable, and his conquest certain; but this weighed little in the scale of Clara's estimation. Her heart was proof against the attacks of wealth and titles, and her hand was not likely to be bestowed where her affections could not follow; but still, though feeling this, she could not but dread the trial that was reserved for her. To decline, would have been to displease a parent who had ever manifested the most unbounded kindness; to consent, would be to blight her own hopes and happiness for ever. It was a trial of duty against inclination; and as such she felt it.

Can it excite surprise, then, when we say that her meditations were of the sombre cast, and that her spirits sank as the hour approached, when they ought, on the contrary, to have risen?

The conversation that was also at this time taking place between Barnwell and Trueman, proved that Clara was not the only one that dreaded the approaching banquet. The latter, whilst fondly imagining that in duty to his employer he had been successful in stifling the unhappy passion that had usurped dominion over his senses, now felt that his boasted indifference had vanished with the occasion that called it forth; and, as a fire that smoulders in concealment for a time breaks out afterwards with twice its former heat and vigour, so did Trueman's love become more ardent and intense through the endeavours made to crush and suppress it.

"You may think it a foolish fantasy, George, that possesses me," exclaimed Trueman, anxious to divert the current of conversation from its former painful channel; "but I would that we had not visited the astrologer's last night. The packet that he gave me was doubtless only intended to raise my curiosity without gratifying it; but it has cost me much anxiety—I will open it this evening!"

"And repent it ever after," cried Barnwell. "No! if its contents are such as only to be made known upon some particular emergency, breaking the seal now may destroy what benefit you might otherwise derive from its inspection; but if, on the contrary, it is as you suspect—a mere quack doctor's trick to obtain customers—it will not hurt by keeping."

"Well, I believe you are in the right there, George," responded Trueman; "but how to reconcile with his apparent reserve towards me the freedom with which he imparted to you your future history, I know not. By St. Paul's, did I believe, as some teach, that purchased prophecies work their own fulfilment, I should infallibly look upon you, George, as a most hopeful candidate for the honour of wearing the irons of Newgate."

A cloud seemed to pass athwart Barnwell's countenance as he endeavoured to laugh away the force of Trueman's observation.

"Nay;" said Trueman, seeing that his words had made an impression he did not expect upon Barnwell, "it was but a jest, man; I place small faith in these same predictions, and would not willingly take one of them, forsooth. But see! here comes one who will be but little pleased to hear us disputing a point like this in preference to executing his behests: I must complete my calculation here, and then have with you for another argument."

The entrance of Mr. Thorogood prevented a reply.

"The packet from Genoa has this moment arrived, Trueman," said his master, "and has brought with it some most important despatches. John Churchill, Duke of Marlborough, has gained the victory at Schellenberg, and the English funds have risen in proportion since the intelligence has become public. Hasten to the 'Change, and buy up what stock yet remains unsold. In a few days the speculation will become productive. On leaving, you may cross the water into Southwark, and obtain the sum due for the last transfer; when, at your return, I shall be happy to receive yourself and Barnwell as my guests above, to witness, and, I trust, approve my daughter Clara's choice."

The two youths bowed in acknowledgment of the invitation they had received.

"You, Barnwell, can remain here," pursued Mr. Thorogood; "your presence will be necessary; and on your return from Southwark, Trueman, I shall, as I before observed, be proud of your company upstairs. I must myself to the Bank; but shall return, no doubt, the first. Were every merchant blessed with two like you, in whom he could place such confidence as I do, bankruptcies would be no longer heard of, and the term 'merchant's assistant' become identified with incorruptible probity and unimpeachable integrity."

"When that confidence, Sir, is abused by me," exclaimed Barnwell with enthusiasm, "may Heaven itself withdraw all favour from me: no punishment can equal the offence!"

"My sentiments are echoed," added Trueman; "but words are but weak arguments—my actions shall speak for me:" and with this he left the counting-house to execute the commands he had received.

The Royal Exchange then presented much the same appearance as it did previous to the recent fire, which in one memorable night levelled this noble structure with the ground, from which, under a Gresham's magic wand, it had so proudly risen. This, the place "where merchants most do congregate," was then in a state of excitement beyond the power of the pen to describe. The South Sea scheme had not, it is true, entered into the fertile brain of its crafty projector; but a hundred other bubbles of less magnitude, but equally as ruinous to those engaged in them, were in the very height of their career. Amongst these stood out, as the most important, the New Greenland Whale Fishery Company, which, with a capital of twenty thousand pounds, was to have illumined the whole of London at less than one half the cost then incurred. For some months the shares were at an enormous premium; whalers were fitted up and sent out on a voyage to Greenland; but neither the vessels nor the money ever returned to the shareholders: and the ingenious contriver of the scheme, one Abel Colton, an unprincipled adventurer, had the gratification of retiring with the spoil he had acquired to the Hebrides, where he resided for some years afterwards with his adherents in a kind of feudal splendour, and amidst a number of vassals and retainers, after the custom of the old Norman barons, whose manners he appeared anxious to imitate. His death was not the least singular portion of his history: for, having retired to rest one night, after a day's debauch, in a state of intoxication, he arose about midnight under the impression that there was a robber concealed in his apartment. Hastily snatching the sword that was always placed by him at his bedside, he examined each corner of the room in vain for some time, until suddenly turning round, he mistook his own reflection in a looking-glass for a man standing in a threatening attitude with a drawn sword in his hand. Forcibly lunging at his imaginary antagonist, he shivered the glass to atoms with some violence, when a piece flying out struck him on the left side, and, entering his heart, caused him to expire immediately. Other accounts, with greater pretensions to probability, state that there really was one of his servants concealed in the room, who, taking advantage of the intoxicated condition of his master, murdered him for the sake of his ill-gotten gold; be this as it may, however, certain it is that Colton died no natural death;

and many of his descendants who still inhabit the same spot, vouch for the truth of the looking-glass story to this very day.

Schemes as visionary as the above were, as we have before stated, then all the rage. Clothes were sold from off the back, and beds from under the sleeper, in order to enable the buyer to obtain a share in his darling project. The child that could scarcely lisp its father's name talked about making its fortune by speculation, and the old man, bedridden and decrepid, turned his thoughts from heaven to revel again in the imaginary earthly joys that he thought his favorite scheme would afford him. The sick man tottered from his couch; the politician abandoned the affairs of State; the lover forgot for a time his mistress; and the author plied his pen with more than wonted vigour—and for what?—that a fortune might be obtained in one moment that might otherwise have taken years to amass! It was a butterfly that allured them on by its gaudy colours, only to disappoint them in its capture at last—a meteor that stimulated a ball of gold, and was, in reality, a ball of fire which not one who touched returned with unburned fingers; it was, in short, a mania that affected every body, and left few unscathed by its noxious influence.

Amongst those who had speculated largely, but, unlike the rest, invariably with advantage, was Mr. Thorogood. Even now, when others were selling out, he continued to purchase with undiminished success, and, at that moment, retained stock to an amount unequalled by any other merchant in the city. It was for the purpose of purchasing, as the reader already knows, that Trueman was on 'Change; and though, that day, the sellers were numerous enough, the crowd was so great that before his business could be finally transacted, it had grown dark. Turning his attention now to the second mission with which he was entrusted, he bent his steps over London Bridge—then the only one that spanned our noble river—to the High Street of the ancient Borough of Southwark, part of which he had traversed on the previous evening. Calling on the merchant, as desired, and obtaining the sum, no inconsiderable one, that was due to his employer, he set out on his return homeward; but, impressed with a feeling of danger and insecurity, to which his heart had hitherto been a stranger. The road that he had to go was the most lonely and ill lighted of any in the metropolis. Should a robber—psha! what motive could prompt him, and how should he ascertain the nature of his errand? it was wild, visionary—nay absurd—and Trueman laughed in ridicule at the fears his fancy had conjured up. Clara, too, what opinion would she form of him if he gave way to thoughts like these. Clara! ah! it had been as well if he had not thought of her! His imagination wandered: he thought of the merchant's house and the scene of gaiety that it presented. There was the loud laugh of joy and gladness borne on the breeze; strains of music too he heard floating on the air, and wherever the laugh was loudest, and the strain was merriest, there was Clara. Halls blazed with a thousand lights, and joyous groups were seen passing too and fro; light feet bounded from the chalked floor, and the dance drew near its end. A youth of noble mien and stature had chosen for a partner one fair girl whose curls clustered in profusion round her ivory brow, seemed at every moment kissing in wild rapture the snowy pillow on which they lay. Her dancing was remarkable for its sylph-like grace and lightness; a buzz of admiration went round the room—the music ceased—the dance was over—the youth led his fair partner to a seat. He pressed her hand ; she smiled ; he spoke to her father, who with anxious eyes seemed watching the result ; he joined their hands—they kissed with mutual ardour. S'death ! the father was his employer. the fair girl his daughter Clara !

Was that a shadow that flitted past, or was it, like the rest, a delusion of the senses ? That sound was real ! No, it must have been the pattering of the water against the time-worn buttresses of the bridge. How dark it was ; the moon had not yet risen. and the wind that swept by in sudden gusts, had carried away on its wings the lights that had once glimmered through broken lamps before the houses on the bridge - aye houses—for there was then a street suspended in the air, with the broad expanse of heaven above, and a wild gurgling current dashing on below, leaping and exulting on its path, as if in exstacy at the thoughts of the frail forms that it there had hurried into eternity. Here was an opening, too, leading to the parapet—caused by some of the houses being in ruins. There had been a fire ! A fire on that spot ! Red flames had darted into the air, licking the old beams of the wooden tenements with their forked tongues, and consuming, like second Jupiters with their Semeles, whatever they embraced. Crowds had dashed too and fro, with no escape but that the opposing element below afforded, which seemed waiting, like a huge monster, open-mouthed, to swallow what its remorseless assistant in the work of destruction had spared. A fire on *that* spot ! It tore the heart to think of it : mothers clinging to the burning bodies of their children, with the prospect of certain death before them. Two fond hearts straining each other in their arms, as if to part even in death were agony. This was a picture too revolting to contemplate, and Trueman, to change the direction of his thoughts, stepped across the charred planks that bent beneath his weight, and sprang on to a platform that commanded a wide view of the river. It was a fearful scene : all was quiet save the noise of the stream below, as it raised its foam-crested head over the dark, green weed that clung to the mouldering stones of the arch ; and all was dark save the rushlights that, throwing a glare from the windows on the bridge, denoted that in the room to which that window afforded light, some wasted form was gradually approaching its final bourne, or that some sleepless student was bartering his health for learning, and in his struggle for fame forgetting that he must first struggle for bread.

It was a dizzy height to look down from on to the river below, and Trueman was about returning to the road, when he heard footsteps behind him, and turning round beheld, to his astonishment, two swarthy men, who with folded arms and piercing eyes seemed scanning his person with some attention to minuteness and accuracy.

"Oh, it's the youngest we want, sure enough !" cried Meggott, for he was one of the scrutinizers : "upon him, Allen, at once,—get the swag—but mind ! no more violence than necessary."

Immediately upon this Allen threw himself upon Trueman, who, unprepared for any attack, stood quite defenceless and at the mercy of his adversary. Conceiving, however, that some mistake had occurred, he inquired who and what it was they sought ? he being in the most humble circumstances, and, as he had little of his own to gain, so he had little of his own to lose.

"We know that well enough," answered Meggott ; "but we can't stop talking here all night ; yield up quietly the five hundred crowns you received from the merchant in the High Street on account of your master, Mr. Thorogood, or you die ?"——

And suiting the action to the word, Meggott presented a pistol at his head.

"Never ! without a struggle for my life, at least," cried Trueman, snatching at the weapon before him ; but his more wily adversary, anticipating such a movement, suddenly withdrew it. and jerking Trueman to the ground, all further opposition seemed useless.

"Come !" impatiently vociferated Meggott, "I'm sure we've well earned the money, by following you on your track two or three nights. Come ! what does it signify to you ? It an't your own, and so the loss will be your master's, not your's."

"That," answered Trueman, struggling to free himself from the tight hold maintained by the two, " is the reason why I defend it with more anxiety than if it were mine own. What, ho ! watch ! watch !"

" What do you think, my cove," cried Meggott, "that we should not have had you before, if we hadn't been waiting for the watch to go off their beat ? You won't see them again to-night ; and if blabbing is the game you're arter (though I don't wish to be over-harsh with you), I shall just take the liberty of ornamenting your countenance with this bit of a wrapper here."

Untying his own neckerchief, Meggott hastily fastened it over Trueman's mouth, whilst Allen proceeded to rifle his pockets ; but their operations were for a moment suspended by the sound of men and horses on the bridge.

"Damnation !" muttered Meggott ; "we shall be discovered. Come, quick, quick ! the money !"

Thwarting their endeavours as much as possible by his actions (for the covering over his mouth rendered breathing, much less speaking, almost impossible), Trueman with some difficulty decoyed his antagonists on to the platform where he had been standing before they attacked him.

"Hark ! the sounds approach nearer : one moment more lost, and we are ruined," cried Meggott, endeavouring to preserve his footing on the slippery ledge.

It was a fearful thought ; but it appeared the only chance. Trueman gave one glance down into the dark abyss below, and stifling a shudder as he did so, caught his opponent Allen by the throat, and precipitated himself with him from the parapet into the dark, black space beneath him.

"Great Heaven !" exclaimed Meggott, as he concealed himself from the view of those who were now passing, by stepping behind a portion of the ruined building where he stood ; " the grave this night has closed over two desperate churls ; they must by this time be dashed to pieces !"

Had it been low water Meggott would have been right in his conjectures ; but the reverse being the case, the two bodies, after sinking in their immersion about twenty feet beneath the surface, rose to the top almost unhurt, and unbruised. The kerchief, twisted over Trueman's mouth, proved the means of his preservation ; for whilst Allen, almost suffocated by the convulsive grasp of his throat which Trueman maintained, was yet involuntarily swallowing immense quantities of water, Trueman was enabled by breathing through his nostrils to rise with but little inconvenience.

A few guttural sounds from the throat of Allen, told Trueman as plain as language could speak it, that they came from the mouth of a dying man. His clasped, bony fingers strained together till the very blood seemed oozing out at the pores, appeared supplicating Trueman to release his hold. He did so, but it was too late; the blackened face and stiffened form showed that death had done its work, and the morning tide, that washed the sides of the public-house in Lambeth Marsh, brought to the lawless gang their late boon companion, Tom Allen, a stark and livid corpse.

CHAPTER V.

LOVE.

Oh! then, methought what pain it was to drown,
What dreadful noise of water in mine ears,
And sights of ugly death within mine eyes.
                                    SHAKSPERE.

'Twas but a waking dream this love of yours,
Wherein you made your wishes speak, not her's;
In which thy foolish hopes strove to prolong
A wretched being, and in which thy brain
Rock wild conceits into some ripened form.
So children on a sick bed idly play
With health-loved toys, which for a time delay
But do not cure the fit.
            ROWLEY'S LOVE IN IDLENESS. (1609.)

TRUEMAN, on releasing himself from the unhappy man who in the convulsive agonies of death still clung to him with fearful tenacity, struck out from the shore, which, being an expert swimmer, he soon reached with but little difficulty, although in a state of considerable exhaustion. Pausing to ascertain the safety of the money that had tempted his assailants, he discovered that his clothes were saturated with blood, and passing his hand over his brow, found that in the force of his descent he had struck his head against one of the buttresses that, jutting into the river, served to break the stream that rushed through the arches. Imagining, however, that the wound, was one not likely to be serious, Trueman resolved to hasten homewards, and, accordingly, thither bent his steps; but the exertion that he had undergone, and the loss of blood he had suffered, soon began to exercise an influence over him, and before he had threaded the tortuous windings of St. Paul's Chain, he felt his whole frame sink under the combined effects of the injuries it had received. Stanching, however, with his handkerchief the blood that flowed in profusion from the wound, he still hurried on, and finally found himself to his great satisfaction, before the house of Mr. Thorogood.

Lights were blazing from the windows, music enlivened the scene, sedan chairs, and the clumsy one-horse chariots then in fashion, crowded the road, whilst the pathway was occupied by the attendants on these vehicles, who were amusing themselves, during the time they waited for their employers, by carousing with the servants of the adjoining houses. Crossing the road, and elbowing his way through the crowd with what little strength he had remaining, Trueman at last gained the portico of the mansion he had in view, The music ceased—there was a pause—a shadow appeared in dark outline upon the blind, its waist encircled by another's arm; the figure moved—it was Clara; the other was——but Trueman's sight became dim and confused, the street appeared vanishing into air, strange ideas whirled through his brain, and fearful phantoms flitted before his vision. He raised his hand to lift the knocker, but the effort proved too much—he reeled back staggered and fell.

"A murdered man!" burst from a hundred voices at once, as torches gleamed through the air upon the bleeding body of Trueman.

"What ho! watch! watch!"

The crowd increased.

"What is the meaning of this uproar?" inquired the merchant, throwing open the window above.

"There is a youth murdered at your door," replied one of the bystanders; "the assassins have escaped."

"Arouse the watch —let the city constables be called," exclaimed the merchant; "the body may be brought in here until identified." and with that the speaker closed the window and disappeared.

A scene of the most indescribable confusion now took place. Some positively affirmed that they saw the blow struck, and that the assassin was a young gallant in a slouched hat and slashed doublet, who was, they said, no doubt incited to the commission of the rash deed by jealousy of the success of his rival in some love affair; and these added, that immediately afterwards the air became filled with a sulphureous and noisome stench, and on looking round the figure of the gentleman in the slashed doublet was found to have mysteriously disappeared. Others averred that the deed was committed by himself. But whilst opinions as diversified as they were numerous began to be formed on all sides, the unfortunate cause of them was allowed to remain untended and almost uncared for.

The door was now opened, and the helpless body of Trueman conveyed in by Mr. Thorogood's attendants, none of whom, however, in consequence of the clotted gore that covered his countenance, were able to recognise his features as familiar.

"This way!" cried Mr. Thorogood, descending the stairs. "Let the body be taken in the counting-house; you, Clara, remain behind—such scenes fit not a tender maiden's gaze: it is unfortunate that we should have to-night been interrupted, just at that crisis too when your future lot in life was half determined on ; but our duty, Clara, to ourselves and to our Maker demands that the life of a fellow-creature should be cherished as our own."

Reaching, with these words the place were Trueman's inanimate form had been deposited, the worthy merchant sent for a surgeon, and discovering from his heaving breast and warm frame that life was not yet extinct, proceeded to bathe his temples with a liquid composed of two most opposite ingredients, vinegar and honey, both then supposed to be of incalculable value to the professors of the healing art.

The surprise and grief of Mr Thorogood on finding that the person imagined to be dead was Trueman, was beyond all bounds. He upbraided himself with being the cause of his injuries, shed tears of gratitude to Heaven for his providential escape, and learning from the surgeon that tranquility alone was required for his recovery, enforced the most strict regulations on his household to that effect.

Whilst the patient, under such treatment, gradually recovered, let us turn our attention to the other actors in the scene enacted during Trueman's absence in another part of the building.

In the *saloon* of the merchant a gay and brilliant throng was assembled. All that wealth could do, or taste accomplish, was manifested in the nature, and style of the decorations. Gorgeous candelabras, shaded by flowers of every hue, and from every clime, flung lustre on the group beneath. Vases laden with the choicest exotics diffused their perfume over the apartment. and side-tables bent beneath the weight of dishes filled with pyramids of the rarest offerings of Pomona. The walls were decorated with pictures, chiefly selected from the works of the old masters; and from the richly-ornamented ceiling was suspended two dazzling chandeliers, which, combined with the candelabras already mentioned, seemed by the reflective power of their lustre to realise the fabled description of the 'hall of a thousand lights.' In the inner apartments, the same attention to the elegance and costliness of the decorations was to be observed. Tapestry shaded in grateful folds the antiquated beams and grained architecture of some, whilst in others imitated branches of palm and date trees and the tasteful groupings of the most rare and curious plants, contributed to give a spectator the idea of having suddenly entered the precincts of one vast and leafy forest. Strains of the softest music, so artfully contrived as to leave the hearer in doubt as to their earthly origin, proceeded from invisible musicians at every turn, and induced its listeners by different passages to the supper-table, where viands alike attractive to the palate and the eye, invited the guests to partake of the excellent repast with which they had been provided.

Leaning in an evidently studied attitude on a marble pedestal supporting the sculptured figure of Mercury, stood Sir Robert Otway, already mentioned as the most persevering suitor for the hand of Clara. He was still what the world called young and handsome, though aged both in look and demeanour. Chesnut locks fell in graceful carelessness over a brow as yet unwrinkled by care, and his manners were such as to insure him an invitation and a welcome wherever he went. His residence on the continent, where, by the way, he had first seen and admired Clara, furnished him with an abundance of those light themes for conversation so anxiously sought after by those desirous of pleasing the opposite sex; whilst his gay, thoughtless mode of delivering them proved that he was without the usual adjuncts to the household of a married man. We have already said he had no incumbrances—if we had included in the catalogue of those things that he had not a heart, we should have been equally correct. The wily and insidious manner in which he administered the subtle poison that he sought to instil into the mind, rendered his designs less apparent and his victims less guarded than they otherwise would have been. Title, he considered, would do much; but wealth, he thought, would do still more; and with this view he had continued his attentions to Clara, with the end, not of ultimately marrying her himself, but of rendering her incapable of uniting herself with another. It was for this purpose that he had toiled night and day to design and execute his project that he had endeavoured to weave a web round the unsuspecting girl, so intricate and complicated, that its disentanglement would be a task of no ordinary difficulty. Sir Robert Otway, in short, was one—and in our own days we can find

his parallel—who seemed to think that the guilelessness of woman was given to her only that she might be more easily betrayed; and that her charms were bestowed only to impart gratification to her betrayer. There are even now hundreds of titled libertines in the world, who, like Sir Robert Otway, hover around the fairest works of creation, for the sole object of destroying them, and who, with the honey at their lips, carrying in their hearts the sting.

Whether ideas similar to these suggested themselves to Clara, we know not; but each time he approached she shrank almost intuitively from the contamination of his touch. Condemned by the usages of society to be his partner in the dance, she yet loathed while she despised the man to whom she spoke. To have assigned a cause for this involuntary dislike would have taxed her ingenuity too far; but she felt its influence, at the same time that she was perplexed to know why or wherefore. It was not her love for Trueman, evidently; for he—yes, she was quite convinced of that—he was no more to her than a brother—a dear brother, it is true, but still no more. She knew nothing of Sir Robert's character or former life, and therefore it could not have arisen from the impressions her mind had received from the accounts she had heard. It was not his ceaseless importunities,—those she could have endured, or at least been indifferent to. Here, then, ye metaphysicians, arises a question for ye to solve:—By what strange feeling is it in the human breast that, the same moment that love is inspired by one person, hate is by another; and both without any previous knowledge or apparent reason? Is it not a species of human electricity—an illustration of animal magnetism? Clara felt that the riddle could not be solved, and left it, as we must be content to leave it, a mystery.

Barnwell had in the meantime met with one in the assembly of the night whose person and features were not altogether strangers to him. This was no other than our military hero in the waggon, Major Mullins, of the Tamworth Militia, who had obtained an invitation that evening as the friend of one Colonel Allison, himself a companion of Sir Robert Otway. Recognizing immediately his fellow-traveller, the Major took the first opportunity of explaining to Barnwell the cause of his being so powerfully influenced by his devotions to Bacchus on the occasion when they last met. He particularly informed him of the high station he held in his corps, and the very high opinion his corps entertained of him; and how, in consequence of the high opinion and the high station both together, a grand dinner had been given to him on the occasion of his going up to town to present a petition to court, bearing reference to some great and glorious privileges being withheld and disputed that formerly belonged to the ancient and honourable troop composing the Tamworth Militia. How, that upon his health being proposed, there was a death-like silence pervading the room; and how, upon his health being drank, this said silence was made most ample amends for by the general clattering and turmoil that was kept up for at least a quarter of an hour afterwards by the knives, knuckles, and glasses of the ancient and honourable troop composing the Royal Tamworth Militia there and then assembled. How he, kindly communicated to them that *that* was the proudest and happiest moment of his life; and how, that if he left nothing else to his children but a recollection of that evening, they would feel fully satisfied with the same, and renounce all other heir-looms and legacies whatever. Of these and many other things that occurred upon this occasion the Major descanted most voluminously; but when he arrived at that portion of his story involving his personal appearance in the wagon, a mist seemed to envelope the Major's narration that conveyed but a very remote idea of the affair to his auditor; a confused recollection of parting glasses, broken bottles, inverted chairs, and furniture generally, multiplied by two, was alone remaining – the rest was as much forgotten as if the Major's tablet of memory had been well washed in the waters of Lethe, and afterwards hung up on the shores of Oblivion to dry.

" Now," said Mr. Thorogood, taking his daughters arm within his own, and retiring to a less-frequented part of the saloon, " the time has come, Clara, when 'tis fitting you should make choice of him who is to be your future husband. Here are assembled those who would deem the hand of the merchant's daughter a worthy accompaniment to their rank and titles. I have (as you know. Clara) no wish to bias your opinion, but would, as a father, suggest that you should select one whose rank may confer credit upon me, and honour on yourself. I am not now what I was. Daily I find my increasing infirmities remind me that I am approaching my final doom. Ere I am snatched from you for ever, my child, I would see thee happy in the possession of one who would love thee as tenderly as I love thee, and who, when I am gone, would be to thee as a father. Such a one I believe I have found—he is—"

"Here!" cried Sir Robert Otway, who, having surmised the nature of their discourse, conceived his presence was required, and now stepped between them.

" My sentiments," replied Mr. Thorogood, " could not have been more exactly, though they might have been less briefly expressed. It *was* Sir Robert to whom I alluded."

" Then hear me. Clara!' replied the other. " With your father's sanction I now offer you my heart and hand. The ardour of my love waits not for idle dalliance in words. Say, fair maiden, that you consent to be mine, and all I have is at your disposal." The colour rose in Clara's cheek for a moment as she released her hand from the tight grasp with which he held it, but changed soon afterwards to an ashy paleness. She was at last gathering courage to determine a refusal, when at this juncture a disturbance, the cause of which our readers are well aware took place before the merchant's house, and interrupting the conversation, drew Mr. Thorogood to the casement, and prevented her reply.

"Come, Clara!" cried Sir Robert!" I interpret your silence as the proverb gives me leave, and thank you for its courtesy. A kiss, as signet to the bond, and then!"--

" Hold, Sir!" exclaimed Clara. " If you are not already aware of the sentiments I entertain towards you, you shall no longer plead ignorance as your excuse. Had aught else been wanting to furnish me with a pretext for declining the honour you intend me, your unmanly. ungenerous conduct of tonight would have furnished me with an excuse sufficient. Farewell, Sir! and that this may be our last interview is all I wish; all that you ought to desire:" and as this was said Clara left Sir Robert to muse on her departure.

"So! so!" he at length exclaimed; "is it thus my offer is spurned—despised, when all I thought secure. But no matter; what persuasion fails to do *force* may accomplish: here, Allison, a word with you"—and beckoning his companion the two entered into deep and earnest converse, at the conclusion of which they departed together.

The detention of Mr. Thorogood below caused the company to disperse at an earlier period than was originally intended; and the chimes of old Bow church had scarcely sounded the hour of midnight, ere the whole of the merchant's guests had departed. The supper (for in these days the good old citizens of London kept earlier hours than at present,) had taken place at ten; and by that time Major Mullins had given most incontestible evidence of the strength and potency of the merchant's wine. Gradually descending the stairs by clinging to the banisters on the way, and vociferating occasional snatches of the most popular ballads then in vogue, the Major at last succeeded in getting again into Cheapside, where leaving him in the care of one of the faithful guardians of the night, whose watchbox he had taken possession of in mistake for his own lodging, we proceed to relate what farther passed at the house he had just quitted.

No sooner did Clara discover the wounded person to be Trueman. than her feelings experienced a strange and sudden revulsion. Her happiness appeared now to depend entirely on another. If Trueman ceased to exist. all hope, she felt, would depart with him; and feeling this, her anxiety became proportionably great for his recovery. Nightly did she watch the pillow of the invalid with an untiring solicitude that love alone could have prompted and maintained. It was a pleasing sight to see the pure and disinterested girl leaning over the wasted form and pallid features of her lover while he slept, to see if a rosier hue had fallen on his cheek, or if his pulse throbbed slower than before. During the fever which attended his illness, Trueman's mind wandered frequently to the past, and the dark form of the astrologer seemed ever foremost amongst the objects that flitted athwart his vision. Clara thus frequently heard her own name breathed with an ardour that of itself denoted the spirit with which it was uttered; and as she reasoned with herself the propriety of disclosing her sentiments to Trueman, she felt that her love for him was somewhat stronger than that she would have borne for a brother.

In the meantime Barnwell had the unlimited command of his master's business. Large sums of money daily passed through his hands; and from the assiduity and attention that he exhibited in the punctual discharge of his duties he gained a character for industry and integrity that reflected on him the highest credit. His name became known to all, as that of one willing to sacrifice his own interests to those of his master, and anxious to further every object calculated to benefit his employer's trade. For services such as these Mr. Thorogood was not ungrateful. He forgave Barnwell the remaining years of his apprenticeship, and at once placed him on the same footing as Trueman. promising, in addition, that when age and infirmities compelled him to retire, he should leave the business to be entirely divided amongst them. Barnwell, thus stimulated, was more than ever desirous of attending with assiduity to his duties. He toiled early and late, and supplied the vacancy

DELAMOTTE Sc

occasioned by Trueman's sence with additional exertions on his own part.

Nor was Mr. Thorogood unmindful of what Trueman had suffered on his behalf. On hearing the adventures of the night detailed, he thanked him warmly for the defence he had made, and insisted upon his retaining the five hundred crowns he had so gallantly preserved, as a slight compensation for the bodily injuries he had in consequence received. Relating also, as soon as the state of Trueman's health permitted, the result of his sudden appearance on that evening, together with its

being the means of interrupting Sir Robert Otway's declaration, Mr. Thorogood remarked, that the day of his daughter's marriage would be the one that terminated his connection with business, for on that day he intended, he said, to retire from the turmoil and anxieties of a merchant's life into some obscure village, where he might pass the remainder of his days in calmness and contentment. Thus smoothly did affairs progress at the merchant's house; but a glance at what was occurring elsewhere will show that the same aspect was not presented at Lichfield, to which place, with the cele rity of a theatrical scene-shifter, we now change the scene.

For some time after Barnwell's departure, Alice Travers directed her steps each day towards the eminence which they were together ascending at the commencement of our opening chapter. Impelled thereto, perhaps, by wishing the scene to revive, when revisited, a portion of the sensations that attended their former interviews, she had yet another motive which induced her to choose that path in preference to the rest; it was the path that led to the spot where Barnwell had sworn to her eternal constancy; and it was here, near the tomb by which Barnwell had hallowed his vow, that she would pause and again peruse those letters from him which she had received. One evening, while thus engaged in reading his last fond epistle, she fancied she heard a rustling of the branches that, waved by the passing breeze, sent forth a lonely and mournful sound. Startled by the circumstance she immediately rose, and retraced her steps; not, however, without hearing, or imagining, the sound of approaching footsteps behind her. Reaching at last her peaceable abode, situated in the suburbs, on the southern side of the city, she entered with a feeling of dread and timidity, which she could neither account for nor repress. Closely barring and fastening the latches of the door, she threw herself on her couch, feeling, in the literal and painful sense of the word, that she was indeed alone. Her situation was certainly one by no means to be envied. She was in a large and roomy mansion, detached from all adjoining houses by a spacious garden, which separated it from the high road, and which, overshadowed by tall and thickly planted elms, imparted a still more secluded and desolate appearance to the house. Her father had been some days on a visit to Stafford, whither he had journeyed, for the purpose of deciding his legal right to some landed property to which he was by inheritance entitled. The male servant he had taken with him, and the other, a female, had that night been sent for by her mother, who was represented to be on her death-bed. The sole inmate of the mansion was therefore Alice. Night advanced, and she closed the shutters, fancying as she did so, however, that grim faces peered out, as if to watch her movements, from the foliage that encircled the casement. Lights were placed upon the table, and the fire (for the weather was such as to render the presence of one necessary), sent up its cheerful blaze and reddening glare, as if in contrast with the dreary look of all things else. Alice listened for some time; but nothing save the monotonous ticking of the clock, and the occasional crackling of the faggots on the fire, occurred to interrupt her meditations. A strange feeling of dread and loneliness crept over her. Even a dog or a bird would have been company. A chillness, too, would suddenly extend itself through her frame, and force her to involuntarily shudder at what she felt. Taking up a volume of her favourite poet, she abandoned herself to reading, determined to wait until her attendant returned. An hour passed, she knew it was no more, for she had counted every vibration of the pendulum, but it seemed to her like ten. The fire, too, wooed her to repose; and laying down her book upon the table, she sank, for a time, into a soft and gentle slumber. Dreams wild and visionary, in which figures of the most frightful and fantastic forms danced before her, soon, however, disturbed her

rest. She awoke, it was suddenly, and in the midst of her sleep. Some sound must have roused her. The candle flaring in its socket, and the fire existing only in a few expiring embers at the bottom of the grate, showed that it was long past midnight. The room appeared darker and more dismal than before. Strange faces seemed to be looking down upon her: and the old time-worn portraits which hung upon the walls seemed frowning more fearfully than ever. It was a time to make others more prone to boast of bravery than a poor weak and defenceless girl, tremble at the fancies their imaginations would conjure up. Hark! There was a sound of footsteps on the stairs. It approached! They would surely not murder her. They! Yes; many persons were at hand. It was evident, by the clamour that they made, detection was not feared. The neighbours could not be roused. If an alarm was given, there was no one to heed it. Alice felt that her fears were not altogether visionary; and as she examined the door, to learn what protection it might afford her in the hour of need, to her mingled surprise and horror she discovered that the bolts had been withdrawn, and the lock destroyed. There was no time to pause; so placing against the door what moveable articles of furniture she could find to serve as a barrier to their progress, she opened the window, to afford, if occasion should require it, a chance of escape. One moment more, and a loud crash proclaimed that the door was forced. Alice hurriedly sprung upon a chair, and in another instant would have cleared with a sudden bound the distance between the window and the earth, had she not been withheld by a powerful grasp from behind. Shrieking with affright, the startled maiden, pale and trembling, confronted her pursuers. They were four, arrayed in robes of camlet, and with their visages concealed in masks. Disregarding her inquiries to know for what purpose she had been disturbed, and why the outrage had been committed, the ruffians stifled her cries for mercy and assistance, as they hurried her from the apartment, by fastening a handkerchief round her mouth, and dragged, rather than conducted her, into the open air. Her energies here failed to support her, and she fainted; but this circumstance weighed but little in the minds of her companions, as they continued to force her onwards. On recovering, she found herself in a carriage, borne along at a rapid rate, over a rugged and uneven ground, but in what direction she was travelling, she saw nothing to afford her the slightest idea. Both doors were firmly closed; and through the windows nought could be discerned but fields skirting the road on either side, and illumined by a few twinkling stars, that diffused an uncertain light over the broad expanse of sky that bounded the horizon. For what purpose she was designed, Alice knew not; no word had escaped their lips to serve her as a clue. She had wronged no one wittingly, and if she had, revenge would have been exercised in a different manner, To what cause, then, could she assign her present abduction? Why was her hitherto quiet and happy home violated, her rest disturbed, and herself forcibly carried off she knew not whither, and guessed not wherefore? Her father too! what would his feelings be to learn his child had mysteriously disappeared, and no trace left of her? She now felt the full force of her misfortune, and her grief vented itself in a burst of scalding tears. This seemed to afford her some relief; and regaining her presence of mind, which for a time she had lost, Alice hastily examined the interior of the vehicle, to see if perchance a stray paper might have been left there calculated to unravel the mystery. Her search, however, proved unsuccessful; and she was about yielding herself despondingly to her fate, when something glittering in the straw beneath attracted her attention. Stooping to pick it up, Alice found that it was a poignard of rare and curious workmanship, on the hilt of which was a cipher, with initials, but so elaborately interwoven, that the letters could not be deciphered. A suspicion that some fearful deed had either been committed or intended, flashed across her brain, and she determined to adopt instant measures for her escape. Dashing the blade through the window, the broken glass fell in fragments on the road, and aroused by its sound the driver leaned over from the roof to ascertain the safety of his prisoner; being satisfied of which he continued to drive on until, pausing at a low public-house by the road side, he drew up the vehicle, and descending from the box entered the house before them. Alice now hoped that fortune had favoured her designs, and passing her hand through the aperture she had made in the window, endeavoured to detach the fastening of the door. It remained, however, immoveable, being acted upon evidently by a spring, the position of which was unknown to her. The cold air that now fanned her fevered brow, gave token that the grey light of morning was making its appearance in the East; but no passing traveller crossed her path to enable her to raise a cry for rescue. Whilst meditating on her unhappy situation, the door of of the ale-house opened, and the driver who had before entered the house, now returned in company with another. Taking a key from his girdle, and unfastening the coach-door, he hurried Alice into the small sanded parlour of the hostel in question, and leaving her there to muse upon her unexpected situation, retired with his companion, apparently for the purpose of consulting with some one in the room above. Alice was not long kept in suspense: returning footsteps were immediately heard, and soon after, one whose dress and demeanour bespoke his superiority over the rest, entered the apartment where Alice was seated, and addressing her in a tone of commiseration, told her that she had nothing to fear unless she continued a resistance that might be fatal to her, and must be useless. It was in vain that Alice supplicated him to explain for what purpose she had been brought there, and why she had been thus at an unseasonable hour torn from her home to journey at such times and in such company, but upon these points he remained obstinately silent, and evaded each question with the tact of one experienced in such matters. Offering her some refreshment, of which however she declined partaking, the stranger remained for some time in deep and earnest converse with the two who had conducted her thither, and who, with their faces still concealed by masks, were awaiting with some anxiety the orders he might give them.

Returning to the carriage, Alice was constrained to enter by the menacing gestures of her unwelcome companions, but not without making many ineffectual endeavours for her escape. A sign from the stranger, however, checked the unnecessary violence used, and reminded Alice of what he had before cautioned her.

" To what place now?" inquired the driver.
" LONDON!" responded the other, in a deep-toned voice; and the wheels of the vehicle were once more in rapid motion.

CHAPTER VI.

THE HERO AND—THE HEROINE.

Mystery? why life itself's a mystery.
Love is a mystery and its causes too:
The universe at best is but a world
Shrouded in mystery from its birth to end;
And death, the greatest mystery of all,
But ends our mysteries by creating one
No mortal yet could fathom.
            The Alchemist, 1610.

There is no life on earth but being in love;
There is no study, no delight, no business,
No intercourse of sense or soul,
But what is love! I was the laziest creature,
The most unprofitable sign of nothing,
The veriest drone, and slept away my life
Beyond a dormouse, till I was in love;
And now I can outwake the nightingale,
Outwatch an usurer, aye, and outwalk him too;
Stalk like a ghost that haunts about a treasure:
And keep awake o'nights; and all through love.

            Woman's a Devil, 1670.

Whilst Trueman was gradually recovering from the effects of his accident, our hero was at the same time raising himself in the estimation of his employer, and no business of any importance was transacted, or new speculation made, without Mr. Thorogood making Barnwell the principal agent in the affair. Under these circumstances his importance to the merchant increased daily, and his presence in the counting-house was deemed indispensible to the welfare and interests of his employer. Trueman, who had observed with much pleasure the assiduity displayed by Barnwell, each day gave him repeated proofs of his friendship; and urged by a recollection of Alice and the delight with which she would view the progress he was making in London, our hero allowed no opportunity to pass, calculated to rivet the links that bound him to his employer, and on every occasion showed by his zeal and undivided attention that he was worthy of the high regard and esteem bestowed upon him by the worthy merchant.

It was at this time, when a fair prospect of future fame and fortune seemed opening to Barnwell, that an incident occurred, which however trifling in itself, became afterwards the means of overthrowing all the long-cherished hopes in which he had so fondly indulged, and changing the current of his destiny to one fraught with the most gloomy fears and anticipations.

Returning one afternoon from an important mission with which he had been entrusted, Barnwell was hastening down the thoroughfare that led to his master's residence, when his attention was arrested by a crowd that collected round the door of a house in the Poultry, increased in tumult and numbers every moment. Curiosity inducing him to cross over, he ascertained that the disturbance arose from a robbery that had taken place on that spot, the perpetrator of which had however escaped undiscovered. A watch had been most skilfully abstracted from the pocket of a passenger, and suspicion had of course rested upon those that were the nearest to him when the theft was committed. A female attired in the most costly apparel that the age afforded her, and of surpassing beauty, had, by chance, been present at the time, and against her, as she was unattended, insinuations were thrown out that, if true, reflected greatly upon her character. Feeling this, and with an earnest wish to rescue her from the aspersions that were now beginning to assume a serious aspect, Barnwell made his way into the midst of the crowd and inquired upon what ground the accusation had been made. Finding that it rested upon a very slight foundation, Barnwell expostulated with them upon the unjust course they had pursued, and as he was well known to most of those who were present, his arguments were suffered to prevail, and the concourse dispersed. Thanking our hero in accents that fell upon his ear like strains of the sweetest music, the fair adventurer gratefully accepted the offer of his arm, and willingly accorded to him the permission he requested to conduct her to a place of safety.

As they progressed onwards, Barnwell took an additional interest in her discourse. From her he learned that she had been but recently in England, and that an unhappy difference with her family, arising from an unwillingness to unite herself with one that they had chosen as her husband, had determined her to throw herself entirely upon her own resources. She told him of the gay and festive scenes she had witnessed in France, of the delights that sunny clime afforded, of the enchantment arising from a continental residence, and finally dwelt with some rapture upon her fortunate encounter with one to whom, she said, she should feel eternally indebted. As this was uttered, her eyes beamed almost unconsciously upon Barnwell; but finding his, gazing with ardour in return, she turned them half-confused towards the earth, a crimson blush at the same time mantling her cheek, and imparting to her the only grace that might have been previously deemed wanting.

"She is *very* pretty," thought Barnwell to himself; "would that I had never seen her or had never loved."

"You seem sad," remarked his companion.

"It was to think," he replied, "that my happiness in your society must so soon terminate. The nature of my avocation will soon require my presence elsewhere, and then I must leave you."

"Nay," responded the other, "then ought I to despond too, did I not know and feel that the pain of parting with an object belov——, esteemed I mean, only heightens the pleasure of again meeting."

"May I then hope that the separation gives pain to both?"

"That," she answered, "is more than I said; yet I know not why maidenish coyness and reserve should repress the finest emotions of the human heart; I do feel a reluctance at parting, which, however reluctant I may be to confess, I cannot disguise from myself. The avowal may be deemed abrupt and unusual, but I am used to express the sentiments I feel, not those the usages of the world would teach me. I am a desolate being, without one object on which to lavish my regard, and therefore the more likely to become impressed with a warm feeling of gratitude to my preserver. You, on, the contrary, are perhaps happy in the possession of all you wish for and desire; loving and beloved in return, life has strewn roses in your path, where it has only planted thorns in mine."

"Fair maiden," exclaimed Barnwell, as he observed a tear trickle down the blushing cheek of his fair companion; "you judge me falsely, if you think my happiness unclouded. It is dimmed by a remembrance of what you must suffer. If my humble endeavours could tend to ameliorate your woes or soothe your sorrows, know that for the future you may command them as your own."

"Thanks, generous youth; your own heart will reward you for the kindness you have shown me. But of all hope my mind is now bereft, and I resign myself to that unhappy destiny which Providence has decreed should be mine."

"But why this despondency? Fortune, that today witholds her favours, may shower them upon us to-morrow. You do wrong to chide the fickle goddess, when she may have a bounteous gift in store we know not of."

"Her greatest boon," responded the other, "has been already bestowed. It was given at the time she caused you to cross my path. I thank you—from my heart I thank you—for the interest you have evinced on my behalf, and the recollection of it will gild my future days with joys I dreamed not of;—but see," she cried, pointing to a range of buildings then bounding the south side of Lincoln's-Inn-Fields, "I have reached my destination, and the moment has arrived when we must separate. Farewell."

"At least," urged Barnwell, "you will not leave me without saying when we may again meet."

"I cannot—*dare* not," was the reply. "I must begone whilst yet I have the power."

"But I implore you not to leave me in this suspense," continued Barnwell. "I now indeed feel that you have interested me, and I would fain know more. If I am entitled to ask a favour in return for what you have been pleased to call my kindness, let it be by naming the time and place for a future interview. Grant, I beseech you, this my sole request."

"Since you will have it so, and reck not the consequences, so let it be; for the appointment, let this time and place suffice, in three days' time."

"Three days! why, 'tis a century by Cupid's calendar;—to-morrow."

"Well then, to-morrow, if such be your wish. You will be punctual?"

"To the moment," exclaimed Barnwell, and impressing a fervent kiss upon her hand he allowed her to depart, but not before, however, she had promised to be herself there punctual at the time and place appointed. Barnwell watched her receding figure as she left him, until it finally disappeared behind some of the houses in Portugal Row, when lost in a maze of conjectures he turned back and proceeded homeward. That night was a tedious and anxious one to Barnwell. He felt that he was fairly enamoured of the fair stranger he had seen, and that his affections had that day taken another course. Her beauty it was that perhaps had made an impression at the first; but her winning looks and attractive graces, had contirued to ensnare his unsophisticated heart more securely than aught else. His love for Alice dwindled into a mere attachment, when placed by him in comparison, and he looked forward with an anxious heart to the hour when he would again meet the object that had so suddenly and effectually engrossed his affections.

Sir Robert Otway was in the interim deeply engaged in concerting and arranging schemes for punishing what he styled Clara's obstinacy; and day after day he formed and discarded plans and resolutions, the sole tendency of which would have been to have inflicted some vast and irremediable injury upon the innocent and uᴇsuspecting girl. On the very afternoon when the events just narrated took place, Sir Robert Otway was busily occupied in sipping his chocolate at White's Coffee House, in St James's Street, when he was aroused from his meditations by a voice which he at once recognised to be familiar to him. Raising his eyes, they fell upon the figure of Colonel Allison, who, to judge from his appearance, had that moment returned from some distant journey.

"Ah, Allison!" exclaimed the baronet, "I rejoice to see thee back at last. I was beginning to quake for thy safety, man. Where, in the name of Satan and his followers, hast thou been so long?"

"On no one's errand but your own, Sir Robert," responded Allison; "the prey was difficult to find, still more to secure; all however goes now as you would wish, and our enterprise has been completely successful."

"Fortune I thank thee! But we will talk of this anon. Waiter! two pints of wine here. But who, i'faith, is that strange animal out yonder, twisting his hat into triangles that Euclid himself never dreamed of;" enquired Sir Robert.

"Oh! our friend the Tamworth Major; he accosted me as I entered, and wants sadly to speak to you before the other visitors, that he may appear a person of consequence; I humour him as I would a child, for despite his eccentricities his services may be useful."

"Oh! let him come by all means," cried Sir Robert, as the Major looked inquiringly at the speakers. "I pledge you, Mr. Mullins, with all my heart."

"*Major* Mullins, if you please, Sir Robert," suggested that individual, insinuating himself at the same time into a seat:—"Major Mullins of the honourable and ancient company composing the royal troop of the Tamworth Militia, and at present—"

"A companion of the renowned baronet Sir Robert Otway," interrupted Allison, dreading the prolixity of his friend's discourse.

"The same," continued the Major, "which to be is an honour that I have long aspired to; Sir Robert, I have the supreme felicity of drinking to your health and happiness."

"Your acquaintance seems somewhat overcome by his new-found honours," whispered the Baronet to his friend, on the Major filling the emptied chocolate cup in mistake for the wine glass, and quaffing its contents without noticing the impropriety.

"One glass more, and it will suffice to ensure his insensibility," returned the other; "by that means we shall be enabled to give him the slip, and arrange our plans for—"

"Come, I'll give you a toast," muttered the Major, heedless of what was being said beside him: "here's to the merchant's fair daughter Clara."

"Ha!" cried Sir Robert, "does he suspect? Psha! it was but chance. Well, here's Clara the merchant's, daughter for whom, by the way, I shrewdly conjecture, Major, you have a sneaking kindness."

"Who? I! Oh? upon the honour of an officer of the Tamworth Militia, I deny the charge, Sir Robert; if the fair maiden is unhappily the victim of a misplaced attachment, and I am the unfortunate cause, why I regret it, and can say no more; but, to my thinking, the young clerk there, Trueman, was more favourably spoken of by her than I deemed necessary."

"'Sdeath! did I think so, his life should pay the forfeit of his temerity," exclaimed Sir Robert, his eyes flashing fire with rage.

"I fear I have angered the baronet," observed the major to Allison, whilst he vainly endeavoured to preserve his equilibrium.

"It will be over in a moment," replied the other, seeing that his opposite companion had relapsed into a fit of meditation: "I have frequently seen him thus: it is an infirmity of temper to which we are all more or less subject, and with him it tarries but for the moment."

"Allison!" at length exclaimed Sir Robert, "I would fain a word with you. This military churl is now nearly unconscious of what is passing, and we can speak without fear of observation. The merchant's daughter must be mine by to-morrow night—nay, *shall* be so, if my instructions are obeyed."

"On that you may rely; but how is it to be achieved? I see no way to accomplish your object, save by violence."

"Are rope-ladders and dark lanterns entirely out of fashion?"

"Nay, if that's your mode, the task is easier than I deemed; but how to plant the one or use the other?"

"Listen! At the back of the merchant's house is a square quadrangle, to which access may be obtained by climing over a wall in the next street. Once there, the rest is safe. Clara's room may be entered, and herself conveyed to my mansion in Mary-la-bonne Fields."

"'Tis a daring and hazardous project."

"And therefore," cried Sir Robert, "the more fit to be undertaken. Were it otherwise, I would spurn it as beneath me. This sleepy pig-headed major ———"

Three snores from that individual showed that he appropriated the compliment.

"——— may be of some assistance to us. We will attempt it to morrow; the waning moon now shows herself but little, and the darkness of the night will prove our best safeguard. Midnight to-morrow shall be the signal for our enterprize. In the meantime let us drink to its success."

And with that the two present filled and drained their glasses, as an accompaniment to the toast.

"Come, Allison," cried his companion, as soon as the above had been disposed of, "we must depart, or we shall be too late to join the party I spoke about. A pool at basset, or quadrille, may enable us to pass the evening away with some profit and pleasure, and the time bids us depart. Let us leave this sottish major to the enjoyment of his slumber; and now for a narration of your last country exploit."

Quitting the coffe-house, they turned into Pall Mall, Allison beguiling the way with an account of the last expedition in which he had been engaged for the baronet, and which, as it might be considered somewhat premature to introduce here, we reserve for a future opportunity. Reaching at length one of the most notorious of the Pandemoniums then in existence, standing upon the ground now occupied by a well-known club-house in that locality, they passed through the green-baize folding-doors into an elegantly fitted up apartment, where, leaving them, engrossed by the mysteries of the Faro-table, we return to Cheapside, in order to furnish the reader with the circumstances attending Barnwell's recent adventure.

The hour at length arrived, when the appointment was fixed upon to take place, and with the moment Barnwell made his appearance on the spot where the fair being who had haunted his visions on the previous night was also expected to appear. He was not long kept in suspense; a light tripping step soon announced her presence; and it was with no slight sensation of pleasure that he beheld her once again at his side, with beauty, if that were possible, increased by the interval that had elapsed. The conversation that ensued between them need not be detailed; let our readers, from their own experience, imagine the glances exchanged and the fond words uttered on the occasion, and they will form a tolerably fair estimate of what really took place. Barnwell now learned, that, from adverse circumstances and a failure of other resources, she had been driven to the stage, as a means of subsistence, and that she was then engaged at the Duke's Theatre, in Portugal-row, where she had to perform that evening. Accepting the proffered offer of an introduction behind the scenes, Barnwell conducted her to what would now be called the stage-door, then termed the Players' Passage, usually filled at that period by an assemblage of the most celebrated wits and bloods of the day. This theatre, which was built upon the site of ground now occupied by the extensive premises belonging to the well known firm of Spode and Copeland, was at the time of which we write, almost the only fashionable place of amusement in the metropolis. Divided only into boxes and pit, for the comparatively modern introduction of a gallery was here unknown, the theatre nightly presented a scene of much attraction, to which the bright galaxy of beauty which adorned its circles contributed in no small degree to aid. Its noble portico, rebuilt after its destruction by fire in 1700, with redoubled splendour, by an architect named Crafford, to whom many of the most elegant structures in that portion of the metropolis owe their erection, was supported by four pillars, in the Corinthian style of architecture, and was composed of a kind of granite, which imparted an air, of massive solidity to the whole, that rendered it at a first view, highly impressive. Supported by a pedestal, on the summit stood the statue of Shakspere, with the motto, "He was not for an age, but for all time;" its original destination having been intended to be the hall at the entrance, but removed from thence to make way for a bust of the Duke of Marlborough, upon whose patronage, and that of the court, the theatre chiefly depended.

Early as it was in the evening when Barnwell arrived, visitors had already began to assemble; for the performances then commenced and terminated at a much earlier period than at present; and vehicles rattled over the pavement in dozens, laden with the choicest beauties of the realm. Following his fair conductress, Barnwell at length found himself in the green-room, where he beheld himself surrounded by a motley assemblage of actors and authors, whose persons, though of course not familiar to him, impressed him with a high regard for the importance of their station.

"He you now see turning over the leaves of a manuscript play," said his guide, "is Mr. Betterton, the manager and tragedian; at his side stand Doggett and Lloyd, the two comedians, whose services he would be loth to dispense with, inasmuch as they are the favourites here. The one leaning upon the mantel-piece yonder," she continued, pointing to a young man with a pair of full expressive eyes, is Mr. Gay, who wrote the prologue for our new tragedy produced last night—the play, is his that the manager is now reading, and you may see by his anxious glances how desirous he seems to obtain his good opinion. The two who have just entered are Vanbrugh and Congreve the comic writers; the latter is the author of the play now to be performed. The one in the sailor's dress is Mr. Powell, of some little notoriety for his duelling propensities and talents as a singer; whilst the person he is speaking to, rejoices in the appellation of the poet-player—having dabbled in both arts without doing much in either; Cave Underhill is, however, no bad companion, for one willing to hear the good things that come out of his mouth, and willing to pay for the good things that go into it."

Continuing her observations upon the company in the same light playful strain, she was about describing to Barnwell the nature of her own employment, when her attention was diverted by a tap with a fan upon her shoulder, and a voice exclaiming,

"Why, Nell, who, in the name of Fortune, have you here that so engrosses your time, that you can spare none for dressing? The bell has already rung twice, and you open the second act!"

"What, Kitty Wilton, my tragedy-heroine!" replied the party addressed: allow me to commend to your protection my brother, who for the first time makes his appearance upon any stage here to-night?"

Barnwell was about explaining the allusion, when a look from his companion deterred him.

"Then, my dear Eleanor Merton," responded the other, "your *brother*—ahem!—shall be well disposed of, I promise you; but away with you to the tiring room, for our friends in the front grow somewhat impatient, and in a few moments the curtain will rise—you have no time to lose."

"Then now to test the efficacy of my toilette!" said Eleanor, as she requested Barnwell to wait her re-appearance at the wing, and hastening down a passage that conducted to the rooms she was in quest of, she left the merchant's apprentice to ponder on the strange scenes to which he had been admitted as a witness.

The motley nature of the dresses, and the effect produced by the characteristic costumes worn by the performers, struck our hero with considerable surprise, from their strange variety and novelty. The din of voices, the noises produced by the arrangement of the scenes, and the numbers that passed to and fro, almost bewildered him with the singular impressions they conveyed, and threw him into a state of astonishment from which he was only aroused by a sudden pressure of his arm; which causing him to turn round, he beheld a female whom he had no recollection of seeing before.

"What, Barnwell, don't you know me in my player's guise?" asked Eleanor—for it was her—

"who would have thought a few minutes would have made such a difference in you?"

"Nay!" cried Barnwell, "that question should have been mine: the difference is in yourself, not me; but wherefore this dress? and why this new disguise? for such I must style it, though it may heighten your former attractions rather than conceal them."

"All in good time shall be explained," replied the actress: "stand on one side whilst the comedy is being represented, and I will tell you all; but where is Kitty Wilton, in whose company I left you when I went to dress?"

"She left me to join that dashing cavalier there," answered Barnwell."

"Sir Henry Vernon!" she replied: "it is as I suspected. The treacherous girl shall repent this interference!"

Without giving Barnwell time to ask her to explain her words, Eleanor Merton left him to perform her duties on the stage, and was soon afterwards lost in the whirl of ideas consequent upon the part she enacted. Barnwell heard the round of applause that greeted her appearance upon the stage, and wondered within himself why, with rank and fortune at her command, Eleanor should have chosen him in preference to the rest; but glad as he was she had done so, his own self-love—of which no breast is entirely destitute—supplied him with an answer to his question. He believed her to be open, generous, and confiding, he *knew* her to be lovely; and her conversation now sparkling with smart touches of humour, and anon delighting him with its poetic fervour, so enchained his affections and won his heart, that the infatuated youth deemed hours minutes that were spent in her company, and minutes hours when she was away from his side. It would be out of place here to enter into a long account, however interesting it might be to some, of the performances of that evening; but a glance at the principal features it presented, falls naturally into the current of our tale.

It has been already said that the comedy was Congreve's: it was his "*Love for Love*," then just produced. The breadth of the incidents, and the indelicacy of the repartees, so far from making the actress or hearers blush for their grossness, served only to increase their merriment, and it was with some feelings of pain and regret, that Barnwell thus saw the rules of decorum violated, and his own somewhat strict sense of morality shocked. The age was then, perhaps, no more vicious than at present, but the habits of society were more lax, and its habits of decorum less stringent than now. A *double entendre* of rather more than doubtful tendency, would often save a piece in those times from condemnation, and it is a notorious fact, that one farce was played at this theatre upwards of fifty successive nights, solely on account of an incident being introduced which we cannot do more than merely refer to. But this is a digression.

Around the proscenium, tapestry was skilfully suspended in graceful folds, so arranged as to impart a neat appearance to the house without destroying the passage of a sound. From the roof above the stage, three massive gilt chandeliers were hung—the only mode of imparting light to the scenes then adopted; and at the sides were arranged the few musicians who composed the orchestra—consisting of two violins, a flute, and a kettle-drum

When the performances had terminated, Eleanor bade Barnwell farewell, stating that her residence was too near to impose upon his kindness further, and hoping that he had been amused by what he had witnessed, made preparations for her departure. Replying in the affirmative, and wishing her good night, he left the theatre, musing on his way homewards, on what the sequel of his adventures might be, and how long a time would elapse before they again met.

Soon after Barnewell's departure, the actress, whose appellation the reader is already aware of, took her departure also in a sedan that was awaiting her arrival in the passage below. The audience had by degrees effected an egress through the narrow portal once more into the open air, and the stage that had before presented a bright and dazzling scene, was now involved in almost Egyptian darkness. The loud laugh, and ribald jest, that forced its way from the green-room, however, showed that the building was not entirely deserted; and the mingled sound of voices that, echoing against the opposite wall, returned in confused syllables to the hearer—for there was *one* patient listener at the door, and caused her ever and anon to suppress a rising exclamation of impatience at the delay, or to chide the speakers for having tarried longer than their wont.

At length the door was opened, and the whole party rushed out.

"Now, my Bart'lemy droll concocter," cried the foremost, addressing himself to a sedate middle-aged man behind: "you Elkanah Settle, the city Laureate, I mean—give us not the slip to-night, as you value your existence. Thou hast a knavish trick, man, of slipping out of a supper party at times, which is most ungentlemanly, and exceedingly unpoetical; is it not my roystering ballad-grinder, Tom D'Urfey," he continued, accompanying the interrogation with a hearty salutation on the shoulder.

"Certainly Mr. Congreve," chimed in the one spoken to. "'Tis old Bacchus that wreathes with the laurel—the vine. Give me him for *my* muse and take back t'other nine."

"A poet like D'Urfy, that quotes his own verses," said a voice at his elbow, "is wise, for he is the only person that can do it with ease or pleasure."

"There snarled surly Dennis the critic," cried another; "a plague o' thy tongue, man; it will one of these days raise thee an enemy who will not cease till he has vanquished thee on thine own ground."

"It will not be Mr. Southern, then," continued the satirist; "since in each of his tragedies he has always taken other people's ground, and originality of idea is thus out of the question."

"No more delay," exclaimed a third, "I prithee: my wishes are at the Rainbow already."

"Well said," continued the first speaker; "thou art in the right, my young traveller to Parnassus, by name and nature still *Gay*; let us on, and, perhaps, you will now impart to us the continuation of your hints and maxims for walking the streets of London, as we can illustrate your precepts by our practice. Have a care, Mrs. Bracegirdle, and Mrs. Barry," continued Congreve, saluting two actresses who were at that moment quitting their dressing-rooms; "a petticoat would be in somewhat dangerous company here! Where is Sir Harry Vernon—is he not with us?"

The question was left unanswered; for the fair

listener already mentioned, had whispered tidings in Sir Harry's ear, as he left the green-room with the others, that had caused him to make his escape from his companions with no time for ceremony. A hurried kiss, hasty glance, and a "farewell, my dear Kitty Wilton," was all that passed between them.

As the rest of the company now quitted the theatre, a song was trolled that roused the drowsy watchmen from their slumbers, and contrasted strangely with the preceding tranquility of the street. Singling out the harmonist from the crowd, they found the noise proceeded from a tall good-looking personage, who, with a friend of his linked arm in arm, were proceeding in the same direction as the others. Saluting Farquhar, for he it was, with a hearty welcome, and bestowing a patronising glance of recognition on his young friend Colley Cibber, Congreve communicated his intention of repairing to their old place of rendezvous, whither the two others gladly consented to accompany him.

On reaching the Rainbow Tavern, in Fleet Street, the jovial assemblage maintained a "nimble exercise of wit" amongst each other, that, aided by the excellence of the liquors, contrived to keep them there until day-break. The charms of Congreve's conversation was indeed said to have been so great, as to induce Henrietta, Duchess of Marlborough, to console herself for the loss of his company when he died, by having an automaton, or statue of ivory, formed as large as life, and made exactly to resemble him, which being brought every day to table with a wine-glass placed in the hands of the figure, was caused by means of mechanism to bow to her, and nod in approbation of what was said. If to him, then, we add that around the festive board were gathered Vanbrugh, the poet-architect; Tom D'Urfey, the lyrist and song writer; Southern, the author of *Oronooko*; Settle, the city Laureate; and George Farquhar, whose *Beaux Stratagem* was then in the height of its career at Drury Lane, we shall find a knot of choice spirits collected, whose nightly orgies here savoured more of Feasts of Apollo than Festivals in honour of the jolly god. But these were not all. Here, when the current number of the *Spectator* had been dashed off, came Steele and Addison, to unbend themselves after the cares of literature, with Colley Cibber, then gaining more notoriety as a young statuary than as a dramatic poet; Aaron Hill, Dennis, Gay, and a host of others who revolved like satellites around the larger stars, partaking of their brilliancy, and reflecting it on others. With such companions as these, we say, it is not to be wondered at that night was merged into morning; and when they at last sallied into Fleet Street, St. Dunstan's clock was chiming seven, and the sun was beaming brightly down upon them with all the freshness of a fine spring morning.

CHAPTER VII.

BARNWELL'S FIRST STEP IN CRIME.

Say is this being one that's called a man?
Has he a heart to feel as others feel,
And human senses fashioned like the rest:
Or is a demon from some all-wise aim,
Allowed to walk the earth in human shape,
And torture mankind in their own resemblance?

Massinger's Fatal Dowry.

'Tis an old house: the crazy hinges creak
With being unused, and not a rafter throws
Its streaching arms athwart the cobwebbed roof,
But its imbedded in the rust of time.
Could these but speak they'd tell a tale would
  make
The youthful blood to curdle in each vein,
And freeze the lazy current in their sire's—
But happily this is spared.

The Alchymist.

THE morning following Barnwell's visit to the theatre Trueman, instead of his usual light-hearted gaiety and cheerfulness, made his appearance in the counting-house with a sad countenance and heavy heart. A circumstance like this failed not to make an impression upon Barnwell, who, to do him justice, took a lively interest in the welfare of his friend, and he accordingly embraced the first opportunity of their being alone to inquire the reason of this alteration in his spirits. His question was at first met by an evasive reply; but upon being further pressed, he acknowledged that his reason for so feeling had a deeper source than he was readily inclined to confess.

" I have been, George," he replied, "dreaming all night about this same astrologer, whose mysterious packet has so long engrossed my waking thoughts, and have at last come to the determination of opening it, at all hazards. A time can never be more appropriate than the present, when Mr. Thorogood has declared he will no longer defer his daughter's nuptials."

"But has Clara consented to become Sir Robert Otway's bride?" inquired Barnwell.

" She at least expresses her willingness to accede to her father's wishes," answered Trueman; "and those tended to recommend him as her husband. I would willingly surrender my happiness, if I thought it would secure her's, but I fear that her future fate is now irrevocably fixed."

" But this said packet?"

" Is here." continued Trueman, removing it from his vest, and breaking the seal: "I shall now learn what information the astrologer has it in his power to afford."

" 'Tis of a somewhat singular nature, even in the wrapper that enfolds it," remarked Barnwell.

" And its contents bear out your observation, George," rejoined the other, hurriedly running his eyes over the paper: "the words and import are alike mysterious, and seem to imply some danger of which I am as yet ignorant. Listen!" and he read as follows:"

" *Young man beware! The Hawk is ready to prey upon the Dove and waits but the opportunity to make her his victim. The bow is already strung— the arrow is about to fly, and will soon wing its way to one whose heart is already penetrated by a shaft from Cupid's Quiver. Let that be the only one whose wound she may have to dread. Be prudent and be cautious!*"

"That last injunction, methinks, is somewhat unnecessary, considering what precedes it," said Trueman, after a pause: the danger is moreover concealed, and I know not from what quarter to apprehend it may come."

"It evidently refers to Clara," suggested Barnwell; "she is in peril, and must be warned of what threatens her."

"But its import gives me not warrant to excite alarm in one whose feelings at this moment require more to be calmed by consolation, than disturbed by fears that may after all turn out visionary. Would that I knew how to act—how to decide!"

Here Mr. Thorogood entering interrupted the conversation, and the rest of the day passed off without any particular occurrence worthy of narration.

Night at length dropping its sable mantle over the earth, brought rest and tranquillity to the world at large, and lent its soothing balm alike to all. In the merchant's house the inmates had long since betaken themselves to sleep, and a profound silence reigned undisturbed throughout the mansion. Clara, however, was far from partaking of its halcyon influence, and for some time continue to bedew her pillow with tears that fell, despite her anxious efforts to suppress them. While thus indulging in grief at the unhappy situation in which she was placed, a gentle tap at the door aroused her from her reverie, and inquiring who was there, was surprised to hear the voice of Trueman.

"It is I, Clara!" he said, "sleep not to-night—some impending danger hangs over us—I will be at hand should you require aid, to succour and attend thee: once more, farewell!" and with his returning footsteps showed that any further question had not been waited for.

"This is something strange," thought Clara to herself. "Danger! whom have I injured—with whom have I an enmity? Ah! Sir Robert Otway, he might—pshaw!—he would not dare to molest me here."

Whether her apprehensions were correct or not, we shall presently see.

The chimes of St. Paul's had scarcely sounded the hour of two, ere a couple of figures emerged from behind a wall that had hitherto concealed them, and, as if anxious to escape observation, proceeded stealthily towards Cheapside. Turning down a bye-street that opened to them on the right, they at last paused before a house where a chaise was already standing, apparently awaiting their arrival, when applying the butt-end of his riding-whip to the door, the foremost one dealt a succession of vigorous blows to the surface of the crazy portal, that made the old house ring again. This operation was not long without producing a satisfactory effect upon its inhabitants, for a very few minutes had elapsed ere a light appeared in the room above. Soon afterwards the light was no longer seen, but a slow, creaking noise betrayed the fact of the window being half-raised to allow the inquirer an opportunity of reconnoitring the party below. The scrutiny, however, seemed perfectly satisfactory, for the window was immediately closed, and a pair of clumsy feet, encased in slip-shod boots, were heard hastily making their way down stairs. A lumbering sound, indicative of the withdrawal of bolts, followed, and at last the battered door, creaking on its hinges as if in complaint of the treatment it had received, opened wide enough to allow the visitors to enter.

"This vay, Sir Robert, this vay!" said a voice evidently belonging to one of the Jewish persuasions: "you are later, much later, than I expected, and I had nearly gone to bed; but, however, better late than never, Sir Robert, you know, and therefore I am delighted to see you here at last. This vay—I left the candle up-stairs, so that my letting you in might not be noticed; but, by the beard of my fathers! you seem determined by your knocking to let all Cheapside know of your arrival here."

Alternately muttering to himself, and speaking to those he conducted, the Jew led the way along a narrow passage, that admitted only one to pass at a time, towards a winding stair-case, the frail condition of which threatened every moment to cause it to give way with those who ascended it. Stopping short before a door on the first landing, their guide selected a rusty key from a bunch at his side, and opening the door invited them to wait there till he returned with a light. The two strangers had, however, scarcely entered, ere the door closed with a loud noise, leaving them in darkness and in a state of uncertainty as to the probability of the other's return.

"He surely would not play us false!" muttered Sir Robert from between his clenched teeth: "I liked not at first his reluctance to admit us; and his behaviour now, notwithstanding his seeming deference, savours of anything but anxiety to assist us in our project, I half repent my determination, Allison, of choosing him as an accessary; my life, however, shall be dearly bought!"

And with that the speaker drew his glittering weapon from the scabbard, and as a gleam of light shone through the crevice of the door, his companion saw him trying the temper of his steel on the boards beneath him.

"Your fears are unfounded, Sir Robert," answered his associate. "Hark! the old curmudgeon is returning, and if I may judge from one of my senses at least, brings with him a light. He is here!"

The words had scarcely escaped his lips, before the Israelite had entered, bearing in his hand a taper, which he placed upon a three-legged oaken table in the middle of the room.

"The door, I find, has become closed during my absence," said that individual: "a strong draught from the open window has caused it, I suppose, to shut," he continued, finding his observation fall unregarded on the ears of his auditors; "the wind moans mournfully through every casement, and is apt to play some strange pranks in an old house like this. I one night fancied that—"

"Hush! what sound was that?"

"It is but the sound of which I was speaking; but of that anon. You are determined, it seems, to carry off this girl of whom you last night spoke."

"At the hazard of my life!" answered Sir Robert; "is all in readiness for our departure?"

"Everything; but supposing the old man should awake—you would surely not attempt to —"

"Murder him, I suppose you were going to add?"

"Aye! Consider my conscience, and the suspicion that would attach to the house."

And as the old man said this the candle that had previously burned dimly, threw a sudden glare of light around on the lonely chamber, lighting up the features of the three who were present, and revealing in their countenances all that exulting passion, avarice, and cupidity could represent.

"Well! here is more gold to satisfy the cravings of what thou callest conscience," said the baronet, throwing down a weighty purse upon the table, which the Jew eagerly snatched up; "and now show us the wall that you say once gained makes the entrance to the merchant's house so easy."

"Then follow me this way. Here is a lantern to aid you in your progress; the ladder you will find there already—it was conveyed thither at my request."

At that moment the candle was extinguished, and a loud noise as if of falling furniture succeeded.

"'Sdeath!" exclaimed the baronet; "there is some one concealed in the room."

"'Tis but the wind," added the Jew: "the lantern will give us sufficient light to direct our footsteps. Come! be cautious and be silent."

Opening a door, till then unnoticed by his companion, he conducted them through a lobby at the back to another flight of stairs, descending which they arrived in the yard below surrounded on each side by a wall of some height as well as thickness. Here they passed; while throwing the rope-ladder over the wall and causing it to catch upon the opposite side, the Jew informed them that all was ready, and promising to await their return, assisted the two others in their ascent. This was accomplished with but little difficulty, and dropping gently on the opposite side, Sir Robert and his companion alighted, when they proceeded to reconnoitre the premises. A dark mantle seemed to obscure the heavens, and even the very stars that had previously studded the sky, like so many diamonds set in jet, now withdrew their lustre, as if in horror of the act about to be committed. Here and there a stunted tree shorn of its leaves, and blackened by the smoke of the metropolis, bent to and fro in the passing breeze and startled them by its sound; but the general aspect of the place was as still and gloomy as a burglar could have possibly desired for the performance of his nightly depredations. A light had glimmered for awhile in Clara's window as they descended, but had now become extinguished, and dreading no further interruption, they commenced putting their design into execution. Hastily examining the brick-work surface of the house, Allison found a staple, driven in doubtless for the purpose of allowing Clara to suspend her favourite canary-bird (then deemed a rarity) in safety without, and with the assistace of Sir Robert he succeeded in attaching thereto the ladder which was to enable them to ascend. The latter now began to try the fastening of the cords, and finding them capable of bearing his weight, reached at length the window above him. With the aid of a chisel he was soon enabled to detach the slight fastening of the casement, and in one moment more found himself in the presence of the sleeping maiden. Overcome by fatigue and watchfulness, Clara had been surprised into slumber as she sat: and now with her head pillowed by an arm as white and spotless as her own reputation, she seemed the very personation of the sculptor's idea of sleeping innocence. The light that had before excited some alarm in his mind, he now discovered to have proceeded from a flickering rushlight, that having become exhausted, had burned down into its socket and extinguished itself. Suppressing an emotion of pity, that had for a moment taken possession of his breast, as Clara moved her lips, apparently in the performance of some sleeping orison, he raised her motionless body in his arms and bore her towards the window. The action, however, caused her to awake, and shrieking with terror she strove to extricate herself from the arms of her captor. Still he relinquished not his prize. The window was gained—passed—and his foot was on the last step of the ladder, when a blow from behind felled him almost senseless to the earth. Raising himself to encounter his assailant, he found to his surprise that he had disappeared, and Clara with him. No time was now to be lost; it was plain that the family had become alarmed; so hastening with some difficulty over the wall, he again returned to the Jew's house, where he found Allison and the Jew anxiously awaiting his presence once more among them. Listening to a few brief words of explanation from the former, who stated that hearing footsteps below he had endeavoured to make him aware of his danger, and had been accordingly obliged to retrace his steps—Sir Robert heaped curses on the heads of his companions, and throwing himself carelessly on the seat of the carriage that had still remained at the door, he was driven with great speed through Watling street and over the stones of St. Paul's Churchyard, as if the rapidity with which he travelled bore him from the contemplation of a deed which he regretted only on account of its ill success.

Trueman, to whom Clara (as the reader perhaps already imagines) was indebted for her deliverance, immediately on carrying her to a place of safety in her own house, returned to ascertain whether the blow he had inflicted, had, as he anticipated, proved fatal. Finding no trace left of Sir Robert's escape; for the wily spoiler had removed the ladder with him; he was at a loss to proceed, and spent some time in a fruitless search about the premises, but, as may be expected, with but little chance of success. Despairing at last of obtaining any clue to the name of this midnight intruder, a glittering trinket on the ground met his eyes as he was returning, and on an inspection (as minute as the darkness of the night would allow him) he discovered it to be a ring, and one apparently of some value, as a large diamond that sparkled in the centre of it would seem to testify. Secreting the jewel in his vest he returned to the house, and impressing upon Clara the necessity of preserving the adventure of the night as a secret from her father—at least for a time—he betook himself to repose, convinced that a second attempt upon Clara's liberty was not likely to be made that night.

The following morning Mr. Thorogood dispatched Barnwell to his banker's, that he might there obtain a sum of money necessary to meet certain engagements which the merchant had entered into; and desiring Barnwell afterwards to call upon a stock-broker in Sweeting's Alley, Cornhill, with whom he was to leave the greater portion, Mr. Thorogood complimented him upon the satisfaction he felt when entrusting him with a commission like this, and recommending him to pursue the path he had chosen, bowed kindly to Trueman, who had just entered, and retired to his own apartment.

"Mr. Thorogood seems well pleased with the attention you have lately shown, George," remarked Trueman; "whither art thou going now, my fellow labourer in the field of figures, eh?"

"Merely to the banker's," responded Barnwell; "but where, Ned, did you get that diamond ring from?" he continued, as the valuable in question dropped from Trueman's vest: "you are somewhat careless with it too, considering that the brilliant is one of larger size than ordinary."

"'Tis a mere trifle," rejoined the other, attempting to replace it without being seen; "a bauble that has but little intrinsic value in itself, and one not worth keeping, were it not for the associations connected with it."

"As I suspected," rejoined Barnwell: "the gift of some fair damsel, whose bright eyes outshine in your estimation the jewel that she bestowed. A marvellously handsome pledge of her love in truth; would that I were similarly honoured with such a trifle!"

"Nay, George! I would not have you labour under a false impression either. See! it is but a ring after all, and one that carries with it, I can assure you, no such pleasing reminiscences."

"By Heaven, I should know that ring! It is one I have seen worn by Sir Robert Otway."

"Sir Robert Otway!" exclaimed Trueman, in some astonishment.

"'Tis his, I would stake my life," added Barnwell; "how came it in your possession?"

"You shall soon know all, George," replied Trueman; "at present it involves a secret that I must not—*dare* not betray."

And as these words were uttered, Trueman, meditating upon what he had heard, became apparently unaware of Barnwell's presence.

"Well, Ned! since there seems to be some mystery hanging over it, I will not attempt to penetrate the veil: but I must be gone to execute Mr. Thorogood's commands; so for the present, my hero of the diamond ring, farewell; when I return I shall expect to hear of some strange adventure having taken place in connexion with it?" and so saying, Barnwell waved his hand and departed.

"Strange enough," mused Trueman, as he replied to the gesture of his friend. "Sir Robert, then, as I anticipated, is the depredator who would have robbed my employer of a treasure his baronetcy could not replace. And this is the favoured suitor for whose hand Mr. Thorogood would yield the happiness of his daughter! Well! well! if all were known there might be some little difference in his intentions; and it *shall* be known when the time serves!"

The entrance of a merchant who had some transactions with Mr. Thorogood here interrupted Trueman's meditations.

Barnwell having proceeded to the banker's, obtained the money, and set out for the stockbroker's, who, when he called, was absent from home, and learning that some time would elapse before his return, Barnwell turned his steps in the direction of Lincoln's Inn, in the hopes of seeing the fair form and features of her who had a short time previously made such an impression on his heart.

On arriving before the portico of the Duke's Theatre, and scanning with his eye the bills, that were then, as now, pasted on its portals, he found, to his great delight, that the name of Eleanor Merton was among those displayed in the flaring capitals, announcing the chief actors and actresses in the entertainments of the evening. Crossing through the adjoining court to the Players' Passage, which his former visit had rendered familiar to him, Barnwell inquired if Miss Merton had yet arrived, and receiving an answer in the negative, waited anxiously for her appearance. The pause of a sedan chair before the door, and the withdrawal of the curtains inside soon revealed to him the object of his search: and as Eleanor, on seeing him, welcomed him with the most unbounded acknowledgments of his kindness in calling for her, he did not regret the time he had thus occupied. Entranced by her manner, Barnwell entirely forgot his appointment with the broker in the evening, and to Eleanor's wish that he should go in front to see her perform, great was the pleasure with which he responded "Yes."

The performance that night served only to inflame his passion the more. His eyes wandered not from her even for a second, and he treasured up in his imagination every look, word, or glance, that he fancied was directed towards, or had the most remote allusion to him. At length the curtain fell, and with eager hopes and a beating heart, Barnwell hastened, as he was instructed, back to the stage-door, where he found her already waiting for him.

The conversation that passed between them, on leaving the theatre, turned chiefly upon the pangs each had endured during the other's absence, and so rapidly had the moments flown that it was not until he was aroused to a sense of his situation, by an exclamation of his companion, that Barnwell perceived he was in Shoreditch.

"Here," she said, pointing to a neatly-built edifice, that stood back from the street, "is my destination for the night. This is the unromantic abode of her whom you have but now styled your soul's idol. Can you still offer her up sacrifices, when you find that she possesses no woodbined bowers in which to receive them."

"My sacrifice," answered Barnwell, "is one that, I trust, needs not such adventitious aid to render it acceptable; my sacrifice is a fond heart, worthy, I hope, of the shrine at which I would bestow it."

"But the humble roof that claims me for its tenant is one scarcely good enough to receive you even as a visitor," continued Eleanor, "much less to be the temple where oblations like these are to be made."

"The true Aladdin's lamp, is the presiding goddess that transforms the poorest and most humble cot to a palace worthy of a monarch; in you, Eleanor, we have an instance of what I have stated. In your presence all things feel your influence, and become, like you, things to be loved, cherished, and admired."

"Nay, Mr. Barnwell," rejoined Eleanor, "the compliment is as unmerited on my part as it is enthusiastically delivered upon yours. If I hear another such, you must give me leave to doubt your experience in these affairs of the heart. A beau educated in Paris, and fresh from a morning's ramble in the Mall, could not have extemporized so well. The academy of compliments must number you henceforth amongst the most prominent of its contributors."

"Such words from such lips," replied Barnwell, "seem to convert even flattery into a virtue; but I must rouse myself from these visions of happiness and return to cold reality. The neighbouring bell reminds me of the lateness of the hour; Eleanor, farewell."

"Stay! your kindness deserves at my hands treatment better, at all events, than this: I have to request your company within. After your walk, a slight refreshment may not prove unacceptable."

"Eleanor, how gladly I would accept your invitation did my duties permit me the pang with which I tear myself from your side will testify; but my return has been expected long ere this, and I dare not remain."

"Farewell, then," cried Eleanor; "I now to my grief measure the full extent of your love. Little did I think, after all your protestations that your hours were spent more happily in the society of another—that for her your more sincere endearments were reserved; that for her you relinquished the company of one, whose heart had so guilelessly become yours, and whose prayers were alone breathed for your welfare; whose love——but this is idle converse," continued the speaker, dashing away a tear from her eyelids as she spoke. "I am addressing one who feels not the pang he inflicts, whose hand reels not with the stroke his own axe hath made; one whose thoughts are engrossed by the blandishments of a being whose fortune I envy, but whose choice I admire."

The suddenness of this appeal so startled Barnwell that it was some time before he could summon to his lips a reply. Once, indeed, the words recalled Alice to his recollection, but banishing the subject so soon as it occurred, as one painful to him, he endeavoured to remove the suspicions of his companion whose passionate harangue had terminated in a burst of tears.

"Eleanor!" he exclaimed with energy; "sooner than you should believe me false, I would resign fame, fortune, reputation—nay, life itself! Do with me as thou wilt; henceforth I know no other guide or monitor but thee."

"And you are still anxious to manifest by your actions that your words play me not false? Well! well! I will not teaze you further, George; I had not quite so volatile an opinion as that I must confess—but come! let us in to supper; the light there has proved our voices have created some small attention however."

And with this Eleanor, as soon as the door was opened, led the way, followed by Barnwell, to a room elegantly furnished on the first floor, where a supper, comprising at least neatness and simplicity in the arrangements of the viands, was prepared ready for their reception.

"I am but an indifferent hostess," remarked Eleanor, as she motioned her guest to take his seat at the table; "and one not overburthened with attendants it would seem—but I trust to your kindness for finding an excuse for the 'meagreness of this poor board,' as our friend Congreve hath it."

Barnwell, however, wanted not an apology for the entertainment. After his first reflections upon the consequences of his not having returned to Cheapside had become drowned in the genial wine with which his hostess liberally plyed him, he seemed to dwell only with rapture upon the conversation of her who was seated at his side. In proportion, however, as his hilarity increased, her cheerfulness decreased, and it was with mingled sensations of surprise and regret that Barnwell noticed and inquired the cause of this despondency.

"It is of little moment, my dear George," said Eleanor in reply, as if endeavouring to rally her spirits; "I am often thus, and believe it to be a weakness, as I know it to be impossible to control. The animal spirits that have buoyed me up through the fatigue of an arduous night's performance, will naturally, on subsiding, give way to a languor instead."

"To-morrow!" exclaimed Eleanor, as the syllables falling from her lips seemed to freeze as they were delivered, and to chill the fears of her auditor; "to-morrow I shall never see!"

"Eleanor, what mean you? This wild, unsettled look; this altered tone alarms me; tell me, I beseech you, what causes your afflictions—and teach me how I may relieve them!"

"Listen then," answered Eleanor; "but, remember, you have forced from me this narration, and that I yield it not willingly. I believe at our first interview I told you that, having fled from my family, I had nothing but my own exertions to depend on. I told you true; but I should have added, that a cousin, whose wealth enables him to injure where he might protect, and blight those hopes that he might ripen, has earnestly offered, upon several occasions, his hand to me in wedlock. His wealth he thought would command success, as his person had attracted attention; but, another having usurped that place in my affections I should

have desired to have bestowed on him, he was refused. On the night we were last at the Duke's Theatre, he had, during the whole of the time, watched us, and had I not have misled him by hastily availing myself of the sedan I found below, when I so abruptly parted from you, he would infallibly have sacrificed you to his vengeance. As it is, he has prevailed upon my landlord to distrain for the arrears of rent due to him, and to-morrow I am, with the exception of yourself, without a friend—and, save the damp field and the crowded street, the refuge of every vagrant, without a home! Here my lot is now cast; here shall I end my days! yet brightened by the reflection that I was acting in accordance with the dictates of my own heart, and with my woes alleviated perhaps by knowing that his prayers would occasionly invoke blessings upon a name as yet unsullied and unspotted. I have defrayed the expenses of to-night with the few last coins I possessed, and feel better in so doing—since my last happy hours will be spent in your society. I am well aware I am exceeding the limits of maiden modesty in thus acknowledging a passion that I ought to have concealed: but attribute it to the native warmth of the country where I was brought up. I am thus disingenuous, because I know my confidence is not ill-placed, and I have now only to beg, in conclusion, that we may henceforth part—perhaps never again to meet. Your path, I trust, may be still prosperous; whilst mine seems on every side to be only one of misery —and one in which I would most willingly involve your happiness."

Barnwell who had watched with much interest and anxiety the different transitions of countenance that Eleanor exhibited during the above recital, was moved by the narration he had heard still more, when he learned that he it was who had been however unwillingly, the cause of her misfortunes.

Beseeching her to control her tears that now coursed each other rapidly down her cheek, he vowed to aid her by every means in his power; and recollecting at that moment the sum of money that he had in his possession to pay over to the stockbroker, Barnwell hurriedly drew it from his vest, and falling on his knees to Eleanor, begged of her to accept the proffered sum, and by that means free herself from all anxiety that she felt on the score of her pecuniary exigences.

"Take," he cried, "the only remedy I have in my power to afford! Here is a sum large enough to defray all that he requires: sacrifice not, I implore you, your happiness to one who is incapable of appreciating the treasure he would possess, and whose aim is alone the possession of beauty, the superior qualities of the mind connected with which he would not discern or value as they deserve to be valued."

"I cannot take it, or accept your offer," answered Eleanor. "I have no claim on you for this, and therefore no right to rob you of it."

"Rob!" thought Barnwell; "there is something in that word that moves me mightily."

"Nay, I must not accept it," she continued; "we had better part—painful as the separation would at least be to me."

"Part!" echoed Barnwell; "never! Hear me, Eleanor, I never loved till now—you have instructed me what the passion of love meant—you have infused into my soul a desire to which it had hitherto been a stranger—and to bid farewell, when I fondly hoped we met to part no more—I cannot, will not think of it. Your happiness must be purchased at any price ; and your refusal. whilst it would not benefit you, would plunge me into the deepest misery and despair."

" Then as such I take it, as a temparary loan to meet to-morrow's fate. But this kindnes from one I would not willingly term a stranger—yet when the date of our acquaintance is considered but little more—overpowers me unexpectedly as it arrives. That a day may come when an opportunity will present itself of making a suitable return I firmly hope—till then believe me I am not insensible of your favours."

" When shall we again see each other ?" eagerly inquired our hero.

" With to-morrow's eve, if so you will it," replied the other.

" And till then, my hopes are entered but in one —that one being Eleanor Merton."

" They stile me here by another name. Merton is but my theatrical title," smiled Eleanor.

" Then your real name is—"

" Milwood !"

Some time had elapsed after the above conversation had taken place, when, pursuing his way westward from Bishopsgate-street, might have been seen a figure, whose rapid strides and uncertain motion showed that the party in question was but ill satisfied with some occurrence that had recently taken place, and was endeavouring to escape even fron self communion.

As he progressed onward, his meditations became audible ; of their import the following will serve to give the reader an idea.

" Fool ! madman that I was," muttered the passenger, " to risk my employer's money so long in my possession. I, that have honours heaped upon me for my probity ; one in whose confidence the strictest reliance was at one time placed ! *Was ?* Aye, too true, it will be now no longer. I am a pilferer—a common robber ! nay, worse than that, I have added ingratitude to my list of crimes. But then Eleanor——her love cannot be too dearly purchased : She is now happy : but by what ? By my ruin ? Nay, the money may be yet made up. I shall have an opportunity of replacing it, and no one will be the loser. Yes, Eleanor, I have acted right in securing your felicity, though it were bought at the expense of my own peace of mind."

Thus commenced Barnwell's first plunge into the abyss of crime, in the intricacies of which he was soon irrecoverably lost. This was his first stepping-stone to guilt—his first attempt to stifle the remonstrances of his conscience.

Were we inclined to moralise, much might we say upon the danger attendant on yielding to impulses like these, that mislead where they ought to guide, and which, by playing the sophist with our conscience, teach us to proceed, step by step, into crime, until grown callous by repetition, the mind becomes more vitiated and depraved, until it is ultimately invulnerable to the "small still workings" of the silent monitor.

But we are digressing ; and having in our next chapter to follow the fortunes of one in whom Barnwell was at the early period of our narrative somewhat interested, we leave our hero for the present at the door of his employer's residence, with the grey light of morning gleaming in the east, and the stars one by one twinkling their last lustre ain the azure arch of the western horizon.

———

CHAPTER VIII.

THE DEPARTURE.

Alas ! how short is life,
If we compute alone those happy hours
In which we wish to live ! Our seventy years
Are filled with pains, diseases, wants and woes,
And only dashed with love, a little love—
Sprinkled by fits, and with a sparing hand,
Count all our joys from childhood e'en to age
They would but make a day in every year.
Oh ! would that the kind gods alone would give
These seventy days, and take the rest away !

Time's a Tell-tale.

Then haste ! conduct me to the lovely mourner
Who weeps in silent houurs her woes away ;
And, whilst I kiss away the pearly drops,
Suck from her rosy lips the fragrant sighs,
And check the uneasy throbbings of her breast,
With other pangs her throbbing heart shall heave,
With other dews her swimming eyes shall melt,
With other sighs her panting breast shall heave,
'Till all her sorrows are absorbed in Love.

Dryden's Conquest of Granada.

The carriage that contained Alice continued its progress through the marshy lanes and thoroughfares leading to the metropolis, with unabated speed, and relaxed not the rapidity of its motion until the wheels rolled passed the " leafless trees of Tyburn." Here the increasing number of vehicles rendering a slower pace necessary, the driver changed the direction of the horses' heads to the left, and soon gained the open space, then known by the appellation of Mary-la-bonne Fields. Here the carriage stopped in front of a noble mansion, the architecture of which evidenced the wealth and taste of its possessor : it was built with that peculiar description of freestone so much in vogue during the reign of James the First, about whose time tradition reported the first stone of the structure to have been laid ; certain it was that the antiquity of the edifice contributed in no slight degree to impress the beholder with an idea of its stately importance ; and as Alice gazed from the small window of the vehicle where she sat on the vast building before her, she felt her heart tremble at the forebodings her imagination had conjured up, and again wondered for what fearful trials she was reserved.

Descending from the outside, her conductors led her through the ample portal into a spacious hall, fitted up with every regard for comfort and convenience. Leaving her there whilst one went to apprise his master of her arrival, Alice became a prey to thoughts of the most torturing and conflicting nature. Never before having been to the metropolis, she would not have surmised even the place of her destination, had it not have been for the directions she had heard given from one to another on the road. Her reflections, however, were speedily suspended by a summons from one of the attendants who had conducted her thither, to accompany him to an apartment above.

Considering that to refuse would not benefit her unhappy condition, she allowed herself to be led along a Gothic corridor towards a door at the end, which leading to a flight of stairs, they ascended, and Alice soon found herself in the apartment they were in quest of.

Reclining on a sofa in an easy attitude, with one

leg crossed carelessly over the other, appeared a young man, who, from the graceful negligence and elegance of his attire, was evidently him whom the attendants called master. Motioning the servant to withdraw, he requested in mild and gentle accents Alice to be seated, and seemed at first struck with the pallid colour that had displaced the roses on her cheek. Instead, however, of complying, Alice threw herself on her knees before him, and in tones that trembled in silver sweetness as they were uttered, supplicated him she addressed, to restore her to the happy home from which she had been so forcibly abducted.

"Miss Travers," said he, "rise: it is I who should bend in that position before you—I who should kneel and adore a being of such beauty. You ask *why* you have been brought hither: I will tell you: it was to make you happy—to place rank and riches within your reach—to elevate you to that situation you ought to occupy, and to give to the metropolis a fairer jewel than any it at present can boast of. Alice I *love* you!"

"*You!*" almost shrieked Alice, as she rose, indignant at the behaviour of him whom she had hoped would have proved a friend; "know, Sir, that my love is not bought with such allurements as those you hold out to me! If that is the motive for bringing me hither, one possessing less sagacity than yourself might have known that force may destroy, but it will never create love."

"You then reject my offer?" exclaimed the other. "Well! 'tis no more than I expected. I heard of the foolish passion that had taken possession of your heart; but pause before you refuse one whose only aim is to make you—"

"Miserable!" interrupted Alice. "To be your's would make me so. Wealth is of little value in my estimation, save as it procures the means of happiness in others. You have adopted a course that redounds neither honour to yourself nor to your menials. You may behold me poor, degraded, and an outcast—you may withhold from me the means of subsistence, and banish the light of day—but never shall you see me your mistress!"

"By heavens, her passion only inflames her beauty!" said the other only to himself, as the energy with which the above had been spoken recalled the colour to her cheek! "she must—she *shall* be mine! Hark ye, Miss Travers, this idle declamation will avail you nothing, for my reasons in having had you conveyed here in preference to urging my love at your own abode, I am the best judge; you may learn them perhaps hereafter. I would not be over-harsh with you either, and attributing your present repugnance to my wishes to the effects of youthful folly and imprudence, I am willing to give you time to reconsider of the opportunity now afforded you; and for that purpose you will be provided with suitable apartments in my mansion—but excuse me, if the restraint I shall be compelled to use, should give you the idea of being a prisoner, rather than a willing and an honoured visitor."

"Sir," answered Alice, "whoever you may be—your mien bespeaks your descent—your abode shows that you are wealthy—but your present conduct convinces me you are a villain. You have robbed me of a father's care, brought me here unprotected and alone, and would now avail yourself of a pretext for forcing me to consent to what I most abhor."

"Nay, you mistake," replied the other; "I only give you a longer period to consider of my offer; that once known, your fate for better or for worse is sealed."

"You know it now," cried Alice: "I never will be yours."

"Proud girl;" he exclaimed; "this vain and useless opposition will but ensure your detention. Here, Jervis! Andrew! conduct this lady to the Picture Gallery, where for the present she must remain; you answer, remember, for her security."

Abandoning all further attempt at ingratiating himself with Alice, the speaker flung himself back on his couch, and with the consciousness of having his victim safe in his power, was soon lost in a train of thought that the recent events suggested.

The two attendants who had been summoned waited not for further orders to convey Alice to the room named, for leading her through numerous passages to a spacious suite of rooms which bore the designation of the picture gallery, they there left her, with an intimation that she would find what refreshments she required in an ante-room adjoining, which had been already prepared for her reception.

As soon as they had gone, Alice tried the fastening of the door, but found, to her dismay, that it defied all her attempts to obtain an egress. The room in which she was appeared to have been built some years previously to the other part of the building, being detached by a wing from the main portion, and ornamented with curiously carved cornices and Gothic ornaments, that threw a singularly venerable aspect over the whole apartment. It was illumined by one large window, placed at such a height from the ground, however, as to render all hopes of an escape by that means entirely nugatory. In the ante-chamber, like the room itself, decorated with pictures, which were chiefly portraits of venerable warriors in most formidable suits of armour, Alice found, as had been stated, a table, covered with what viands she might require; and not having partaken of anything since she had left Lichfield, Alice availed herself of this opportunity of making a repast calculated to fit her frame for the trials that awaited her. Thus invigorated, she commenced an active and minute scrutiny of the apartment, to see if an opportunity for escape was afforded her by the structure of the room. Determined that she would undertake or endure anything rather than become subservient to the wishes and desires of one who possessed no claims on her love or esteem, she allowed nothing to escape her calculated to further her designs. The gloom or evening surprised her in the search, and suspended her operations. Hoping that morning would aid her endeavours, she that night sought a refuge from the cares of life in sleep, and the following day was about renewing her investigations, when a ray of light falling upon a portrait before her, startled her with its surprising resemblance to reality. On a closer inspection, Alice found that the features were not only striking, but were also familiar to her, and impressed with a firm conviction that she had seen the original somewhere, she scanned the expressions of the countenance more narrowly. The portrait represented a young man, apparently in the prime of life, with the flush of manhood on his cheeks; and with dark wavy hair falling in careless profusion behind. A point lace collar, hung in graceful folds around his neck, and his habiliments betokened the wearer to have been one holding some military commission. Around his waist had been painted a belt, in the centre of which, near where it might be supposed to have been fastened, appeared a small clasp, or minature locket, visible only to a near view, which struck Alice as being singularly similar to one in her possession. Detaching the locket from her neck, and comparing it with the one represented in the picture, she found they were exactly alike. Whilst pondering on this singular coincidence, she recollected that her mother, on giving her the trinket, had stated that it formerly belonged to a near relative, who under peculiar circumstances, which she had never heard detailed, had had another made exactly alike. Alice was, however, not prepared to find it so near her, and was therefore at a loss to conceive how the picture could have come into her oppressor's possession. Another surprise was, however, in store for her. Placing her own locket upon the other, to ascertain the similarity of the size, she was astonished at feeling it give way with the pressure, and still more, when adding to the force she had previously bestowed upon it, Alice found that it communicated with a spring, that, being pushed on one side, allowed the portrait to revolve upon a pivot, and disclosed to her equal gratification and surprise a long winding passage, the extremity of which was lost in the gloom that prevailed. Addressing a brief but fervent prayer to Heaven, as a thanksgiving for the means of escape that she doubted not was now opened to her, Alice determined to postpone her departure till the evening, when the inmates of the mansion, being wrapped in slumber, would render her absence from the room less certain of instant detection, and would allow at the same time the darkness of the night to favour the secresy of her elopement.

The strict decorum with which she had been treated since her arrival also, convinced her that no immediate violence was to be dreaded, and formed another inducement for her deferring until then the project she had in view. Passing the afternoon in making preparations for her departure, she was soon after aroused by a loud knocking at the door, when, replying that the visitor might enter, the same person to whom she had been conducted on the previous morning appeared before her, and with a tone of gallantry as haughty and imperious, however, as that he had before assumed, demanded of her an answer to his suit.

" I am here," he continued, " again to urge your compliance with my wishes. You have seen that I am opulent—you now learn that I am not insensible to the attacks of the tender passion—tender, forsooth, since it makes even me bow down a suppliant before the throne of beauty."

" It may not be out of place," said Alice, " if while listening to these words, I should inquire the name of him who utters them."

" Hum! you may call me now Arlington," answered the other. " What you may one day call me, depends upon your decision, which I await."

" It remains unchanged," rejoined Alice, " and will do so while I am here. Dost thou think that the caged bird feels more attachment to its keepers by being preserved in a wiry prison, than when, clearing unrestrained through the broad and ample field of sky above, it repays them with a joyous song? Why, then, by force endeavour to command feelings that would change sooner, doubtless, if more scope was allowed them for the purpose?"

" You talk idly, Miss Travers," pursued the self-styled Arlington ; " remember, you are in my power, and might at least place some small restraint upon your tongue ; but you women, in that respect, are true advocates of liberty—ye reck no bonds, save those you put on others. Once more, will you be mine ?"

" Never ?"

" Then here you must remain for one day more ; at the expiration of that period, if you still continue obstinate, force shall place in my possession what I was willing to obtain by free will. Till tomorrow, proud girl, farewell !"

As soon as the noise of the bolt as Arlington retired, manifested that he had not neglected the usual precautions for her security, Alice seated herself under the old arched window, anxiously awaiting the appearance of the evening star, when she might bid adieu to the gloomy chamber where she sat. As soon as that bright luminary rose in lustrous majesty into the cerulean vault of heaven, diffusing around its twinkling rays, and sending hope to the bosoms of the loving and the loved, Alice arose, and hastily trimming a lamp that had been left on the table, touched the spring concealed by the locket in the portrait, and sliding back the picture with a strange feeling of curiosity to know whom it represented, found herself once more in the passage already mentioned. The cold air, that, rushing up the avenue, threatened every moment to extinguish her lamp, convinced her that it had an outlet at no great distance, and also that its existence must be unknown to the present possessors of the hall—as the Picture Gallery would not have been in that case selected as the place best calculated to secure her person.

Shading the lamp with her hand, Alice continued her progress along the passage for some time, following its tortuous winding in breathless anxiety, until stopped by a massive iron door, which seemed to have an immediate communication with the road beyond ; but all attempts to force it open were made in vain by the trembling maiden who exerted her energies for that purpose.

Ascertaining that the current of air she felt on her first entering was caused by an opening in the grated bars above, Alice was compelled, after some time spent in deliberation, to retrace her steps, hoping that in her room she might discover a key that would fit the rusty lock. As she was returning Alice beheld a door in the side that at first had escaped her observation, and sliding back the panel joyfully left the passage for one of narrower dimensions, but less exposed to the wind. Traversing this likewise, it brought her to a flight of stairs that had seemed constructed for the express purpose of baffling discovery : they were built in the corkscrew form, and seemed so as to form part and parcel of the other portion of the building, that a cursory observer would have passed them unnoticed. Guided by her lamp, Alice ascended, and finding at the summit another panel which, like the former, yielded easily to the touch, discovered that it led into a large and spacious room, the furniture of which, magnificent in decay, showed that the apartment had evidently been fitted up as the most splendid of any in the house. The room, however, now presented a most forlorn and miserable aspect. It had been apparently unoccupied for nearly a century ; and the ancient tapestry that mouldered at the touch, brought with it dust and cobwebs in such vast quantities as to compel Alice to retrace her steps a few paces lest the lamp should

be extinguished. A harpsichord, and some loose pieces of music laying on the floor beside a broken music stand, denoted that a female had once honoured the room with her presence, and the conjecture was further corroborated by an unfinished drawing that, with the pencil near it, remained almost concealed from sight by the dust on the inlaid table.

At the further end appeared an inner room, which from the curtains that enclosed it, seemed designed as a sleeping apartment. Drawing aside the tapestry, Alice was horror stricken at finding the bed clothes, which had been half-turned down, as if some one had arisen from them in haste, covered with large spots of blood. The pillow was spotted in like manner; and on bending nearer, Alice found several handfuls of hair as if torn up by the roots, strewing the carpet at the foot of the bed. Rushing from a scene so full of horror, she opened the shutters of the other room, and as she did so, suddenly felt her arm seized forcibly from behind. Shrieking with terror, she turned round to face her assailant; but soon after smiled as the cause of her groundless fears displayed itself in a roll of damask that, falling from the ceiling as she opened the shutter, had twisted itself round her arm, and had thus occasioned her terror. To her mingled joy and surprise Alice found, on looking out from the window, that it was scarcely twenty feet from the ground, and that it overlooked a green mound at the back, where, on alighting, she might regain the country beyond. This wing, which was on the other side to that where she had been confined, had long been closed under a reputation that it possessed of being haunted, and consequently not one of the domestics were ever known to have passed it after nightfall.

This much Alice had gathered from the conversation of the servants who had brought her to the Picture-Gallery; and taking advantage of the popular impression, commended herself to the protection of Providence, and made preparations for her escape. Unbinding a shawl from her waist, and fastening one end of it to the iron grating that fringed the window, Alice tried it several times, to ascertain its capability of bearing her weight, and then flinging the other end out of the window, commenced her descent slowly and carefully.

Her task, however, was of more difficulty than she anticipated, for owing to the darkness of the night, Alice soon found that she had deceived herself in the depth she had to fall, and, bewildered by fears, was at last compelled to release her hold of the scarf—and fell. There was the rushing sound of a body dropping through the air, and a heavy bound on the grass beneath. A red tint lined the eastern horizon—birds began to carol forth their matin songs—flowers enclosed their drowsy petals to the sun—daylight, in short, began to dawn, but the scarf still remained fluttering in the breeze above, and its owner, benumbed and senseless, lay extended on the ground below.

CHAPTER IX.

BARNWELL'S INTERVIEW WITH HIS UNCLE.

Money! thou bane and antidote of good,
Thou moral pestilence, devised by him
Who erst from Heaven spread sin and shame on all!
How many souls are bartered for thy dross?
How many hearts are warped from Virtue's path?
How many hopes are blighted by thy power?
And hearts, souls, hopes and all exchanged—for what?
A demon coin, that kills where'er it comes!

All is not Gold that Glitters, 1670.

Come, come! good words, mine host. She is
A noble lady—great in blood and fortune,
Fair, and a wit; but of so bent a phantasy,
That she thinks nought a happiness but to have
A multitude of servants; and to get them,
Though she be very honest, yet she ventures
Upon those precipices that might make her
Not seem so to some prying narrow natures.

Rowley's Match at Midnight.

BARNWELL arose the morning after his visit to Milwood a prey to feelings and reflections of no very enviable character. He had betrayed the confidence that his employer had placed in him, had forfeited his own good opinion, and had destroyed by one blow his peace of mind, as he feared, for ever. That he felt consolation, however, in believing that he had alleviated another's wants, it must be admitted, but he had done so in a way that all

his sophistry could not palliate or justify; and his only hope was that, by an unexpected remittance from his mother, he might replace the sum he had *borrowed*—stolen was a somewhat harsh word—and restore to himself peace of mind and quietude of conscience. But whilst consoling himself with this idea, little did he imagine that by degrees he was involving himself in a labyrinth of crime from which there was no moral clue to assist in self-extrication.

The precipice of guilt yawned before him; one false step—one irresolute movement, and his return to the paths of rectitude would become difficult, if not altogether impracticable. He dwelt earnestly on the events of the preceding evening. The present was a period to him full of high hopes and ambitious desires; and fond and ingenuous as he was, Barnwell found that he had yielded intuitively to the promptings of a mind easily excited, and that he had thought but little of the ultimate ill effects conduct such as he had been guilty of would produce. His brain was racked with wild and tumultuous throbbings, and seemed almost to burst with the weight it contained.

Was he entrusting his honour, his character, his respectability, his present happiness and future prospects, to her who would rightly appreciate them, and feel the responsibility that would be entailed? It was a question he could not answer. Was the bosom that he fondly imagined throbbed responsive with his own, a shrine worthy of the offerings he had placed there? Would she, in return for what he had yielded, sympathize in his welfare, and share in his griefs? He feared to hazard a reply. Love such as he wished—expected to obtain—would have indeed proved a noble return for all he had suffered. Love—true woman's love—love that still smiles when fortune frowns, when friendship fails, and when calumny crushes, is indeed a treasure—worthy to be cherished—aye, even worshipped, and he who can boast *such* love, has a mine of wealth in his possession that will conduce more to his real happiness than all the fabled talismans of the East, or the golden ore of Potosi or Peru. But, alas, for our hero! the meteor that had flashed across his path was one calculated rather to dazzle than to lead—to bewilder with a delusive glare, than illumine his road with a certain lustre. It was a light that served only to guide him into a maze of error, from which he could find no outlet.

Milwood in the meantime rejoiced in the success of her schemes, and the good fortune she had met with, and flattered by the attentions Barnwell had shown her, thought only of plans by which she could more securely ensnare her victim. Her sole object was to possess herself of money, and for that purpose she had stopped not short of anything save actual murder. But as her subsequent conduct we shall yet have occasion to speak of, we reserve our further comments.

Trueman, who with the mystical events of the ring, and its concomitant circumstances fresh in his recollection, did not at first observe the altered demeanour of Barnwell, soon perceived that his companion's spirits were more depressed than usual, and inquiring the cause, was surprised to find that, for the first time, his friend refused to place confidence in him.

"I cannot," said Barnwell, endeavouring to evade the question, "at present reveal the cause of my unhappiness; but another time, Ned, you shall know all. In the meantime if you value my friendship, and your own quietude, you will not seek to learn further."

"Your answer is sufficient for me," replied Trueman; "I would not intrude into any one's private griefs, but doubted only what those were in which I could not participate."

"Trueman," pursued Barnwell, "you would shun me, I fear, did you know all; avoid me as you would one inflicted with the plague, and scorn me as a reptile. But your last words have determined me; you shall hear all, and much as you will blame me, you cannot reproach me more than my conscience has already done."

The few words that were exchanged between them, only served to render Barnwell more dissatisfied than ever with his conduct. Gladly availing himself of the hour when it was his duty to go upon 'Change and watch the fluctuating price of stocks, Barnwell departed before Mr. Thorogood made his appearance in the counting-house, fearful that questions might be put to him relative to the cause of his prolonged absence the preceding evening, which he could not answer. Returning from his mission, he began to reflect on the best mode he could adopt of restoring the sum he had appropriated; and not wishing to reveal his irregularities to his mother, determined at last upon seeing his uncle, who resided in Camberwell Grove, and entreated him to lend him the amount required. Immediately acting upon the resolution he had formed, Barnwell, instead of returning direct to Cheapside, crossed over the Bridge into the Borough, and proceed thence to Camberwell, considered by the citizens of that day as a small village, that far removed from the bustle of the metropolis, was especially adapted for rural retreats and villas for retired merchants.

On arriving at the residence of his relative, Barnwell, who had not seen him for some time, at first hesitated upon calling; but remembering the urgency of the case, and the necessity he was under of obtaining the sum that day, he overcame all scruples, and announced his name to the domestic who opened the door, with a request that he might see his relation immediately. He was accordingly shown into a room, the antiquated furniture of which manifested the peculiar taste of its owner. Whilst pondering on the appearance of the apartment in which he was seated, his meditations were interrupted by the sound of footsteps proceeding from the hall, and soon after his uncle himself made his appearance.

Mr. Ezekiel Barnwell was a venerable individual, attired in the old fashioned garments of that day, with a fine open countenance, furrowed, however, by the unerring plough of old Time. Bred a merchant, his partiality to mercantile pursuits was displayed even in the arrangements of his household, where ledgers and day books constituted the chief ornaments, and the state of the money-market his chief topic of conversation. Greeting his nephew warmly by the hand, he requested him to resume the seat, which Barnwell had quitted in deference to the age of his relative, and taking a chair at the opposite side of the table, entered into conversation.

"I trust," said Mr. Barnwell, "that you are not neglectful of your duty, George. A merchant should have his name and honour as unspotted and as pure, as if his life depended upon his integrity.

I have heard and approve of the zeal you have manifested in your employer's behalf."

"I shall at least endeavour to merit the commendation," responded our hero, not over pleased with the tenor of the foregoing speech.

"By so doing, you will find your own advantage," pursued his relative; "I intend making you the heir to what little property at my death I have to bequeath."

"Your kindness deserves my warmest acknowledgments," replied George. "The object of my visit is to seek your aid."

"Then it is granted at once," continued the other: "if I can be of service to my poor brother's son, you know you may command my assistance. I vowed at his decease to take you under my protection, and I will act up to the promise I then made, as much as if your parent were still living."

Our hero, confused by so open an acknowledgment, was for a time almost at a loss how to proceed; recovering, however, his self-possession, he was compelled to add falsehood to his previous indiscretions, and at last stammered out a reply that he was in want of some money to send to his mother, who had written to him desiring such a communication, and added, that it was only under such a pressure of pecuniary difficulties, that she would have sought for assistance from one who had been before so liberal a benefactor.

"Say no more," said the benevolent old gentleman; "Providence has placed in my hands the means, and I should be wanting in the common duties of humanity, if I withheld my helping hand when it most required. Name the sum she desires."

"Twenty pounds will be amply sufficient," rejoined George.

"Then take it; I have here thirty pounds. It is her's; and may it relieve the wants of one who has a natural claim to my assistance."

"My kind, generous uncle, how shall I ever repay this benevolence?" exclaimed George, moved even to tears by the liberality of his relative.

"By acting in accordance with your dying father's precepts," replied the other; "and, when you have the opportunity, by doing the same for others."

"I am beholden to you for more than life itself," said George; and again thanking the generous old man for the kindness he had evinced, bade him farewell, and left the house, overjoyed at the success of his visit.

Light and joyous were his steps homeward. He had now in his possession the means of replacing the sum he had taken from his employer, and he accordingly at once determined to hasten to the broker's with the money that should have been delivered on the previous evening. On London Bridge, over which his road lay, he paused awhile to observe the brilliant effects of the setting sun, that, after illuminating the face of heaven with its glowing refulgence, was sinking its broad red disc behind the houses in the west. The river was studded with boats laden with articles of merchandise, and presented a peculiarly animated scene. In the distance appeared Old Saint Paul's, with its cross and dome burnished with the last beams of the departing luminary; and farther down the river then unobscured by any other bridge, rose in pomp and splendour the steeples of St. Dunstan's and St. Martin's, the lofty spire that at this period marked the situation of the Savoy, and the gilded towers of the Old Abbey in Thorney Island. It was indeed a scene to be looked upon, even by those who "were native here and to the manner born," with feelings of interest and gratification. To Barnwell it came with a soft and soothing influence that wrapped his senses for the time almost in forgetfulness; and he became again sensible of the scene around him, he found twilight had shaded the metropolis with its dull and laden hues, and that the moon, yet young, was sailing gallantly along the broad firmament with a group of light gossamer clouds in its train, and marking its aeriel course with a flood of radiance that seemed to dip the distant prospect in a sea of molten silver. Our hero, anxious to reach home before nightfall, lost no time in proceeding towards his destination; but as he did so, gave way to a train of thought that his reverie on the bridge had been mainly instrumental in exciting. He had wandered on thus for some time when he found himself, to his surprise, within a few doors of Milwood's residence.

"There would at least be no harm in calling," thought Barnwell, as he looked up to the window, where a light cast its cheering glare upon the curtains that decked the casement—"I shall be home yet in time;" and as he murmured these words to himself, he applied the knocker with somewhat more severity than usual to the oaken door before him. After an inquiry, which was replied to in the affirmative, had been made by Barnwell, to know whether the object of his visit was at home, he was directed up stairs, and soon found himself before Eleanor, who, probably anticipating his arrival, had bestowed that evening more than usual attention on the careful decoration of her person.

"I am quite delighted to see you again, my dear George," said Eleanor; "this is kind of you to pay me a visit so soon—soon, I say, with reference to the time that has really elapsed, though to me it has seemed an age."

"To see you is a pleasure almost unexpected, though not unhoped for," replied George: "I doubted whether I should have found you at home."

"Why, I have resigned for a season my theatrical duties, in order that I may more securely enjoy the society of one for whom I would yield tenfold as much," responded Eleanor.

"Indeed!" cried Barnwell; "and he is—"

"Yourself George! Need you ask?"

The youth caught her to his arms, and in a fond embrace imprinted numberless kisses on her lips.

"You found the trifle of yesterday serviceable, I trust," said George, perceiving the glances of his companion directed towards a sideboard, on which had been somewhat ostentatiously displayed a few articles of female apparel, apparently not long escaped from the hands of the manufacturer.

"Aye, that did I," rejoined Eleanor; "and you see the use I have made of the surplus. Does this tint meet your approval? Love, they say, views all things couleur de rose, and this should not prove an exception."

"It confers equal credit on your taste and choice," remarked Barnwell, somewhat disappointed though he scarce knew why, at the use to which the sum had been put, that had cost him a day of so much trouble and anxiety to replace.

"Stay! I have a present likewise for you," continued Eleanor, not pretending to notice the expression of her admirer's countenance. "'Tis a simple gift; but one, I trust, not less acceptable on that account."

"The gift derives its value from the donor," replied George, as he received from the hands of his enslaver a small minature, at the back of which was a spring, that, being pressed, flew open, and revealed an inner case, in which was a lock of hair.

"It requires no diviner's art to say at once the hair and portrait are alike your own," said Barnwell, after a hasty glance at the minature and its contents; "such eyes, such hair, no other could possess."

"Nay, you flatter now; but glad am I it meet with your approbation. You think it like, then?"

"As thy second self."

"It was done for me by a young artist, who calls on me occasionally: he is reckoned an adept in his profession, and paints likenesses to perfection," continued Eleanor.

"Your eulogium is indeed well bestowed," smiled Barnwell, "if this is a sample of his handicraft; whilst I have the copy at my side, I shall scarcely miss the original."

"You will sup with me to-night," said Eleanor' flinging her arms round his neck, as if to induce him to stay.

"Nay, I must be even now gone," returned George, "I have spent the time here so rapidly, that I forgot the hour. Farewell, my dearest, for the present: and rely upon it, I shall avail myself of the earliest opportunity that favours a repetition of my visit."

"It is yet early," said Eleanor, reproachfully; "you surely will not depart from me so soon?"

"It is but for a time," urged Barnwell in reply, endeavouring to release himself from her embraces; "I will be with thee to-morrow at this hour."

"Then, if it must be so, farewell! at least think of me when I am no longer before you."

"That admonition was somewhat superfluous; you monopolise the whole of my reflections:" responded George; "I live but in your sight!"

"And yet so anxious to quit it," laughingly added the other. "Well, well! I know it is not your own desire; so adieu! but mind, fail not to-morrow."

Barnwell hastened down the staircase towards the door, and made his way with speed towards his employer's. Had he tarried awhile as he descended, he might have heard a suppressed laugh of exultation and a voice that thus soliloquised:—

"Poor youth! were he less fond of me I should be more willing to continue this; but, as it is, I could almost find it in my heart to pity him, in consideration of his age and attachment. My oath must, however, be kept inviolate, and he must share the fate of the rest."

But Barnwell did not hear this, and he reached Cheapside, perhaps, all the happier in consequence. On arriving in the room destined to be his place of rest for the night, his first impulse was to ascertain the safety of the money given to him by his uncle.

Examining first one pocket, and then another, he, with each renewed search, betrayed greater feelings of fear and disappointment; and at last, infinitely to his surprise, was compelled to feel that he had no longer the sum in his possession. Again and again did Barnwell cherish the hope that the pocket-book in which the notes had been placed was yet lurking in some unexplored corner of his vest; repeatedly did he scrutinize the contents of his outer pockets, eagerly did he scan the farthest recesses of his inner ones, but in vain ; the sought for article was nowhere to be found, and Barnwell's visions of content and happiness, were now faded into the air from which they had originally sprung.

"Robbed!" said Barnwell to himself, as he sank on a chair with the firm conviction that further searches would be useless. "Robbed of what I had endeavoured so anxiously to obtain, and deprived of that I had so fondly hoped would have preserved my name and honour unblemished! 'It is more than I can bear. Curses on my imprudence that caused me to loiter on the Bridge ; it must have been there that the pilferer took advantage of the opportunity afforded him, and robbed me of my reputation. And yet," continued Barnwell, musing on the events of the evening, "I felt, or fancied that I felt it secure when I called upon Milwood. Surely she has not—oh! no—her heart is too pure, herself too kind to warrant the commission of an act like this. Shame on me for harbouring such suspicions against one whom calumny should not taint. I almost deserve my fate for thinking so, even for a moment."

Continuing his reflections in the same strain, it was with a weary heart and tortured mind, that Barnwell that night courted the gentle pressure of his pillow. The prop that had hitherto sustained his hopes, had been taken away; the support of his honour was gone. He had not now the means of replacing the sum due to Mr. Thorogood, and there was no mode by which it could be in time obtained to prevent discovery. To be branded as an ingrate —a felon, and abstracter of his employer's hard-earned gold! He could bear anything but *that*. To see Eleanor look upon him with an eye of scorn, to bear the freezing glances of his friend Trueman, and meet the reproaches of his poor mother, these he could not endure, and all things must be sacrificed rather than be subject to an ordeal like this. There was, indeed, *one* way open, but he would not —durst not think of it—at least, not then—some other time, perhaps, when the emergency was greater, and his thoughts more composed—but now he was in a fever of excitement; his recent loss had so worked upon his mind, that he felt his body partake likewise of the influence; and his parched lips, and quivering hand told plainly of the raging passions that racked his breast.

Sleep, however, at last brought its refreshing languor to his aid, and plunged him into a forgetfulness from which he did not recover until the morning had become somewhat far advanced. He was aroused by a summons from Trueman, who, bringing him a letter that had that day arrived by the early post, expressed surprise at the unwonted delay of which George had been guilty on the previous afternoon.

"Mr. Thorogood himself, George, noticed the circumstance," continued Trueman; "and desired me to relieve your mind from any anxiety you may feel on the score of his forgiveness, as he is always ready and anxious to overlook errors as venial as these are."

"He is ever a kind master," responded Barnwell; "but I will explain the cause of my detention to him directly, when he will see he has but little reason to chide me for the delay—it was caused by the absence of a merchant that day on 'Change."

"I will tell him so," returned Trueman ; "but pardon me, George, if I take more than a friend's liberty in saying that I doubt the accuracy of your answer. You are not sufficiently well versed in falsehood to neglect truth. That crimson flush and hesitating speech are tell-tales that need no accuser ; but I must return below, and rely on it, George, you shall not complain of my want of diligence in colouring your inattention to the best of my ability."

"Even he suspects my sincerity," remarked our hero, as Trueman left the room ; "but he tells the truth nevertheless."

Scanning the letter with an eager eye, he found that it was from his mother, and contained a detailed account of the abduction of Alice, the circumstances attending which are already known to the reader. The writer added, that the father of Alice, surmising that the metropolis was the destination of his daughter, had proceeded there without delay. Doubting however whether she had been carried away by violence, or with her own consent, and in either case she stated he had left Lichfield with a determination never to again return until he had sought her out, and punished the instruments of her flight.

To Barnwell this caused but little uneasiness ; he had taught himself to look upon the love he bore Alice as the effects of a boyish passion, which a succeeding intercourse with the world had naturally cured. He thought not of the possibility of another assuming that place in his heart that he formerly had reserved for her—of another usurping the attention he had previously bestowed upon Alice. No! he attributed to his own superior discernment what was merely the effect of inconstancy, and the ardour of his love for Milwood, he looked upon as the best excuse he had for forgetting the companion of his early years.

Trueman, who was earnestly arguing with Clara the propriety of communicating the recent outrage of Sir Robert Otway to her father, was at that time actuated by feelings of a very different nature. He was strongly dissuaded from such a course by Clara, on the grounds that, until they had stronger proofs than the mere circumstantial evidence of the ring having been found there, it would be better to remain silent, lest the merchant should attribute the statement of Trueman to have arisen from unworthy motives. Acquiescing, at length, in the views Clara entertained upon the subject, Trueman desisted from urging the point further ; and was about leaving the apartment when Mr. Thorogood entering, desired an immediate conference, exhibiting, at the same time, an anxiety in his countenance, to which it had hitherto been a stranger.

"Trueman," said the merchant, "having placed every confidence in you since you came into my office, I see no reason why I should withold it now. Unless I can procure certain papers within a month from this time, you behold in me a ruined man. I have been lately, as you are aware, speculating rather deeply in the funds ; the whole of my property is, indeed, concerned in these uncertain undertakings ; and the only opportunity I see of rescuing myself from the seeming ruin that is impending over my house is, to gain certain documents of great political importance that, by influencing the court of Queen Anne, will produce a corresponding effect in the money market."

"Where are they to be met with?" anxiously inquired Trueman.

"That I shall soon ascertain," said the merchant, "having adopted measures for that purpose ; and now, come with me into my study, where I can impart to you my instructions without the chance of their dropping on the ear of some unwished-for listener.''

"When is it probable I should be required to commence my journey?" asked Trueman, as he accompanied the footsteps of his employer.

"With to-morrow's sun-set you may hold yourself in readiness; in the mean time, the papers I have to show you are here;" and the merchant led the way to his private room, where, leaving them earnestly engaged in conversation, we return to one who possesses, at this period, some little claim on our attention.

CHAPTER X.

THE ESCAPE.

The morning's sun now rising in the east
Begins to dye the clouds with roseate hues,
As if the day did blush for the strange deeds
Its sister night had witness'd in its course;
And as the dew in drops did gently fall,
And moisten with its damp the arid ground,
A poet's fancy might proclaim them tears,
And write an ode to check this matin grief.

Eastward Hoe, 1697.

THE sun had indeed ridden high in the heavens ere Alice became sensible of the dangers by which she was environed. Smoke was rising lazily into the sky from the chimneys that, though at some distance, rose above the trees, and marked the neighbouring abode of man; and clear and cloudless was the blue sky that threw its azure canopy overhead, and gave light and gladness to the world beneath. The day had dawned in all the majesty of Spring, and the birds, the untaught choristers of nature trilled their plaintive warblings from the dew-laden boughs with redoubled sweetness and energy.

"Alice, to whom the events of the previous day appeared more like a dream than the result of occurrences that had in reality taken place, felt some difficulty in recalling her scattered senses to her aid, and to persuade herself that she was not labouring under a delusion. An attempt to rise, however, soon convinced her to the contrary; for though fortunately she had escaped from broken limbs, some severe bruises yet remained to mark the reality of the fall. A glance upwards to the window, where her scarf still waved to and fro in the passing breeze, only served to bewilder her still more; the height was so great that in the day-time she would certainly have deemed it madness to have thrown herself from the casement. Collecting her energies now to assist in her flight, Alice, weak and trembling, fled from the scene of her recent captivity. Regardless of what path she took, so that it led her from the old mansion, her steps were directed towards a line of trees to the left that seemed to tower above the rest like the leafy guardians of a road but seldom trodden by the foot of man. Turning up here, and continuing her progress in the same direction for some time, she came to a path that winding its way in a serpentine manner over a hill, she determined to trace its course, satisfied now that there was but little cause to fear pursuit. This hill she soon reached, and gaining its highest elevation was well repaid by the beautiful and commanding view of the scene around her.

In the distance appeared the straggling houses and ill-built streets, that marked the prospects of old London, with its forest of spires shooting up into the air, and its quaint old-fashioned chimneys which could then be plainly distinguished at that distance, as the smoke they vomited forth was not in such large quantities in those days as at present. Old St Paul's, the monument, and the flaunting ensign that waved above the turrets of Northumberland House, to mark the presence of its owner, were all sought for and recognised by the fair fugitive, who endeavoured, in the contemplation of a view like this, to forget for a time the anxieties that agitated her own breast.

Stretching away in the distance far beyond the houses, and forming a deep blue undulating line in the horizon, rose the Surrey and Kentish Hills, seemingly almost as unsubstantial and ideal as the clouds that rested on the summits, and threw their boundary into broader outline. Here and there, sparkling like a silver thread, might have been seen the Thames, proceeding on its sinuous course between verdant banks and brick-lined shores, now leaving the osier beds of old Chiswick, with its gentle ripples as bright and clear as the fair maiden's eyes who watch its progress, and anon dashing its muddy waters against the beams that formed the buttresses of London bridge, now losing itself behind the houses, and now reappearing amongst the trees beyond, swelling each time larger and larger, until at last it mingled with the salt waves and tumultuous foam of the English Channel.

Turning her attention to the opposite quarter, Alice beheld a somewhat strange and pleasing alteration in the prospect, the quiet Arcadian repose of which contrasted greatly with the busy appearance of the other. Cottages embosomed in the vale below, wreathed around with ivy or evergreen, that seemed the very abode of rural happiness; homesteads thatched with straw, in true country fashion; and farm-yards where the feathered inmates spoke well for the condition of the proprietors: these were the chief objects of attraction. Above rose clumps of trees, that imparted beauty and variety to the landscape, and formed a natural link with the thickly-wooded country beyond; whilst in the foreground, pasture lands, and the snow-white blossoms of the almond-tree, then in bloom, diversified the scene, and charmed the eye of the spectator.

But let not the reader delude himself into the belief that this is the prospect he will have now, when, taking advantage of some invitingly sunny morning, he provides himself with a hearty breakfast and an oaken staff, and journeys forth, to explore the beauties of the ground we are describing. If he does, we give him warrant beforehand he will be most grievously disappointed.

The Hill indeed remains there still, but the prospect is gone—swallowed up in a vortex of bricks and mortar. London now stretches its gigantic arms to the very foot of the mound, shutting out the contemplation of green trees and meandering rivulets, and presenting us instead with a clumsy combination of brick-built tenements, the leases of which, as a board in the vicinity informs us, give the buyer possession for a century bating the last year. The trees have long been cut down and uprooted to make way for gentlemen's villas and stuccoed mansions; and a railroad company have undermined a portion of the Hill, for the purpose, one would imagine of experimentalising upon the probable tendency of earth to fall inwards. The cheerful sounds of the farm-yard are superseded by the shrill whistle and uneasy bellowing of the steam-engine : and where gardens once redolent of blossoms and fragrance existed, a public house has been lately built, with skittle grounds and concert-room complete, and boards displayed in front, alluding to something having reference to the New Police Act, and the twenty-fifth of George the Second. Such is the effect of time.

A few years more, and a green leaf may be exhibited in London as a rarity, and a tree itself be thought worthy of a niche in the British Museum. Innovation, with its seven-leagued boots, is yet advancing : where his step may next rest, it remains for the rising generation to discover. But to return to our narrative.

Alice, who had become for a time almost lost to a sense of her own woes, in her admiration of the scene, now felt more acutely the loneliness of her situation, when she contrasted her present feelings with those she experienced when gazing, with Barnwell at her side, on the prospect that had hallowed their last meeting. She was then sad, it was true, but it was as the cloud that obscures the face of heaven for a time only, to make the succeeding brightness more apparent ; and her sadness besides, was not the effect of past misfortunes, but merely arose from a shadowy foreboding of those to come. Barnwell she still believed constant ; and her thoughts were therefore brightened by the reflection, that he would sympathise in all she had suffered, and do all in his power to alleviate her sorrows. Her first impulse was to go to Cheapside, and see him there ; but, upon a more mature consideration, she reflected that her tale, wild and improbable as it was, might appear a fiction ; and that even if it was believed, applying to her lover for assistance and advice would be open to observations that might bestow rather too warm a colouring on the circumstance.

Feeling faint with langour and fatigue, Alice now descended the eminence, and selecting a path to the right, soon found herself in the precincts of a small village, which she was informed by a board, as she passed, bore the name of Hampstead. Anxious to procure shelter for the night, which was now coming on apace, Alice selected a small but neatly-built hostel by the road-side to be the object of her inquiries.

Addressing herself to the landlady, a buxom, rosy-cheeked dame, on the umbrageous side of forty, who was standing at the door watching the wayfarers as they passed, and greeting each that she knew with a smile and a nod of recognition, Alice begged to know if she could be accommodated with an apartment for the night, adding by way of explanation, that having missed the vehicle that was to convey her back again to the country, she would be compelled to remain there until she could aprise her friends of her situation.

"Aye, marry !" returned the hostess to Alice's question, "the Seven Bells was never yet known to turn away a customer, even of the other sex, much less one so young and pretty as yourself. But you seem fatigued and pale ?"

"I have walked far," said Alice, "in the hope of regaining my friends ; and the unwonted exertion has been, I fear, too much for me. I am faint and weary."

"Then come in, and partake of some refreshment," continued the hospitable lady : "we are just sitting down to tea ; and you can share our meal—aye, in good sooth shall you—and I shall charge you nothing for it either," she added, seeing that Alice was about giving a refusal : "so don't let any fears about the reckoning stand in your way. I have been poor and friendless myself once, and know what it is ; so come along, and take care of the step as you go down. There ! Bless me, how you tremble ! Well, here's a fire and all. Now, no thanks—I won't hear a word, I tell you ; so fancy you are at home, and do as you like."

Continuing her observations in the same strain, and anxious to prevent Alice from replying, the dame led the way to a snug little parlour behind the bar, fitted up with ample shelves and cupboards, where were arranged in the most unexceptionable order, tea-cups, milk-jugs, horn-tumblers, ale-glasses, then considered a novelty, and other useful articles of domestic economy, tastefully varied at certain intervals by sundry divided lemons and nutmegs, the future flavourers of divers liquid potations. Over the mantel-piece was the portrait of a female, attired in all the majesty of point lace and ample ruffs, that Alice had but little difficulty in indentifying as the youthful likeness of the present hostess ; and around it were suspended specimens of her early embroidery, consisting of rough representations of scriptural subjects that it would have been perhaps somewhat hazardous to mention, had the artist not taken the precaution of attaching the explanations beneath. Whilst Alice was thus casting her eye over the contents of the room, the proprietress of the Seven Bells was busily engaged in making preparations for the evening meal, which being completed, a few calls brought a third party on the scene, in the person of Mr. Ralph Royster, the husband of the lady before mentioned, and for whose entrance she had prepared Alice with a few prefatory observations.

"My husband Ralph," said the hostess, "is you see, my dear, a strange compound of idleness and good nature, of which, however, I believe, the latter has the advantage. It was a lone thing, I thought for a widow to reside by herself in a public-house which so many of the opposite sex frequented, so I determined to marry again ; and having enjoyed my liberty after the death of my first husband too much to be ready to resign it without a struggle, I chose for my second one who would never interfere with the business at all, but allow me to be as much by myself as if I was in reality a widow again. In this I succeeded to a nicety ; and I am delighted to say I have now a partner who spends the one half of his time in the skittle-ground, and the other in the parlour—serving all the purposes of a husband, in protecting his wife, without bringing with him the usual trouble and inconveniences."

The entrance of the individual in question here interrupted the landlady in her remarks, and caused Alice to turn from the contemplation of what had been said to the figure that now appeared before her.

Ralph Royster was, in fact, considerably younger than his, in every sense of the word, better half ; and this at once gave her an advantage that she otherwise would not have had. He was a tall and somewhat stalwart specimen of masculine humanity, with a round, florid countenance, expressing as much as a cipher divested of an accompanying unit, and was attired in one of the rough jerkins usually worn by the peasants of that day, corresponding with the shooting jacket that forms the customary habiliment of our present sportsmen. Without noticing Alice, Royster drew towards him a seat, placed for him in a remote corner of the room, and commenced making a formidable attack on the edibles of the table, consisting of substantial viands, that would put to shame the light formalities of the tea-table equipage at the present time. The repast was concluded in silence ; and at its termination, Royster rose, and renewed his skittle conflict in the arena at the back of the house, appropriated to that purpose.

" You see the life I lead here," said the hostess ; " it may seem dull to you, but to me it forms my chief happiness."

" You are fortunate in your selection, at all events," remarked Alice ; " scarcely one husband in a hundred would interfere so little in your business."

" And for that reason I prefer Ralph," returned the other : " but come, you are fatigued, and repose may be desirable. My niece is no longer with me, and her room will be at your service."

" I thank you," rejoined Alice, " and avail myself of your offer. Sleep will be a welcome visitor to those eyes, that have been lately seldom closed."

Following the landlady up a flight of stairs, that led to a neat but plainly furnished room on the first landing, Alice took the pen and ink from the table, bade her hospitable friend " Good night !" and retired to rest.

On closing the door, Alice, before she began to disrobe, drew a chair nearer the table on which the writing materials had been placed, and commenced a letter to her father. She described the manner of her departure from Lichfield, and the consequent imprisonment and escape, at full length ; and concluded by stating where she was then residing, and the difficulties she had to encounter Appending in a postscript, her wish for an immediate reply, Alice laid down her pen with a feeling of satisfaction and pleasure at having now adopted the means of ensuring a speedy interview with her parent ; and offering up a thanksgiving to Providence for her safe deliverance from the danger that had so lately environed her, and for the blessings she then experienced, increasing fatigue and languor warned her of the necessity of repose, and she soon sank into a calm and tranquil slumber.

The following morning Alice awoke with a strange, dreary recollection of the events of the preceding day. The bright sun that darted its early beams through the white and spotless curtains of her room, seemed to recal to her mind the place of her birth, and the scenes amongst which her youth had been so joyously passed. The chirping of birds, the cackling of poultry, that indicated the proximity of a well-stocked farm-yard, and the occasional lumbering sound that marked the transit of some heavily-laden waggon—all brought to her recollection her own room at Lichfield ; and when she saw the graceful wreaths and nodding tendrils of the vine, that threw its tender branches around the casement where she sat, fancy almost impressed her with a belief that the plant was of her culture, and the wreaths of her own twining.

The landlady, Mrs. Tabitha Royster, received her at the breakfast-table with undiminished expressions of kindness and regard. Ralph had quitted early in the morning for town, in order to obtain a fresh supply of malt, and his usual seat being therefore unoccupied, Alice had an opportunity of speaking to her hostess, without feeling the inconvenience of explaining circumstances to a third person. She now, therefore, briefly informed her, as far as was absolutely necessary, of the causes that led to her present situation, and entreated Tabitha to send off the letter she had written without a moment's delay.

" Aye, marry ! that will I," returned the good-natured hostess. " Dickon, our stable boy, shall ride off this very moment to London, and consign it to the care of the Staffordshire waggoner there without delay. In the mean time, till the answer arrives, make this place your home. I wish my niece Cicely was here again, to keep you company, but she is now married, poor thing, and a long way off. Those flowers near your window were planted by her hand."

It required but little exercise of the imagination, on the part of Alice, to picture the young florist training up the plants with an anxious eye and an untiring hand, watching their growth day by day, and marking the gradual opening of the buds as they blossomed forth, until she had brought herself at last to look upon them as old friends. And, then from her own feelings, Alice painted the contrast—when the day arrived that transformed the blushing girl into a wife, and brought her new objects to interest her mind, and new cares to depress it—how the plants grew untended and uncared-for—how weeds thickly sprung up in the once well-trimmed parterre—and how the buds had blossomed into maturity, with no watchful eye to mark their progress, and the leaves had fallen, with no friendly hand to arrest their decay. Alice thought of this, and instituted a comparison between these floral emblems and her own hopes. She had found a likeness between them on the preceding evening, and had already compared her brightening prospects to a rose that just culled was blooming in a vase upon the mantel-piece, redolent of all its native freshness and fragrance ; Alice turned towards the shelf now, and found the flower had *withered*.

Days passed away in rapid succession ; and as each terminated, the fears and anxieties of Alice increased. She could not divine the reason of her father transmitting to her no reply : and though for some time she cherished the hope that it was only on account of his intending to see her in person, even at last that hope gave way, and a season of doubt and foreboding succeeded.

Remarking at length the increasing despondency of Alice, the landlady of the Seven Bells took the earliest opportunity that offered itself of inquiring the cause of her sadness, and receiving for answer, that it arose from her present inability to defray the expenses incurred, she desired Alice not to render herself uneasy upon that account.

" You have been of infinite service to me, since you have been here," said the benevolent old lady, " in supplying the absence of my niece, whom otherwise I should have much missed : and therefore I had previously made up my mind not to charge you for what little you have consumed. If you would continue here until the communication you expect arrives, you need be under no apprehension that it would add to your expenses : on

the contrary, I should feel myself indebted to you for your kindness."

Alice, who was almost at a loss to express her gratitude, gladly accepted the proposal; and many were the blythe swains and gay gallants that from that time refreshed themselves with a tankard at the Seven Bells, for the sole purpose of having a glance at the pretty barmaid who handed them the liquor.

It was towards the decline of a day that had been characterised by more than usual serenity, that a horseman, whose exhausted animal bespoke the speed at which he had been ridden, alighted at the door of the hostelry in question, and called for a stoup of brandy. As Alice supplied him with the potent fluid, she saw the stranger scan her features closely, as if recognising in her countenance some extraordinary resemblance. Confused at the circumstance, and never remembering to have noticed the stranger before, she retired, and gave place to the hostess, who, bustling up to the door, betrayed by her manner the annoyance she felt at what she considered to be the impertinence of her visitor.

"Tell me, good dame," inquired the horseman, with the air of one who asks more from curiosity than from any other motive, "how long has your pretty lass been an inmate of thy dwelling?"

"Marry!" rejoined the hostess, perceiving by Alice's manner that she wished to disguise her real station—"I think a matter of some nineteen years come next Lammas-tide."

"Why, she must then have been a mere child!" laughingly exclaimed the stranger.

"Thou hast hit it to a nicety," returned the other, "and art surely, by thy shrewdness, a professor of the conjuror's art. She was indeed a child when she first came here; for, according to the best of my recollection, she was born in the house."

"'Tis strange!" muttered the horseman to himself, as he sprang on the back of his steed; "but the likeness is almost unaccountable."

"The reckoning, good sir," interrupted the landlady; "thy memory needs jogging."

"Truly it does," smiled the other; "but I will make amends for it: here is that which will nobly repay thee for thy trouble;"—and flinging a well-filled purse into the hands of the hostess, he clapped spurs to his steed, and in a few minutes was out of sight.

"A well-behaved gallant, by my troth," said Tabitha, as she jingled the coin in her hand, and watched the receding figure of the stranger; "a man of some good standing in the county, and well to do in the world, I'll be bound. But how's this, child?" she continued, observing the pallid countenance of Alice; "this hath ruffled you. Unfeeling creature that I was, to study my own wishes before I had provided for your safety! It is growing dark and you need repose."

"I am better now," murmured Alice, in tones that almost contradicted the tenor of her words; "the air has revived me."

"Try some of this cordial: it possesses a marvellously strange power of strengthening the weakened frame: and is reckoned by old Sam Grayling the sexton an excellent restorative, I can assure you," said Tabitha, pressing upon her a flask containing the liquid in question.

"Thanks! my kind friend," replied Alice, as she sipped the revivifying contents of the phial, more in compliment to the landlady than in accordance with her own wishes; "I need repose, and will avail myself of your permission to retire. Of late, I have been somewhat subject to these attacks."

"Well, Heaven bless thee, my child!" returned the good dame, "for I love thee as tenderly as if thou wert, in sooth, of my own flesh and blood. Take thy lamp and book up with thee; but, prithee, be careful of both."

Returning the salutation of the landlady, and promising attention to her parting admonition, Alice retired to her own apartment, which wore an aspect, at that period of the night, that harmonized in every respect with her own feelings. Leaning upon the open casement, (for the window had been raised during the day, for the purpose of admitting a free current of air), she surveyed in silence the prospect that opened to her view. A dark, grayish mantle seemed to shroud the sky, excepting where the horizon was marked by a long narrow strip of light, that threw the distant objects into strong relief. The distant tinkling of the sheep-bell, and the dull drone of some whirring insect in its drowsy flight, alone broke the monotonous stillness. It seemed to remind Alice of her once happy home—of the last night she had spent there, and of the strange scenes she had witnessed from that time; and when she retired from the casement, and closed the window, it need not be a matter of surprise that the heart of Alice was heavy, and that her eyelids were bedewed with tears.

Wishing to divert her attention from the scenes that now crowded on her memory, Alice sat down, and, trimming her lamp, endeavoured to turn the current of her thoughts to the matter in the book before her. Upon her table was a looking-glass, of a larger size than ordinary, that mirrored in its clear and polished surface the whole of the window behind her, the curtains of which she had forgotten to draw down.

The volume that engrossed her attention was *Milton's Paradise Lost*, then beginning to be appreciated by the reading world, in consequence of Addison's notices of it in the *Spectator*. Alice had been reading for some time, when the bell of the neighbouring parish church began tolling the hour of twelve, reminded her of the lateness of the hour. Gently raising her eyes from the book to the lamp, the oil in which was fast waning, she was frozen with horror at a sight that then met her vision. Reflected in the looking-glass before her was the face of a man with dark, shaggy eyebrows, and bushy whiskers, peering in at the casement, and watching her every moment. Alice gazed for some time in a state of stupefaction on the fearful image, as it appeared to her in the mirror, and saw that his eyes followed hers in every direction. What was to be done! To give the alarm by voice would be useless, as the hostess and her husband had retired long since, and there was no bell that communicated with the other portion of the building. Still the two eyes glared on her's, like a couple of burning embers, and seemed to scorch her with the fierce glance they conveyed. Her bosom heaved, her temples throbbed, her brain reeled, the furniture seemed floating past her—and uttering a loud but involuntary shriek, Alice fell senseless on the floor; and the expression of the face in the glass was varied by an exulting smile.

———

CHAPTER XI.

MILWOOD.

Gulielmo.—Constancy! what word is that?
Why, man, there's no such thing as constancy.
The vane that changes with each wind that blows
Is far more certain than a woman's heart,
The brittlest reed that e'er bow'd to the gale
Is more to be depended on than her.
Then think no more of what a woman says,
When she professes love to more than one;
Her mind is like the needle, that still turns
To where the attraction's strongest.

                    'Tis Pity she's a Bad One.

Oh, woman! woman! how couldst thou assume
So fair a form, for deeds so damnable?
Some lurking devil sure did sway thy thoughts,
And urge thee on to mischief!

                    The Deceiver Deceived, 1741.

IT is now time to unfold to the reader the mystery attendant upon Milwood's behaviour. When woman becomes vicious—when she throws off that "angel garb of innocence" in which Heaven has arrayed her, and dons instead the sable robes of vice—her fall is sudden, not gradual; her tastes and habits, it is true, become vitiated by degrees, but her descent from virtue to vice is the work of a moment: and such was Milwood's!

An intense love of admiration, its usual concomitant, a fondness for dress, and above all an insatiate thirst for conquest, constituted Milwood's leading foibles. To one of these sources the after-currents of her life might invariably have been traced. Man she regarded as a toy, intended to amuse and delight for a time, and then to be thrown on one side for a new bauble, and in its turn to be displaced by its successor. Unequalled powers of dissimulation, and a consummate knowledge of human nature, were the tools with which she worked; and in a most artisan-like manner were they handled too—for, to carry out our metaphor more fully, her designs were invariably conceived and executed in first-rate style. Statesmen, philosophers, lawyers, actors, authors, and artists, had each in their turn fallen victims to her seductive wiles, and confessed themselves vanquished by the power of her tongue. Nature had endowed her with a person in itself sufficient to command attention; and art, aided by long practice, had enabled her so to disguise her real sentiments as to leave them if not unthought, at least unexpressed. Possessing a rapid succession of ideas, and having a copious supply of words in which to clothe them, her conversation if not always brilliant, was nevertheless interesting. With a quick perception of the ludicrous, and the power to avail herself of it in company, she was yet very sensitive to opinions expressed in like manner with reference to her; and her badinage was therefore exercised more in private than in public, where, though the field of observation was more confined, the amusement was less dangerous.

A perfect mistress of all the arts that fascinate mankind, she lost no opportunity of testing their efficacy upon all with whom she came in contact; and there were few indeed who came away unscathed.

Deceit and hypocrisy were in her carried to their greatest extent; and the sophistry with which she would throw a veil over her indiscretions, when discovered, would in a better cause have extorted the highest admiration. Her features were fashioned in somewhat of a Jewish mould, with a broad expansive forehead and arched eyebrows, that shadowed beneath their long silken lashes a pair of lustrous orbs, that seemed to float in a sea of their own brightness. Not content, however, with the roseate hue that Nature had planted on her cheeks, Art had been called into requisition, for the purpose of making the carnation tint still more striking. Her form might have been cavilled at by a sculptor whose ideas of symmetry were formed upon the Grecian model; but her figure, when not criticised according to these notions of the ideal, would certainly have been pronounced if not faultless, at least nearly so. As she was now viewing her form in a glass that mirrored the decorations of her apartment, already mentioned to the reader, perhaps thoughts such as these passed through her brain; at all events, the nature of her reflections may be surmised from the following conversation that took place between herself and her attendant.

"How like you this cap, Hester; sits it jauntingly enough? Think you it will entrap the heart of any of the gay gallants that have of late honoured my poor room with their presence?"

"Think, Madam!" replied the Abigail; "I would stake my hopes of getting married on its success; and I am sure you would not have me be more confident than that. I should pity the poor youth Barnwell, as you call him, if he were to see you now; were he not already smitten, that dress would move him mightily."

"Tut, tut, girl! dress may provoke the contest; but it is the tongue that must decide the victory. Have any cards been left for me to-day?"

"Mr. Stanley, the young artist, has called twice, Madam, and expressed some little surprise at finding you absent."

"When he next calls, say I am unwell—that I am not at home—anything, in fact, that you think of first. I have made use of the miniature that he presented me with, perhaps, for a different purpose than that which he intended; but it matters not: I wish, however, not to see him again."

"I understand, Ma'am: he is to be rejected like the rest; but with reference to the rich old baronet, Sir William Brandreth?"

"Should he call, admit him; though if he again presume to offend me with his paltry five-pound presents, I shall scruple not to let him follow in the wake of the rest."

"Hark! there's a knock at the door," exclaimed her attendant; and looking at the person of the visitor through the window, added—"as I live, Ma'am, it's the old hunks himself; as if to verify the old proverb."

"Let him in, Hester, immediately," said Milwood.

"You are sure to do that," muttered the other, as she left the room, "and so will save the trouble; but, however, it's no business of mine, and that's one comfort."

Milwood hastily viewed the arrangement of her person in the glass before her; and throwing herself into a graceful attitude upon the sofa, awaited the coming of her admirer.

Sir William Brandreth was one of those wealthy, unprincipled debauchees who reck not health, time, nor money, in the pursuit of their object, pleasure; and care not by what means they gratify their unlawful passion, so that they *are* gratified. Debased and enervated alike in mind and body, he deemed himself still capable of exercising the finest faculties of both; and though feeling his powers glide from him daily, and age and infirmity stealing on apace, lived as if he could still act with the same impunity as of yore, and eke out his brief span of existence to eternity. It is a pity that the class we describe departed not with the century of which we write.

"My life! my charmer!" mumbled the old rake, as he advanced; "how glad am I too see the once again! I seem to have begun a new existence in thy presence."

"It would have been little harm if such had really been the case," thought Milwood to herself, as she allowed him to kiss her hand.

"I have been looking out for a cottage for thee," continued the superanuated love-maker, "where we may pass our days amidst the cooing of doves, and the sighing of gentle zephyrs, that fan the rose leaves near us—fit emblems of peace and happiness. Lik'st thou the treat I have in store for thee, love?"

"It is at least romantic," said Milwood, revolving in her mind how she could best turn the projects of her antiquated beau to her own advantage; "I should have imagined that Sir William Brandreth would have preferred the noise and bustle of a London life to the retirement of a country village."

"Aye! before I knew thee, my charmer, I might have done so; but now I pant for domestic felicity and quietness. I would keep thee all to myself; and let not those gay striplings whom I have heard buzz around thee, rob thee of any of thy smiling favours."

"*Heard!*" interrupted Milwood, rising from the recumbent attitude she had previously assumed, and drawing herself up to her full height—"heard! how dare you, Sir, upon hearsay, cast a stigma upon my character? Am I not to be believed, when I assert that you are the only visitor I have? Is my reputation to be assailed by rumours that I have not the power to control, but which those who know what envy can effect may easily account for? But I deserve these suspicions, for having confessed so guilelessly an attachment to yourself. I ought not to complain of your unjust reproaches, though Heaven, who knows the secret workings of my inmost soul, knows how wrongfully my conduct is impugned."

"Nay, sweet, I meant not to reproach thee when I said this," replied the other, confused by the torrent of tears that had followed Milwood's speech; "I believe thee, I do indeed; and as an earnest of it prithee take this case of jewels, to deck thyself with at thy leisure."

"They are valueless to me," sobbed Milwood, "without the heart that should accompany such gifts; but since you say you did not intend this insult, I accept them as a guerdon of your word: but 'twas unkind of you to suspect mine honour."

"Nay, nay, I'll think no more of it; and henceforth ———"

Here a loud knock at the door suspended the meaning of the sentence.

"Oh! what in the name of fortune will become of us?" hastily whispered the attendant, as she abruptly entered, "here is Mr. Barnwell, Madam, at the door; shall I say you are from home?"

"Nay, that would never do," answered Milwood; "you admit him, and I will find a way to get rid of the other. You may be surprised at what has occurred, Sir William," she added aloud, as the party addressed seemed somewhat startled by the mysterious behaviour of his companions; "but when I tell you that the person, whom you have just heard has arrived, is my brother, who has returned unexpectedly home to-day, your astonishment will cease. He is of a somewhat hasty disposition when the fit is on him, and where he to find you here it might be perhaps productive of bloodshed. Leave me then, my dear Sir William, for the present; and when he is gone, I will send to you again."

"Anything to please thee, my little Sultana," returned the other, "though I must confess I do feel surprised at not having heard of this brother of yours before."

"Nay, no remonstrances, Sir William; fly at once, before he ascends the stairs: for your own sake—for *my* sake, depart without further delay."

"I am gone, then. Farewell, my charmer! You remember your promise, to send to me when he has gone. A plague take the interloper! Such a cottage thou shalt have, bless thee! all covered with roses and lilacs, and—well, well! I see you are impatient. Farewell! my fascinating little decoy-duck I shall see the anon;" and, urged by the importunate gestures of Milwood, the old Baronet took his departure, not before, however, he had soiled the gloved hand Milwood extended towards him with a few clumsy kisses.

"Thank Heaven, I am rid of him!" said she to herself. "Now to prepare for the merchant's clerk, my more youthful swain."

So saying, Milwood assumed a more pensive appearance, and when Barnwell entered seemed deeply engaged in reading.

"Eleanor," said our hero, as he advanced, "I am not, I trust, intruding?"

"*You* intrude!" reproachfully uttered Milwood, as she rose from the table to meet him: "that, George, you can never do; I am always pleased to see you here at least."

"I have called to ascertain if I left my pocketbook here last night?" pursued Barnwell in desponding accents, as if he anticipated an answer in the negative.

"No! George, that indeed you did not—but you have lost nothing, I hope?"

"No matter—a mere trifle!" sighed Barnwell, as unwilling to explain the nature of his loss as to inflict pain on Milwood by suspecting her: "but you had company here when I arrived?"

"Company! nay, I had none: there are few who visit the abode of the poor and the humble. Stay! you must mean my uncle—true, he left me, I think, as you arrived."

This was said with such an appearance of artlessness, that many, more suspicious and wary than Barnwell, would have been deceived by the plausibility of her statement.

"I was not aware you had so near a relative," observed George.

"If I have not before mentioned his name to you," said Milwood, "you must impute the neglect to want of due courtesy, and to no other motive. He is a jeweller, and has presented me with these brilliant ear-rings as an Easter present."

"A gift worthy of the hand that receives them," said George in return; "but I fancied that his face was familiar to me upon 'Change, where I had heard him styled by the appellation of a baronet."

"Can he suspect?" thought Milwood; but, though much confused, she changed not colour: "I must be cautious here. True!" she said aloud; "you have, I see, noticed the resemblance that prevails between the two; it has been indeed sometimes a matter of much dispute among their respective friends which they had seen—but upon a closer view you may soon distinguish the difference—one being taller and more robust than the other: but, to change the subject to one more pleasant, I wish to visit Spring Gardens one day this week—will you accompany me?"

"Need I say with what pleasure I shall do so? When have you arranged to go?"

"The day after to-morrow," responded Eleanor; "I expect to meet some friends there, but should prefer being in your company."

"Gladly I accept your proposal, and will be true to my appointment; but I must now depart, since my avocations are now likely to require more strictly my presence than ever. I could not, however, permit even one day to pass unsunned by your smiles." And as the enamoured youth said this, he tangled his fingers in her luxuriant tresses, and impressed a passionate kiss upon her responsive lips. "Farewell, Eleanor!" he cried, as he fixed his eyes stedfastly on hers," and strained her to his heart: "you have exercised a strange power over me of late, and I need indeed all the love you bear me to sustain me in my trials; but I do not think you would play me false—I cannot believe that you would desolate the heart that loves you, tear up the flowery hopes that blossoms in my path, and plant a group of thorny cares instead—I say I cannot deem you capable of such cruelty, and would not willingly accuse you of it; but forgive me if in my frequent thoughts of you and happiness dark clouds of doubt and fear have hovered trembling around, and caused me to doubt the real emotions of your mind. Eleanor, do you *love* me?"

The eyes of her whom he addressed gradually became, as Barnwell proceeded, suffused with moisture, and for a time she seemed almost incapable of replying, but dashing a tear from her eyelids as she spoke, her features were suddenly lit up with animation, and her voice became more firm, and her tones more impressive, as she thus replied:

"George, this looks not well coming from you. Had I been so taunted by another, I could have borne it, but you who have experienced such repeated proofs of my devotion, from whose knowledge I withheld nothing, and for whom I have rejected the most brilliant offers, it is ungrateful of you, at least a harsher term I will not apply—but to doubt my sincerity, to question the ardour of my love, and to throw a stain upon my name, by causeless fears like these, stabs me to the heart. If you knew what I suffered when hearing this, even if I had been worse than you imagine me, even then, you would pity me; but why should I reveal my griefs to him who no longer will relieve them—rather shall my sorrows remain locked up in mine own breast, until they eat away their prison?"

Barnwell, attributing the vehemence of her emotions to a strict sense of female decorum, which he fancied he had offended, though he scarce knew how, apologised to her for what he had said, urging that she had taken a more extended meaning for his words than he had in reality intended to convey. Her heaving bosom and deep-drawn sighs manifested the passions that perturbed her breast, and caused

Barnwell to regret still more the imputations he had unwittingly given utterance to. At last, however, upon Barnwell's repeated assurances that he was now confident in her love, and doubted not her sincerity, Milwood rose and embraced him, both darting love-laden glances with their eyes, and exchanging with their lips mutual tokens of forgiveness.

"You will not fail, my dear George, in your appointment with me," said Milwood, perceiving Barnwell impatient to depart.

"Not for worlds!" responded Barnwell; "for they would but poorly repay me for thy absence. At what hour shall I see thee?"

"At six precisely," answered Eleanor.

"With the last stroke of the hour you may expect me; till then, farewell."

Again pressing her to his breast, and in a fond caress pilfering a score of kisses, Barnwell departed.

"Poor youth!" laughed Milwood, as soon as he was gone; "thou art most sorely duped. Come forth, my Abigail, and share the joys of thy mistress! Has he reached the door yet?"

"Aye, in sooth, has he," replied her confidant; "and in as joyous a mood as ever bridegroom danced in at a wedding, he sprang over the threshold as though he had taken lessons of Signor Carlo, the Spanish jumper; and pressing a crown piece into my hand, bade me attend incessantly to your comfort, and let you want for nothing. If he continue in the pace he set out with, he has reached Cheapside long ere this."

"Thou art a good girl, Hester, and may find this adventure profitable to thee; I have a plan by which we can carry on our schemes with more security, and one that I will reveal it to thee anon, but now time presses. Is my sedan ordered?"

"I have taken care that it awaits your orders," answered Hester. "You are now going to the theatre to see Mr. Oswell, the performer, I presume?"

"Thou art surely a witch, Hester, and I will have thee burned for one," smiled Eleanor in reply. "I *am* going to the theatre, and for the self-same purpose you have mentioned, too."

"Aye, Madam, there you have been entrapped yourself. If you pretend love to others, you feel it there for him."

"True, Hester; though I know not why it is so. He possesses not half the attractions either in mind or body to be found in any one of my other beaux, and yet I love him more. He was the sole tie that linked me to the stage, and it was through him that I was inititiated into the mysteries of the green-room—but, beyond that, I have no inducement to even speak to the man."

"You forget that he is married."

"Aye, there perhaps lies the reason. To gratify a womanish feeling of pride and vanity, I piqued myself upon obtaining that man's love, despite the difficulties that beset me in my path. I had to contend against the attractions of his home, of his wife, of his child: I vowed to myself that I would ween him from all. I kept my word—I DID so; he is now deprived of all that throws a halo round the hearth of domestic bliss. His wife, though every way superior to myself, (and I confess the truth, for the purpose of showing how art can triumph over virtue) is deserted, his child dead, and its father my minion—paramour—call him what you will—but I have succeeded in my task, and I am satisfied. I gloat over the misery I have caused—banquet on the ruin that I see has marked my progress—laugh to scorn the idle remonstrances of prating moralists, and run riot in my shame. Ha! ha! there is pleasure in all this that your duller brains wot not of."

Hester, who was too accustomed to such vehement outbreaks to pay them any undue attention, busied not herself in remarking upon the tendency of her speech, but patiently awaited the orders of her mistress, receiving which the sedan was brought round to the door, and Milwood, who had by degrees calmed the natural violence of her disposition into tranquility, now again called into requisition this power she possessed, and drawing down the inner blinds of the vehicle, to screen her from observation, was hurried off at a rapid pace to the theatre in Duke's Row, Lincoln's Inn Fields.

In thus affording the reader an insight into Milwood's character, we have been compelled to disclose some melancholy and startling chapters in the history of human nature. We could have laid bare still more, but the details of the life of a woman such as Milwood, however interesting they might be, would jar upon the eye and ear with their seeming improbability. Let not the reader so delude himself—the world still teems with occurrences such as we have described—motives as vile still lead to the same results, and, in fact, human nature is still the same, and the race of Milwoods is not yet extinct.

CHAPTER XII.

TRUEMAN'S MISSION.

Quick saddle and comparison your steeds!
We will to horse, and breathe the free air,
The country give us. Let no thoughts of home
Disturb your fancies aught; but let hot love
Grow cool, and whimper at its own fireside,
Ere it s all check you in your enterprise.
Come, come, my pupil, dost thou hear me now?

Tricks on Travellers, 1632.

What, my young student, wouldst thou study now
That you've not learn'd before? Is't Alchemy?
Mark how yon blushing girl converts her words
From air to gold, as dropping from her lips
They catch the listening ear of her fond swain.
Is't Witchcraft? Dare the witchery of that form,
And mark how potent is its magic spell.
Is't th n Astrology? Tut, tut! those eyes
Would make star-gazers of one half the world,
And keep the rest in darkness Leave then these
To grey-beards who thus waste their midnight oil,
And study thou Great Nature's fairest book—
The book of Nature, where a woman makes
The fairest page of all.

Old Play.

THE preparations for the departure being now completed, Mr. Thorogood impressed upon Trueman the necessity of secrecy in the business he was about to transact, and gave him the letter and documents necessary for the fulfilment of his mission.

Accordingly Trueman lost no time in complying with the wishes of his master. To Clara he bade adieu with a heavy heart: he feared lest his absence was alone wanting to consummate the nuptials between Clara and Sir Robert Otway. He dreaded lest the merchant, suspecting the attachment he bore towards his daughter, had resolved to ensure him a prolonged stay in the North, whither he was going,

and thus at once frustrate all his most ardent hopes. At one time he determined upon revealing all he knew of Sir Robert's villany, and thus effectually prevent the possibility of her being his bride; but in this he was overruled by Clara herself, who, for the reasons she had before stated, preferred circumstantial evidence, that was more decided, to the mere accidental circumstance, as it might upon explanation have proved, of the ring having been found on the merchant's premises the same night as he attempted abduction. In that case he considered that her father himself would hasten the match, and so hurry on a result that both desired most anxiously to avert. Under these impressions, therefore, they determined to await the effect of time; and, after exchanging the most ardent embraces and the most passionate protestations with the object of his devotion, Trueman renewed his vows of constancy with redoubled fervour, and departed in sadness to rejoin Mr. Thorogood in the hall.

"Well, farewell, Ned! and may thy mission be prosperous!" cried Barnwell, who was at the door, as he grasped the hand of his associate with warmth; "I shall miss thee much."

"Not more, George, than I shall regret your absence, I can assure you," answered Trueman. "I have arranged all my accounts with Mr. Thorogood, and received from him, in return, a compliment for my regularity. I should recommend your doing the same, and thus, when I am again with you, we shall be enabled to run on smoothly once more together."

"I will endeavour to do as you wish," stammered Barnwell in reply, colouring up with the recollection that when the books were inspected, his conduct would be known. The circumstance was, however, unnoticed by Trueman, who springing on to the back of the horse that was to be his companion in the journey, was engaged in testing the accuracy of its gear and appurtenances.

"Here," said Mr. Thorogood, handing him a pocket-book, "you will find ample means of defraying the expenses of your journey, and here," continued the merchant, extending towards him a folded paper, "you will find further instructions how to act. Now, Heaven make thy journey prosperous, and thy return home safe and speedy!"

"Amen, Sir! with all my heart," returned Trueman; and bidding adieu with his lips to Barnwell and the merchant, whilst he waved his hand at parting to Clara, who sat at the window above, with a beating heart and moistened eye, watching his departure, Trueman gave his impatient steed the rein, and the receding sound of his horse's hoofs, as they clattered over the rugged surface of Moorfields, soon gave token that the distance was fast increasing between the clerk and his employer.

Crossing what is now called the New Road, and selecting the great northern thoroughfare, as it was then styled, for the continuation of his course, Trueman relaxed somewhat from the speed at which he had hitherto proceeded, and allowed his fancy full play, in embodying the phantoms his imagination had conjured up. He saw Clara, sacrificing her own feelings at the altar of her father's interest—the bride of a man she abhorred. He thought that Mr. Thorogood, embarrassed as he was, would scruple not to yield even his daughter's happiness, if he imagined by so doing he could maintain his own credit as a merchant. He knew that the heart of Clara throbbed with too noble emotions to permit her to perhaps reproach herself at some future period with the thought that she had been the cause of her father's ruin; and then the question presented itself to his mind, was it wrong to love her? *Wrong!* what, to suppress feelings that proved alone the sources of his happiness!—to forego a hope that was the "one green spot" in the desert of his existence, the oasis in the arid plains of his memory's Sahara? Wrong! He could not—*would* not think it so. And yet he could not blind himself to the knowledge, that by continuing the path he had chosen, or rather perhaps had been impelled into, he was injuring his employer. He felt himself acting as a nightly marauder; robbing the person who had been most kind to him of his choicest treasure; meanly ensnaring the affections of her whose hand was intended to be the prize of one more wealthy. And yet, could he resign her without a pang, when his whole soul was devoted alone to her—when his happiness was centred in herself, and her love twined round his very heartstrings? It was a cruel, bitter thought! Rather would he abandon all, than her; give up the hopes of mercantile distinction, that had hitherto proved his fondest aspiration, and, secluding himself from the world that had wrought him so much unhappiness, pass the remainder of his days in ministering unseen to her welfare and meditating unheard-of on the harsh fate that had separated him from her.

Such was the direction of Trueman's reflections; and finding, from the depressing nature of them, that he had been surprised into a slower pace than was compatible with his intention of reaching St. Albans that night, he urged his animal to a gallop, and striking across the country in a westerly direction soon reached the secluded village of Hampstead. It was here, whilst recruiting his own and his horse's strength at the Seven Bells, that he saw Alice, as we have previously narrated, and struck by the extraordinary resemblance that she bore to a miniature which Barnwell had often shown to him as the portrait of Miss Travers, Trueman naturally felt somewhat surprised when he heard from the landlady that Alice had been brought up in the house, and that therefore, as he inferred, the resemblance must have been accidental. Alice, on the other hand, conceiving Trueman to have been in some way connected with the scene of her recent captivity, and fearful that he had been instructed to discover her retreat, was a prey thereby to the most maddening conjectures, little aware that the object of her suspicious fears was the bosom friend and fellow apprentice of him she loved, and would have given worlds to have seen.

Trueman, however, gave the occurrence no more than a passing thought; and after liberally remunerating the landlady for her useless intelligence, and quaffing off the liquor with which he had been furnished, he expedited his steed with a few encouraging sounds, and was soon, for the second time, lost in a reverie of the past.

Day had now deepened into twilight, and the evening breeze, as it whistled acrosss the moor over which Trueman was travelling, became every moment more tempestuous and more shrill. The whirring bat wheeled its circuitous flight each time nearer his head, and the tall trees shook their young leaves in the blast with a wild moaning sound that contributed not a little to the loneliness of the scene. To add to his comfort, a few heavy drops of rain, that fell at regular intervals from a dark black cloud, that loured gloomily above him, gave warrant that a storm was approaching, and excited fearful forebodings in his mind as to the chances of his escape from its influence. The red sun had sent forth at its departure a flaring yellow and sickly light over the horizon that seemed as cheerful as the mock hilarity of a dead man's smile; and night instead of coming on slowly and by imperceptible gradations, dispatched thick masses of vapour as heralds of its progress, in which all the succeeding gloom appeared to have been concentrated. Still Trueman urged his steed forwards: now wishing that he had not forsaken the main road; and again congratulating himself with the thought that he had so providentially fortified his interior man, by which means he had been enabled to defy the malignity of the elements. Still the rain came on faster and heavier; now plashing among the trees and plants that indigenous to the soil skirted the road side, and anon pattering on Trueman's leathern doublet with a force that soon made its wearer sensible of the moisture that it conveyed. Finding from the unbroken state of the clouds above him, that any abatement of the storm was not to be anticipated for some time, the traveller began to look anxiously about him for a shelter from its present inclemency, and espying a light that glimmered from a window a little way in advance, he rode hastily up to the house that presented such a welcome beacon, and found it to be an hostel of rather inviting aspect, and with a promise of every accommodation that could reasonably be required. Trueman accordingly dismounted; and leading his horse to the door, soon gave audible manifestations of his proximity.

The tavern before which Trueman had stopped was one of those old-fashioned, lumbering hostelries that was then common to the country for some miles around the metropolis, and which may still be found, although not in such abundance as formerly, decorating the High-street of our modern boroughs. It had been once the country seat of a wealthy nobleman, but as if to afford an illustration of "to what base uses" even mansions may return, it had been gambled away, with the estate on which it stood, by the only surviving relative; and the buyer not wishing to continue the expense attached to maintaining the family dignity in its pristine splendour, had, with very little trouble, converted the old building into a public house, in which capacity it had seen some fifty winters lodge their snow upon its gables, and as many summers bring to light and life the roses that blossomed round its portals.

The summons of Trueman was not long meeting with an answer. The door was speedily opened; and a good-humoured, rosy-cheeked individual, who acted as Boniface on the occasion, led the horse into the stable, and conducted its rider into the parlour, without more delay than was absolutely necessary to enable them to get to the two places mentioned. The room in which Trueman found himself was what had been once the kitchen of the mansion, but which had since then been doing duty as the parlour —and a wide rambling apartment it was too, with a lofty ceiling and ample fireplace, that now disgorged such heat as to make even the fire-proof visitors, who had gathered round it, withdraw to a more deferential distance. A wide-arched window, standing boldly out in a recess at the further end, admitted light to the room through an infinite number of small diamond-pattern panes, that here and there, damaged by the weather or accident, had at divers periods been relieved by sundry substitutes of brown paper, that, however dextrously disguised by the hand of the artist, were still too apparent to escape notice. Ranged along shelves on the sides of the apartment were brightly-polished culinary utensils, that reflected in their clear and lustrous surfaces the ruddy glow of the fire beneath; and peeping out from under the quaintly moulded cornices were two larger wicker cages, where the feathered captives had long since betaken themselves to rest. Trueman, however, thinking that the change of scene might effectually divert the current of his thoughts, expressed his willingness to remain where he was; and ordering a hot supper and bed to be prepared for him, drew his chair nearer the fire, and cast an observant eye upon the personages who were scattered round it, and who had suspended their conversation on his entrance.

Occupying the left-hand corner of the fireplace was a venerable old man, with white hair and wrinkled brow, that Trueman had but little difficulty in identifying as the old schoolmaster of the adjoining village. He had his arms folded, and his eyes bent down, as if in reflection upon some subject that had been started, and had apparently been unconscious of the arrival of any new-comer, as upon Trueman's entrance he had not expressed any signs of recognition at all. Next to him was a short, middle-aged man, with a sharp perking nose and chin, and two small jet black eyes, that twinkled as he spoke with a kind of unnatural lustre. This was Mr. Ferret, the lawyer; and to look at him as he sat sipping his brandy and water, accompanying each application of his lips to the glass with a fierce smack and a kind of suppressed laugh, one would think him one of the best-humoured lawyers in Christendom—and so he was too, even in general; but upon this occasion he was more than usually facetious, having ejected that day two poor tenants for not paying their rent on the morning it was due, and having, in addition, levied an execution upon a poverty-stricken widow with three young children, at the instance of the undertaker, who had not received the whole of the money due to him for the burial of one of her children. Opposite to the schoolmaster sat a ruddy-cheeked smoker, in the chimney-corner to the right, who, puffing his smoke into the air with a vehemence of jesture that appeared at first perfectly startling, was the representative of the sexton, having officiated for some time past in the former functionary, then confined to his bed by an attack of rheumatism, that left him but little hopes of being able to wield a spade again. Bill Mattock (for so was the deputy styled by those with whom Trueman now came in contact) was one of those light-hearted, careless fellows, who with a merry song would drown all disputes, and banish all cares and troubles in the vapour that arose in eddying circles from the bowl of his pipe. Nature made Bill Mattock a philosopher, and accident twisted him into a sexton's helpmate.

"Come," said Mr. Ferret, to the schoolmaster, as he inserted the poker between the bars of the grate, and gently raising the wooden log that blazed upon the fire, sent up such a bright column of sparks into the air as warmed the hearts and gladdened the eyes of all with its cheering contrast to the damp and cold without—"come, neighbour Lawson, this gentleman won't mind our talking, I

dare say; besides, it may amuse him. Finish your argument about the existence of these ghostly beings that you have been talking of."

"It's no pleasing subject, Master Ferret, for me to speak upon, I can assure you," said the old schoolmaster, slowly and mournfully: "I know too painfully the truth of what I am saying; but, since you wish it, I care not if I do tell you of it, though I remember the time when I would not have spoken on the subject—no! not for worlds; but now I am getting an old man, and my own turn will come soon. Well, well! I shall not detain you long: so listen; and may it make those who hear it pause, ere they enter on a career of guilt like that which marked the life of Jasper Hardyng!"

Trueman, who had become much interested in the appearance of his venerable companion, willingly accorded the looked-for permission to commence, and listened like the rest with an anxious ear and suppressed breath to the narration that we may call—

THE SCHOOLMASTER'S STORY.

"I was a young man," began the speaker, "when the event I am going to speak of took place, but it has left an impression upon my brain as clear and as vivid as if its occurrence was but of yesterday; and from that you may judge of the impression it made upon me at the time. I was like most gallants of that period a wild, thoughtless youth, with no care for the morrow, or reasonable mode of enjoying myself for the day, and having a loose dissolute set of companions, I soon contrived to spend in reckless debauchery the patrimony that should now have been the pillow of my age. Amongst the foremost of these associates of mine, and one with whom I was on greater terms of intimacy than the rest, was one Jasper Hardyng, a young man of about my own age, but far more experienced than myself in the mode of life I was now pursuing. We were both smitten with the daughter of a certain merchant in Eastcheap, whose friendly gold we had often furnished with wings in return for the security which we gave him as his due. I am an old man now, and grey hairs but ill accord with descriptions of female beauty, else could I tell you *how* beautiful Ruth Vaughan was. I loved her—sincerely loved her—and offered to make her my bride, but she preferred my comrade, Jasper, and he knew it. Hardyng's love was the love of a libertine; his sole object her ruin; but still, she loved him, and, although I knew his motives, I was silent. Perhaps a feeling of revenge taught me this hypocrisy; perhaps 'twas natural to me; but silent I was. The result proved to be what I anticipated, and confirmed my worst suspicions: Jasper lived with her for one month, and then deserted her. The next year was the year of the Great Plague, when the hand of death smote all around us, and amongst others it fell on her. That year will live in the recollections of others beside myself, but on none did it fall more heavily. She wrote to me to call and see her at a crazy lodging-house where she was living in St. Clement's. I called. God! I shall never forget that day. On a straw pallet lay the once haughty Ruth—the victim of the destroyer. Her dead child—Jasper's child, had died of the plague—she had taken out of its coffin, and was dangling in her arms. I sickened at the sight, but what followed was still more fearful.

Seeing that I had noticed the livid spot that marked the advent of the plague, Ruth, desperate and insane, and fearing that I should abandon her to avoid catching the infection, rushed to the door before I was aware of her design, and locked it, throwing the key out of the window. I stood like one panic-struck. Death in its most awful and lingering shape awaited me: shut up with one already dead and another dying of the plague, with no hope of liberation but that afforded by a slow and lingering death—oh, Heaven! it was torture! I would have given worlds for a drop of water at that moment. My lips were parched, and I fainted. When I again came to myself I found I was being carried, at night, in one of the dead carts through the streets. Torches glared on each side with a red, unearthly light, like the links of demons, and such for a time I fancied them to be, till the well known cry awoke me to a sense of my situation. How I got there I knew not, but now suppose the door had been broken open by the owners of the house, and the dead inmates of the room—of which I was apparently one—conveyed away. Of that, however, I gave no thought, my remaining strength being now devoted to affecting my own liberation. Watching my opportunity, though weak and disabled, I contrived to drop out unperceived behind, for I feared had I been seen they would have murdered me on the spot in order to prevent my spreading the contagion. The first person I saw on leaving the dead-cart was Jasper Hardyng. I told him of the fate of Ruth. He laughed in ridicule, and called me *coward.* Can it be wondered that I struck him ? He reeled and fell. I dragged his bleeding body to a pit dug near the spot. Before he died, he cursed me—cursed me with his lips from which the blood was gushing like a fountain, and, mingling with his dying breath a horrible imprecation, vowed, if there was a hereafter, that he would follow me on earth to my latest moment. I flew from the spot, but still his image, ghastly and blood-stained, was present to my sight. I sought the clear sky and the green sward of the country - but he kept his word—for twelve successive nights he appeared before me, calling down vengeance on my head for having slain him ere he had repented his misdeeds, and telling me he was suffering the tortures of the damned in consequence. Since then I have tried change and scene and country—have wandered through every clime and every region; but the horrible infliction still haunts me ; I am doomed to expiate my crime by a punishment such as mortal never before felt, and still I have lived on day by day, and night by night, as if Heaven was unwilling to bring my miserable existence to a close. I am now, however, warned of my approaching end : last night Jasper Hardyng again drew the curtains of my bed, and presented his fearful countenance clotted with gore as it was on the morning of our encounter, but it was to tell me my hour had arrived. Before another sun has risen I shall be a corpse! I see you think it a delusion ; think, perhaps, that my sorrows have made me frantic ; but it is not so. Would to Heaven ! I were really mad ; but reason, as if to render my feelings more acute, has throughout my life still maintained its seat. I am now on the verge of the grave. You have wrung from me my history, but it has been given the more willingly that I believe it may be like the poison that works well for some though ill to others. He who visits my grave will find, perhaps, my bones blanched, and my flesh crumbled ; but my soul—where the secret has gnawed my vitals till life has become a burden—will still be the object of Jasper Hardyng.''

As the old man finished his recital, that was only interrupted by his own frequent sobs of anguish, large drops of perspiration stood upon his brow, and his whole frame shook with the vehemence of his emotions, but his hearers moved not.

Staggering, rather than walking to the door, he reached the threshold ; but the exertion proved too much, and casting a fearfully vivid glance behind him, his features became strangely contorted, and he fell heavily to the ground. With the assistance of the neighbours who began now to be gradually moving off in twos and threes, he reached his bed ; but his forebodings were realized, and the next time

the sun streamed into the old man's bed-chamber, it cast its rays upon a corpse.

Trueman finding that he had been left alone in the parlour, and wishing to forget the narration he had heard, hastily dispatched his supper, and inquired for his room. Ascertaining that it had not been slept in for some time, he ordered a fire to be lit, thinking that he would sit up for an hour before he went to bed, and arrange plans for his future proceedings. The servant returning brought him word that his injunctions had been complied with, and now waited to conduct him to his chamber.

The room in which our adventurer was to sleep, appeared to be in a part of the house seldom used. At the noise of their footsteps as they proceeded, aroused from their slumbers, numberless rats who rushed from the arras that in most instances covered the wainscot of the lobbies, as if to ascertain who it was that had dared to molest them in their retreat. At the end of the second lobby, the servant, who rather a pretty specimen of rustic beauty, described the room that was appropriated to Trueman's use, and half-seriously and half-jestingly asking him whether he was afraid of ghosts, lit her own candle that she held in her hand, and wishing him good night, returned at a rapid pace from the lobby to the more inhabited portion of the building.

Trueman found the room to which he had been directed with but little difficulty, and, on entering it, soon saw the reason of the girl's question as to his fear of spectral visitors. The chamber was, in fact, just such a place as a ghost of the old school would have wished to have taken up his residence in : it was wide and commodious, but so lonely as to make the heart of Trueman, as he entered, become chilled with horror. An antiquated piece of furniture with faded curtains and worm-eaten wood-work, supplied the place of a four-post bedstead, and rendered him still less anxious to seek repose. Two full-length portraits of some former possessor of the mansion, hung on each side of the fire-place, and frowned in most majestic sympathy with each other, whilst a closet which on being opened discovered nothing but a heap of rubbish, filled up the recess on the chamber. The fire, however, burned up bright and cheerily, and that was some compensation for the gloom of the other part of the room ; so Trueman drew the chair and table nearer the fire, trimmed the candle, mixed himself some spirits, and began to unpack his portmanteau.

Finding the books he was in search of, Trueman commenced reading, but was soon aroused by a loud noise, apparently proceeding from the closet, that seemed to bear some resemblance to a person endeavouring to force an entrance.

Rising from his seat, he anxiously scrutinized every corner of the apartment, but found all secure. Fastening the door by a bolt, as the lock he thought might be forced, Trueman examined the closet, but finding nothing to excite his suspicions, he attributed the noise to the rats which had before attracted his notice, and laughing at the imaginary dangers such sounds had conjured up, composed himself once more to his task. But it was in vain that he strove to fix his wandering mind on the page that his eyes beheld ; his fancy wandered to the tale told by the schoolmaster, and the possibility of the grave giving up its prey ; and then the fire, aided by the fatigue of a long journey, began to woo him to repose ; the candle diminished more and more each minute, and at last burned down into the socket and extinguished itself.

Then all was dark and quiet, save the pattering of the rain against the window-panes, and the crackling of the embers on the fire; but the silence affected not the slumber of Trueman, for he slept on, still dreaming of plague-spots and apparitions: but fortunate for him was it that he did sleep, else would he have seen standing at the back of his chair a tall figure, gaunt and ghostlike, with a dark shadowy mantle that concealed his features. This strange apparition was rendered still more impressive by being illumined alone by the flickering red light of the fire; and the darkness magnifying its real proportions imparted a truly startling effect to its appearance.

Still Trueman slept on in ignorance of the presence of what might have rendered his slumbers less tranquil than they were, until the weighty pressure of a cold hand upon his shoulder aroused him to a sense of his position. Raising himself from his seat with the confused appearance of one walking from some horrible vision, his eyes encountered the figure, whose mysterious entry we have previously described; and paralised with horror at the sight, Trueman stood transfixed with fear and astonishment. His first impulse was to discharge one of the pistols that he had about his person; his second to inquire the motive of the intrusion; but the action of the being before him anticipated him in both, and he refrained from exercising the power of either his weapon or his tongue.

Making an inclination of the head, and beckoning with its hand, the spectral visitor, if such it was, motioned Trueman to follow. Undetermined whether to obey so dangerous a request, Trueman stood for some moments irresolute, but, at last, summoning up courage to proceed, he snatched up his pistol from the table, and signified his willingness to go on. Leading through a winding passage he proceeded along in silence, keeping the weapon in readiness for any meditated attack that might be made. The passage which they were now threading terminated in a vault, in the centre of which was a trap-door that being open disclosed a flight of stone steps illumined by a glimmering lamp that sent forth a few faint rays over the place where they stood. All that Trueman had heard of the dead haunting the living with their presence, till some mighty secret was imparted to one bold enough to hear it, now flashed across his memory, and he thought of the fearful narrative he had that night heard, with a startling conviction of its truth.

A deathlike silence, unbroken by even the breathing of Trueman, succeeded; but still the figure moved onwards, and, descending the staircase, appeared impatient at his delay. Considering that he could not endanger his safety by proceeding, more than he had already done, Trueman followed his mysterious guide, and, reaching the bottom of the steps, passed rapidly through an intervening quadrangle, and soon after confronted his supernatural conductor in the open air.

CHAPTER XIII.

THE ORANGE TREE, WESTMINSTER.

[strong,
Peppercorn.—How now, ye brawlers! Is the drink so
That, it, perforce, must mount into your heads,
And steal away the furniture thereof?
Or does the valiant soul each boasts he has
O'er boil itself with commendable rage,
And cast its bubbling froth upon the rest?
Fie; fie! for shame! no quarrelling 'mongst friends!
If ye must fight, go fight the watch, ye knaves;
They'll find employment for ye.

Dick with the dirk.—Well! well! be cool, good Master
We had a bout of swords just for the nonce—   [Peppercorn.
But nothing further.   Fighting is our food—
The very sustenance by which we live—
The atmosphere itself in which we breathe.
Then, why debar us from such provender,
Which, if we have not, death would sure ensue?

The Bully of Alsatia, 1697.

WESTMINSTER! ever venerable, ill-built, and ill-inhabited Westminster! what volumes might be written descriptive of the deeds that have been done within thy precincts; what folios might be filled with details of the scenes thy crooked courts have witnessed; and what wild fancies might be conjured up from thy dark alleys and gloomy thoroughfares—fancies such as would make stout hearts quail, and young forms shudder—fancies that would blanch the rosy cheek of the fair listener, and check the jest on the lips of the witling—fancies that would create dreams from the impressions they would lave, and fears from the thoughts they would give rise to; but it is not with these that our business lies; we have to recount the wanderings of those that pass its humble tenements unmindful of the associations they bring with them, and to these, accordingly, we direct our attention.

Crossing from the Broad Sanctuary into the Almonry, and threading a maze of dirty hovels and crumbling almshouses that skirted the adjacent thoroughfare, were two ruffian-looking personages, from whose stealthy manner of progression it might have been gathered they were from some cause or other anxious for concealment. With this object in view, they could not have selected a better path than the one they were now pursuing. Here and there a flickering oil-lamp, calculated more to mislead than to guide, shed an unsteady glimmer upon the surrounding huts, but the darkness was throughout the greater part of the road so intense as to cause sundry misgivings on the part of one of the pedestrians as to the probability of their reaching their destination in the direction they were then taking. It was scarcely an hour past dusk; but the narrow lanes so completely shut out the light of day, as to occasion the inhabitants to burn lights as well when the sun was above the horizon as when it was below it. The traveller's doubts, however, were speedily set at rest by the increased confidence with which his companion proceeded at every turn, and as he paused to ignite a short pipe thrust between his lips, at a coal-shed on the way, he found that his associate was in advance some dozen yards before him.

"Come along, Mark!" said the foremost, addressing him; "thou art ever a laggard when business is afoot, though I'll give the credit for the most active industry when the wine-cup's afloat. Hast thou no pluck in thee, man?"

"Why," returned the other, as he came up to the speaker, "you don't consider, Jack, that we have journeyed many a wearisome mile to-day, and I'm tired. But wherefore this haste?"

"Thou shalt know anon," answered Meggott; for it was him; "and then thou wilt be satified, I trust: in the meantime consider that, if our comrades leave the Orange Tree before our arrival there, we might as lief have remained down at St. Alban's, for what good we should be like to do; but come, rouse thee, man! a hot supper awaits us yonder, and each step instead of diminishing adds to my appetite."

Continuing their progress at a more rapid pace than before, they soon reached a smoky, poverty-stricken region, that appeared the very abiding-place of crime in its worst shapes, and known to the dwellers therein and the neighbourhood around, by the appellation of "Palmer's Village." Here they stopped awhile before a low, dingy public-house, the sounds that proceeded from which gave evidence of the scenes of riot and revelry that were taking place in the interior.

Arresting the arm of his companion who was entering without ceremony, Meggott cautiously approached an aperture in the smoke-begrimed red curtain that was slung along the window, and communicating to Haydon his intention of watching for a few moments the conduct of those inside, the two took up their station on the exterior, where, for a short time, we leave them, to glance at the proceedings of the inmates of the room into which the footpads were now gazing.

Seated in various postures around a few crazy oaken tables scattered in different parts of the parlour, were a group of ill-conditioned "tobymen" relieving the ennui of the evening by gambling. Dirty packs of cards that had been dealt round so often as to deface the images on most, were in the hands of each, and the nature of the stakes might be determined from the liquor supplied in abundance to every player. Dense clouds of smoke rose heavily into the confined atmosphere around them, and rendered the objects almost indistinct; but eyes beheld them used to such a medium, and they played on, therefore, unmindful of the thick vapour around. The ale-jugs and bottles were taken and refilled again and again; glasses were replenished, as each moment passed, and the conversation became less quiet and more general. The motions of the speakers began to be more governed by the laws of gravity, and, by degrees, the drinkers one by one disappeared from the chairs and stools on to the sanded floor beneath. Oaths and imprecations interlarded their discourse more freely, and the tumult of voices, each struggling to be heard, caused the words to be confused into a meaningless torrent of sounds.

Three of the card-players, whose heads were as yet proof against the potency of the liquids, were pursuing their game with greater ardour than the rest, in a remote corner, watching each turn of the cards as if their very existence depended upon their present success, and demonstrating by their gestures the interest with which they surveyed the progress of the game, and the little heed they took of what was going on at the further end of the room.

"Come," said the elder one of the three, at the conclusion of one of the rounds, "you are

lucky, Jem, to-night; burn me if I don't think you've struck a bargain with the old one!"

"That makes us quits," added the second, as he handed a few bright coins to his companion: "one more game, and we'll leave this flash ken to take care of itself, while we roll ourselves down eastward."

"With all my heart, Clayton," returned the first speaker; "else will Jem Brooke here with his new fakements turn me out empty. So another game, and then to business!"

The game was recommended; glasses were again refilled, and bottles were again emptied. The game was concluded—the winner was the same as before.

"Clayton," suddenly cried one of the losers, prefacing the name with an expletive we care not to repeat; "there's roguery in this! Jem has cribbed some cards to-night from the pack, or my name's not Harris, that's all!"

"Who says that is a liar!" returned the party accused.

"There are two words to that bargain, Jem," quickly uttered the other: "say that word again, and I will cram your teeth down your throat for it."

"Come, come," interposed Clayton, "heed not what he says; we have more urgent calls upon our time than petty quarrels such as this. It's getting late."

"Well! well!" said Harris, "I'll be with you: your hand, Jem; I would not quarrel just now with one of my oldest pals—say there was no trickery in your play and I am satisfied."

"I call Heaven to witness there was none!" replied the burglar, elevating his right arm. The action betrayed him; the removal of his hand caused his roguery to be known, and the few cards he had secreted in his vest fell fluttering to the ground.

The countenance of Harris changed, his lips quivered, but no sounds came therefrom. Clayton himself moved not, but stood like one transfixed at the knavery of his associate, who confounded at the sight of the cards was looking moodily on.

The silence was soon broken by Harris, who, threatening to hurl the trickster to the earth, gave vent to his rage in language too vehement for repetition.

The blood of the other now began to boil, and throwing himself on Harris, Brooke dealt a succession of blows that would have been, had any reached their intended destination, the means of reversing the nature of the threat just given.

"Peace! peace! ye turbulent knaves," cried Clayton, interposing himself between the combatants: have ye no better target for your blows than each other's bodies? Although Jem did handle his fixing cap, its no reason why his head should suffer for it afterwards."

"Pshaw!" cried Harris, ceasing to prolong the encounter; you'd not wing a hawk though you saw it carrying away one of your own chickens. I hate such milksops!"

"Well! henceforth I am as mute as a milestone," cried Clayton, "and when I again do a friendly deed, why somebody may tell me of it—that's all."

During this speech, Brooke, unmindful of the cowardice of the action, had stolen behind Harris, and was in the act of raising his arm to strike him when he was arrested by the powerful grasp of Clayton, who, surmising the probability of such a circumstance, was prepared for the consequences, and restrained the blow.

"Now, Mark," said Meggott to Haydon, "is the time for us to enter: this brawl may end seriously else;" and pushing aside the door, that yielded to their pressure, the two encountered the group we have attempted to describe.

"Shame on ye for idle dullards!" exclaimed Meggott as he carefully surveyed the position of the trio, who released their hold immediately on the entry of the new comers. "Shame on ye! I say, for witless brawlers, who let the liquor get the better of their reason. What! Harris, Brooke, Clayton, do you forget your old pals Meggott and honest Mark here!"

A hearty shake of the hand given by Clayton and Harris, and a scornful glance bestowed upon him by Brooke, proved that such was not the case; and the four (for the originator of the uproar had left that side of the room) were soon earnestly engaged in conversation over a fresh supply of liquids that had been brought in, and were, in addition, doing their best to lessen the quantity of sundry substantial viands that mine host of the Orange Tree had introduced in a dish as a no very unwel come companion to the fluids already there.

All the demands that an unruly appetite could by any possibility make upon the good things provided, were duly honoured, and the dialogue recommenced.

"I have purposely waited till the rest departed," said Meggott, casting a furtive glance around, as if fearful that some stray word might catch a listener's ear that was not intended: "I say I have waited to tell you that the plan I was speaking to you about, Clayton, is now ripe—the crib I mentioned may be cracked to-morrow, and we four be all that share the booty or the knowledge of it."

"Where does it lay?" inquired Harris.

"At Hampstead, and is known by the sign of the Seven Bells. I have beat about the house for some nights past, and find that there's nothing to fear from those who live there, as the house is only inhabited by an old lady, her husband, and a pretty lass who acts, I think, as barmaid. I peeped into the young girl's bed-room the other night, and frightened her nearly out of her seven senses, though how it was she saw me I don't know."

And a brutish laugh succeeded the empty taunt.

"But the swag?" impatiently cried Clayton.

"Is as safe as Tyburn," responded Meggott, "and will be made up chiefly of plate, watches, and other things which we may turn into cash as easily as possible. I've arranged already with a Jew for their disposal."

"And when do you propose setting out?" asked Harris.

"To-morrow morning, and remaining there for the day," said Meggott; "the cart will be in readiness by ten."

"Then at that time we'll start," answered Clayton. "Two had better go down first to lull the beaks off their guard, or else we may be nosed."

"That also I have determined on," said Meggott;" and we two will go; you and Harris can meet us there—the place I will appoint. There is another little affair in hand which I have left to Haydon to continue, that at first I thought bid fair to turn out well, but now changes a little. No matter! we'll speak of that at another time. Remember! at ten to-morrow."

And with that the thirsty quartette maintained an interchange of toasts and a consumption of fluids, that abated not till day-break, when each flinging himself down on the low bench, that was continued round the sides of the parlour, sought, in that position, a few hours' slumber, to prepare them for the business of the day.

Morning, however, came at last, and with it bright beams and cheering smiles of light. The few stunted plants that reared their smoky and leafless stems above the dirt that, confined within four bricks, to represent a flower-pot, had vegetated for years in the parlour-window of the Orange Tree, actually seemed that day to have discarded the dirty-brown colour in which the branches usually appeared, for a bright coat of green, that seemed truly to bring with it heart-refreshing reminiscences of summer and green fields, and all the delicious associations connected therewith. The poor linnet, too, that imprisoned in its wiry prison, had hitherto only sang a sorrowful tale of its capture and present bondage, now began to change its plaintive note for a joyful burst of song, and after a few preparatory trials, as if to essay an almost-forgotten accomplishment, hailed the glad sunshine, and the warmth it brought, with a flood of melody that might for its sweetness have been trilled forth in one of nature's fairest spots, and under one of Heaven's bluest canopies. The smoky walls themselves even seemed to partake of the revivifying influence the sunbeams cast on all around, and looked less smoky and more cheerful; whilst the table, strewn with remnants of the previous night's debauch, such as broken pipes, cracked glasses, and other indications of revelry, presented a far less nauseating appearance to the eye of a spectator than might have been otherwise the case.

Giving a few hearty slaps to the sleepers' shoulders, Meggott, who was the first to awake, having altered his previous determination, soon roused the whole party from their slumbers, and in a very short time they were ready to proceed.

Leaving the Orange Tree to the right, they turned down Artillery Row, towards where it branches off in the direction of Tothill Street, and taking advantage of a by-way here, came, after the threading of many tortuous alleys and courts, into the precincts of the Almonry—now vulgarly corrupted into Ambury.

The Almonry of those days, as may be imagined, presented a few different features to those that perhaps the reader will now see, if he, defying the pleasant badinage of certain rosy-cheeked young ladies who, attired in robes of varied hues, and boasting of shoes and stockings where the fissures are NOT "few" or "far between," will, no doubt, entice him into a free and easy conversation unrestrained by the trammels that society imposes—we say, if he, defying all this, can screw up his courage to what Macbeth has denominated the "sticking-place," and provided himself with a friend, and a cudgel in case of "accidents," will explore the sacred limits of this region, he will find that, even in its present state, it will well repay him for the trouble, and that its crumbling tenements and old-fashioned architecture still possess interest and poverty sufficient to gladden the heart of an antiquary or a poor-law commissioner.

The Almonry, properly so styled, is a large open quadrangle, at the back of Tothill Street, and eastward of the Broadway, with a number of courts diverging from it to all points of the compass, and garnished on every side by lofty four-storied houses, that seemed to threaten destruction on all who pass beneath. In some, long wooden balconies and galleries form a communication from the exterior of one house to that of another, and impart a truly foreign appearance; whilst the extended articles of domestic apparel, that having undergone the ordeal of soap and water, are spread upon projecting poles from window to window, and waive in the breeze that finds its way down there and keeps on continually whistling as if it could not find its way back again, resemble the chivalric flags and ancient pennons that erstwhile welcomed the wanderer back from the "Holy Land." A pavement, the component parts of which appear to be oyster shells and cabbage-stalks glutinized together with a certain adhesive preparation called mud, and a pump, the water of which has ceased to flow for ages, the Almonry still can boast of; but the introduction of gas and policeman has done much to alter the character of the place, and the "night-rufflers" and "day-squeezers" that our forefathers feared so much in days of yore, are now to be no longer heard of within its precincts. A polite inquiry after the health of one's maternal parent, a similar interrogatory as to whether you are supplied with soap, and a few other playful little sallies of that description, that are occasionally indulged in, constitute all that the visitor has now to fear, "provided always," as the lawyers have it, he runs not headlong into danger of his own accord.

Here it was that the first printing press ever known in England was established by Caxton, who printed thereat the first book ever read in a printed form, entitled the "Game at Chesse;" here it was that Chaucer wrote a considerable portion of his "Canterbury Tales," and gathered ideas for the others; here was it that Savage, the poet lived, and nearly died—for in a night-brawl here he was within an ace of being murdered; and, lastly, here was it that our Knights of the Road, Meggott, Clayton, and Harris, were patiently waiting for Haydon to return with the tools of their profession which Haydon kept in his room for the use of the gang. They had not, however to wait long; the tools were brought, and obtaining the cart they required, all four now availed themselves of the vehicle's assistance, and urging the animal to its full speed were conveyed at a rapid rate towards their destination."

It was by this time late in the afternoon, and the silver crescent of the young moon had already gemmed the blue sky in the east with its presence. The back lanes having been chosen as the best suited to conduct them to their destination, they encountered none save an occasional straggler on foot, or a labourer returning homewards from his daily toil; and this circumstance, added to an indulgence in sundry potations whilst they were proceeding, caused them to become slightly more uproarious than their previous designs of secrecy might seem to warrant. Mark Haydon, who was ever foremost in echoing a sound of hilarity from others, gave vent to feelings of this nature now, and impelled thereto by the requisitions of his companions, trolled forth, adapted to a popular air of the period, a "right merrie" song, which, as it will serve to give the reader an idea of the excuses then framed for following the "profession" of a thief, we subjoin as above:—

SONG OF THE HIGHWAYMAN.

Let moralists prate that to rob is a crime
That deserves, when it's done, to be punished in time,
You shall find I will prove the reverse in my rhyme.

     Tra, la, la; tra la.
     A Highwayman's life for me!

The moon robs the sun of its heat and its light,
The earth robs the moon, which, of course, serves it right!
And mankind rob the earth, such a prig to requite.

     Tra, la, la, &c.

Each cloud robs the sea, all its moisture to drain!
And the earth robs each cloud of its booty, in rain!
Whilst the sea robs the earth of its treasure again.

     Tra, la, la &c.

That the atmosphere's robbed from the flowers, you'll learn
They depend for their life on its aid, you'll discern,
But the air of their fragrance robs them in return.

     Tra, la, la, &c.

The miser himself robs throughout every clime,
And to heap up his riches robs youth of its prime;
One is robbed of his name and another of time.

     Tra, la, la, &c.

Death robs us of life in an unpleasant way!
And the grave robs all life of its troubles, they say!
But the worms in return rob the grave of its prey.

     Tra, la, la, &c.

This, I think, is enough angry feelings to smother!
Since here I have proved, without much care or bother,
That throughout all existence we rob one another!

     Tra, la, la, tra la.
     A Highwayman's life for me!

"Hold!" cried Meggott, seeing the white spires of the village church of Hampstead peeping above the thick foliage of the trees that surrounded it: "we must be near the crib that we are going to crack to-night. A few minutes will bring us within a dozen yards of the spot—so, caution, my pals! and success is certain."

Allowing the horse to increase its previous canter into a gallop down the hill before them, they diverged a little to the right, and Meggott's supposition being found correct, the cart was put up at a dingy-looking ale-house at hand, the seclusion of which seemed to further their objects of concealment, and the burglars entered, determined to await the arrival of night when they could put their plan into execution.

The intervening hours were spent in drinking and revelry. Glass after glass was sent merrily round, and bottle after bottle emptied; but it seemed to exercise but little effect on the heads of those present. Darkness at last came on, and out the four sallied to reconnoitre the scene of their intended robbery. The stars had studded the firmament with jewel-like brilliancy, and the night-breeze, as it whistled cheerily over the heath, fell on the ear with a strange unearthly sound, as if the guardian spirits were aware of the act about to be committed, and warned the inmates of the tavern of the fate that awaited them. The cart had been left in the hands of Clayton, and the rest moved stealthily onwards in the direction of the Seven Bells.

The chimes of the village church now showed the hour of eleven to be passed, and the depredators began to cast anxious glances around to ascertain that their own safety, in case of alarm, was provided for. But all was quiet, save the baying of some watchful house-dog too far distant to interfere with their designs, and the scene appeared so serene and tranquil, that the very falling of a leaf would have carried with it an audible sound to the ears of those that listened.

"Now then, hand me over the *insinivator!*" cried Harris, passing his hand rapidly over the exterior of the window to discover where the fastenings were situated; "all's quiet and as right as a trivet."

"Well! you star the glaze if needful, and I'll take care of the 'vallytles,'" interrupted Meggott. "Mark here can keep watch; and, harkee, take care of one of my bull-dogs for me in case of a queer card turning up! Is everything ready?"

"All right!" was the response, and to work the burglars proceeded. The shutters were soon detached, and an entrance effected through the window. Meggott climbed in, and assisted by the lantern that Harris held, surveyed the position of the spot in which he stood.

It was the parlour behind the bar into which Alice was inducted on her first visit there, and contained little beside sundry articles of plate, which Meggott possessed himself of without scruple. Espying, however, a closet half-open, to the left, his experienced glances soon detected a small iron box secured by a strong padlock. This he at once surmised to be the place where the money was kept, and, summoning Harris to his assistance, he began most vigorously to assail the lock with one of the instruments he held in his hand. For some time, however, its strength baffled him; but a violent wrench at last enabling him to succeed, a bright display of gold and silver met his delighted gaze, and a further search revealed a packet of bank-notes that had been before concealed by a secret drawer. Appropriating these, and giving instructions to Harris to do the like, the till next became the object of his attention. To open this a knife was necessary, and, seizing a large carving knife that was on the shelf beside him, Meggott so skilfully applied it that all its resistance was soon overcome, and the drawer flew open with a loud noise. Its contents, however, disappointed him, a few silver and copper coins being all that he found therein, and he was about closing it again with an oath or two, when footsteps on the stairs alarmed him.

It appeared that Mrs. Royster, the landlady, hearing strange noises below, which she was at a loss to account for, had risen from her bed, and was now coming down the stairs to ascertain the cause of the unusual sounds. The light directed her.

"Hush, Jack, douse the glim!" cried Harris; "the crib's roused."

All was utter darkness.

"Help! murder! thieves!" exclaimed Mrs. Royster, at once perceiving the danger in which she stood.

"Oh! if it's to blow the gab you're after, that dodge must be silenced," said Meggott, who, with the knife in his hand, endeavoured to stifle her cries with a towel that he found near him.

Alice, now waking with the disturbance, and fearing that some fearful deed was being committed, crept softly down stairs, and, learning the position of affairs by leaning over the bannisters, hastily returned to her room, where some fire-arms were kept, and taking from thence a couple of pistols which she knew to be loaded, roused Ralph Royster, who was asleep, and snoring most lustily in his own room, and hurried back to the landing.

"Now then, Harris," cried Meggott, "be off with the swag through the window—quick! d'ye hear?—and I'll follow. D—n the woman! how she clings to me!"

"'Sdeath!" exclaimed Meggott; "I shall be roughly here, if I stop—at all hazards I must go, and, if nothing else will release me, this must," and drawing the sharp blade of the carving-knife across the throat of the unfortunate woman, the heavy fall and groan that ensued told the murderer that his object was gained, and Alice that her kind friend and protector had ceased to exist.

Without stopping to ascertain more, Meggott snatched hold of the lantern Harris had left behind him, and seeing Haydon waiting for him threw to him the plate he had been able to secure, and jumped through the window after it. Alice, scarcely knowing what she did, now discharged the second pistol, which missing Meggott, for whom it was intended, struck Haydon on the shoulder, and causing him to utter a loud exclamation of pain, felled him to the ground. Meggott, on hearing the report, turned quickly round, and seeing in one moment Haydon's unfortunate situation, he raised him on his shoulders, and bore him towards the cart, where Clayton and Harris were waiting anxiously expecting their arrival.

The neighbourhood had by this time become alarmed, and, accustomed to depredations of this nature, the cry of "robbery" and "murder" was soon responded to by a dozen voices from the neighbouring houses, the inmates of which, notwithstanding the lateness of the hour, were in a few moments up and ready to secure the assailants.

The fugitives, however, were far beyond their reach. Satisfied with the booty they had obtained, although it had not turned out equal to their expectations, the burglars made their escape from the scene of action at a pace that set pursuit at defiance, and, in less time than the narration of it has occupied in telling, the cart was seen leisurely jogging over the stones that marked the road of the leading northern thoroughfare. This altered pace was, indeed, necessary, for the jarring motion of the previous few minutes had so increased the danger arising from Haydon's wound, that it was deemed advisable, at all hazards, to allow the vehicle to progress at a gentler rate. To have summoned the assistance of a surgeon there, would have been to have ensured instant detection, and there was no alternative, therefore, left but to convey him back to the Almonry.

Although the pain was excessive, a few heavily-drawn sighs alone escaped the lips of the wounded man, to tell the agony he was suffering, and these were at long and distant intervals. Meggott had stanched the blood with his handkerchief in the first instance, but the jolting of the cart had caused the wound to bleed afresh, and the unhappy man was, therefore, now wallowing in a pool of his own blood. By the time they reached Westminster the day had begun to dawn, and the burglars, who had scarcely exchanged a word on the road, began to look cautiously around them to ascertain that their proceedings were not watched.

Haydon, and it was fortunate for him that such was the case, had swooned from the loss of blood some time before they had passed the Gothic edifice that told them their journey was at an end. They had, therefore, no difficulty in conveying him to his room—a scantily-furnished apartment in a dilapidated house that reared its unsightly front among the other crazy hovels with which the Almonry abounded.

Leaving him on a straw pallet, that was the humble substitute for a bed, Harris went in search of a brother of the gang—one Andrew Warren—who added to his skill in thievery sufficient medical knowledge to enable him to tend those unfortunate fellows of his craft who required his services.

The two soon returned together, and Warren, after narrowly scanning and probing the wound, commenced preparing the remedy a case like his demanded. The bullet was found to have lodged in the flesh just beneath the shoulder-bone, and its extraction was accomplished with as much difficulty to the operator as pain to the patient. It was, however, done at last, and the healing liniment was then applied. This seemed to afford the wounded man some relief, for his respiration became more easy, and his frame more composed than before. His eyelids seemed weighed down with sleep, and, under the advice of Warren, he was allowed to fall into a deep and tranquil slumber.

Meggott and Clayton now left him under the care of the two others, and hurried down to the Minories with the booty they had obtained, in order to effect its disposal with the old Jew fence. A few words served to clench the bargain between them. and, although the plate and notes were disposed of at one-fifth of their value, the two declared themselves satisfied with the transaction, and soon departed some pounds the richer for their night's adventure.

In the parlour of the Seven Bells a sad and mournful assemblage had collected.

The morning sun was streaming merrily in through the window and flinging its bright rays on the blood-stained carpet, as if to render its contrast with that and the tear-filled eyes of the group who were scattered around still more striking. It is a mournful sight when the orb of day, that should only light up things fair and pleasant to the eye, throws its beams upon a dead body; but when that body is a murdered one, it comes with a still stronger and more painful sense of the mockery conveyed. The goldfinch in its humble wicker-cage, whose cheering notes had, erstwhile, gladdened the heart of her whose inanimate form lay stretched beneath, had been hushed in its matin minstrelsy by Alice who had thrown her handkerchief over its welcome prison, and now, as if conscious of the melancholy event that required its silence, the poor bird drooped its head pensively down, and ceased even to pick up the scattered seeds that the kind hand of its mistress had strewn on the previous night over the bottom of its cage. Ralph Royster, who to do him justice, loved his wife dearly, had, overcome by his grief, thrown himself into a chair, where, with his face shrouded by his hands, he appeared lost to all sense of the presence of those around him; and Alice had pillowed the head of the ill-fated landlady on her lap, whilst the surgeon, who bent over strove, but in vain, to recal animation to her stiffened frame. The other spectators of the sad scene were such as a knowledge of the melancholy appearance had brought together, and amongst these was a dead silence preserved, save when an occasional whisper of pity or horror burst from their half-closed lips, indicative of the anguish they experienced.

The exclamation of the surgeon, however, who after repeated trial now proclaimed that life was indeed extinct, produced a change of emotions in all. They had each hoped, as all will hope when the forms of those we love seem nearly clasped by death, that some vital spark yet hovered about the body to be fanned into life and motion—that some lingering breath of life was yet remaining to be recalled into the breast of the dying one; but now when they knew too well that all hope had fled—that all expectations of her surviving was at an end, and that they should never again behold the good old dame alive, a thrill of grief and horror pervaded the whole assemblage, and the awful silence that previously prevailed was changed to a deep-toned murmur of sorrow and regret. Alice, who had been, perhaps, the most sanguine in her anticipations, gave vent to her hitherto smothered feelings in a burst of scalding tears that brought not their usual relief to the heart of the weeper. Her bosom was torn amidst conflicting emotions; her mind maddened by the sense of sorrow and loneliness that now came over her. Had her own life been required to save that of her late kind protectress, how willingly, how gladly would she have laid it down to have done so. But this train of reflection increased rather than allayed the feelings of anguish that perturbed her breast; and overcome by the thoughts that crowded upon her at that moment, she uttered a loud cry, and fell senseless to the floor. The wonderful fortitude and presence of mind which she had displayed throughout the night, now entirely forsook her. The re-action had taken place, and the pallid cheeks and colourless lips of the fair sufferer, told how keenly she felt the loss of her they all deplored.

By the advice of those around her, she was borne off to bed, and a couple of elderly females, whose previous acquaintance with Alice furnished them with the preference for so doing, volunteered to watch at her side until she recovered. The rest of the neighbours finding that their services could be dispensed with, or were no longer required, now departed to lay the particulars of the affair before a magistrate, a couple of farmers who lived near at hand alone remaining to protect the house and furniture.

Alice continued in her trance for some hours, and then, instead of being better from the sleep, the surgeon pronounced her to be in the first stage of a raging and burning fever, from which, he said, it would be extremely doubtful if she ever recovered. Four long days and nights, however, passed away, and on the fifth night she awoke with the fever gone, Her first symptom of returning consciousness was the identifying of the room in which she was, and then came a vague, a very vague recollection of what had happened. Yes! there was the same spotless pillow on which she had before slept—the same clear, white curtains that had before been drawn around her, and the same latticed window—yes she recolled *that*—through which the horrid image had glared upon her. And then a feeling of fiery, unquenchable thirst came over her. Her throat seemed parched and scorched, as if burning lava had beed poured down it; and a sense of weakness too she felt, but why or wherefore she knew not. It was night too, and candles were lit and the fire lighted; two females were bending over the fire and watching

the simmering of some preparation they were making. Why should they be *there?* Had she been ill—so ill as to require nurses to attend her? Her mind became again, for a time, bewildered. The two watchers were in conversation—it was carried on in a low and subdued tone—but she could still hear them talk, and gently withdrawing the curtains of her bed she listened to their discourse.

"Ah! its a sad and awful affair," said the apparent elder of the two, as if in reply to some observation her companion had made; "its a sad thing, Goody Kent, but I hope they will be able to find out and punish the ruffians."

"They say, Margery, they have got a clue to them," returned the other; "one was wounded, for great clots of blood were found upon the green grass in the morning, and a marked handkerchief was found close by; but we have lost a good neighbour—rest her soul!"

"Aye!" continued Margery, "the coroner's jury did right when they returned a verdict of "Wilful Murder," for murder it was, and a most horrid one, too."

"They say the burial is to take place to-morrow —it will be a sad day for those who knew her— poor Tabitha Royster! her death will make many a heart grieve."

"Then it is no dream after all!" almost shrieked Alice, as she started from her pillow: "no fearful vision that had disturbed my slumbers, as I was hoping, but horrid reality."

"What, my pretty lass Alice!" exclaimed Goody Kent, "art thou indeed recovered? Now, Heaven be praised for all its mercies! how glad am I to see thee again in thy senses; but there," she continued, seeing that Alice was almost frantic with a recollection of the fearful night; "there, you must'nt agitate yourself. Mr. Powell, the surgeon, has ordered that, in case you awoke, you should be kept very quiet, and not disturb yourself. Here is some sage-tea that he said you ought to drink, and that we have been preparing for you."

"Tell me first, I beseech you—pray of you, is Mrs. Royster indeed dead?" cried Alice; *murdered* she would have said, but the word seemed to choke her.

"Aye, and more's the pity! but come, you must not take on so; we all must die at one time or other; and she perhaps has only been spared some years of trouble that we know not of—I scarcely expected to hear you speak again."

"Oh, heaven! to what agony am I yet doomed!" ejaculated Alice, as the full weight of her misfortune burst upon her.

The next morning brought with it more than usual anxiety to the inmates of the Seven Bells. It was the day on which its late owner was to be buried. Alice, who had arisen entirely recovered from her severe illness, was allowed, in consequence of her importunate entreaties, to join the funeral procession, and it was with a sad heart indeed that she paid this last duty to one from whom she had experienced so much kindness. The train was a long and mournful one. Ralph, by virtue of his intimate relation with the deceased, followed the coffin; then came Alice, and Cicely, Tabitha's niece. A body of the neighbouring villagers by whom she had been most sincerely respected brought up the rear, and in this order they arrived at the village church. The discourse of the clergyman who officiated on the sad occasion seemed more than usually touching and solemn, but it was not until the first shovel-full of earth had been thrown upon the coffin—that deadening sound that seems to sever the connecting link between the living and the dead—that Alice suffered a tear to fall. It was then, when an awful silence stole over the whole group—a silence broken only by the grating sound of the sexton's spade in filling up the grave—that an ungentle hand was laid upon the mourner's shoulder, and a voice struck chilliness through the frames of all assembled:—

"Miss Travers," cried the new-comer, who was the magistrate of the place, "*I arrest you as an accessory to the murder of Mrs. Tabitha Royster!* here is the warrant for your apprehension."

Alice heard no more, but falling into the arms of Cicely, who was fortunately at hand, became like one death-struck.

Of the cause of the interruption, and the consequences attending it, we shall speak more fully in a future chapter.

CHAPTER XIV.

BARNWELL AND MILLWOOD VISIT VAUXHALL GARDENS.

Herrick.—Pooh! pooh! man, don't tell me; I'll swear
And I will prove her so, or lose my life!   [she's false,
Though crafty as the earth-imbedded fox
When it turns round to 'scape from its pursuers,
Her double-dealing shall stand all-confessed;
And when her villany is bared to view.
You'll wonder and admire how men could be
So deeply gulled by subtlety so foul.

Forsyth.—Good Master Herrick, you deceive yourself!
Her plots, if plots they are, are far too deep
To be unr velled by a moment's care.
Didst ever climb a greasy pole, or eat
Hot hasty-pudding with a two-pronged fork,
Shave with a pair of scissors, or essay
To clean your boots i'the morning with a tooth-brush?
If you've done one or any of these things,
You'll know how hard it is to find her out.

Heywood's Fair Maid of the Exchange: With the
Merry Humours of the Cripple of Fenchurch.

"Is it not near the hour when Mr. Barnwell should call, Hester?"

"It is now within a quarter of an hour to six, Madam — the time when he should be indeed here."

"His absence alarms me. Sure, no foul mischance is keeping him away!"

"I am glad to hear you so anxious that he should arrive safe and well."

"Tut! tut! girl; I meant not that; I care little with what fate he meets, so that my object is gained. I was only fearful that something had come to his knowledge with reference to me that deterred him from keeping his appointment. He may be dead for aught I care, so that he provides me with some more money."

Need we explain that the speaker was Milwood, and the person she addressed, her attendant.

"Hark! there is a knock at the door," exclaimed the Abigail; "it is the very stripling we were talking of."

In another moment Barnwell was announced.

"George, my dear George," said Milwood, rising to meet him; how anxiously I have awaited thy coming! Each minute seems an age, when those we love are away; and I was fearful that thou wast unwell—had met with some sad accident; nay, a thousand things I imagined; but glad am I indeed to see my fears thus set at rest."

"I have been detained on business," responded Barnwell, returning the fond caresses which she lavished on him; but I am even now, by some minutes, earlier than the time we mentioned."

"It may be so," cried Eleanor: but when you are away the time hangs heavily on my hands, and I then fancy you are unmindful of your promises, and heedless of what she must feel whose only happy hours are spent in your society."

"Nay," said George, "let this be a token that you are not forgotten by me in your absence;" and so saying he plucked from beneath his vest a watch of curious workmanship, with which Mr. Thorogood had presented him in the first year of his apprenticeship: "it will serve you to mark the progress of time, my dear Eleanor, more carefully."

Millwood, seemingly overcome by gratitude to Barnwell, at first let her moistened eyes alone speak her thanks, but, after a short pause, as if only then finding words to express her acknowledgments, she threw herself on his breast, and thus addressed him :—

"George! you know, well know, that my love is neither created nor increased by trinkets such as these. I love you for yourself alone, but I cannot overlook your kindness in thus bestowing a thought upon me when I am away. As a proof that your affection is as strong towards me when I am absent as now, I accept it, and may Heaven reward you for your kindness to one who feels that she cannot thank you sufficiently."

"Come, come," said the attendant; what loiterers ye lovers are; the time has come when the entertainments at Spring Gardens commence, and ye'll be too late to witness the performance of Signor Carlo, the celebrated Spanish Jumper."

"Thou sayest truly, Hester," returned Millwood. "Come, George, we will depart; the evening has already far advanced—but there will be time yet to take a pair of sculls from London Bridge, if we delay not by the way."

"Have with you then," rejoined Barnwell; "I am ready on the instant, and wait but for your toilette to be completed."

"That is a task of no great difficulty, nor long duration either," said Milwood, putting on one of those ample satin hoods then so much in vogue among the fashionables of the day; "there! how do you think I look?"

"More charming and fascinating than ever," replied Barnwell; "you appear to impart grace to what you wear rather than that the outward adornments of dress increase your own beauty or attractions of your person."

"Compliments again, Mr. Barnwell; really you improve each day in your courtier-like accomplishment: was not my heart already gone, I am afraid these words would make you a purloiner of another person's property."

Whether Milwood had intended the allusion in the way it was taken by Barnwell, or had thrown it out hap-hazard as a random observation, it matters not, for the result was in either case the same. The sentence had struck a chord in Barnwell's breast that ceased not to vibrate for some minutes afterwards.

"Come, George, we are laggards," said Milwood, observing Barnwell's altered demeanour; "it will be dusk almost ere we set out, and if we are to get there by water, there is not a moment to spare."

"I crave your pardon for my inattention," replied Barnwell, "but I had become somewhat oblivious; we will depart this instant:" and giving his arm to Milwood, they left the house, Hester having received some previous instructions in a whisper from her mistress.

It being one of those light and cloudless evenings when the delicious coolness of spring seems blended with the more vigorous warmth of summer, and when nature, as if rejoicing in such an atmosphere, appears to put on its fairest aspect, the streets were thronged with many a goodly group of well-dressed citizens, who, with their portly dames and smiling offspring, had sallied out to enjoy the freshness of the gentle breeze that wafted the smoke gaily over the houses, as it trifled among the brick and mortar outlets that crested their tops. Their object was one—pleasure; but not so their destination. To those who cared not for distance, the *Mother Red Cap* held out its at-

tractions, whilst nearer the city were the concerts at *Peerless Pool* and the magical diversions of *Merlin's Cave.* Some wended their way to Mr. Sadler's far-famed *Music House ;* and others, more soberly inclined, travelled westward, to explore the museum of *Don Saltero's.* But all, as if rejoiced at resigning for a time the dingy closeness of some city alley for the freer space of an open thoroughfare, wore upon their faces that joyous look that told the happiness that lurked beneath.

Beguiling the walk with casual remarks on the passers-by, Milwood continued her conversation in a tone of hilarity that induced Barnwell to remark he had never seen her in a more blithesome mood, and begged her to assign a cause. But their arrival at the London Bridge Ferry interrupted the dialogue, and he was therefore content to leave the question unanswered.

"Skulls to Westminster, good gentlefolks, or Southwark?" cried one of the watermen.

"Ranelagh. Chelsea, or Spring-gardens?" exclaimed a second, bowing to the ground.

"Here's a boat fit for Queen Anne herself to travel in," pursued a third. But their self-expressed eulogiums seemed to exercise little influence on the minds of the new comers, for, selecting the wherry belonging to one who had remained silent amongst the rest, Barnwell handed Milwood down the steps, and the two were soon afterwards seen gallantly proceeding up the river on the road to their destination.

Swiftly and skilfully did the waterman ply the sculls, and, aided by the tide, they reached Vauxhall-stairs within an hour after their departure from the city. That one hour had, however, brought darkness with it, and the delay of a few minutes would have rendered the journey by water not quite so safe as the passengers might have desired. Ascending rather a steep declivity, Milwood and Barnwell soon found themselves in front of the edifice that, beneath its ample arches, led the visitor into a scene of splendour which, even then, might have impelled a stranger with a warm imagination to believe fairy-land.

Disbursing the sum demanded at the doors for admission, Barnwell proceeded with his fair companion to the Gardens, where myriads of objects on every side met his enraptured gaze, that for a time nearly bewildered him with their novelty and lustre.

The scene was so different to the dull counting-house in which our apprentice had been for the best part of his time immured since his arrival in town, that it can scarcely be wondered that his senses became for a short period intoxicated with the new delights they opened to him, and he continued to turn from one object to another with increased pleasure and surprise at every change of attraction that met his view.

Spring, or *Vauxhall Gardens,* as they are now termed, was indeed a spot aided both by nature and art to delight and enchant the eye. Long rows and chains of lamps, resembling so many festoons of fire, hung in pendent wreathes from every tree, and connected whole groves together with their continuous links of brilliancy. Music filled the air, and birds twittered from every bough, as if in unison with the orchestral melodies that burst from the Rotunda. Advancing up the avenue, the eye beheld a grand vista, about nine hundred feet in length, formed by lofty elm and sycamore trees, each so profusely hung with the variegated lamps we have before alluded to, that the oriental fable of

Aladdin's garden of jewels seemed more than realized. At the end rose a colossal statue of Aurora, gilded, and bathed in a flood of light that was artfully contrived to proceed from the water round her, intended to represent the dawn of day. Further on were statues of the four seasons, each with their appropriate emblems, and also lit up by lights concealed from the eye of the spectator. To the left appeared the Rotunda, a wide and spacious edifice, constructed with such art that sounds never vibrated under it; the music, of course, being heard in consequence to greater advantage. Its interior was fitted up in a style displaying the greatest splendour with the greatest delicacy of ornament.

The roof, or ceiling, was adorned with painted festoons of flowers, terminating in a point, and so naturally coloured as to give them the appearance of reality; and these, ranged round the dome on every side, imparted to the whole a very pleasing and natural effect. The walls, where not painted, were lined with looking-glasses and mirrors, so skilfully contrived as to throw each object into a double reflection, and thus present an apparently interminable prospect.

In what was then termed "The Grove," mechanical pictures and transparencies, intermingled with Chinese lanterns, of a curious and fanciful designing, peered from every thicket; and at the further end, an organ pealed forth its volume of sound to attune the mind of the visitor to the highest pitch of admiration. Wildernesses at the back, crowded with sweet-briar, groups of violets, rose-trees, and wild plants, loaded the air with their fragrance; and here the nightingale, an unseen minstrel, poured forth its plaintive notes on the ear of the enraptured listener, mingled with the gushing of crystal fountains and artificial cascades, and the cheerful and melodious chimes of the bells of St. Mary Overy.

To add to the fascination of a scene like this, fair forms, as beautiful as the Houris of Mahomet's Paradise, hovered around the spot, and presented faces of so lovely a description, that, had Zeuxis again to attempt his picture of Venus, it would have been from here, and not from Greece, he would have selected models to compose his image of perfect beauty.

With Milwood, Barnwell explored every nook and recess that presented an object, however trivial, to fix his gaze on, or attract his attention. His brain actually reeled with delight, and Milwood now rejoiced to perceive her victim in a fit state to further her designs. Feigning fatigue and languor, she took our hero into one of the alcoves, or wine-boxes, that were erected round the gardens, and expressing a wish for some refreshment, Barnwell called for, and obtained, a bottle of hock, the liquor then most in vogue. This was soon disposed of, for, unused to strong potations, Barnwell partook of the liquid more freely than discretion would have allowed him, had he known its power, and another soon shared the fate of its predecessor.

Milwood now artfully turned the conversation on the splendour of the attire worn by those that passed by, and recommended Barnwell to appear in a suit more fitted, as she said, to display the graces of his person. His present garments were, she continued, antiquated and behind the spirit of the age; and his employer, she insinuated, was bound to supply others, so that there could be no harm in appropriating what was in reality his own:

but while the temptress was thus pouring her subtle poison into the ears of her victim, it will not be amiss to glance at what constituted the dress of those that she alluded to.

The gallants of that period wore their coats cut straight before and reaching below the knee, embroidered with lace in front, and generally buttoned to the bottom with ample cuffs that turned half-way up the arm. The vest reached also to the knee, and was most frequently laced with gold or silver, adorned with frogs or tasselled buttonholes. The *culottes*, now dignified by another name unmentionable to the ears of the softer sex, fitted close and tied below the knee; whilst the shoes, with their large buckles, high heels, and square toes, rendered the operation of walking by no means a thing of easy achievement. A ruffled shirt, long cravat, and three-cornered hat, completed the adornment of their upper man; and long flowing perukes, frosted with powder, appeared to swell the head to an enormous size. It is worthy of remark, that these said wigs, by the way, were regulated in size by the eminence of the wearer; an attorney, for instance, never presuming to wear a wig as large as a barrister: and a physician would have deemed it a disgrace to his craft had he seen a petty dealer in medicine so be-wigged as himself. A shake of the head then indeed was ominous to all other heads in its immediate vicinity, for a cloud of meal-powder was sure to be dispersed by so energetic an action. But, to return: the ladies appeared in all the majesty of long and flowing robes—a fashion doubtless borrowed from Albert Durer, the Swiss painter, who represented an angel in a flounced petticoat driving Adam and Eve out of Paradise—with ruffles long and doubled, and hair frizzled and curled to a formidable extent. The flowing *coife*, or rather veil of the finest linen fastened upon the hair, fell behind, and continued till the high projecting headdress was restored after a discontinuance of nearly fifteen years. The bosom was either entirely exposed, or else carelessly shaded with gauze—an indecorousness that caused great offence to prudent fathers or ladies whose necks no longer vied in whiteness with the down of swans. The large tub hoop had scarcely begun to be introduced, but where it had been, the apology was its great coolness in summer; though, as Swift says, it was no more a petticoat than the tub of Diogenes was his unmentionables. It was large enough, indeed, in circumference to have concealed a moderately sized gallant, and to this use history relates it to have once been put, for it is well known that Henry the Fourth, of France, was saved from assassination by hiding himself under the hoop of his Queen, Margaret of Valois.

We have been thus diffuse, in order to convey an idea to the reader of the scene that presented itself on the night in question to Barnwell's view, and unaccustomed as he was to mingle in assemblages so refined, a new passion seemed to spring up in his breast, of the existence of which he had never before dreamed. This passion was the love of dress, and for the moment that Milwood instilled this feeling into his mind, he panted for habiliments equal in costliness to those he saw worn by the wealthy visitors around him.

This was a skilful movement upon Milwood's part, and ere long we shall have to trace its effects. She well knew the reigning foible in her own breast, and by implanting a similar one in his, she thought that her own passion was more likely to be gratified. Nor was she wrong in her deductions, as will be afterwards seen.

Barnwell, heated by wine, and intoxicated with the delights that night had opened to him, was now ripe for encountering any danger, and overthrowing any obstacle that stood between him and the gratification of his wishes. He felt that his life had been hitherto passed in a sphere too limited for enjoyment; and he now determined, at all hazards, to drink the cup of pleasure to the dregs.

Incited by Milwood, who still kept adding fuel to the flame, he drank deeply, and as each glass was drained, the thirst for liquor increased. He laughed boisterously at his own occasional attempts at wit, and sang and talked alternately. An elegant supper was provided at Barnwell's wish, and more wine after that was called for and drank. Milwood cautiously blended with the vinous beverage, an admixture of water. But Barnwell persisted in swallowing it as pure as it was brought him. It was then, as coin after coin was slipping from between his fingers, that a person of elegant and fashionable exterior rose from an adjoining recess, and entering the alcove where they were seated, familiarly accosted Milwood.

"Ah! Captain Vavasour," exclaimed Milwood in reply, "how delighted I am to meet you here! Permit me to introduce you to my friend, Mr. Barnwell."

A mutual bow acknowledged the introduction.

"Have you long returned from Paris, Captain?" continued Milwood, addressing the new comer.

"Only since yesterday," was the reply. "I little anticipated the pleasure of seeing you so soon, I must confess."

"This gentleman was one of my earliest acquaintances," remarked Milwood to Barnwell; "and I may add," she continued, glancing significantly at the person opposite, "he was at one time the only protector I had."

"The lady overvalues my poor services," observed the Captain; "but, to change the subject of conversation—allow me to call for a pint of Rhenish—may I ask how the entertainment of the evening has amused you?"

"To me," responded Milwood, "it would have seemed irksome, were it not for the excellent company I have had; but my friend here has expressed his delight in the highest terms."

"I am rejoiced to hear it," replied the other; "though, for mine own part, I care little for scenes of this description, having been satiated with them on the Continent; but perhaps the gentleman would prefer a pastime of a more exciting description—say cards or dice, for instance?"

"I thank you, sir, for the offer," answered Barnwell; "but to me both remain a profound mystery."

"Impossible! you are surely jesting," exclaimed Vavasour, with well-feigned astonishment, — "a gallant of so noble a mien and bearing cannot be ignorant of an amusement so refined."

"I am afraid he speaks the truth," rejoined Milwood; "but I must not lessen him in your estimation; a few lessons from so efficient an instructor would qualify him for encountering the adepts of St. James's."

"Since you desire it, it shall be so," returned the Captain; "I have a pack of cards in my pocket, whereby I can render the intricacies of the game apparent in a moment."

Barnwell hesitated.

"You *must* play," whispered Milwood, "to preserve the character I have given you: it would be ill-bred and churlish to refuse. Besides, the chances are equal; you may win: and then think of the profit you would acquire, and the triumph that would be yours in vanquishing a player like the Captain."

The lure thus thrown was successful. Barnwell, who was paying the expenses of the evening, as perhaps the reader already imagines, with his master's money, saw a faint glimmering of hope that by these means he could replenish his own exchequer, and replace the sums of money he had at divers times abstracted from his employer. Buoyed up with this expectation, he eagerly swallowed the bait, and, flushed with wine, became as anxious to play as before he was willing to avoid it.

And here it may not be amiss to remark, lest surprise should be felt at Vavasour proposing a game at cards in a place of public resort, that it was a common practice at this time to wile away the interval between one song and another with a hand at Basset, L'Ombre, or Piquet. The laws for the suppression of gambling in theatres and places of public amusement being not enacted until nearly twenty years after the period in which these events took place.

"Come!" said Vavasour, dexterously sorting the cards, "we will have a trial at the noble game of Bragg; the play is easy, and the chances are most in your favour as an inexperienced player, since chance in this predominates over skill."

"With all my heart," responded Barnwell; and the cards were shuffled and dealt.

"Cospetto!" cried the Captain, as he glanced at the cards in his hand; "Luck has indeed, young sir, been favouring you now. I can make not even so much as a pair royal."

The playing proceeded, and Barnwell won.

"You clear the pool, sir," exclaimed Vavasour, as the game reached its termination; here are the fruits of your labours." And he handed five bright crown pieces to his successful adversary.

Barnwell, delighted with the success of his first game, readily replied in the affirmative to Vavasour's desire for a second, and remained with strained gaze and beating heart watching the cards, as they fell in array before him.

This game likewise concluded in a few moments, which, brief though they were, seemed an age to the anxious mind of the youth who thus passed them. The cards held were different, but the winner was still the same.

"Now, by the bones of St. Chrysostom, young man, your play is fortunate! The fickle goddess seems to have sheltered you beneath her wing with a truly motherly care, and little recks what becomes of me. Well, *n'importe*, never mind, Fortune's wheel cannot present every spoke uppermost at once, and there lies my consolation."

Such were the words uttered by Vavasour, as carelessly shuffling the cards, he marked with an experienced eye the elated manner in which Barnwell received the intelligence of his victory. Another game was now commenced.

The stakes were doubled.

The cards having been cut and dealt round afresh by Vavasour, who took upon himself that office, in consequence, as he alleged, of Barnwell's inexpertness, the game was renewed, and this time our hero found himself the loser.

Again was the same effort attended with the same

result, and again was Barnwell obliged to confess himself vanquished; but heedless of the entreaties of Milwood, who implored him to leave off whilst it was yet in his power to do so without further risk, he continued to hope that his former good fortune would return; and the better to ensure his ultimate profit, the original stakes were this round quadrupled.

"You play boldly," observed the Captain, "for a beginner, and merit victory for your bravery; but pause, ere you hazard a sum like that now before us."

But Barnwell was now too eager in his wishes to consider the risk he ran, and this his companions well knew. Like all incipient gamblers, he looked only at the bright side of the prospect, and dreamed not the possibility of their being one more gloomy; the thought of foul play turning against him never occurred to him for a moment.

"One ace, king, knave, and a pair-major!" exclaimed Vavasour; "you have lost the game!"

Barnwell seemed stunned by the words. He continued to gaze on the cards for a brief interval in a kind of stupified astonishment bordering on delirium, and then, the consciousness of his loss flashing on his mind with the speed and withering effects of lightning, he uttered a loud groan, and, pressing his moistened palm to his fevered brow, as if to assure himself of its reality, he buried his face in his hands, overcome by mingled feelings of remorse and despair.

"Come, come!" cried Milwood, "you have been unfortunate, George; but, remember, I warned you not to play when I saw the tide running against you; another time you may win all back, and then——"

"Your friend seems unwell," interrupted Vavasour; "a bumper of this sparkling Rhenish may revive him."

Yielding to the entreaties of Milwood, our hero quaffed off the intoxicating beverage at a draught, and forgetting for a time the cause of his unhappiness in the fond caresses which she lavished on him, again became as madly joyous as his corresponding sadness had before been intense. But his laugh was the wild burst of merriment that flows from the lips of a maniac—his joy the furious hilarity of a drunkard. From wine he sought and found a temporary relief, and as each returning ray of reason shot through his frenzied brain, he dispelled it with renewed applications to the bottle before him.

Some female acquaintances of Vavasour were now introduced into the box, and the remainder of the night was spent amid scenes of riotous revelry and debauchery, that spoke little for the taste of those engaged in them.

Such was the state of mind that Barnwell was now in, that what would have before created within him feelings only of absolute disgust, now constituted the sources of his greatest enjoyment. He participated with Milwood in all the follies in which his associates so recklessly indulged, and with the transit of every hour became more and more regardless of decorum.

Dawn was, however, now breaking in upon the scene of their night's revelry, and, summoning a coach, Vavasour handed Milwood and Barnwell into the vehicle and departed, not before, however, making an appointment for a future interview with the first, and warmly expressing the most sincere friendship for the latter.

The clumsy carriage that contained them, rolled at a most tardy pace towards that part of the city in which Milwood's dwelling was situated, and having disgorged its fare, the two passengers—the deceiver and the deceived—entered the house already rendered familiar to the reader; and here for the present we leave them—our heart sickening at the description of what then and there ensued. The revolting endearments, passionate caresses, and open manifestations of the vilest of all affections—mercenary love—which Milwood lavished on Barnwell, need not be recorded by our pen; their existence alone is all that we dare hint at; and gladly turning from so revolting a scene, we pursue our narrative in another chapter.

CHAPTER XVI.

DISSIPATION AND INFATUATION.

Oh! Gambling, damned vice; the fatal spring
Whence ruin gushes in a thousand streams;
How many victims wilt thou more require
To glut an appetite so foul as thine?
This world had been, indeed, a world of bliss,
Had men not yielded to thy cursed power,
And Adam still had been in Paradise,
Had thy ambition been to him unknown.

The Fatal Hour, 1774.

This world's a large-sized gaming-house, and all
The men and women in it merely gamblers.
Fortune holds the stakes, and often gives
To those that least deserve. Fate casts the dice,
And pleasure is the pool for which we play,
Love acts as croupier, and misfortune cogs
The die as thrown upon the board of life!
Heaven acts as umpire, and observes our play!
And when grim death stalks in and seizes all,
We yield our tables, and the game is lost.

Old Play.

Of all the vices that the mind of man ever yielded to, or imagined, perhaps the most destructive in its immediate causes and ultimate effects is that of which we have above spoken. Gambling, the most insidious foe to man that man ever yet encountered, is alike pernicious to the habits of the individual and the morals of the community. It is the key-stone to the arch of Ruin, and the sum lost at the gaming-table, reversing the nature of the prerogative of mercy, is *twice* cursed; it curseth him that gives and him that takes. It is as the serpent that fascinating the senses by its glowing colours, waits but the opportunity to make the gambler its victim. Little by little does the passion lay hold of the human heart, till growing with its growth, and strengthening with its strength, it usurps entire dominion over his whole frame, and ultimately hurls the unhappy mortal to destruction. The gambler lives in a perpetual atmosphere of excitement; the thirst for play is quenched not by the intoxicating libations that he pours before the shrine of his idol. Life to him realizes the horrors of the infernal regions. A Pandemonium of misery and torture exists in his own breast, and the few glances of happiness that he now and then may enjoy, are but as the rays of sunshine that beaming athwart some barren waste brighten up the prospect for a few short seconds, and then abandon the scene to greater gloom and wretchedness than before. Like the fabled talisman of the Egyptian enchanter, Fortune holds out to his gaze delusive prospects of a mine of wealth that can never be reached. Resembling the *mirage* that gladdens the eye of the traveller on the arid deserts of Arabia, his fondly cherished hopes of happiness disappear before a nearer view, and he lingers on a wretched existence uncheered by all that can render life happy, and sinks into the grave the follower of a phantom that eludes his grasp.

Such is gambling even in its best form; but, when the system of foul play that then existed, and was openly practised in defiance of the legislature, and the cries that were made to it for suppression, is taken into consideration, the monstrous deformity will appear still more hideous. The various hangers-on at the gaming-tables of the day, who obtained an excellent and comfortable livelihood by victimising some "Lamb" or *Pigeon* as the phrase now goes, out of his hard-earned gold, were, generally speaking, composed of the very sweepings of society. The whole tribe of sharpers, known by the generic appellation of "Rooks," and subdivided into jilts, huffs, hectors, setters, pads, biters, divers, lifters, filers, budgers, droppers, and cross-tilers, were men who were equally ready to rob a man of his money, or deprive him of his existence; to pick a hole in his purse, or pick a hole in his body. Versed in all the nefarious arts of palming, cogging, topping, and slurring, they added thereto an intimate acquaintance with the workings of the human heart; and, under a show of civility or kindness, worked upon their unsuspicious victim till he became enmeshed in a web from which extrication arrived too often only when it was too late. The better to aid them in their schemes, and further their diabolical intentions, an association was most usually formed with some depraved and abandoned female, who officiated as a decoy-duck, and lured the "pigeon" to his ruin. One of these moral pests—one of these human leeches—was Vavasour; his companion in infamy,———; but we must leave the reader himself to supply the hiatus, having matter more pressing on hand yet to dispose of.

The uneasy occupier of a couch, that brought with it neither repose to the body nor tranquillity to the mind, lay Barnwell, a victim to the most maddening reflections, and the most raging passions. It had been morning—not the first faint blush of early dawn—but broad, open daylight, ere he had returned to the merchant's house; and now, on his bed he lay, tossing his restless frame from side to side, as if anxious to obtain oblivion in what was most denied him—sleep. Oh! the pangs and tortures of that hour!

The dissipation of the preceding night had been followed by a parched tongue, and a fevered brow. His eyes seemed burning in their sockets, and his hand trembled with the vacillation of an aspen leaf; but this was nothing to the agony he endured in his mind. His heart was racked by the thoughts that now poured in profusion upon his brain, like torrents of melting lava from the crater of his memory. The reflection, that money so wrongfully obtained, had been so foolishly appropriated, seared his very heart. How glad he was that Trueman was not there to reproach him for his extravagance, or know of his misconduct; and his mother—that kind and affectionate parent, who had on the day of his departure from home invoked blessings on his head, how rejoiced he was, she as yet knew not how little he deserved them. The merchant, too, who had acted with all the

kindness of a father towards him, was *this* a return to make him for his kindness? He dared not pursue the subject further. It seemed goading him into madness; so, with an aching head, and a still more aching heart, he rose to resume his duties below.

Feigning indisposition, a plea that was most unsuspiciously received by Mr. Thorogood, Barnwell plunged himself at once into the duties of his office, hoping by these means to escape from his own thoughts, but it was in vain, the scene of its accompanying effects, seemed ever present to his vision. Dusk however at last arrived, and burning with impatience to again see Millwood, he gladly availed himself of the opportunity, a commission of some little importance being placed in his hands, afforded him, for passing an hour with her in whom all his hopes of happiness were alone bound up.

Milwood, who well knew the influence she had over him, received him with her usual bland and affectionate demeanour. The events of the previous night were but briefly alluded to, and that in such a pleasant vein of jocular hilarity that almost reconciled Barnwell to the part he had taken in the affair. She descanted largely upon the delights of scenes like those they had there witnessed, and painted pleasure in so alluring a guise, that, enchanted with the picture, Barnwell paused not to inquire into the stability of the colours, or examine the unsound nature of the canvass upon which they were pourtrayed. Man's best privilege, she contended, was the enjoyment of the present hour, and ridiculed the idea of allowing obstacles, however great, to stand in the way of such enjoyment. The world was formed for man, not man for the world; and, therefore, there could be no harm in applying that to our uses which Nature, she asserted, designed.

Reasoning such as this, false and sophisticated though it was, failed not to have its due influence upon our hero. He began to consider that the line of demarcation that separated the paths of virtue from those of vice, was but an imaginary barrier that had its origin in the absurd dogmas of priests and moralists. Surely, he reasoned, one whose heart is so pure, whose mind is so well-informed, cannot be deceived. Virtue he regarded as a visionary deity, worshipped most where least understood; and vice he began to look upon as something if not absolutely to be followed, at least to be admired. Where then, thought he, can be the harm of applying that to my own uses, which, if not missed, can never be regretted?

Oh! false and delusive sophistry, how many more besides Barnwell have yielded to thy pernicious influence!

"I have just been thinking, George," said Millwood, after a short pause in the conversation, "that this silken dress of mine has become somewhat antiquated and old-fashioned, and that I had no right to lecture you on your attire, when there was so much room for improvement in mine own."

"Last night I saw no blemish in it," replied Barnwell, "even when contrasted with the robes of those that passed us, and now, when you alone are by, it seems to savour more of the costly fashion of the day than ever."

"I thought perhaps you might wish me to be more elegantly dressed, that I might not disgrace you, George, in your new habiliments; but I plainly see now that your love is becoming colder to me. You refuse me the least favour.''

"If to obtain you that you call a favour, I must not—will not grant it, but think of some more striking proof of my affection than the mere purchase of a new dress: think how I may display more openly the ardour of my attachment; and believe me, Eleanor, the prize you name is yours.''

"Nay,'' said Milwood, who was not so easily to be thrown off her guard when she was determined upon the possession of anything, "I did but jest, my dear George; but the subject seems to annoy you; let us change it. You have never heard me sing yet, and here is a ballad which I have been practising over before you came. The words and music are both of my own composition; but I am afraid they will fare but poorly when you remember the charming melodies of last night.''

And so saying, Milwood, without further preface, drew towards her a harp, that ornamented one portion of the room, and running her taper fingers carelessly over the strings, breathed forth, in accents most tender and touching, the following words, accompanying each sentence with a glance that sent new flames into the heart of Barnwell, and raised him for the time to the highest pitch of ecstacy.

THE FORCE OF LOVE.

Since love hath lighted at our eyes
    A pure and holy fire,
Sure 'twere a sin if thou or I
    Should let this flame expire.
The sacred fires of old ne'er felt
    Their flames at all decayed:
And when the priest before them knelt,
    They sacrifices made.

    Then Love, like them, should ever prove
      As lasting and as clear,
    And sacrifices made for love
      Should ne'er be valued here.

If thou perceive thy flame decay,
    Come! light thine eyes at mine:
And if mine own should fade away,
    I'll pluck fresh fires from thine.
No lover's, nor no bridegroom's mirth
    With mine compared can be:
They have but PIECES of this earth,—
    I've ALL THE WORLD in thee!

    Then Love like vestal fires should burn
      As lasting and as clear:
    And sacrifices in return
      Will ne'er be thought too dear.

As the last dying cadence melted again into the air from which it had been called forth, Barnwell continuing to gaze in silent admiration on the singer, as if fascinated to the spot, allowed a considerable pause to take place before he ventured to destroy the spell that music's enchantment had woven around him.

"Eleanor!'' he at last exclaimed, "you exercise a strange power over me, so strange that I doubt sometimes whether you derive it from heaven or elsewhere. Even now I stand rooted to the spot, infatuated with your person, spell-bound by your voice, and delighted with the mastery you have obtained over one of the sweetest of instruments. The thrilling words and heart-stirring melody that I have just heard seems to enthral me more deeply than ever. You behold me, a willing captive, in your power, secured by the strongest of all chains —those forged by love.''

"Then,'' returned Milwood, laughingly, "for the sake of the wearer, these said chains of yours shall be but links of roses after all; but tell me, do you think I shall ever be a favourite with the Muses?''

"An thou art *not*,'' said Barnwell in reply, "there would be but one reason for it, and that is a kind of envious jealousy lest you should surpass each in her own art: but we were speaking just now of a dress—it is yours; I can resist no longer.''

"You know, my dear George,'' rejoined Milwood, "that I accept it only as a guerdon of your love for me: but I see you are anxious to depart— let it not be long ere we meet again.''

"Absence carries with it its own punishment; I am a prey to the most wretched gloom and misery when I am away from you.''

"And I should not speak with the candour that is natural to me,'' cried Milwood in return, "did I not re-echo your sentiments. The poets have fabled Time with wings; but, to my thinking, when absent from those we love, he should be pourtrayed with leaden ones, that impede rather than assist its progress.''

"I shall see thee again ere long,'' pursued Barnwell; "till then, thou knowest, Eleanor, I am thine alone!''

"And I call Heaven to witness, that my thoughts, George, stray to none but thee!''

"It is growing late,'' exclaimed our hero; "I must be gone; each minute may prove serious else to my employer's interest.''

"Then farewell!'' sighed Milwood! "though I would yet willingly make thee a truant to thy trust by detaining thee in these arms. When shall I have the dress, love, that we spoke of?''

"To-morrow!'' answered Barnwell, "I will send it thee.''

And bestowing a dozen kisses on her lips, and receiving as many fond caresses in return, the love-stricken apprentice departed.

"*To-morrow!*'' mused Milwood, as she sat at the window, watching Barnwell's departure. "Then I can join Vavasour at the masquerade, as I promised; that will be fortunate. Let me see; a gold ring studded with brilliants from Sir William Brandeth; another miniature from Mr. Stanley, the young artist; five pounds from Vavasour, as my share in my last night's adventure; and a new dress, which, if honestly come by, cannot cost less than ten—no bad day's work, methinks. My admirers had need have purses pretty well furnished, for I call upon their resources to no small amount. The chimes of St. Paul's are now striking eight. No one will call to-night, I should imagine. Here, Hester, run with this note to the theatre, and tell Mr. Oswell I shall be happy to see him after the performances are over.''

"I understand, Madam,'' replied the attendant, and departed.

"If I hear of his writing any more letters to his wife, I must discard him,'' thought Milwood; I once fancied that I *loved* that man, and though the foolish passion has long since left me, I should be vexed to think he is beginning again to sigh for domestic happiness. New plans must be thought of to detain him in my power. Well! well! this is a strange world, in sooth, to boast man for its lord when a woman thus can mould him to her will. Man! our toy, our mockery, our plaything —a puppet that moves indeed, but only as we pull the strings—and *he* to boast of the power he possesses!—ha! ha!—how soon would I reduce the

proudest of them to my feet, and make an emperor my abject slave! But can I be blamed for exercising the power I possess? Can I be thought worse of for turning that power to my own ends? No! I, like others, have been deceived, neglected, trampled on, but I have returned with tenfold interest on the sex the injuries I have received from one. I have fought them with their own weapons; defeated them on their own ground. Who is now the victor? I *have* loved—;" and here a cloud passed athwart the countenance of Milwood;—" have known what it was to crouch, in submission, before the tyrant's foot; but I now assume the passion for my own purposes—to become the instrument of my own vengeance—though it has left its unerring sting behind. Yea! the clouded sky may brighten to the sun; the flower we pluck may once again find root; but woman's love once proffered, once refused, turns on itself its scorpion sting, and withers with the heart from whence it sprung."

Such were the meditations of Milwood. In her better moments she thought often so, but these occurred but seldom.

Now—or else the darkness was deceiving—huge tear-drops, each scalding as they came, chased each other down her cheek, and blistered the leaves of the book that she held, more for appearance sake than for the purposes of reading, in her hand. But this momentary gush of feeling was as transient as the thoughts that called it forth. As if ashamed to confess, even to herself, so much weakness, she hurriedly checked with her handkerchief the moisture of her eyes, and, hastily lighting the lamp on the table, became absorbed—or at least appeared to be so—in the contents of the book before her.

We must now return to Barnwell, who was seated alone in the merchant's counting-house, pondering over the events of the last few days. Money, *more* money, must be obtained, but how or where he knew not. His former resources—the witholding of sums that he had received on account of his employer—were if not altogether inaccessible, at least at that moment of no avail. An immediate sum must be obtained.

It was late; the household were all at rest—what if he were to borrow—aye, only to *borrow*—a few coins from his master's well filled bureau? They would not be missed before he could replace them. The room, too, was near his own. He knew the chest was carefully locked up, and secured at the top of the house; but a chisel would overcome all impediments. A chisel! lucky thought; the carpenters had left one behind them that very day. He would but try—only *try*—whether he could open it. It was under his protection—implicit confidence was reposed in his honesty—but what of that? he had a right to participate in what he had himself been the means of accumulating; and, therefore, there could be no harm. At all events, he would go thither and see that all was secure, there could be no danger in *that*; and up the flight of stairs that led to his own room Barnwell accordingly proceeded.

He listened at the door of his employer's bed-chamber; all was quiet; Mr. Thorogood slept; he was, apparently, wrapped in the wild intricacies of some feverish dream, as the suppressed breathing and occasional startle in the midst of his slumbers, denoted. The next room was Clara's: he listened; she was not asleep, but writing—it was a letter perhaps to Trueman. He could plainly hear the sound of the pen as it travelled rapidly over the paper and traced thereon the thoughts that emanated from the mind of the fair writer. There was a footstep. Psha! it was but the echo of his own. He proceeded onwards; the room was now gained wherein the treasure had been deposited. There was no one to see, or watch him. Yes there was ONE; but he would not think of that. The light was burning dimly; but he could see the desk that contained the prize he sought. He had brought up the chisel, too, in his hand—almost unwittingly had he brought it—but there it was. Well! he would but see whether it could be opened with so simple an instrument. The lock was forced; the desk flew open. Hush! there was a noise; a figure, too, had darted athwart the room. Psha! the noise was that of his own chisel—the figure his own shadow as he passed before the light. He raised the lid, and what a bright vision of wealth was revealed to his gaze. He would but take one bag—only one—and yet *two* out of so many would not soon be missed—he could replace them both at the same time. There! he would shut the lid down, and return; why was the desk so hard to close? it opened easily enough. But the pressure required to bring the lock back to its original position brought clammy drops of perspiration to his brow. It used not to be so. That picture, too; why looked the old magistrate so frowningly at him, following his every motion with his sightless eyes? Could a mere canvas

portrait read his thoughts, and be a witness against him? A cold shudder ran through his frame. He replaced the desk in the closet from whence he had taken it. His key that had opened it quietly before, now grated in the lock. Did his hand shake? He had closed the door on entering it; but it was now open; was it fancy? or did the wind force its way in? How cold it was! he had just felt so warm, too—a sultry, unwholesome warmth, as if he had been stifling from want of air. Now he was freezing; the money, however, was in his possession. Yes! yes! he had succeeded—but at the price of what?—his happiness—his moral rectitude! He sought his bed; but not to sleep. No! rest was denied him. Now and then he sank off in a slumber, it was true; but it was only to wake up again soon after, in the midst of some frightful dream.

FROM THAT TIME BARNWELL FELT HIMSELF A ROBBER!

CHAPTER XVII.

THE SOOTHSAYER.

[being dwells?
George a Green.——Know ye the spot where this strange
Eglamour.——Aye, marry, do I to my sin and sorrow:
'Tis in a gloomy pit o'ergrown with briars,
Close by the ruins of a shaken abbey
Torn with an earthquake down unto the ground:
'Midst graves and grots that crumble near the charnel-house,
And fenced with slime of caterpillars' kels,
And knotty cobwebs rounded in with spells.
Thence steals she forth to find relief in jogs
And rotten mists that hang upon the fens
And marshes of damp Lincolnshire's crowned lands:
To make ewes cast their lambs, swine eat their farrow,
Sour the milk so maids can churn it not,
Writhe children's wrists and suck their breath in sleep,
Get vials of their blood, and where the sea
Casts up its slimy ooze, search for a weed
To open locks with, and to rivet charms
Planted about her in the wicked feat
Of all her mischiefs, which are manifold.

          The Lincolnshire Witches. 1636.

WHILST these events were taking place in London, Trueman was proceeding towards his destination with such speed as seemed to demonstrate how nearly he had the merchant's interest at heart. The mysterious figure that had accosted him in the old tavern, near St. Alban's, had, it will be remembered, lured him on through dark vaults, and subterraneous passages into the open air, but here, when he anticipated some important result from so singular an interview, the phantom, if such it was, disappeared, leaving its mission unfulfilled, and Trueman to return bewildered and disappointed to his unpressed pillow. How this was caused will be afterwards explained; but to Trueman's fevered imagination the event appeared to him of some supernatural importance. The next day he refrained from mentioning the subject to his good-humoured host, who received every stranger with a smile and a jest; but he determined, nevertheless, to examine the sides of his apartment minutely. The aperture, however, was so skilfully contrived as to render all his attempts at discovering the entrance to the passages he had traversed perfectly fruitless, and he was, therefore, content to leave the hostelry with the mystery that hung over it unravelled. Passing through the town of St. Alban's, with its dark mansions of red brick, and its venerable abbey screened by a lattice-work of ivy, Trueman again soon found himself riding alone on a hedge-skirted road where there was not a house to relieve the monotony of his journey for miles. Still Trueman urged his horse onwards, and during the close of the third day that had passed since his departure, Trueman found himself entering the fenny confines of Lincolnshire. Lincoln's lofty spires gladdened his vision that night, and tasting the sweetness of a quiet night's repose, Trueman awoke on the following morning with a frame quite invigorated and restored, despite the fatigue he had so recently undergone.

After viewing the principal objects of interest in this ancient city, and transacting the business he had to do for Mr. Thorogood in the town, our traveller again proceeded onwards, and turned his horse's head towards Yorkshire. Leaving the town by the clumsily built gateway known as Newport-gate, Trueman crossed a spacious heath overgrown with thistles and teazles, and passing through Wharton arrived late in the afternoon at a small village named Croxhill. Seeing that his steed received proper care and attention, he determined to avail himself of the opportunity the unusual serenity of the evening afforded him for exploring the ruins of the neighbouring abbey of Thornton, and, accordingly, resigning his horse to the care of the proprietor of the humble inn at which he had stopped, Trueman proceeded, on foot, to an object which possessed for him so much interest and attraction.

Following the windings of a grassy path, that led down to a gentle slope towards the south, Trueman came in sight of the ruins of which he was in quest. From the remains few could doubt that this had been the site of one of the most magnificent abbeys in England, and enough was still standing to show that a sum had been expended on its decorations, that, well bestowed in charity, would have gladdened the heart of many a poor pilgrim who, hungry and foot-sore, had since been turned away with an empty blessing and a parroted prayer. At least so thought Trueman, as he gazed with awe and admiration upon those gorgeous memorials of priest-craft and clerical wealth. It appeared originally to have consisted of an extensive square surrounded with a deep ditch and high ramparts, as if serving for occasional military defence as well as pious warfare. The Gate-house, which formed the western entrance, was yet tolerably entire, and was still flanked by brick walls having loop-hole arches, terminating in two round towers, between which a draw-bridge once swung. The front was richly ornamented with cornices, niches, and statues—the latter rendered not a little grotesque by the occasional loss of a member, headless saints kneeling with fractured joints to angels who could none of them boast the usual compliment of legs or wings, and isolated hands with an unequal number of fingers appearing to silently reproach the arms that kept at such an unseemly distance. Here, too, had frowned the massy portcullis; parts of the great wooden doors being still pendant on their hinges—the sport of every wind. But what gratified Trueman's vision most was the roof, that displayed in its wild and fantastic architecture a curious combination of the most quaint embellishments with the most simple ground-work. The arches were finely groined: the ribs supporting which were elegant brackets enriched with flowers and figures. Here and there peered out from among the curiously carved wood-work a half-length image of the human figure, so distorted in countenance as to represent the being in purgatory. The Chapter House, adjoining, was of an octangular shape, and highly decorated, having round it, under its handsome windows, an arcade consisting of pointed arches with cinque foiled heads, and in the centre of each an ornamental trefoil pendent drop.

Thither Trueman proceeded, and as he gazed upon the havoc that time had made in reducing to dust the once lofty walls of this costly edifice, reflections on the vanity of human grandeur and the unerring progress of the spoiler of Time, came thick upon him; and he turned from the contemplation of the outer walls to the Refectory itself.

"Alas!" thought he, "how many hours and years have passed since human forms have gathered round that table, or since its surface has been illumined by lamp or taper. There rang the jocund laugh; there was the festal song sent joyous round with wine; and there, perhaps, did the oily monks apply those welcome offerings of gold to uses, of which the pious devotees who gave them never dreamed. The cross and crozier have yielded to the mattock and the spade; whilst the once costly tesselated pavement is now overspread with a slimy green mould; and the proud towers have sank, like their builders, to the ground, and delved for themselves a grave in the yielding surface of the earth beneath. And this is the end of man's proud ambition! This is the goal to which all his wishes tend; and this the realization of his most ardent hopes! How sad a monument of human vanity; how melancholy an illustration of human frailty!"

"Thou thinkest truly!" exclaimed a voice at Trueman's side: "thou hast read aright this page of worldly wisdom; and now profit by the moral it conveys."

Trueman started from his position with no little celerity; he had been unaware of any person being in his vicinity, and as the shades of evening had darkened the fabric where he stood, he was unable, at first, to ascertain from what quarter the voice came. The sound of footsteps, however, soon arrested his attention, and in another moment he recognized in the countenance of the person who stood before him the familiar features of Edmund Fuller, the Astrologer, of Lambythe Marshe.

We say he recognised; but it was that kind of recognition that implies a faint recollection of the features themselves, but accompanied by a very indistinct idea of the person to whom they belong. And that this was the case with Trueman will excite little surprise, when we inform the reader that Fuller now appeared only a middle-aged man, when he thus accosted the traveller, with straggling chestnut locks displacing the long white hair with which Trueman had seen him before invested, and the furrows that Time appeared then to have made in his countenance, either entirely removed, or so little apparent, as to render his appearance younger by some thirty years.

"May I ask to what cause I am indebted to so strange an intrusion!" inquired Trueman.

"It is an intrusion, I grant," answered the other; "but I trust, nevertheless, not an unwelcome one. I saw you pass the road leading hither, and so came in search of you, expecting to find you here."

"So far you have not been disappointed," continued Trueman; "but in what manner I can have interested you in my wanderings I am yet ignorant."

"That you shall not have long to learn, young man. Edmund Fuller disdains to raise curiosity without, at the same time, gratifying it."

"Fuller! True, the Lambeth astrologer."

"The same. But though this were a fitting scene for my narration, it is not here that it must be told. Night is now coming on apace, and to tarry here might place our persons as well as health in jeopardy. My own dwelling lies not far off, and there, an' it so please you, we will discourse of these things further."

"I attend you," returned Trueman.

In another minute they had reached the outer gate of the abbey.

Their course lay down the hill, of which we have previously spoken, and at another moment might have presented objects to Trueman's vision which, under different circumstances, would have arrested his attention. From the eminence which they were now descending were seen innumerable lights — dancing, as if in joyous unison over the heath before them; now fantastically illuminating with a faint blue light the tangled brakes and brushwood that skirted their path; and anon hovering over a marshy tract, and then dispersing themselves into brilliant coruscations of fire that appeared stationary for a few moments and finally subsided into darkness. These Trueman at once recognized as the ignes fatui, or wills-o'-the-wisp, held in such awe by the common people who, ignorant of their origin, attributed them to the sportive freaks of elves and fays that were supposed to have made that district their abiding place. As they proceeded, these meteoric exhalations became less frequent, and lights of a more settled description gleaming from the window-casements of the cottages below, assumed their place.

But Trueman's mind was too much occupied to allow of his noticing the rapidity with which this transition had been effected. He imagined, though he scarce knew wherefore, that the expected communication bore some reference to Clara, and dark fears of doubt and misgiving crossed his thoughts. The silence of his companion afforded him no relief, for, from this circumstance, he concluded that the unwelcome intelligence of her union with Sir Robt. Otway was about to greet his ears.

Whilst engaged in ruminating upon this subject, he found, however, that they had reached their destination; and entering the cottage, which Fuller pointed out to him as his abode, the astrologer placed some refreshments upon a table, and handing towards him a seat, thus commenced the conversation:—

"You cannot be ignorant, young sir, that on a previous acquaintance I rendered you a somewhat important service by preserving, at least for a time, the fair fame and perhaps life of a certain damsel in whose fortune you appear to be deeply interested. How I acquired the information which enabled me so to do, is not at the present moment an object of much importance; nor should I have even alluded to the circumstance now, were it not that I am about to request a favour in return. A certain Baronet, one Sir Robert Otway, is about forming a matrimonial alliance with the daughter of the merchant whom you serve. Nay, start not; I am not now juggling with the fiend; my knowledge is derived from no such unearthly sources, I assure you; but

this marriage must never take place—nay more, it never can take place, provided we understand each other. Am I right in supposing you would do all in your power to oppose this hated contract?"

Trueman assented with willingness, glad to find that as yet his worst surmises had not been confirmed.

"Then listen! This Baronet is a libertine—the worst of libertines—who recks not by what means he can gain the accomplishment of his wishes, so that they are accomplished at last. He has endeavoured to ensnare the affections of an innocent and unsuspecting damsel—by name Alice Travers—at first by fair means, or what he styled fair; but finding these not succeed, he has had recourse to foul. Her escape from the toils he had woven round her has proved to be but temporary; she is now on the brink of a precipice that yawns in readiness at her feet. Her ruin appears inevitable, but her doom is not yet sealed. Of this girl you must have some knowledge, as she was affianced, whilst in the country, to a friend and fellow-apprentice of your own, who was with you on the night of your visit to me in the Marshe. He is, as far as I can yet learn, ignorant of the fate that awaits her; and must remain so; her salvation being required to come from other hands. The place of her present abode is unknown to me, though it cannot long remain so; but I wish to derive from you the intelligence that I should otherwise gain elsewhere. Can you aid me in my inquiries?"

Trueman briefly related his encounter with Alice at the Seven Bells, already related to the reader, and added an opinion that he was now perfectly convinced of the identity of Miss Travers with the barmaid who had attended him on the occasion of his passage through Hampstead.

"I find my surmises then confirmed," returned the astrologer; "I suspected that the information herein conveyed was false."

And drawing from his vest a letter, he placed it in Trueman's hands to peruse the contents.

He therein found, to his infinite amazement, a minute detail of the flight of Alice from her home, with a circumstantial narration of her having fied towards the North in company, as the letter stated, "with a young clerk of questionable repute, named Trueman. employed by Mr. Thorogood, a merchant in Cheapside."

The writer detailed at great length the motives that induced her to take this step, and these were related to have arisen from a passionate infatuation and unconquerable love for the companion of her guilt, with whom "she had been in habits of close intimacy for some time."

The letter purported to come from one Allison, who could furnish proofs of these allegations, and was addressed to Colonel Travers.

"You need not trouble yourself to contradict these assertions," pursued Fuller, as soon as he perceived Trueman had finished reading the epistle; "I knew the greater portion of them to be false, and suspected the rest; I only wonder that they were heeded so much as they have been. That some little attention has been paid to the statement, you will perceive, when I tell you that Colonel Travers has followed you on your route, with the expectation of recovering his lost daughter, by these means. Indeed, he has already arrived at Croxhill before you; be it my task to undeceive him. Of the motive that induced the instigator of this fabrication to send the Colonel on so fruitless an expedition, I am not quite so confident; but I have my suspicions that it has been the portion of a deeply laid and cunningly devised plot: the schemers shall, however, find, that crafty as their machinations have been, they may yet be outwitted by the very means they have adopted to further the success of their own project. To do this, your aid will be necessary, and I think I may command it. Your route now lays towards Edinburgh, whither my best wishes will accompany you. The merchant's plans for preserving the honour and credit of his house are not unknown to me, and it may lay in my power to be of some service to you on your arrival in the Scotch capital. Take with you these letters; they will serve as the medium of introduction to the persons of whom you are in quest. Nay! no acknowledgments, young sir; deliver these as they are directed, and the knowledge that I have promoted your welfare and your employer's interest will be of itself sufficient thanks. The object of my interview is now gained."

" I am grateful for your unexpected kindness, indeed," said Trueman; " but you have left me still in ignorance of how I can be of any service in rescuing Miss Travers from the perils by which she appears to be surrounded."

" Until I am certain what the precise nature of thes perils may be," answered Fuller, " I cannot enter into the subject further. I now only wished to secure your co-operation in case it should be found necessary. Further information of what course is to be adopted will be contained in letters that shall meet you in Edinburgh."

" One thing more and I have done," cried Trueman; " when I last saw you, I beheld a venerable and age-worn man whom Time had appeared to have used most rigorously; I now see a person whose advancement in years is scarcely to be observed. How am I to reconcile this contrast ?"

" By knowing more of human nature and human exigencies;" answered the seer, and continued with a smile, " this innocent masquerading has been often practised for more dishonest purposes than those for which I adopted it. Disguise I found necessary, and I availed myself of its aid."

" Then I am to conclude that astrology and the jargon by which it is conducted is a farce; an imposture; in short, as embodied in yourself, a mere trap to catch the unwary, and a trick to delude the ignorant."

" Nay," exclaimed Fuller, his countenance radiating with rapture as he spoke, " not so ! The glorious science has beheld in me one of its most ardent devotees. Night and day have I pondered over the dazzling truths which it unfolds, and arisen from every study more deeply impressed with the unerring certainty of the noble doctrine that teaches us that our actions are ruled and our fates governed by the planets that shine above us. I know that the world despises and ridicules our profession: that men of learning have carped at it, and that others have fancied, with a kinder interpretation, that we deceive, being deceived. But the time is not far distant when its value will be acknowledged, and its influence felt and its study appreciated; when man will be able to read the stars as some glorious book placed by Heaven in the spacious firmament, to be perused by all who will take the trouble to study its language; when evil may be averted or lessened, and good increased; when, like the Chaldeans of

old, we shall foretell the fate of empires, and govern the progress of coming events : when—but you will pardon this rhapsody, young sir, for it proceeds from one who is a sincere and ardent lover of the science he professes—who looks up to it as a mistress, and adores it as a god. It has been only treated as chimerical by those who have never estimated its value, or studied its truths, and these I am content to leave blessed in the darkness of their unhappy ignorance. See here," he continued, throwing open the casement and revealing a wide expanse of sky studded by innumerable constellations twinkling with the superabundance of their own brilliancy; " see the bright orbs that unfold their mysteries to us, if man would not blindly close his eyes and shut his ears to the lessons they convey. See the planets as they roll onward, each in its spacious orbit, and reflect if there is not something ennobling in connecting each with our own destiny; and looking upon each as the face of some familiar friend on whose cocntenance we gaze with rapture, and whose changes of expression we observe. Night is thus rendered doubly lovely to us by the associations it brings with it, and twice as much to be adored as the garish eye of day. Who would not penetrate into the Arcana of that science that thus repays its votaries ? Yonder is Orion's belt, gemming the glorious firmament with its triple lamps; there, to the north of it, shines Betelgeux, the star that shed its light upon my birth, and the orb that will watch over me when I die; and, as my soul wings its way from the frail mortal tenement that now contains it, towards its final destination, that star will receive it on its wanderings, and guide the etherial messenger to heaven. But I weary you by my discourse; and without a heart enthusiastic in its love of astrology, like mine, beats responsive to the sentiments I express, it may appear wild and absurd. I have been led into an expression of my opinions somewhat rashly, but it was on a subject that is in itself inexhaustible. Astrology an imposture ! No ! there may be some errors in the calculation it brings with it; but its mighty truths can never fail to strike conviction to the heart of him who is willing to explore its mysteries, and who has patience to investigate the science as it deserves to be investigated."

The kindled eye and excited frame of the speaker indeed well attested the earnestness with which the foregoing speech had been delivered, and Trueman bade adieu to the enthusiast, with regret that the conversation had been brought to a termination, rather than with a sense of tediousness at its having been continued so long.

" If astrology be, indeed, the chimera that some say," thought he, as he journeyed homeward, " it is, at least, a science that brings man in communication with the heavens, and raises his ambitious thoughts far, far above the dull grovelling earth on which we move. If it is, indeed, a delusion, it is a pleasing and profitable one; for though it may have a tendency towards fatalism with some, it can only increase, in a well-regulated mind, man's love and veneration for the Being who rules the stars, and whose mandate called them into existence."

The length to which the interview had been prolonged had merged night into morning, and in the east Aurora had already begun to " unbar the golden gates of light." It was the hour when elves break up their fairy court, and when, at the command of Oberon, Titania with her train of sylphs forsake the grassy glade and mossy dell for the recesses of their own sacred caverns; when Queen Mab and her attendant sprites take wing to other spheres, and "chasing midnight as she flies, pursue her round the globe; when each tiny fay, brimmed with the over night's potations of pure dew, drank from the inverted chalice of the blue-bell, shrinks from the careless gaze of passers-by, and then for very fear creeps into a neighbouring acorn-cup, and allows the wanderer to pass; when Puck no longer lures the unlucky traveller with his treacherous light, misguiding him to bogs and marshy fens, where, mocking him with jeers and subtle antics, he leaves him to despair. It was the hour when the morning star, peeping over its azure banks of clouds, warns the joyous groupe their revels have an end till Cynthia again resumes her sway, and bathes the world in genial moonlight.

> " To rest! to rest! the herald of the day
> Bright Phosphorus commands you hence; obey!
> The moon is pale and spent, and winged night
> Makes headlong haste to quit the morning's sight,
> Who now is rising from her blushing wars,
> And with her rosy hand puts back the stars."

But, alas! fairies, and all the delicious associations connected therewith, have fled—sepulchred in the tomb of every-day life. Steam-carriages have expelled them from the earth, Nassau balloons routed them from the air, and steamers with their roaring paddles, have ploughed up their coral caves in the deep. Iron trams, diverging to all points of the compass, have stretched their Briarean arms athwart each sequestered dingle and fay-hunted dell, likening England to the intricacies of one vast gridiron. Fairies have indeed departed, banished by the march of intellect and utilitarian philosophy; but they have yet a monument worthy of them. They are treasured up in our earliest recollections; their memories are embalmed in our hearts and cherished in our fondest associations, despite the power of animal magnetism and the advancement of mental "philosophy." Ghosts vanished when gas appeared, and we think they showed their good taste in so doing; but the attraction of Fairyland still lingers around us, clinging to our hearts and loath to quit its abiding place in the storehouse of our memory. What Winsor did for ghosts, James Watt has done for fairies; steam has out-oberoned Oberon, and the enchantment has fled. The fairy *Hegira* may be dated from the introduction of boilers and pistons, and we have too much cause to fear that the era of their return to "merrye Englande" is as much involved in mystery as their present place of refuge.—Wherever they may be, our benison go with them!"

CHAPTER XVIII.

A SCENE IN NEWGATE.

Here from my prison will I view the world
As from an eminence, where I may gaze
In peace upon the plain mapped out below:
Behold the springs that move this vast machine,
And study well the lessons they convey.
Then shall I see how Justice with one hand,
Receives the bribe that lets the rich man 'scape.
And with the other signs the fatal deed
That hangs the peasant: then shall I, too, behold
The Poet wearing out in nightly toil
His youth in fruitless searchings after Fame,   ['rous
And how when Fortune smiles, and Fate seems prosp-
The o'er-taxed thread that wedded him to life
Snaps its frail fastenings, and he loses all:
And if his fame lasts after his decease,
'Tis like the shell that shines not in the dark,
Until the living form that gave its birth,
Lies rotting in the grave. Then shall I see
The statesman guilding true the helm of state
With party breezes bellying out the sails:
Behold the Patriot, anxious much that man
Should share (kind soul!) fair equal joys with man,
Filling his purse with others' hard-earned wealth,
And crying still for "Justice:" see how knaves
Grow fat and prosper, whilst we honest men
Exhaust our lives in poverty and toil.
But conscious worth and innocence repays
Our sufferings yet, and Providence is kind
In sending Death to terminate our woes.

The World's my Prison, 1703.

WE left Alice, at the conclusion of a former chapter, in a situation of no little perplexity. It will be remembered that, on the day of the burial, she was arrested by the magistrate as an accessory to the murder that had been committed, and we now proceed to show the cause that led to this proceeding.

Sir Robert Otway, by means of his agents, having discovered the refuge that Alice had taken in the house of Mrs. Tabitha Royster, after her flight from his mansion—for it would be idle now to disguise from the reader that Arlington and Sir Robert Otway are *one*—sedulously endeavoured to ensnare her once more in his toils. Abduction, by force, from a place like Hampstead, where his person was so well known, would have been attended with too much of danger and difficulty to render so hazardous an attempt advisable. Whilst actively engaged, however, in fabricating schemes for her detention, the circumstance of the murder taking place at so critical a moment, furnished the wily Baronet with the means by which he could attain his object. He saw clearly by the details that he had heard, that a chain of circumstantial evidence would be wound round her, so complex and intricate, as to render her escape from its meshes a matter approaching to almost sheer improbability.

The probable obstacle of her father's interference in his project was easily removed by the letter sent by Allison at his instigation, and this, as we have shown in the last chapter, succeeded beyond their utmost expectations. Of Barnwell he had no apprehensions, for though he knew that Alice was betrothed to our hero, and would most likely seek an interview with him, he was satisfied at the same time with knowing that he had not the power, even if he had the will, of extricating her from the perilous position in which she was placed. It was on the day previous to the burial taking place that Sir Robert Otway, in a casual excursion to Hampstead, heard of the murder and the circumstances attending it, and at once conceived the idea of rendering it subservient to his designs. For that purpose he had an interview with the nearest magistrate, and so forcibly pointed out the suspicions attached to Alice, that he had but little difficulty in persuading the legal functionary to issue a warrant for her detention immediately. He argued upon the careful manner in which Alice had abstained from giving particulars of her family or connections; the singular, not to say suspicious, circumstances attending her first introduction to Mrs. Royster's; the opportunities she had for assisting in a deed of this description, and the slight probability of a stranger unknown, and, according to her own account, friendless, resisting a temptation that came with such a powerful inducement to make her an abettor in the robbery—for the murder he looked upon, and he was this time right in the conjecture—as a thing by no means contemplated, in the first instance, by the plunderers.

He dwelt particularly upon the circumstances of Alice on the night of the murder not being roused from her slumbers until the burglars had had a fair opportunity of escaping, and then coming down in her evening dress—which seemed to show at once that she was prepared for what was to happen, and had preserved her attire accordingly.

This, though it was purely accidental, inasmuch as Alice had been reading late on the night in question, according to her usual custom, and had allowed sleep to steal on her while thus engaged, in consequence of which she did not wake till aroused by the cries of her mistress—was allowed by Mr. Hugh Clinton, the magistrate, to be weighty evidence against her, and from that moment he was wavering in his opinion as to the criminality of Alice.

"Besides," argued the Baronet, "she, as far as I can gain from the villagers, had viewed with favorable eyes the host of the Seven Bells, Ralph Royster himself, and, therefore, the removal of an obstacle so fatal to the advancement of her interests, as Mrs. Royster, would be regarded, by her, as advantageous rather than otherwise."

"True! most worshipful Sir," exclaimed the clerk, who was noting these things down in the book he held before him, and who invariably made it a rule to coincide in the opinion of the last speaker; "the gentleman is right."

"But the discharge of the pistols—" suggested the magistrate.

"Was a feint—a blind to her real object," answered Sir Robert. "Remember! the first, as she has said herself, flashed in the pan when the life of her mistress might have been saved, and the second was fired when, from the neighbourhood being alarmed, some demonstration of resistance was necessary. It appears to have wounded some one, it is true; but a woman's hand can seldom ensure a good aim: and I, therefore, conclude it was a random shot that gained an unlooked for destination."

"Most correctly argued," cried the clerk, again addressing himself to the cumbrous quarto that received his lucubrations.

"Your arguments stagger me, I must confess," returned the magistrate; "and I should be wanting in the duties of my office did I not inquire into this sad affair more minutely; but these are but conjectures you must remember, Sir Robert, that are far from being decisive."

"Aye! that's certain again," muttered the scribe.

"Peace! Gabriel," continued Mr. Clinton, "thy tongue grow wearisome. I was saying, Sir Robert,

that, before we proceed to extremities, we should have grounds more relative than these on which to base our opinions."

"Were these wanting," said the Baronet in reply, "I should not have been here. In thus coming I have been actuated, as you perceive, only by the best intentions—namely, those of furthering the ends of justice. I am merely suggesting certain things which appear to have been overlooked—for Heaven knows I would wrong no one wittingly. I cannot pretend to compete with your worship in legal knowledge, profoundly as you are skilled in the mysteries of the law; but while asking for a stronger proof of the unfortunate girl's delinquency, you seem to have forgotten the finding of a handkerchief clotted with blood, and found near the house on the following morning."

"True, it was her handkerchief, and marked with her own initials; but she declares that it was left on the night in question in the bar, and that, therefore, it must have been taken by the burglars."

"And is it likely," insinuated the other, "that on this night alone it should have been left? rather suppose it to have been thrown from her window as the signal for the depredators to commence their operations."

"Most likely," chimed in the clerk, who, in consequence of the previous rebuke, had since attested his entire concurrence with each speaker by his eyes alone; "most probable."

"Peace, Gabriel, I again say," exclaimed Mr. Clinton; "you forget that we have no audience now where you may display your wisdom;" and continued addressing himself to the Baronet; "your remarks appear to me feasible; and, anxious as I am to discharge my painful duties honestly, I cannot withhold longer my determination to issue a warrant for her detention. It appears to me that the person is in some way, at least, implicated in this sad affair. Here, Gabriel, hand me a paper to fill up; her real name is——"

"Alice Travers!" said the Baronet.

"Gadsooth! you seem to have some knowledge of this misled girl."

"Why," returned the other, somewhat confused, "I have heard her name frequently mentioned in the village throughout the day, and so it comes to me as familiar as my own. You will excuse me appearing further in the affair, as important business call me back to town this very night. I wished only to render my aid in seeing this horrid mystery unravelled."

"Your motives are most laudable," rejoined the magistrate; "and your selection of me for the vehicle of your surmises confers upon me the greatest honour. I will not detain you from your journey longer, Sir Robert, but trusting it will be a pleasant and speedy one, proceed to avail myself of your kind suggestions."

"A garrulous blockhead, muttered the Baronet, as, after exchanging the usual compliments, he gained the open air; "he might have seen my drift before: but no matter, the train is now laid—the explosion will soon follow."

"We must set about this matter instantly, Gabriel," remarked the official, after Sir Robert's departure.

"Most decidedly," acquiesced the clerk; and the document was forthwith made out and presented—its effects are already known.

Mr. Hugh Clinton, though a magistrate, was a

man of no sound penetration—an anomaly not less frequent in our own day than those of which we write—else would he have seen through the flimsy arguments made use of by Sir Robert, and treated them accordingly. As it was, his whole soul was absorbed in the importance of the station to which he had arrived, and aught tending to increase that importance was most greedily seized and availed of. Thus, he fancied, that arrest of Alice would not only gain for him the credit of possessing great penetration, but at the same time gratify his own self love in increasing the dignity attached to his office. He foresaw, also, that by so doing, he should raise himself in the opinion of Sir Robert, to whose patronage he looked up, and in whose estimation he felt exceedingly desirous of holding a high place.

Motives such as these still lead to the same results; and could we trace back to their native spring the actions of most of our modern heroes, we should doubtless find that, where the world has given credit for great discernment and disinterested patriotism, the real incentives to action have been unbounded vanity and inordinate love of self.

Of the manner in which the unexpected intelligence was conveyed to Alice, we have already made the reader aware, and the mode of dealing in cases like this being then much more summary than at present—the accused had no other opportunity of justifying herself than by strenuously asserting her innocence—in the earnest belief of which all the bystanders heartily joined—and surrendering herself to the officers of "Justice" was forthwith inducted into one of the cells at Newgate—there to await her trial at the sessions.

In the romance, as well as in the reality of life, the progress of events bears a marvellous resemblance to a drama, where, at every turn and phase of the story, the scene changes, obedient to the prompter's whistle, and new characters appear on the stage, displacing those who preceded them, to be in their turn succeeded by those who follow. How often do we see in real life a man nursed in the lap of affluence, and yesterday lolling indolently on a damask couch; to-day eating the bread of labour, and struggling through all the ills attendant upon a life of hopeless, bitter poverty? How often do we see a statesman, now on the pinnacle of fame, the favourite of his monarch, and the admired and envied of all beholders, wielding the sceptre of nations in his grasp, and looked up to by millions as the arbitrator of their disputes, and the ruler of their destinies. You think that man happy; fancy, perhaps, he will be always thus. Tush! wait but the changing of the scene, and you shall see this Wolsey disgraced, despised by the very people who before so eulogised him, and his place and fortune bestowed upon some more fortunate trial, who will, in his turn, share his predecessor's fate. We have seen a man who swayed for years the destiny of Europe, who overturned former empires and created new, and who was within an ace of acquiring the ambitious title of the "Conqueror of the World"—we have seen this very man, as the changing of the scene, exhiled in shame and sorrow to a sea-girt prison, where, with but two sharing his banishment, out of the many hundreds who had participated in his prosperity, he breathed his last in an island, where his sighs, wafted by the ocean breeze, could alone reach those most dear to him. From happiness to misery, from wealth to poverty,

from fame to ignominy, there is but one step; the shifting of the scene brings us either one or the other; and when at last life's curtain drops, it is a matter of little moment to the principal actor, whether the drama in which he has been engaged has presented more of the former than the latter, or whether he has been applauded or condemned for playing the part assigned him by the manager —Fate. It is so with us at the present moment. We have seen Alice happy at first in the enjoyment of her own peaceful home, then passing a few weeks of rural tranquillity at Hampstead; and we have now to play the scene-shifter, and transport her to the recesses of Newgate, where, for a crime of which she was innocent, fortune had doomed her to experience an accumulation of misery, that, when contrasted with her former life of peace and happiness, seemed indeed the very height of wretchedness and woe.

On a low mattrass, scarcely raised above the cold stony surface of the prison-cell, was seen Alice, endeavouring to snatch from slumber a few hours of peace and repose, which her walking moments denied her. Her sleep was the sleep of innocence —calm and unbroken, save by an occasional sigh that escaped her lips at intervals, as if some heart-rending sorrow, that, pent up in her bosom, would corrode the place of its confinement, was seeking to find egress by her lips, and thus relieve the mind of the fair sufferer of a burden that could not be otherwise than wearisome.

But she was not alone; another was bending over her, watching with anxious eyes and beating heart each movement of the slumberer. This was Cicely, who, conscious of Alice being free from crime, had daily visited her since her incarceration, and endeavoured to soothe by her conversation and attention, the many woes to which her companion was a prey.

A slight movement and change in her position manifested to Cicely that the slumbers of Alice had terminated. She raised herself up from the couch, and casting her eyes languidly around her with that uncertain gaze that seems to betoken the mind returning to its former consciousness, soon became aware of the presence of Cicely.

"Now this is kind of you, Cicely," said Alice, thus to cheer me with thy presence so early."

"You have slept somewhat longer than your wont," returned Cicely, "else would you have said I had been late in my arrival."

"I have indeed slept soundly," continued Alice: "but knew not of the hour. I have had dreams, too—such pleasant dreams, dear Cicely—that made my hours of sleep seem spent in Heaven."

"I trust 'twill prove a good omen; but see here," cried Cicely, placing in the hands of Alice a bouquet, "here is a present for you, given to me, for you, by a gallant gentleman who accosted me in the outer court."

"Ah! from Barnwell, perhaps," eagerly exclaimed Alice, trusting that the letter she had sent him had hastened his arrival.

"I could not hear the name by which he was addressed," replied Cicely; "but from the deference paid him by Mr. Lockyer, the jailor, I fancy he was a person of some rank and opulence. But see! here is that, that may unravel the mystery." And plucking from the flowers a note, Cicely placed it in the hands of Alice, for perusal.

The countenance of Alice glowed with indignation as she possessed herself of its contents. It

was signed " Arlington," and expressed in the strongest terms the affection which the writer felt for Alice. No allusion was made to the escape from Marylebone; but the main points of the epistle turned upon the protection which he could afford her in the event of her compliance with his wishes; and a postcript was added, to the effect that he would himself wait on her to receive her reply.

"And am I sunk so low?" cried Alice, her voice swelling with emotion; " am I so far reduced below the level of my sex as to require insult to be added to injury? Oh! would that I had some kind friend to aid me in the wreaking of my vengeance! one who could avenge my wrongs, as well as share my sorrows."

" You have one, Alice, in me," said Cicely, moved even to tears by the grief of her companion, " who already sympathises in your sufferings, though I know not how I can relieve them. But that letter is from————"

" A villain !" interrupted Alice, "who is the cause of all my present anguish; who forced me from my peaceful home, and kept me a close prisoner until fortune enabled me to escape. A villain who is————"

" Here !" exclaimed a voice behind them, and, turning round, Alice beheld her persecutor in the person of Sir Robert Otway.

" This is somewhat ungentle language to use, fair lady, in the absence of the party whom you were so highly eulogising just now. I was in hopes my floral missive had prepared you somewhat differently for my arrival.

"Neither your presence nor your note, Sir, can I consider as welcome," observed Alice, "your garb and the rank in which you move should have at least taught you that, thus to intrude into the society of two females, unlooked for and unsolicited, is a breach of good manners, if, indeed, nothing else."

"I crave your pardon, Mistress Alice, if I have aught transgressed; but I am willing to overlook past circumstances, and think only of present ones. You require my aid, and I am here ready to offer it."

"Aye, on conditions that even *you* dare not trust your tongue to express while your eye rests upon the form of her you would injure. But know that I am still inflexible in my determination. I never can, nor will be your's."

"Poor, misled girl! You injure but yourself in acting thus. You are accused of a crime of which I believe from my very heart you are innocent; but—"

"*You* then believe I am not guilty. Oh! bless you for those words, but my o'er-fraught heart is breaking."

"Nay! hear me out. I say you have been charged with the commission of a crime you probably never committed; but the evidence is strong against you. There is not a single witness you can call to prove your innocence. Death, then, or, at least, a lingering life in other climes, will be your fate, for your judges are already predisposed to consider you as guilty. Choose, then, between the freedom I now offer you, and an ignominious punishment—choose between a life of happiness with me, and a doom that, though prolonged, is yet inevitable."

"I *have* chosen!" exclaimed Alice, energetically. "I will await my trial, and Heaven will prosper the event."

"Still stubborn and unyielding," cried Sir Robert; "then you must receive the reward of your obstinacy. But look, the prison doors are open. Bribes and golden persuasives have wrought me a free passage hither, and will you hence? Here are the keys of the outer gates."

"What if I were to make known your dealings with the jailor?"

"It would avail you nothing, fair informer; the minor officials are already in my interest, and their masters would not credit an imprisoned criminal in preference to my testimony."

"True, indeed!" sobbed Alice; "oh! leave me, I beseech you, to my fate."

"Not until I have received my answer."

"You have heard it already. I will consent to the loss of my life rather than of my reputation. I am conscious of my own innocence, and I will abide the result."

"You play a bold game, madam, so do not blame me if you lose it; but, trust me, you will yet repent this foolish pride."

"Never!" cried Alice; "I am fixed in my resolve."

"Then I take my departure; but the more unwillingly, however, that my mission has been attended with no good result. I came to save your life, Miss Travers, not to take it; but I perceive my presence here grows wearisome. Once more, I humbly take my leave."

And the clanking of the chains as the turnkey on the outside made fast the door, told the inmates of the cell that their visitor had daparted.

CHAPTER XIX.

SAMPSON SKELTON'S TALE.

Have ye no tale of ages long gone-by,
No fairy legend brimming o'er with fun,
Or story of a haunted tower drear,
Wherewith to chase away care's leaden hand,
And cheat dull time of many a sluggish hour?
Come! Come!—I know thou hast—unfold! unfold!

Old Play.

BEFORE we can return to Barnwell, it will be necessary for the advancement of our story, and in order the better to preserve the continuity of the narrative, to see Trueman a little farther on his journey towards Edinburgh. We left him in our last chapter at Croxhill, whither, after bidding adieu to his friend the astrologer, he had returned that night. The next morning saw him in Ferrybridge, and passing through Northallerton and Darlington, he soon, by easy stages, arrived at Durham. Twenty miles of hard riding carried him into the county of Northumberland, and without stopping at Newcastle longer than was absolutely necessary for the refreshment of himself and horse, he proceeded onward through Gosford and Morpeth to Alnwick, where he put up for the night. Another day enabled him to reach Tweedmouth, a considerable village on the north side of the Tweed opposite to Berwick, where he reined in his steed, his heart glowing with satisfaction at beholding the borders of Scotland stretched out before him. It was late in the evening of the next day when he arrived at Broxburn, and falling in on the road with a traveller bound to the same city as himself, they both agreed to pass the night at that place, rather than encounter the keen easterly wind at that time blowing across the heathy waste with no gentle force, accompanied by chilling gusts of sleet and hail. The welcome fireside, however, of the country inn soon restored warmth to the limbs of the travellers; and the stranger—by name one Sampson Skelton, and by profession an itinerant salesman—took advantage of their being comfortably housed, and a good supper being disposed of, for letting forth a flood of anecdote and legendary lore that made Trueman not regret the companionship of one who proved so instructive a tutor in the superstitions of the soil. Drawing a chair nearer to the fire, and bidding Trueman do the same, the anecdotist recalled to his recollection a gigantic obelisk or cross which they had passed in the course of the afternoon, and adding that there was a somewhat strange story connected therewith. Skelton filled his pipe, replenished his glass, and commenced the following narration; which we prefer, however, giving in our own words, as being less diffuse, and more free from the peculiarities of dialect, than when it emanated from the lips of the narrator:—

THE STORY OF THE FAIRY CROSS.

A LEGEND OF NORTHUMBERLAND.

Many days ago, when the world was by some hundreds of years younger than it is now, he who looked over the wide domain of Harrington, would see towering above the tall elm trees that clustered around it, a spacious and noble castle with turreted battlements, and lofty towers that, built upon the summit of a commanding eminence, and overlooking the country for miles round, presented a fair and beauteous prospect to the eye of the beholder.

The proprietor of this stately castle was the renowned Knight, Sir Launcelot Gamhon de Hohmbugg, a Norman Baron, who had at the period our tale commences but just returned from the Holy Wars, bringing back with him both honour and wounds, testimonies of his valour, in which we are bound to say that the latter predominated. The Baron was a fierce, muscular man, with a mouth as wide as his own moat, and garnished with whiskers and mustachios as threatening as the spikes of his own portcullis: he was a cruel man withal, and exceeding proud and haughty in his demeanour; but he possessed one attraction that brought many a gallant Knight within his castle, and acted as a sort of counteracting agent to his own repelling power. This was his daughter Madeline. A fair and beauteous creature was she, fashioned by Nature in one of her happiest moods, and so mild and amiable in her disposition, that one would have wondered how so tender a branch could have been grafted on so stubborn a tree, did not report say—but that is no business of ours—let it suffice for the curious to know that the Holy Wars were of a very long duration in these days, and even Baronesses might then sometimes miss the presence of their husbands, so that if any *faux pas* was committed, why it was a very common fau't at this period, and there's an end of it.

But Madeline was far from being dutiful, with all her good qualities; for, during her father's absence, she had fallen in love with one Walter Annerley, a young peasant residing on the estate; and love being a pit, that however easy it may be to fall in, is not so easy to fall out of, it very naturally occurred that when the Baron, Sir Launcelot Gamhon de Hohmbugg insisted upon her marrying the man he had selected—the very counterpart of himself—she as obstinately refused, and cherished her affection for Walter with more ardour than ever. The Baron was a man however, not to be gainsayed in anything that he had once set his mind upon, and, accordingly, without asking his daughter twice, he gave a grand entertainment in honour of her nuptials, and invited the neighbouring Barons for miles around to partake of his hospitality.

The Baronial Hall was fitted up in a style that benefitted the occasion, and huge garlands of misletoe and yew-berries—for it was winter—decked the old-fashioned lamps that hung from the ceiling and the benches on which the guests were seated. A large boar's head, flanked by portly flagons of ale, each with a roasted crab hissing in its centre, occupied the place of honour opposite the host, and a series of dishes containing brawn, stuffed peacocks, quails garnished with bay-leaves, and a huge sir-loin of beef sprinkled with sprigs of rosemary, furnished the centre. Nor was the necessity of liquids forgotten. Sack was distributed in formidable beakers, each containing a quart, from a fountain at hand, and these were emptied at a draught; whilst songs and jests floated gaily from one to another, and gave rise to peals of merriment that might have been heard beyond the Borders.

But these sounds of merriment were before long suspended by a report at first arising from the lobby, and then gradually spreading itself over the body of the Hall, to the effect that the Lady Madeline, who was that night to have been married, was nowhere to be found. Great was the amazement depicted on the visages of all by this unexpected ntelligence, but when it reached the ears of the

Baron, he got absolutely frantic with rage, and learning from a trembling vassal of his household, that Madeline had escaped in company with young Walter Annerley, he at once determined, notwithstanding the darkness of the night, to set off in pursuit of them. Never was such consternation and confusion known, as that exhibited now in the mansion of the Baron. Everybody ran in everybody's way in pursuit of everything, and, as is usual on such occasions, brought back nothing.

The feast was broken up into " most admired disorder," and ten of the fleetest steeds in the Baron's stables were saddled simultaneously for the pursuit. No sooner were the saddles placed on the backs of the horses, than the baron himself and nine of his guests jumped upon the backs of the saddles, and, learning the direction taken by the fugitives, soon left the castle walls far behind them.

On, on, on, they go, guided by the pale light of the full moon that now emerged from behind a dark cloud, as if anxious to be a witness of the scene; and many miles of rugged and uneven ground had been passed over, when the Baron found that he had far-outstripped his companions, and that he was now left alone to continue the search. Nothing daunted, however, by the discovery, and certain that the objects of his vengeance could be at no great distance, he rode on at an unabated speed, and traversing a winding road that led over a wild uncultivated district known as Haggerstone Marsh, his eyes were soon gratified by the sight of a light glimmering before him, as if carried by a man on horse-back; and this he at once set down to be the lantern of Walter and Madeline.

Following the course taken by the welcome beacon, he diverged considerably from the main road, and betook himself to a narrow winding pathway that was overgrown with thick bushes and briary plants, threatening the horse on which Sir Launcelot rode with many a promised fall, and creating many an unpleasant stumble. Still onward he went, until the increased ruggedness of the waste made further progress on horseback impossible; and thinking from the depressed position of their light, which now appeared but at a hundred yards' distance, that they had done the same, the Baron turned his steed adrift on the marsh, determined to overtake and secure the fugitives on foot. And now did the perplexities of his journey come fast upon him. The narrow strip of pathway became so closely intertangled with briars that the Baron's dress was torn to shreds at every pace he took, and anon, when piteously complaining to himself of these impediments, the ground would yield under him, and immerse him in a bog from which self-extrication was a matter of no small difficulty. Then the light which before seemed so near that he could almost touch it, now moved off to a considerable distance, and by the time the Baron had taught his baronial limbs the uses of a run, huge drops of perspiration trickled down his brow, and he began to sigh for the peace and enjoyment left behind him at his own mansion.

After a fatiguing chase had thus been maintained with spirit on both sides for upwards of an hour, the Baron began to find his energies give way, and he grew tired and breathless. Battling with the Saracens and Paynim Knights was a trifle compared with the arduous exertions of this night's pursuit, so he wisely determined to give up the chase, seek out his steed, and return to the castle. No sooner, however, had this resolution been formed in his mind, than the lantern that had before appeared at least three miles off, was seen dancing at his side. Yes, there it was; but to the horror of the Baron it seemed conveyed along without any visible agency. The undulating motion was exactly that which would have been produced, had it been carried in the hand, and evidently gave the idea of a person walking with it. On looking down, however, the Baron found that, instead of being placed in the hand, it was fixed upon the head of the traveller; and further scrutiny developed a small, dwarfish, little old man, scarcely two feet high, with wrinkled countenance and hobbling gait, as the carrier of this said lantern. Chagrin and vexation at discovering the error into which he had been led, soon gave way to feelings of amusement and wonder at finding such a mysterious and comical personage carrying a light over a lonely moor at an hour so irregular; and the result was that the Baron, after minutely surveying the diminutive person at his side, haughtily inquired if he had observed the two persons he described as Walter and Madeline, pass that way.

The comical looking old gentleman replied at once in the negave, but asked the reason.

The Baron explained.

"Tush! is that all?" returned the comical little old gentleman: "leave it to me; I will undertake to bring them to you."

"*You!*" contemptuously uttered the Baron, as he eyed the manikin at his side: "why," and here he imparted a peculiarly strong emphasis to the personal pronoun, "why I have been unsuccessful."

At this allusion to his personal dignity the comical looking old gentleman waxed exceeding wroth; the lantern seemed to increase in size, and the body under it enlarged correspondingly.

"Am I big enough now?" cried the voice that formerly belonged to the body of the comical looking old gentleman.

But the Baron could make no reply through fear and astonishment.

Still the figure went on getting larger and larger —lantern and all—like we see sometimes in our phantasmagoria exhibitions at the present day. The legs stretched themselves out to a length most marvellous to behold, and the body became greater in proportion. The head magnified itself to the size of a cart-wheel, and the lantern would have filled a moderately sized room.

"Am I big enough now?" roared the giant, in accents like the rumbling of distant thunder.

But, if the Baron was dumbfounded through fear and surprise before, he was now doubly tongue-tied. He essayed to speak; but his tongue clove to the roof of his mouth.

"What no answer again! then let this teach you better manners for the future." And elevating a cumbrous club in his hand that had during the last few minutes grown from a sprig of holly, he dealt it with unerring precision on the Baron's head, and felling him senseless to the ground the figure evaporated.

When the Baron recovered, he found the wan moon flinging her pale beams over the wide expanse of waste around him, but revealing not the proximity of a single human creature. The intense cold began to benumb the baronial tips of the Baron's fingers, and he resorted to an expedient, familiar to the labourers of the present day, but then only just introduced into England, the great secret of which appears to consist in endeavouring to throw the right arm as far over the left shoulder as possible and *vice versa*.

Considerably invigorated by this plebeian process, the next thing was for the Baron to regain his horse. This was a task of no very easy achievement, as the Baron's notions of topographical identity about this spot were slightly confused. Like all other tasks, however, it must have an attempt made towards its accomplishment; so selecting the road deemed most likely to answer his expectations, he once more set out on his journey with very different feelings and with a very different object in view.

New dangers, however, here appeared to environ him. As he proceeded, frogs and toads, of a size considerably larger than ordinary, amused themselves by playing at leap-frog over the Baron's shoulders; and this was an indignity the noble scion of the great house of Hohmbugg was not disposed to put with. Clearing a score off his hat with a vigorous shake, that seemed to dislocate nearly every bone in his body, he proceeded to exterminate them from his shoulders; but just as he did so, the treacherous ground sank under him, and the Baron found himself up to his arm-pits in a huge cavity filled with a damp, clayey substance, that clung with tenacity to his already chilled frame.

"The fiend take these pitfalls!" ejaculated the Baron, petulantly—for it must be remembered that Barons swore in those days as well as in ours.

"Ha! ha! ha!" laughed a thousand voices from every side.

"Ho! ho! ho!" echoed a thousand others, more distant.

The Baron looked up. He was convulsed with horror and amazement. From every crevice in the plants around him peered forth a fearful face. Some indescribable shapes were squatted on toadstools; others, poised upon the unbending rush that supported them, grinned with a fierce, unearthly grin down upon him; and the rest, fantastically spreading their fingers before their long hooked noses, wagged them with a kind of demoniac exultation. But this was not all: a figure, dumpy and deformed, with a head thrice the size of the body to which it was attached, sat cross-legged on the decayed stump of an old tree, and, at every renewed laugh, whirled himself round on the pivot beneath him with surprising celerity—a species of rotary exercise in which the others most cordially joined.

"Ha! ha! ho! ho! you are the Baron de Hohmbugg, eh? that runs after the true lovers at midnight on St. Agnes' Eve. Ha! ha! ho! ho!" and again was the fantastic form of the sprite on the stump whirled round with boisterous delight.

The Baron, now recollecting for the first time that it *was* St. Agnes' Eve, became impressed with great feelings of fear and terror. His teeth rattled against each other with a cold, chattering sound, and his knees knocked audibly against the clayey soil in which they were imbedded, whilst other unequivocal symptoms of trepidation were added to those that preceded them.

"Ha! ha!" shouted the imp; "the Baron is getting courageous, eh? Who'll help the Baron out of the pit?"

"I! I! I!" echoed a thousand and one voices.

"One at a time, please, good people," remonstrated the sprite who had first spoken—"what excellent fun it is. Ha! ha! ho! ho!" and again did the subtle imp spin himself round upon the stump with increased celerity; a motion which the rest on the bulrushes, as they had done before, instantly imitated.

"Aye! in the name of St. Agnes aid me in getting out of this confounded bog," supplicated the Baron, hoping that the hour of his deliverance was at hand.

"Ho! ho! help the Baron, eh! who would help no one else. Ha! ha! come hither, Hobbinol—aid the Baron to get out of the bog."

A short, dumpy elf, with large green goggle eyes set in a very red face, here tumbled out from amongst the crowd, and tweaking the baronial nose of the Baron with treacherous pinches, at last firmly grasped the nasal promontory between his hooked thumb and finger, and raising him by this means to a considerable height above the earth, kept him suspended in mid air.

"Oh! gramercy, most courteous sprite," uttered the Baron, with plaintive tones; set me down whence I came, I beseech you."

No sooner said than done—though the mode was different from what the Baron expected. The thumb and finger were unclasped, and the heavy form of the noble Sir Launcelot fell—fell—fell through the air, until, by a heavy splash and suffocating plunge, the Baron was engulphed in the very bog from which he had so lately been taken.

"Ha! ha! ho! ho!" shrieked the sprite on the stump; and again did the huge head of the sprite revolve with its satellite, the body, on the stump's axis, an example followed, as usual, by the rest of the elfish troop, each on their respective pivots.

"Oh! release me from this torment, and all my barony shall be yours," spluttered the Baron, through the marly lumps of dirt that had splashed into his mouth.

"Here! take then this stick," cried the elf with crossed legs, "and get astride it—you will see what will follow;" and breaking off from the stump a small branch of some twelve inches long, he flung it to the Baron.

The Baron did as he was told, and the sprite proceeded.

"Now say after me these lines:—

Hie thee away, travel back to the moon;
Puck hastens with thee, so hie away soon.

No sooner did this magical distich escape the lips of the Baron, than he felt himself dart at one bound up into the air. The earth began to look smaller and smaller; all objects had disappeared from its surface, or had mingled into one undistinguishable mass, and clouds that he had just before looked up to with awe at their height, now, offering no barrier to his progress, appeared miles beneath him.

"How like you this mode of travelling, Baron?" enquired a small, squeaking voice behind him, and turning round, the Baron's eyes beheld the sprite whom he had left upon the stump below, perched carelessly upon the lower end of the branch.

"Now, my malison light on thee, thou treacherous imp!" ejaculated the Baron; "I asked to be upon the earth, not in the air."

"Civility, Sir Launcelot, if you please," responded the sprite, with a grin. "Look down and see where you are!"

The Baron did as he was desired, and the sight rendered him so giddy that he grasped the magic stick on which he was mounted with the grasp of a vice, to prevent himself falling off.

They were travelling through the regions of space, where a dim kind of twilight pervaded the atmosphere, and enabled distant objects to be just distinguished. The earth, coloured like our modern globes with lines of red and blue, appeared the size of an orange, far, far, beneath them. The planets above were becoming larger and larger, and the moon, which they left to the north, shone like a huge ball of gold. The sun was altogether invisible, as it had no immediate power of refraction, and the only light they had of any brilliancy on their journey was once, when a comet whisked rapidly by, with its long tail of brilliancy, and passed so near to the voyagers that they were obliged to bow their heads to escape the collision that would have otherwise ensued.

"Well, are you satisfied, Baron, with your aerial trip?" inquired the sprite.

"Perfectly!" cried the Baron in reply, rendered almost breathless by the rapid rate at which they were journeying.

"Turn the stick round, then, and we will descend," exclaimed the elf; and doing this at the imminent danger of a tumble, the alteration in the motion soon told the Baron that he had succeeded in the experiment.

Down, down, down they went with increased force as they encountered the attraction of the earth's gravity, until they were but a few miles from the surface of the globe.

"We must remain stationary a moment," suggested the imp, "until England comes under us; we are now over the very capital of China."

"Wonderful!" thought the Baron to himself; but fearful that a remark would displease his supernatural companion, he was content with *thinking* his admiration.

The earth revolving on its axis at last brought the county of Northumberland exactly beneath their feet, and here the word was given to descend. The rapidity with which they sank was so great that the Baron was obliged to close his eyes lest the air should tear off his eyelids, and when he again opened them, after feeling a heavy blow from the concussion with the earth, he found himself perfectly alone in the middle of a richly cultivated field, with a summer sun beaming warmly upon him, and both the stick and the sprite gone.

Not knowing what to think of this, he enquired of a labourer who was journeying to his work, in what part of the county he was in, and learning to his infinite gratification that the Castle of the Hohmbuggs was situated at only a quarter of a mile's distance from the spot on which he then stood, he sat out in that direction without the loss of a moment.

On arriving before the walls of the castle, he found, to his infinite amazement, the aspect of the place completely changed. The porter at the drawbridge knew him not, and the servants of the place, when he represented himself as the Baron de Hohmbugg, actually laughed in his face, and ridiculed what they termed his unaccountable assurance. The moat was dried up and overrun with weeds, and time appeared to have spread over the turreted towers a coating of lichens and stone crop that wrought a marvellously different appearance from that it exhibited when the Baron last saw it.

As he was ruminating upon this strange occurrence, he happened to cast his eyes over the plain, and he beheld, to his infinite amazement, the lady Madeline and her husband, as he imagined, riding up to the castle, as returned from hawking, arrayed in all the pomp and majesty of state. The dresses were, indeed, different to those usually worn by them; but he could not be mistaken, he thought, in the likeness, and, accordingly, rushing through all the obstacles that opposed him, he seized hold of the lady's bridle, and demanded the resignation of the castle to him.

"To the earth with the bold caitiff!" furiously cried her husband; and aiming a blow at him with his falcon-cane, would inevitably have succeeded in his object, had not the prudent withdrawal of the Baron on one side caused the blow to miss its intended destination.

"Hold! I command you," cried the astonished Sir Launcelot. "I am your father, Madeline—the ill used Baron Sir Launcelot Gamhon de Hohmbugg."

"You!" shrieked the lady, with mingled laughter and surprise. "My name is, indeed, Madeline—for I was called so after my poor grandmother—but I myself closed the eyes of my late father. Besides, Sir Launcelot has been dead these one hundred years."

"Stay! one word, then, I beseech you! The Lady Madeline—this relative of yours—did she marry one Walter Annerley?"

" 'Tis true she did."

"Then unhappy mortal that I am; *I have been a century in the air,*" and rushing from the astonished groupe who imagined him to be mad, the Baron disappeared from sight, and was never heard of afterwards, except in the Christmas tales of young lovers, who told it as a warning for their parents not to interfere in the progress of their affections. Some, indeed, who would overthrow the whole doctrine of fair agency, have been found, who asserted that the real Baron was drowned in one of the bogs on Haggerstone Marsh on the night of the pursuit, and that a hundred years after an impostor appeared, who laid claim to the baronial estates; but however that may be, a Cross was erected on the spot where the fairies are supposed to have met with the Baron, and it is called to this very day by the name of "The Fairy Cross." The Castle has, long since, been levelled to the ground, but the race of Hohmbuggs, so far from being extinct, is flourishing in great numbers than ever, and has spread from one county over every portion of the civilised globe. The legend is most devoutly believed by all who reside in the neighbourhood, and there are few, indeed, who would care to encounter the Fairy Cross after midnight on St. Agnes' Eve.

By the time Sampson Skelton had finished his narrative—the substance of which we have given above—the glasses had become empty, and the fire was waning; so bidding his entertaining companion good night, Trueman sought his chamber, and in a few minutes was dreaming most vigorously of Clara, the astrologer, and the fantastic vagaries of Puck and his elfish brethren. The next morning—a warm and sunny one—saw him skirting the "banks and braes" of bonny Dalkeith, and before the old abbey bell of St. Andrew's had tolled curfew out, our knight errant had secured a temporary abode in the North Wynd, Edinburgh.

CHAPTER XX.

TEMPTATION AND DECEIT.

Andrea—Poor youth! I fear me he'll not come to good.
Alcanor—And if he does not, who is there to blame
But your own sex; your false, deceitful sex.
That Jove intended should be man's best boon,
And not his curse— his friend and not his foe.
Oh! did ye know the power ye possess
For good and evil—how ye sway our hearts
To right or wrong, and make us doubly blessed
Or doubly cursed—you'd pause ere you did lend
Your power supreme to aught that smacked of vice,
And turn the scales of Fate to Virtue's side.
Oh! would that woman would remember this,
And ponder on the moral that it yields.
                                    Old Play.

IT is one of the few privileges possessed by novelists—and Heaven knows they ought to have some—that when their characters are withdrawn for a time from the eye of the reader, they are still supposed to be actively engaged in their various occupations, although no actual mention of them is made; in the same way that our heroes and heroines recorded in the pages of history, have each ate, drank, and slept, without their so doing having been taken notice of in the writings of the chronicler. In like manner has Barnwell continued to visit Milwood, and plunder his master, alternately, though the winding track of our narrative has compelled us to overlook for a time his nefarious proceedings, but now that the opportunity is afforded us, we hasten to put the reader in possession of what ensued after the robbery at his employer's, satisfied with the guilty accomplishment of which robbery our last account left him.

Alice who still entertained a strong conviction of Barnwell's constancy, had, immediately on her imprisonment, dispatched a letter to her betrothed, in which she briefly stated the circumstances under which she was accused—her innocence—and the trial that awaited her. She also requested our hero to see her without delay, as she wished through him to let her father know the unfortunate situation in which she was placed. On reading this letter, Barnwell, obeying the impulse of the moment, and remembering the fervency of their early love, set out with the intention of seeing her immediately, and for that purpose chose the road leading to the prison. On his way however he encountered Milwood, who learning the nature of his mission, and dreading a renewal of their previous intimacy, which would overthrow all her schemes, she persuaded him to return with her to her own apartments, where she stated a slight refreshment awaited their arrival.

When they reached Milwood's residence she forcibly pointed out the impropriety, as she expressed it, of visiting a person, charged with so heinous a crime as that of murder, for the avowed purpose of assisting and befriending her; and pourtrayed in strong terms the stigma that she asserted, must necessarily attach itself to Barnwell if he paid any attention to the letter. But finding this mode of reasoning not succeed so well as was anticipated, she attacked him on a ground where he was more vulnerable, and accused him of inconstancy towards herself.

"Yes George," exclaimed Milwood, throwing a passionate fervour into her delivery—"well I know that this feeling of kindness and protection that you evince for Miss Travers, is but the return of the love you say you once felt for her. This wish to aid her is but the effect of a former passion reviving, and a present one growing less ardent. You would see her—once more behold her, and renew your former vows; impress again those lips that murmured words of passion back to you, and again clasp that form whose faultless symmetry has left its imprint on your heart. Well! be it so. Take her—may you be happy! I *had* hoped that our mutual promises of truth and constancy would not so soon have melted into air; had hoped that the love you professed for me would have proved more lasting; but no matter—" and here the speaker dashed a succession of tears from her eyelids as she spoke—"my selfish feeling that you might be ALL my own is gone now; I yield back to its rightful owner a heart that no more belongs to me, and give it gladly to ensure its possessor's happiness, though the struggle costs me mine own."

"Dear, dear Eleanor, you wrong me much—you do indeed—" said Barnwell, deceived by the vehemence of her address and the apparent sincerity of her speech—"I look upon Miss Travers now more in the light of a sister than aught else, whilst my love, Eleanor, belongs to you, and you, alone."

"Would that I could think so," sighed Milwood.

"Would that I could prove it more than I have already done," reproachfully cried Barnwell.

"You have it in your power so to do," exclaimed Milwood eagerly.

"How?"

"By not seeing Miss Travers."

Barnwell hesitated.

"Yes," continued Milwood, "too plainly I perceive your love for me has vanished. You would now leave me, in quest of new forms and new faces; you would forget that Eleanor exists—wish perhaps that she never had existed, and care not what her fate may be. But remember, my dear George—for so thou still art to me—when you who thus forsake are by others forsaken—when the love you now slight is in its turn slighted, there is still a hand ready to welcome you, and a being who will sympathise again in your joys and share your sorrows. You have played with a heart till you have broken it, but the fragments of that heart will throb years hence as ardently for you as now."

And here Milwood burst into tears.

This silent appeal which a woman makes when all her verbal rhetoric has failed, is ever found the most effectual.

Tears shed by a pair of bright eyes soften hearts that would be proof against every mode of attack, and prove as effectual as Hannibal found vinegar in melting the Alpine rocks. They strike home to the bosom of the spectator, and he must, indeed, have a heart of adamant who could resist their force. When the Poets fabled Niobe weeping, they transformed her to a fountain to show allegorically that even the marble fount itself would wear away beneath the force of woman's tears.

Barnwell experienced the full effect of this. He felt his regard for Alice succumb to the fervent passion he had for Milwood. He first hesitated—then wavered, and finally—but it was not without a severe struggle—protested that if it was in opposition to her wish, he would never see Alice again.

"Yes," continued Barnwell, "I sacrifice all, Eleanor, for thee, and methinks, the pleasure of your society, and the influence of your sweet smiles, more than repay me for my loss."

"Now," exclaimed Milwood, rapturously, "thou art my own dear George once more. Trust me, I shall not forget this kindness. But why in such haste to be gone—is my presence so distasteful to you that you wish to avoid it?"

"Nay, not so," replied our hero; "the stern decree of Fortune calls me hence. I am but now a truant to my trust."

"Well! well! I'll not detain you, but your absence shall be that of the pet bird that its mistress allows to fly no further than the gentle string can lure it back again. I wish to visit Mr. Sadler's Music House this evening, and require you to be my escort thither. Nay, no excuses—I'll not listen to them, without you'd make me question the sincerity of your speech just now. I shall expect you here at six."

"Your wishes form my commands, Eleanor; I shall be ready to accompany you. Till six—farewell!"

"The fervor of a grateful heart go with you;" and bestowing a fond caress on her admirer, Milwood suffered Barnwell to depart.

"'Twas somewhat fortunate," thought Milwood to herself, as soon as she was alone, "that I met the love-sick youth so luckily, else *my* dominion might have been in danger."

"Mr. Oswell, Madam, is below, and wishes to know if you are at leisure to receive him," exclaimed the attendant, as she entered.

"Certainly Hester, admit him instantly."

The abigail accordingly left the the room, but soon after returned with the visitor.

"Ah, my dear Oswell—Hester, you may leave us—how glad am I to find you have not quite forgotten me."

"Surely that were no such easy task," replied Oswell, with a smile; "but I have called to leave you some admissions for the 'Wells' at Islington this evening."

"You have singularly anticipated my wishes," rejoined Milwood. "It was the very place I was on the point of visiting."

"So much more fortunate," said the actor. "I should have been with you before, had not a rehearsal for our new piece at the Duke's Theatre detained me."

"How fares my excellent friend Kitty Wilton; is she still on as good terms with Sir Harry Vernon?"

"They were never so intimate. Since you left he has been more unremitting in his attentions than ever. By the way, he was inquiring after you last night in the green-room, protesting that you had encouraged him in his addresses to you."

"I!" indignantly exclaimed Milwood; "why you well know, Oswell, that I have never bestowed a thought on any but you."

"You have always, at least, led me to believe so," replied Oswell, somewhat haughtily.

"And, in so doing, I have been actuated only by the sincerest dictates of my heart. 'Tis true I have met Sir Harry, laughed with him, danced with him, but what then? Am I to be upbraided for acting in accordance with those rules of politeness that society requires, nay, commands. I did think, Oswell," and here Milwood threw more solemnity, into her manner, "that you placed more confidence in me, than to suppose I should prefer the company of an empty and conceited coxcomb, to one like you requiring but to be known to be admired."

We have had occasion before to point out the great knowledge of human nature displayed by Milwood in her intercourse with the opposite sex;

and we cannot suffer this last speech that escaped her lips to pass unobserved, without directing the attention of the reader to it, as an illustration of this peculiar faculty of turning that knowledge to account. Oswell's ruling passion was vanity. By appealing directly to this foible, Milwood well knew she trampled on the barriers that his reasoning faculties would raise up against her. By making it a handle to aid her own temporary purposes, she knew he would overlook the proofs of her coquetry with which he had come armed, and thus, by a skilful manœuvre, to turn the tendency of the conversation, she ensured his acquiesence in whatever she might assert; and, by flattering his own self love, bandaged the eyes of his reason.

"Well, my dear Eleanor, I believe you, after all," said Oswell, sealing his reconciliation with a kiss; "but who do you intend shall be your beau for this evening."

"Why certainly not you, Oswell, as a punishment for your jealousy. Let me see—how easy it would be to decide did Love direct me—there's a young merchant—by name Barnwell—who has dealings with the broker below, he shall supply your place at my side for the time you are absent."

"*Avec tout mon cœur*," rejoined the actor, borrowing, as was usual then, a few broken words of French to interlard with the more vulgar English, "I shall not be able to meet you there until after our first piece in Portugal Street is over; so I trust your new companion will not, in the interim, supply my place likewise in your heart."

"There is but little fear of that," laughingly added Milwood, "whilst it has so excellent a tenant already; but I see you have not yet shaken hands with the green-eyed monster—not quite ceased to forget the cautions I have given you—come, come, let us have no more of this. It pains me, Oswell, to hear you charge me with this, as much as if I had indeed been really guilty of it. Without you would add to my unhappiness, prithee leave the subject alone."

"Miss Copley, madam," announced the servant, as she entered.

"Ah! this is fortunate. Oswell, I am happy to bring about an introduction between you. Admit her, Hester, immediately."

The fair personage, who was thus announced to the two others in the room, was a dashing female of some three and twenty years. Her hair was braided over her forehead, her eyes full and prominent, with the subordinate features in excellent keeping with the rest. A figure graceful, demeanour unexceptionable, and dress fashionable and costly to an extreme, manifested the visitor to be an ornamental if not a very useful appendage to the community at large.

"My dear Caroline," exclaimed Milwood, "I have the double pleasure of making two friends of mine acquainted with each other. This, Caroline, is Mr. Oswell, a gentleman of whose fair fame report has been no niggard; and this, Oswell, is Miss Copley, an especial friend of mine, and, I need not say, a most delightful companion."

The usual compliments were exchanged.

"Your visit has been peculiarly well-timed," continued Milwood, rattling on with that freedom of delivery in which she occasionally indulged! "Oswell was just complaining of having to wander as far as the 'Wells' this evening without a companion—nay, no frowning my bashful *Archer* when a *Mrs. Sullen* is ready to receive you. Yes, I say

he was positively wishing me to find him one. May I select Caroline Copley to be that one?"

"But the lady, ——" stammered Oswell.

"Will comply with my wish. Is it not so, Carry?"

"I certainly can offer no objection," replied the person so addressed. "But it will be nine before I can join you."

"No matter for that," answered Milwood, "put Caroline into the front of the theatre, and then, when the piece is over, you can go round for her."

"Well, if Miss Copley would prefer it so, I shall be proud of her company," returned Oswell.

"Of course she will," added Milwood; "and now, Oswell, I must enjoin your departure under the penalty of my absolute displeasure. We have a few private affairs to discuss that will render the presence of a third person somewhat irksome."

"I am gone," obediently responded Oswell: "Miss Copley, till the time arrives when I shall see you at the theatre, I am your most obedient—Eleanor, farewell," and imprinting a kiss upon her hand, he took his departure.

"And now, my dear Nell, as one of your admirers has left," said Miss Copley, "allow me to inquire into the success of your schemes with the others."

"It is far beyond my wildest anticipations," replied Milwood; "Man I always considered to be as easily governed as a child that's made to kiss, the rod that inflicts the pain; but I have even succeeded just before your arrival in proving, against the evidence of a person's seven senses, that black is most undoubtedly white."

"Ha! ha! Nell," rejoined the other, "you have most excellent spirits, but your skill in bringing about certain matters have even surprised me. Who would have thought now that what appeared a chance visit upon my part this morning was designed a week ago, and that my visit to the Duke's Theatre this evening was planned between us but yesterday, to further our own purpose. Ha! ha! I can scarce help laughing, Nell, when I recollect how fearful he was that the 'lady' should not accept the offer of 'a pass to the front.' Ha! ha! it pleases me to think on't."

It will be seen from the remarks above given that Milwood's artifice had been again called into requisition for the purpose of enabling her companion in vice to obtain an interview with one of the gallants whose nightly haunt was the vicinity of the green-room, and obtaining for herself, at the same time, the means of diverting Oswell's attention from the familiarities she might bestow on Barnwell. We purposely draw a veil over the conversation that passed between them, as its relation would, in our opinion, neither tend to the amusement nor the instruction of the reader. Suffice it to say, that it chiefly turned upon the conquests they had already gained, the plans they had in progress for ensuring others, and the peculiar habits, dispositions, and resource of those unfortunate beings that had fallen, either blindly or willingly, into their snares. Between the two, however, there was a strong and marked distinction. If Milwood regarded money, she did it only as a means to attain an end; viewed it as a stepping-stone to her vengeance, rather than as the primary source of gratification; whilst her associate in infamy worshipped only the golden image of Mammon, and made all other feelings bow down in subservience to this. If Milwood inflicted a wound,

she did it like a skilful surgeon, without hurting the patient; the other cut less deep, but wounded more. Milwood, on the one hand, strove to win hearts by address and artifice; her companion, on the other, relied exclusively upon the attractions of her person. We might extend the parallel still further, but enough has already been written to distinguish the different impulses that actuated the two. We therefore leave them for a short time engaged in the mysteries of their art, and return to Barnwell.

No sooner had the hour of six arrived, named by Milwood to be the time of their departure, than our hero, attired in a new and and costly suit—the effect of a recent abstraction from his master's coffers—knocked at the door of Milwood's dwelling, and finding Milwood already dressed to receive him, the two sallied forward without a moment's delay towards their destination for the evening. Directing their course across St. John Street, Clerkenwell, Milwood pointed out the site of the old playhouse existing in Elizabeth's reign, and bearing the title of the Red Bull, of which the benevolent founder of Dulwich College, Edward Allen the player, had been the quondam proprietor. A turning to the left, leading to what is now called Myddleton Square, but then open fields, brought them to the " newly-built quadrangle of Lloyd's-row," and passing under the creaking sign-board that marked the proximity of the old-fashioned hostelrie of the *Sir Hugh Myddleton*, they soon arrived within sight of the building they were in search of.

Sadler's Wells Theatre, then called the Islington

Spa or New Tunbridge Wells, was at this time in-
closed within a wall of considerable extent, affording
space for the growth of several clusters of tall and
goodly elms that spread their shade-yielding branches
over the grand avenue.   A gate then faced, as now,
the New River, ornamented with huge brackets of
iron, on which was inscrib d, under a pediment,
" Sadler's Wells."   The old brick house, on the
site of which the present edifice now stands, contained seven windows in front, with angular mul-
lions, and was surmounted by a flat roof concealed
from the eye of the spectator by a triangular erection at the top, on which was adroitly carved emblematical figures connected with the pastimes that
were exhibited in the interior.

In the grounds adjoining, were pedestals and
vases grouped with considerable taste under some
extremely picturesque trees, whose foliage could be
seen with great advantage from the neighbouring
fields.   The river was adorned with tall poplars,
graceful willows, sloping banks and flowers on which
fair nymphs in company with their gentle swains
were seen calmly reclining.   The walls of the theatre
were on one side reflected in the glassy surface, and
on the other might have been observed willows that
hanging o'er its margin drooped their leafy boughs
to kiss their shadows ; capriciously separating every
moment as the passing current seized the substance,
till the elastic branch recovering itself again sprang
into the air and shook a shower of spray from every
leaf.

Then might have been seen, as now, the patient
yet anxious boy with a hazel twig for his rod, and a
bent pin for his hook, bending over the gentle stream
where the clear white pebbles marked the shallow
depth, fishing for minnows : and, further on, came
strains of music wafted by the summer breeze through
the open windows, and making young hearts throb,
and old feet beat, in unison with the lively airs of
" Old Sir Simon the King," " Green Sleeves,"
" John, come kiss me," and the soul-stirring old
English melody of " Sir Roger de Coverley."

Hastily glancing at the objects of which we have
endeavoured to give the reader some faint idea, Milwood and Barnwell proceeded to the interior, where
a new scene presented itself to Barnwell's delighted
eye.   The pit of the theatre was fitted up with wine-
boxes and fruit-stalls, where those who had paid
their money at the doors for admission might enjoy
their pint of wine, given in return for the same, and
listen to the music at the same time—a custom that
continued here until, comparatively speaking, a very
recent period.   The box tier running round the
theatre was ornamented with lozenge-shaped devices,
generally alluding to the union of music and dancing
with the sister arts of poetry and painting.   The
proscenium was surmounted by painted drapery,
above which was the old motto, " Mirth, admit me
of thy crew," and round the entablature of both
columns were tastefully designed groups of figures
representing the delights of the fabulous Arcadia,
and pourtraying the festival of the shepherds and
their shepherdesses.   Francis Forcer, who was at
this period the proprietor, being himself an excellent
musician, retained in his service an orchestra of no
mean quality, either in point of numbers or talent.
The music was certainly of a light and easy nature,
chiefly consisting, in fact of the popular airs we have
before alluded to ; but as these seemed to suit the
taste at this period better than dull, elaborate over-
tures of foreign composers, the proprietor at once

displayed both his tact and judgment, in according
with the fashion of the time.   The House was nearly
filled by the time they had arrived, and before the
ballet was over that appeared first in the programme,
it appeared almost crammed.   The cause of this was,
a new entertainment being offered to the English
play-goers in the shape of " rope-dancing," which
the said Francis Forcer was exhibiting at this theatre,
for the first time in our country, and the novelty
and attraction of which drew an immense concourse
together from every portion of the metropolis.   In
addition to this, there was also the celebrated " Mat.
Miles, the Posturer," and " La Belle Espagnole,"
the beautiful Spanish dancer, whose exquisite face
and figure constituted, after all, the great attraction
of the evening.   This, united with the diversified
amusements of dancing, balancing, juggling, conjuring, tumbling, and divers others feats of skill and
dexterity, will at once account for the multitudes
that had assembled within the walls of the theatre to
witness the performances so rare.

The delight experienced by Barnwell during the
progress of the entertainments almost suspended the
conversation between him and Milwood.   The applause lavished by the audience on the amusements
seemed to his excited fancy scarcely a sufficient tribute to their excellence or variety.   He dwelt on
each succeeding scene with an intensity of pleasure
that amounted almost to extacy, and beheld each
removed with increasing feelings of regret.   A slight
pressure of her arm from behind made Milwood
sensible of the arrival of Oswell, and, turning round,
she took the advantage of Barnwell's attraction to
convey, by raising her finger to her lips, an indica-
tion of secrecy.   Further signs she had not time to
make, for the curtain rising and disclosing a prettily
painted pastoral landscape, a burst of applause and
approbation betokened the presence of Signor Cas-
tarelli, the rope-dancer. Another channel was, however, open for communicating what she wished.
Pencilling, unseen by Barnwell, a few lines on the
back of a letter, she directed with one hand the attention of the unsuspecting youth to the stage, whilst
with the other, she conveyed to Oswell the intimation she had written.   Whatever it was, its purport
was such as to cause Oswell to leave the theatre immediately, and bidding an adieu by gesture to Milwood, who returned it in the same manner, the retiring sound of the actor's footsteps made Milwood
aware that her stratagem had succeeded.

On the succeeding events of the evening we need
not dilate further.   Wine, as on a former occasion,
contributed to intoxicate Barnwell to that extent
that he became, at last, perfectly delirious, and
when the return from the theatre had caused the
cool air to fan his fevered brain into something like
consciousness, he expressed his affection for Milwood in more ardent terms than ever, declaring that
Death itself should only tear him from her.   What
followed must be allowed to pass into oblivion.

———

CHAPTER XXI.

LOVE AND DUPLICITY.

She slept—and rosy dreams of days gone by
Came flitting round the couch whereon she lay
Youth spread anew its treasures at her feet,
And care came limping by on leaden wing,
Till Phœbus, rising from his golden bed,
Shook balmy perfumes from his amber hair,
And scattering light with either hand around,
Robed all the Earth again in Beauty.

The Vision of Valhalla, 1784.

OH! LOVE! thou greatest passion of the human breast—mysterious arbiter of fate below! by what strange agencies are thy effects produced, and where lay those secret springs that thy hand calleth into being, and that power that, like the rod of the Israelite, causeth a stream of happiness to gush from a rock in the wilderness—whence emanates a flood that, like the o'erflowings of the Egyptian river, fertilises wherever it touches, and, to continue the simile, brings, like the Nile, scenes also of desolation and despair? Exhaustless theme of which none yet have tired. A subject that will be written on as anxiously, and perused as eagerly two thousand years hence as now. Whether it is the devoted fervency of a first love—the hallowed recollection of a buried one, or the more staid attachment of after days—the result is the same. Memory clings to the retrospect of these with more tenacity than to the everyday passions that rise and fall as the blood becomes warm or cool, like the mercury in a barometer. Who is there that does not look back upon his first love with pleasure and regret—that does not remember the uneasy throbbings of his heart when the object of its adoration was near; and who is there that would abandon the recollection of these things, and the soothing influence they bring with them, for all the wealth the world could yield them? Not one. They are twined too closely round the chords of that great Æolian harp, the human heart, where the slightest vibration will suffice to call forth the melody within, and where, like Memnon's statue, a lively air follows the rising of the sun of happiness, whilst a plaintive one accompanies the sunset. We say they are too closely intertwined to be severed hastily; and experience proves this. A flower, a song, a word, a few strains of music, or even one note, will restore the link that time has broken; it will recal the presence of the loved one, and the associations connected with the past; and memory, like the golden hues of departing day, will so invest each with a borrowed lustre, that age will forget its wrinkles, and youth its sorrows, in the contemplation of the time when all around breathed of "the purple light of love and young desire."

So thought Alice—and as she thought, so she dreamed. The prison cell became an open landscape, the low mattrass a couch of roses, and Barnwell was at her side, breathing words of passion back to her. Anon the scene changed. There was the sacred tomb by which he had hallowed his vow of constancy; the ardour with which he had sworn eternal faith to her was also ringing in her ears; the flowers faded as she gazed on them, and storm-clouds spread over the previous clear expanse of blue; but Barnwell still remained, pressing her hand to his lips, and reiterating the words that promised a union of their fates for life.

When Alice awoke it was with the consciousness of having lived, as it were, the earlier portion of her life anew. She saw in the shadowing forth of these scenes, the warm impulses that had guided her in her younger days, and looking back upon these, as the traveller who has gained an eminence surveys the country through which he has reached it, she could not but sigh for the tranquility of mind that had accompanied them, and shed a tear for the insubstantial visions that had now vanished. Whilst engaged in these soothing, albeit unprofitable, speculations, Cicely entered and communicated to Alice the information which she had gleaned from a conversation with Mr. Lockyer, the jailor, to the effect that her trial was fixed for the second day from that time.

"Alas!" cried Alice mournfully; "it matters but little, my dear Cicely, how soon my fate is sealed. With no kind look but from you, and no familiar voice to cheer me in my solitude, I might as well have ceased to live, since I have ceased to be loved."

"But Barnwell may yet be here," suggested her companion.

"There is but little hope," continued Alice. "There was a time when he would have flown to meet me—now a strange misgiving prompts me to say, he finds my name a talisman that checks, rather than incites, his progress."

"And is it possible," inquired Cicely, "though unfaithful you can love him still?"

"Possible!" responded Alice, with warmth. "Oh, little, Cicely, do you know the enduring constancy of a woman's heart, if you imagine that even inconstancy on the part of the being it beat for, could change it aught. Those who have loved as I have loved, who have given their whole soul as I have given it, up to a passion that ceases only with life itself, know that *that* love will cling like the ivy round the ruined tower, and relax not its embrace until the mouldering structure lies buried in the dust."

Succeeding footsteps warned her of the approach of a visitor, and the jangling of chains—those sounds that more than aught else convey the idea of imprisonment—announced the arrival of Sir Robert Otway.

"Once more, Miss Travers," he cried, "I appear before you. Nay, frown as you will, it moves me but little. I am here to offer you freedom; and a kind word from you in return is all I ask."

"Your perseverance, Sir, in thus annoying me," returned Alice, "is worthy of a better cause; but for the second, and, I trust, the last time, I inform you that your importunities are useless. I am fixed in my determination, and will abide the result."

"Then so it must be," replied Sir Robert; "though I did think that to see a father——"

"My father!" interrupted Alice, "O say! what of him? Is he here? Can I see him?"

"All in good time shall be explained. I can say no more now than, that by accompanying me you will succeed in gaining an interview. Are you ready to accede to my proposition?"

"Oh! teach me, Heaven, how to decide," cried Alice, kneeling on one knee.

"Let me choose for you!" exclaimed Sir Robert: "with me a life of happiness awaits you—here a punishment that brings disgrace and infamy, will follow. Can such a contrast require a moment's consideration?"

An officer of the prison now entered.

"Miss Travers," said the official, "you have been declared innocent, in consequence of the confession of a criminal, named Haydon, who has proved himself an accomplice in the murder at Hampstead. The governor desires an immediate interview with you."

"Innocent! Confession! echoed Alice, as if doubtful of the sounds which she had heard. "This flood of happiness is too great—now I am indeed free. Inform Mr. Woolmer, the governor, that I will be with him without delay."

"Now, my dear Alice," said Cicely, who had remained a patient listener during the above conversation; "am I not right in telling you that dreams like these are always ominous of good?"

"Aye, Cicely," answered Alice; "but this good fortune is far beyond my utmost expectations. To what cause, I wonder, am I indebted for so strange but fortunate an occurrence?"

Otway, whose chagrin at the entrance of the officer at so critical a moment, had now softened down into a more pleasing expression, here held Alice by the hand, and, assuming s gentler strain, continued as follows:

"Alice, my dear Alice—for so I must tutor my tongue to call you—is it possible that you can doubt for one moment whence this change in your prospects proceeds? Knowing the interest I take in your welfare, can you not at once deem me the source of your liberty?"

"Ought I to attribute it then to yourself?" answered Alice.

"I have already owned as much," rejoined Sir Robert; "but, fancy not that I rest satisfied with this—more shall be accomplished, and your innocence shall be felt and acknowledged by the whole of the metropolis."

"This is, indeed, kind of you; but my father—you say he waits for me."

"Aye! at mine own house."

"I fear me, Arlington, you would play me false."

"Nay," answered Sir Robert, "not so; but, if you doubt me, Cicely shall accompany you. Within one hour I will return, making, in the interim, all necessary preparations for your departure."

"I shall then be ready," responded Alice: until the lapse of an hour, farewell!"

"Remember, I come back to restore you to your father's arms!" cried Sir Robert.

"And with that you will ensure my happiness."

"Aye, or *mine own*," muttered the Baronet to himself, as he left the cell for the lofty passage which led to it.

Alice, immediately after his departure, swayed to and fro by doubts she knew not how to remove or control, hastened to the Governor of Newgate, in compliance with the request she had received. The Governor, who was a man of few words, briefly expressed his regret that evidence so slight should have been deemed sufficient in an affair so momentous. Mr. Hugh Clinton, the magistrate, should, he declared, be suspended from the exercise of his official functions, and all necessary inquiries instituted into the source of the proceedings.

"I have this day," continued the Governor, "received a letter from the country, wherein a hint was given out that a conspiracy on the part of a Baronet was the immediate cause of this detention, and the name itself is placed in my possession, to be used as I think proper. Have you any reason to imagine that the allusions in this letter are correct?"

Alice was at a loss how to reply.

"I see by your agitation, Miss Travers, that these are not the mere idle rumours I imagined them to be. Rely upon my zeal and activity in sifting them to the utmost."

The remainder of the conversation was taken up chiefly by apologies on the part of the Governor, expressing regret that, in accordance with the strict rules of the prison, he had been compelled to withhold from Alice those indulgences to which she had been accustomed; but he stated that if, in any manner then, he could be of service, he would endeavour in that way to efface the remembrance of his former severity.

Alice thanked him, and was about communicating the intelligence of Sir Robert Otway's arrival in Newgate, and the proposition which he made, when a message from the Baronet himself stated that all was in readiness below for her departure.

A hasty acknowledgment of the Governor's kindness was all that Alice had time to make; for her impatience to behold her parent would not allow her to linger on the road.

Accordingly, hurrying down the long flight of stone steps leading from the vestibule, she joined Cicely and Sir Robert! and soon after, the trio were in a vehicle half way towards their destination in Mary-le-bone Fields.

CHAPTER XXII.

DEATH AND RETRIBUTION.

Martyn.—Who is that thinly-clad and wretched being,
That, stretched athwart the straw, miscalled a bed,
Mocks the repose of others with a start,
A fit, or sho k, or wild contortions strange,
That nature shudders at and loathes?
Gerald.—A dying man, sir, one, whose life being spent
In every kind of wickedness and crime,
Now thinks repentance will wash out the sin,
And give him passport unto scenes of bliss.
Poor, misled knave!   The Old Manor House, 1784.

WE have now to request that the reader will accompany us back to the Almonry, where Haydon ever since the memorable night of the burglary at Hampstead, had been stopping, unable, in consequence of his wound, to move. The utmost skill of Andrew Warren, the physician who attended him, failed in producing any beneficial result. Day followed day, and he grew worse instead of better. The wound began to mortify, and assisted by a naturally weak and by dissipation an enfeebled constitution, the most serious effects were anticipated.

It was towards the evening of a warm and sultry day in June, when through the open window gentle zephyrs, breathing of the country and its associations, came struggling up past the narrow and ill-built thoroughfares of Westminster, that Haydon, finding himself growing gradually worse, desired Warren to be sent for; and, on his arrival learned, for the first time, that Alice had been taken up on suspicion of having been concerned in the burglary. Impressed with a firm conviction of his approaching death, and rendered callous by the desertion of Meggott and Clayton, who had left him there to die the death of a dog on the straw mattrass that supported him, he determined to communicate the knowledge he possessed of the affair to Mr. Woolmer, the Governor of Newgate; and, accordingly, without delay gave Warren the note which was to free his conscience from guilt, and save an innocent maiden from disgrace. The interval that elapsed between the departure of Warren and his return was spent by Haydon in absolute purgatory. He felt the icy hand of Death gradually coming nearer, and his whole hopes of future happiness being bound up in the confession of his guilt, he began to fear lest he should die before that confession could be made. All his apprehensions were, however, speedily removed, by the return of Warren, in company with a solicitor and one of the under-sheriffs, who, bringing with them some restoratives, enabled Haydon to speak with more ease than he otherwise could have done.

The table being drawn to the bedside, Mark commenced his narration; the substance of which being merely a recapitulation of the events connected with the burglary at the Seven Bells, our readers are already in possession of. Being testified to by the witnesses, and authenticated by his own oath, the officials took their departure; not, however, without offering Haydon a slight pecuniary assistance—a gift that, though proffered, was not accepted. On being left alone with Warren, he expressed a wish that candles should be brought in, alleging that, in the twilight, he beheld strange phantoms and forms, which were goading him into madness. The introduction of the lights, however, failed to produce the desired effect. Mark Haydon continued to behold the same visions as before, and, snatching at the air in fruitless endeavours to secure the imaginary objects he saw before him, gave utterance to his disappointment in the most poignant cries and exclamations.

" See !" cried he to Warren, as he pointed out a blank space in the air, " see where my poor father, with his grey hairs straggling over his forehead, comes to upbraid me with my early disobedience. Shield me from his vengeance—let *his* hand be not the one that hurls the parricide to perdition."

" Psha !" said Warren, who was gazing on the scene with perfect apathy, " it is but fancy."

" Fancy !" echoed the other, " see there ! Look at yon beauteous girl in her shroud. Do you see her ? She is bending her head towards me. Yes, I am coming ; she beckons me—*love ;* true, I once loved you, but that was before your brother died— I killed him, but what of that ? Faugh ! why change your face to a skeleton's skull ? That's hideous. *I* brought you to the grave ! Tush, it is false."

" Haydon, I implore—beseech you——"

" Whip me, ye devils, with sulphur—lash me with thongs of fire—sit not there at the foot of my bed—grinning so damnably. Ha ! ha ! I can laugh —why should the innocent suffer with the guilty— are you there, Kate ? give me your hand, the road is so dark. I'll go with you, only mind that your brother don't see us. Fiends of hell, why torture me thus—who says I am mad ? My brain's on fire—oh, water, water, to quench my burning thirst !"

" Cease ! Haydon, to imagine these absurd things," cried Warren, alarmed by the insanity of his patient, now manifesting itself in every action ; " sleep will do you good."

" Sleep ! Ha ! ha ! I sleep ! aye, in the grave, with a clod of clay for my pillow—a softer one than

those of down—how dimly burn the candles—bring more in—let me not die in the dark. Do you hear ? why do you draw the curtains so closely round the bed ? Must I be smothered ? Augh ! I am choking. My eyes refuse their office. Come—a song—I'll begin.

> Pass the glass, my brave boys,
> Let each cup be filled high :
> We'll live well while we can,
> When we can't, why we'll die.

Now, then, why don't you join in the chorus· S'death ! do you desert me ? cowards that ye are— is blood never to be worn out ? Come, light the candles—more light still—no answer—dark as my own hopes !—

> We'll live well while we can,
> When we can't, why we'll—"

The lips moved, but no sound came from them ! and when Warren leaned over the bed to look at the body, he found a corpse before him. *Mark Haydon had expired in singing a drunken song !*

Consigned to a few narrow feet of earth in that part of the burial-ground devoted to paupers, and those buried at the charge of the parish, mouldered the mortal remains of the burglar. Although no marble monument records his vices, or blazons forth his crimes, they will live in the recollection of all whose taste for bygone days leads them to a perusal of the criminal calendar of that time.

With the talents and opportunities that he had, and neglected, Mark Haydon might have been an ornament to society ; as it was, he was its greatest curse. Gaming and drunkenness led him to indulge in scenes of riotous debauchery ; and the consciousness of a mental superiority over his depraved companions, pandered to his vanity, and, at last, linked him indissolubly with them.

Well would it be for many of our own day, if this same vanity was less prevalent now than it was then !

Return we now to Sir Robert Otway, whose claim to the liberation of Alice our readers will have perceived, by a perusal of what has preceded, to be entirely the effect of his own artifice. On leaving the prison, the carriage which contained Alice, Cicely, and himself, was driven at a most rapid rate towards Marylebone. On reaching the mansion that boasted the Baronet for its master, feelings were called up in Alice's breast not altogether irrelevant to the scene. She remembered it as the place of her captivity, and the night of her escape came vividly back to her recollection. Cicely, who was, of course, a stranger to the feelings that agitated Alice, beheld it with mingled emotions of wonder and admiration. All further thoughts were suspended by their entrance into the court-yard, where, Sir Robert alighting, assisted the two others to descend, and ushered them into the Gothic chamber, which Alice immediately recognised to be the same as that that received her on a previous occasion. Whether the Baronet read the feelings that existed in her own mind, or merely guessed at them from what was passing in his own, is not certain, but a smile played upon his lips, and his face seemed lit up with unusual animation, as indicative of the pleasure he felt in anticipating at least a triumph over the cherished scruples of Alice.

"Now," cried Alice, "I require the fulfilment of your promise; let me behold my father."

"Fair maiden," responded the Baronet, "I regret that I have been compelled to practise deceit towards you; but, remember that you are the cause. Had you been more complaisant, I should have stood in no need of artifice. Candour compels me to avow that I have not yet seen Colonel Travers, and my ideas of his present residence are about as clear as those of his person; only that I believe him to be travelling towards the North many miles from here."

"Your deceit, Sir, is as cruel as it is unmanly," rejoined Alice; "I am now only anxious to quit thy roof with my companion. I humbly take my leave."

"Nay, not so fast there; thinkest thou that in the moment of my victory I would abandon a prize gained with so much trouble?"

"Ha! what mean you?"

"Simply that, as persuasion has been found of no avail, force shall be adopted instead. You are now completely in my power—you must—you *shall* be mine, and with this kiss I seal the bargain that consigns you to my arms."

"One step—one movement," exclaimed Alice, approaching nearer the window, "and I plunge myself from yonder open casement into the stream below!"

"Rash fool!" muttered the other, "thus I claim you as my bride."

Struggling with Cicely, who endeavoured, but in vain, to oppose his progress, he threw his arms round Alice, and prevented her by those means from putting her threat in execution. In another moment he would have implanted a torrent of kisses on her lips, when an arm, powerful in strength, flung from behind the libertine to the ground.

"Hold!" exclaimed a voice, that smote like ice the ears of the Baronet as the syllables were uttered. "I command you to forego your devilish purposes. Colonel Travers, behold the miscreant who robbed you of your child; Otway, behold in me the brother you have so much injured. Thus do I complete my triumph."

Before the last words had left the lips of the speaker, the anxious father had clasped his trembling daughter to his arms.

"Edmund!" exclaimed the Baronet, rising, "*you* here?"

"Aye!" continued the first speaker? "even me, Edmund Otway—Fuller, the astrologer, or the owner of any other title you may choose to give me, but, by each and all, still your brother—your ELDER brother. That brother whose estates you have plundered—whose property you have arrogated to yourself—whose very name you have soiled with infamy, but who, under the protection of the strong arm of the law, has now returned to enforce that claim which consanguity should have yielded peaceably. Years have passed since we last met, proud libertine, but the blow given by you at our last interview, though unnoticed, has never been forgotten—thus, *thus* have I repaid it."

The Baronet, abashed by the circumstances that had taken place during the last few minutes remained silent.

"Colonel Travers," pursued Fuller, whom we shall still continue to call by his assumed name, as being more familiar to the eye of the reader than the real one of Otway, "Colonel Travers, I told you that by my means your daughter should be recovered;

I have kept my word: we have arrived, it appears, just in time to save her from becoming a victim to the snares of this consummate villain. Nay, Sir Robert, gnash your teeth, frown, and look big as you will, it moves me not: I say we have rescued her from a perilous situation; take the full advantage of it, quit this den of infamy, and return to your own peaceful abode; I will give you a safe escort thither. No thanks! I require them not; and you, fair maiden," he continued, addressing himself to Alice, "let these recent events prove a caution to you against trusting to the protestations of man whose strongest oath is as slight as the gossamer threads that are borne in a summer's eve on the wings of the gentle zephyrs."

"Farewell, Sir, then, if we must part," cried the Colonel, "but we shall meet again ere long, I trust."

"My future destiny is yet involved in mystery," rejoined Fuller; "the planets are inexplicable upon that point; but accident may, and will, no doubt, throw us again together. For the present, farewell."

And, bidding adieu to Fuller, with a trembling voice, and greeting him with a kindly pressure of the hand, expressive of the gratitude she felt towards him, Alice linked herself to her father's arm, and the two departed in company with Cicely.

"Stay!" cried Fuller, in a voice of thunder, seizing the arm of Sir Robert as he was about to follow the fugitive; "you go not for assistance."

"By what right am I detained?" exclaimed the other.

"By the right of justice," answered Fuller. "There is yet atonement to be made."

"Atonement! to whom? by whom?"

"To yourself, and the bleeding corse of the woman you murdered."

"Mur——"

"Aye, well may the word choke your utterance. But come!"

"Whither?"

"*To the Tapestried Chamber*," replied Fuller; and he who looked on those two human forms as these words were uttered, would have seen depicted in the face of the one the most humiliating cowardice, in the features of the other a look expressive of the greatest triumph.

CHAPTER XXIII.

THE LIBERTINE—THE CATASTROPHE—AND THE
DEATH-STRUGGLE.

Now forked flames arise from every side,
And lick the beams with their fantastic tongues,
Consuming in their basilisk embrace
Whate'er they touch: so Jupiter of old,
Enclasping fair Semele in his arms,
Burned up the form that yielded to his touch,
And Death ensued from what should follow Life.
                              Jupiter and Alcmena. 1673.

No sooner had Colonel Travers and his daughter left the fated abode of Sir Robert Otway than, directing their steps towards the road leading to " Tottenham Court," they entered the fields surrounding the ancient thoroughfare of " Old Bourne," or Holborn as it was then beginning to be called, and, making a rapid progress towards the Strand, arrived at " the Angel" in St. Clement's about an hour after their departure from Mary-le-bone. Here finding the " Flying Waggon" just starting for Lichfield, they secured places in the interior, and before nightfall were some miles on the road to their destination. In the course of two days more they entered the goodly city in Staffordshire which Alice claimed as her birth-place, and seen, as she saw it, by sunrise, with its spires and pointed gables gilded by the rising luminary, her heart yearned for the home of her childhood, and anxiously were the momoments counted that brought her nearer to her dwelling. On finding herself once more in her own apartment, Alice gave vent to her feelings in a burst of tears. Her heart seemed overflowing, and each fond memento of days gone by received again and again the effects of the warm impulses of her impassioned soul.

In the interim, the mansion of the Baronet was the scene of strange events. Fuller had led his brother to the Tapestried Chamber, which our readers may remember as the one from which Alice, on her detention here, made her escape, and as the guilty libertine retraced his steps through the narrow vaults and stair-cases that led to the room in question, his blood ran like ice in his veins, and his whole form seemed swayed by the influence of some strange emotion. Impelled by an impulse which he could not account for, to obey the mandates of his brother, Otway at last reached the chamber of where his victim had been murdered, and closing the door with a rebounding sound, Fuller here confronted his companion.

The wing of the building in which this room was situated, had been, as was before stated, closed for many years, under an impression among the domestics, that it was haunted. Until Alice, in her endeavours to escape from the Picture Gallery, had threaded the tortuous windings of the old mansion, no living soul had been visible there since an event occurred which it will be our province, in the course of this chapter, to communicate to the reader.

The ancient tapestry mouldering into dust, as it fell, unbidden, to the ground, the dust enmantled articles of furniture strewn carelessly over the colourless carpet, and the mildewed portraits that, suspended from the sides of the apartment, looked down upon the present intruders in awful solemnity, all imparted to the scene a strange, unnatural aspect; whilst the air, rushing in through the open window that Alice had forgotten to close when she descended, swayed the curtains to and fro with such violence, that it required but little imagination on the part of the two spectators to fancy they had entered unhallowed ground, and that the late spiritual inhabitants, conscious of mortal intrusion, were taking flight to other spheres. The influence of these things was not lost upon Otway. His very blood seemed to congeal as it flowed through the channels of his frame; and when Fuller drew the curtains of the bed, besmeared with the crimson outpourings of life, and revealed the pillow, clotted with the same sanguinary stream, his limbs quailed beneath the weight they supported, and the faculty of speech forsook him.

" Now," said Fuller at length, as he gazed with searching eyes on the glazed features of Sir Robert, " my pilgrimage has ended. Here, if repentance comes at all, should it be offered. In this room that, twenty years ago this very day, a murder was committed that to this hour burns my brain as I recall it to my recollection, should the only recompense you have it in your power now to make, be made. Brother! we have both sinned—sinned in the sight of Heaven and of earth ; but it is not too late to ask forgiveness for that crime we have committed. I have endeavoured to expiate my offence by years of toil and study. Both have, I trust, been accomplished with a good motive, that of benefiting my fellow-creatures. You have continued the same career of seduction and reckless infamy which marked the budding of your manhood. I have waited long and anxiously to see if you betrayed the least symptom of remorse ; it is needless to say I have found none. " See here," he continued, drawing on one side a curtain that veiled the portrait behind from observation. See how the skilful limner has embodied upon canvass that beauty which you destroyed. Mark how yon blue eyes follow the changes of your own, and does not that fair finger point downwards towards the murderer ? Poor Julie Desanges ! sad was your death—sad will be its retribution."

" Edmund," stammered out Sir Robert at length, " I came here back to this fearful room," and here he cast a furtive glance around him, " in compliance with your wish, not because I desired it. If your only object was to pour forth idle protestations to me, and show me a canvass daub, your company is unnecessary ; I will leave you."

" Not before you make the only restitution fate allows you. Here, in this room, where the very air seems redolent of blood, do I demand a hearing."

" I cannot—will not listen more than I have done."

" I ask it not for myself," continued Fuller, " but for the sake of your son."

" My son !"

" Aye ! you are ready enough now to lend a patient ear ; but come, be seated ; my story is none of the shortest, and I lack repose."

And selecting two of the least dilapidated couches in the apartment, Fuller motioned his brother to be seated ; and, drawing his own seat nearer, thus commenced his narration.

" When you first set foot in Normandy, brother, you little imagined the evils that would follow on your path. You remember the little cottage at Valaise, with its trellis-work of vine tendrils, and grove of orange trees—that cottage where you first saw Julie—that cottage where your first protestations of love were made. You offered her your hand, and with a guileless innocence of deception she accepted it. One obstacle yet remained; her poor old father, whose constant companion she had been from infancy, was averse to the match; he could not spare his only child. Under pretext of a summer evening's ramble, you forced her from home, embarked on board a merchant-vessel, and arrived in England. The same day that saw you reach London, witnessed also the decease of her father; his grey hairs bowed down in sorrow to the grave, grief for the loss of his daughter killed him. You loved Julie too well to let her go, but yet refused to marry her. She required a fulfilment of your promise—you apparently consented, and empowered me to cheat her with a mock ceremony. But you were yourself deceived, for the clergyman who united you was in orders."

"Cursed fool that I was," muttered the listener, "not to perceive at once the imposture!"

"Months rolled by," continued the other, "and you were happy; happy in each other's society; but fate decreed that this should not last long. You grew restless and discontented, seeking fresh forms and fairer faces; she reproached you, and you disliked her. Shortly afterwards you found that Julie would soon be a mother; this, instead of adding to your love increased your hate. It would have interfered with all your air-built castles of ambition, and there would have then been a tie too strong to break between you. You see I know your motives now, though I guessed not at them then. Well! well! you were young then, so young that the down of manhood scarce had dulled your cheeks, and you pleaded this as your excuse; may Heaven accept it! Each succeeding day saw you more discontented and more enraged against her, though yourself could scarce assign a cause. Your domestics called it jealousy; said that you were jealous of me, but I knew 'twas not so; you sought for higher and for nobler game; your eyes were bathed in the beauty of a certain Countess, and you forsook Julie. This to her was a death-blow. She grew daily worse, but you cared not for that, and when the infant came at last to life, an old woman, unskilled in surgery, was the sole witness of her agonies. But you were not satisfied with this—her death, likely to be premature, as it was, seemed too tedious for your wishes, and you resolved to *murder* her."

Here Otway, who had hitherto remained in painful silence, uttered an exclamation of remorse.

"Well may you shudder at the recollection of that night—the fatal 10th of July, 1700—a night stamped on my heart with an indelible brand, singeing my brain, as if 'twas torn with red hot pincers. I need not dwell upon the arguments you used to make me an abettor in your guilt. You painted in glowing colours the advantages that would accrue from her death to our family, leaving our joint estates untrammelled; and I—your elder brother—fool that I was, believed it. To me you confided the destruction of the child, whilst you undertook to terminate the existence of Julie—Julie—your *wife*."

"Oh! horror! You goad me on to madness."

"Had you felt then as you feel now, all would have been well; but it was not so. On this very night, twenty years ago, you entered this room comparatively an innocent man, you left it—a murderer. Julie was sleeping tranquilly in yonder bed, her head resting on the snowy pillow that darkened when contrasted with her clear, white neck. Her child was clasped in her arms; nestling, as instinct taught it, close to the bosom of its mother. The noise of your footsteps aroused her; she inquired the cause of our both being there. You asked her to forego her claims to you, and return to Normandy. She refused. Angry words arose. You snatched the child from the arms of Julie, and placed it in mine. When I returned, I found its mother suffocated with the pillow, and you gazing in cold, unmeaning apathy upon her face."

"Oh! never shall I forget that fearful moment," cried Sir Robert.

"How the body of Julie was disposed of you know—buried in a grave, dug many feet beneath the surface of the earth, she sleeps, I trust, in peace: what became of the child you have yet to learn; for in that particular I deceived you. Instead of throwing the helpless infant in the Thames, as was at first designed, I confided it to a kind old lady in the city who had just lost her own babe. Placing it there to nurse, I left a sum of money adequate for the support of the lad when he became of age, as well as some for his maintenance till then. From time to time I paid visits to the good dame, and found the boy grown up a thriving youth, with the name attached of Trueman, being that of his adopted mother. One day, however, I called, and found the shutters closed; the house was to be let, and Mrs. Trueman herself had paid the debt of nature. The lad was gone—no one knew whither; but those on whose information I could best rely, stated that, with the residue of the money left by his supposed mother, he bound himself apprentice to a merchant, and this I have since found to be correct. He is as yet ignorant of his noble birth; here I ask in his name the estate so justly his due, and to which I waive all claim."

"And it is for this fruitless mission you have brought me here? Psha! Edmund, you might have known me better. Was the shade of Julie herself to rise before me, pale and bleeding, and ask me to sign the document that proved him mine, I would not do it! Besides you have no proofs."

"Indeed! say you so? Behold the marriage certificate, and these letters to me, which I have preserved."

"Give, give them to me!" cried Otway, eagerly.

"Not till you do as I desire," replied the other.

"Give me one hour—but *one*—to consider of the proposal!"

"Willingly! In an hour then shall I return. I am going to Lambeth, and shall expect to meet on my arrival here again, an answer favourable to my hopes."

"You will meet, brother, with the answer you deserve," rejoined Otway, significantly, as Fuller departed; but he little thought that the poisoned arrow he was there on the eve of discharging would recoil on himself.

When left alone, his first object was to escape from the recollections the apartment in which the above colloquy had taken place was conjuring up. It had grown twilight too, and fancy imaged to his heated brain strange shapes of spirits and "chimeras dire." Following the labyrinthine wanderings of the adjoining passage, he reached a huge stone staircase, ascending which he gained his private room—an apartment situated just beneath the turret of the mansion that beetled over—and being at the summit of the mansion, commanded through the grated window a wide prospect of the surrounding country.

Here was he wont to meditate on his designs, and it was partly for this purpose that he had ascended thither. But this was not the only one, as will be seen from his subsequent conduct. Unlocking a small bureau, he took from thence a sealed packet, containing the letters and papers connected with the marriage of himself and Julie. A small miniature, being a counterpart, on a smaller scale, of the portrait below, was in the centre, and smashing this to fragments with his foot, he cast the pieces through the iron bars of the casement into the stream below. ·

His next care was to destroy every proof of his nuptials, and to this end he drew near him the lamp which he had lit, and began to try the efficacy of the flame in annihilating the silent witnesses of his crime.

"Now, brother," thought he to himself, a crisis has arrived, which must terminate the existence of one of us at least. Trueman knows not of his near relationship, and the only proofs which would establish his claims are in your hands. Those must be mine. When you return, this trusty door secured with a spring in the interior shall hold you fast; a death, long and lingering, such a death as starvation brings with it, shall be your portion. Then shall we see who triumphs."

he room in which these words were uttered, was an old-fashioned chamber, with an immense quantity of wood-work stretched across the ceiling, supported by huge beams of the same material, and was constructed with pannels of the same inflammable substance. The papers that Sir Robert was now burning, began to send up a huge mass of flame, that, swayed by the current of air from the open casement, soon set light to the curtains of the chamber. Engaged in the perusal of these papers, the progress of the flames escaped his attention, until startled by the sudden blaze of light, that pervaded the room, he turned round, and endeavoured to arrest the increasing fury of the conflagration.

But it was too late. The wood-work had become ignited, and the crackling beams foretold the destruction of the entire building. One fearful crash ensued, and a large rafter, embraced by wreaths of fire, fell down athwart his shoulder. It was an awful moment: every object was concealed by dense volumes of smoke; but, assisted by a knowledge of the localities, Otway at last gained the door. It had closed with a spring, and almost overpowered by the heat, and stifled with the smoke, he exerted all his energies to find the clasp. The perspiration poured like water down his face; his very dress had caught, and was smouldering round him; whilst the forked flames, unchecked in their fury, tore down beam after beam, and rafter after rafter, till the whole room became a perfect chaos. At this crisis, when all hope seemed ready to forsake him, he found the spring. His heart bounded again with exultation—he uttered a loud yell of joy—when, in his anxiety to press back the steel fastening, THE SPRING BROKE, and thus barred his egress.

His previous exultation was now changed to deep despair. He shouted for assistance, until his lungs were hoarse with exertion, but in vain, as the servants of his household, in obedience to his own direction, never approached that part of the building. Maddened by the thought of the horrible death which awaited him, he rushed to the window; but one glance sufficed to show him the impossibility of escape by its means. Its height from the ground, and the strong iron bars that protected it, seemed to cut off all hope.

Nevertheless, an attempt must be made. Tearing away the stout grating with such herculean strength, as an emergency like this generally supplies, he found his hands streaming with blood and his nails torn off to the quick. Still he relaxed not his exertions. One by one the bars yielded to his stained hands, where the fingers strained from their very sockets hung drooping down. But the window was now cleared. One bound, and he would precipitate himself to the earth. That were, surely a better death than to endure the torments that then surrounded him; but even in this he was disappointed; for a red-hot beam, slanting downwards, fell upon his neck, and seared a livid mark in its contact. Another moment, and the floor gave way; when suffocated by the smoke, and enveloped in flames, the mangled body of the libertine Baronet fell a charred mass of dust beneath the ruins. The moon rose clear and placid into the wide expanse of blue, showering its silver radiance on the surrounding objects; but still the flames of Sir Robert Otway's mansion burned fiercely and rapidly, until, dying the heavens with an ensanguined sky, a heap of ruins only served to mark its former site.

CHAPTER XXIV.

WOMAN—HER INFLUENCE.

Life's a brief period between two eternities—
That comes we know not how, and goes we know not whither;
Held without thanks, and given when oft we know it not;
A thread—extended whilst we sleep—and valued least
When most required: a dream of mingled hope
And cankering care, that guiles us for a while
With pleasing visions, till it snaps itself,
And breaks off in the midst.   Old Play.

PLUNGED deeper and deeper into Vice, Barnwell began to grow callous to every virtuous emotion, and satisfied only with rioting in those guilty excesses which bring with them stupor to the mind, and weakness to the body. Pleasure—not that pleasure that heaven warrants, and earth supplies—but Pleasure with a groupe of evils in its train, and accompanied by the demons Want, Woe, Disease and Death, was his idol—his earthly Deity, and, like a true votary, he cared not what the sacrifices were he made so that they were accepted. He had quaffed deeply of the Circean cup, and, like the companions of the wandering Ulysses, had experienced its bestializing effects. He had swallowed the intoxicating contents of this cup, we say, to the dregs; and now, like an insatiate drunkard, thirsted for more. This perpetual craving for excitement, this morbid desire of illicit enjoyment, is too often the curse and bane of our young idlers about town, fixing upon them an idelible brand of infamy, and bringing them to a premature grave, uncared for, and uncaring. Those addicted to these sottish pleasures, springing, in the first instant, from a venial partiality for social intercourse—as prussic acid, the deadliest poison, is distilled from the innoxious and beautiful blossoms of the almond tree—are generally those whose energies and intellects, if rightly applied, would have gained for them an eminent position in society—that society which they have inevitably and irretrievably lost. Our mighty Babylon—that leviathan world abounding with all that is good and great, and at the same time with all that is pernicious and infamous—teems with instances of what we have set down. Who is there that, amongst his associates, cannot point out one whose talents are thus degraded into a level with the irrational brutes that man is taught to despise and contemn? That seeking for companions in the lowest depths of society, goes onward in his evil course, until his pillow, that might have been smoothed by the gentle hand of the partner of his domestic joys, is damped only by his own fruitless tears of repentance, and he withers out his miserable existence like the blighted tree scathed by the lightning that marks the progress of the destroyer, and should be looked upon as a beacon to warn others of their danger.

In such a position was our hero now placed. We have seen him the favoured assistant of his employer, conscious of his own integrity, and possessing only a fervent wish of advancing that employer's interest, regarded, admired, and respected by all whom he came in contact, winning " golden opinions from all sorts of men," and cheered by a reflection that, whilst he continued in the path of virtue, he might hope at no distant period to gain for himself an eminent station amongst the merchants of his time. It is now the sad necessity of our pen to record the downward progress of the un fortunate youth; to show how, step by step, he sank lower into vice; to trace him gradually casting off every remaining show of virtue; to display the futile sophistry by which he strove to conceal even from himself the digression he was making from the bounds of honour and probity; and finally to describe how these departures from that strict sense of duty to which he had always previously clung with pertinacious adherence, led him ultimately to become pitied and lamented, while he was contemned and despised.

The chief agent in causing this change in his sentiments was, as we have endeavoured to show to the best of our ability, A WOMAN. Did our language furnish us with any other name by which we could at the same time distinguish her from her sex, and yet show that she belonged to it, by that name would we call her. Woman—that ought to be man's solace in his affliction—his partner in his happiness; that providence kindly sent down upon earth, to give us a foretaste of heaven;—woman, that holds a sway mightier than the mightiest emperor; whose kingdom extends further than the widest kingdom—for it is that of the human heart;—woman, this guardian spirit of man's happiness, has, since the creation of Eve downwards, abused the power she possessed, and used it for the torment instead of the benefit of mankind. Instances still occur in which man, bowing down to her absolute dominion, resigns his fate at once to her, and his happiness for ever. A contrast—such contrast as the serene tranquillity of a summer evening's landscape presents to a plain torn by contending storms—appears oft in the reverse side of the question in which woman, brightening like the sun at whatever she gazes on, diffuses her halcyon influence around on all, and scatters with her bounteous hand domestic joys and combined felicity. But, alas! seldom is it that woman can do this: where she ought to be obliging, she is imperious; where she should be firm, she is weak. Her affability degenerates into coquetry, her reserve into prudeness—her very love is an extreme, and her vengeance the same. The golden medium is to her unknown; and she has been by turns the slave and the tyrant of the opposite sex. If these remarks be anything near the truth now, they were much more so at the period of which we write. Then, woman had not gained her proper station in society—that society which now awards her an eminent position. Education was denied her; and the young beaux and fops of the period began to look upon the whole sex as if intended by heaven only to supply their wants, or minister to their pleasures. It is necessary for the reader to consider these circumstances, in order the better to understand what has preceded the present chapter, and to enter into the spirit of what follows. If we are occasionally discursive in our pages, it is only the privilege of the traveller, who, journeying over an undulating country, pauses here and there, to point out objects in the distant landscape, that though at first sight are perhaps considered unworthy of regard, lend new beauties to the prospect, and impart a picturesque reality to the whole.

It was now the very height of summer. Those whose finances enabled them so to do, had long since left the smoke-soddened Babel of bricks and mortar to gain the more cogenial region of the country. The watering-places were crammed by patricians and their families, and the sea-shore was lined by visitors of every denomination, each anxious to inhale the sea-breeze, let the price be even the denial of town luxuries for the remainder of the year. The West End was comparatively deserted, and few even of the old merchants in the City, cradled amidst the rumbling of hackney coaches and the smoke of a thousand and one chimneys, cared to remain in London whilst they could snatch a glimpse of green from their rural villas. A few stragglers, whose avocations or whose inclinations linked them to the town, as we have before said, remained. Amongst these were Milwood and Barnwell. At the residence of the former, with the window thrown open to its greatest extent, sat the two whom we have named. Twilight had stolen on them apace; and the evening star—that herald of love and happiness—had already climbed far into the western sky. Still did Milwood and Barnwell continue to converse; still did they continue to gaze in silent abstraction in each other's eyes; and as if there their aspiring souls found not wherewithal to gratify their desires, the lips would meet at intervals, and interchange communion with soft sighs and fervent kisses. Barnwell had now, in fact, given himself up entirely to the power of love. Of Eleanor he dreamed, talked, wrote and thought. His whole soul seemed bound up in the utterance of that one name. His was no common passion. Had the world, with all its golden stores and glittering attractions been placed in one scale, and Milwood in the other, he would have unhesitatingly chosen that freighted with the latter. His infatuation seemed indeed to have no bounds. From the time when we last saw them at Sadler's Wells, she had been his constant companion. He regarded her as a superior being, possessing more than common power over the destinies of mortals, and as such sought to excuse himself for the influence she held over him. Milwood, on her part, preserved her character to admiration. She lavished on him the most extravagant proofs of her affection, and gained from him solid presents in return. Every term of endearment that the language could afford—every gesture that might be construed into a token of affection—every look that carried with it new fuel to fan the flame in his heart, were all offered in succession, and, by turns, succeeded. Together had they traversed the secluded windings of bricks and mortar—for even in London there are some—that their converse might be unbroken, and their love unseen. Together had they imprinted their footsteps on the yielding grass of Hampstead, and the marshy soil of Islington. Canonbury had welcomed them to its ancient tower, and Highgate had shown them its wells, and, with all this Barnwell had become not only more infatuated, but also more anxious, for the period when he might claim her legally as his, and bind her to his heart as his alone. But this was a turn of affairs Milwood had no inclination to encourage. Her wish was the patriotic one of conducing to the "greatest happiness of the greatest number," and had no idea of making the greatest number, number one.

It was, as we have before described, one of those genial summer evenings in July, when the events we are about to narrate took place. Milwood had thrown her right arm round Barnwell's neck, and he, in return, had detained her left hand, not unwillingly, in his grasp. By a kind of sympathetic influence, and species of human animal magnetism—if we may be allowed for the nonce to coin the Hibernicism—the pressure of that hand had been for some moments the only medium of communication between them. There are times, as your true lovers well know, when this kind of eloquent silence is far more expressive than that language formed by audable syllables, and it was found to be so on this occasion. Milwood, in turn, responded to the pressure of her admirer, as if grateful for the acknowledgment thus shown, thanked it by a kiss. His heart seemed too limited for the happiness that now gushed upon it, and his brain reeled with the delight he now experienced. The world at that moment seemed one vast parterre, Life—a path strewed with roses. Oh! happy—thrice happy—hero of ours, little didst thou think that a serpent lay coiled beneath the flowers, and ready at a given signal, to seize upon the hand that plucked them.

"You have detained me, love, longer than I expected," said Barnwell to Milwood, as he tangled anew his finger in her hair.

"And is my bondage, then, so irksome?" returned Milwood, reproachfully.

"Nay, love, not so; but remember, the money I have in my possession is Mr. Thorogood's, not mine."

"Well! well! it will not diminish in keeping."

"True," replied George; "but it may in returning. Some time ago I had the misfortune to lose my pocket-book in hastening home from this very house."

"Indeed!" exclaimed Milwood, with well-feigned commiseration.

"Aye," resumed Barnwell, "and, what is strange, still, I had almost taxed you with being the cause of it."

"Ha! ha! methinks you must have been truly bewildered with your loss to allow, even for a moment, the existence of a thought so improbable."

"And why?" inquired Barnwell, with some keenness of perception, as his former doubts returning were corroborated by the vacillating frame of her he gazed upon.

But the question was one not destined to receive an answer; for at that moment, the name of Captain Vavasour was announced, and before the words had left the lips of the announcer, that personage himself entered the room.

"Happy to again renew my acquaintance with my young pupil," said Vavasour, after exchanging the compliment of the evening with Milwood.

"The pleasure, I am sure, is reciprocal," answered Eleanor, perceiving that Barnwell remained silent; "the company of so complete a gentleman as Captain Vavasour must always be considered an acquisition to any society."

"Eleanor," cried Barnwell, "I must leave you. You know," added he, in an under tone, "that I do so with regret; but it is growing late, and our narrow streets are not exactly those that one would care to traverse after dark."

"With your permission, I will accompany you," responded Vavasour; "my visit here was only a passing one, to inquire after our friend's health."

Barnwell, whose feelings were divided between an intuitive dislike to his proposed companion, and a jealous disinclination to leave the two together after his departure, at last acquiesced.

"Well! farewell, George, if you must go," said Milwood; "but I shall expect to see or hear from you to-morrow."

"You shall not be disappointed," returned Barnwell. "Farewell!"

And, impressing a passionate kiss upon her lips, Barnwell departed in company with Vavasour. Their course lay for some time through a succes-

sion of narrow lanes, where the houses seemed nodding to each other in their decay, and where the inhabitants of each might literally shake hands with their opposite neighbours; but, emerging from these they soon entered a more spacious thoroughfare, standing on the site of the one now known by the appellation of "the Pavement."

Directing Barnwell's attention to a house where the multitude of lights blazing from the windows, and the noise of revelry within, gave token that its inmates were passing the night away amidst scenes of what they called enjoyment, Vavasour paused, and bade his companion do the same.

"Come!" said Vavasour, "I am somewhat in your debt, young man: the last time we played you lost; it is now time that I should give you your revenge."

"I thank you, sir, for your offer; but I am in haste to arrive at my employer's," returned our hero.

"Psha!" sneered the Captain; "an hour cannot make much difference; besides, it is beneath the character of a gentleman like you to pay such a punctilious regard to time. You should learn to despise these mechanical sons of trade, and participate in pleasure worthy of your age and station."

"But my employer——"

"Tush! away with such a word. This distinction of society is purely artificial; the very trammels that are imposed on youth to repress their natural inclinations. Learn to have a higher ambition than that of a mere shop-boy."

This taunt was not without its due influence on the mind of Barnwell. He yielded, and entered.

This sneering away of honourable principles and conscientious reservations is ever, unhappily too successful. It requires a stronger mind to resist ridicule than many seem to be aware; as an assassin who stabs in the dark and in disguise is more to be dreaded than an open and avowed adversary.

The house they had entered, the reader needs not to be told; was a gambling-house. Its avowed title of "THE CITY HELL,"—a place, by the way, to which our present pandemoniums are indebted for their modern appellations, sufficiently pointed out its nefarious objects. A long passage, illuminated at intervals by brilliant rows of lamps, led to a spacious saloon at the end, in which our adventurers now found themselves. Tables covered with green baize, and each lit up by a single oil lamp, shaded with ground glass, were ranged across the room. Waiters, with refreshments, flitted noiselessly behind the players, who were too intent upon the game to care much for any other stimulants than those afforded them by cards or dice. It needed but little persuasion on the part of Vavasour to induce Barnwell to play. He was already infected with the passion for gaming; and this is one that, like the fabled shirt of Nessus, adheres to the wearer till it causes his destruction. He saw the piles of shining gold raked by the fortunate winner to his side, and he panted to obtain, like him, a prize so great. The tables were soon selected, and the dice rattled in his ears, like the shattering teeth of fleshless skeletons. The marker's cry of "seven's the main," resounded through the room, and no heart throbbed more responsive to the echo than that of our hero. Instructed by Vavasour, he played long and earnestly. For a while, as on a former occasion, Fortune seemed to favour him, and his spirits rose in unison. But this was but the flickering sunbeam of the moment. A long course of careless ill-luck succeeded. The inverted dice-box trembled as he threw its ivory contents upon the baize. His hands shook, like the dying leaf waved by the Autumnal wind, as he again possessed himself of the damning implements of the craft.

He threw—BLANKS!

With that throw, he had lost one hundred pounds!

Furious and maddened he rose from play. Vavasour, seeing the forthcoming storm, immediately, upon obtaining the money, left him to his fate. He raved like a maniac, and swearing to the croupier, who gazed in apathy upon the scene, as one used to such, vowed that he would regain his master's money, or lose his own life in the attempt. The other players rising, a scene of indescribable tumult and confusion arose. Some few, who, like himself, had been plundered of their little all, took part with him. Chairs were broken, tables smashed, and lamps extinguished in the affray; but, like most tumults that are violent, it was but of short duration. Some of the victimised, either willing to put up with their loss, or not caring to regain it, ceased, as if their courage had been spent, to take any active part in the contest, and Barnwell soon found himself aided alone by a young man, whom he had observed, like himself, eager to gain accumulation of wealth by the occurrence of one lucky moment. But, what could their slight assistance avail against the united force of numbers? They were overpowered, repulsed, and driven—yes, driven—from the narrow passage into the open street; they turned these to face their cowardly assailants. A street brawl was of too common an occurrence in these times to attract much attention from the passers-by; but a party of watchmen, whose beat was in the vicinity, in the hope of retrieving their previous character for neglect by present interference, took Barnwell and his friend, upon the charge of the others, into custody, for creating a disturbance. Little disposed to put up with such a result, our hero at first expostulated—then resisted; but this, instead of bettering their condition, only caused them to be more unceremoniously treated; and the two were hurried forthwith to the station for the night—then familiar to all criminals and street-disturbers under the somewhat formidable title of the old "Clerkenwell Roundhouse."

CHAPTER XXV.

CONSTANCY AND DEVOTION.

See how the moonlight sleeps upon this bank,
As if 'twas lulled by yonder rippling stream:
Whilst seeming grateful for the soothing sound,
It pays it with a flood of silvery light
That, dashing on in wavelets to the shore,
Breaks up the darker shadows. Fit emblems these
Of minds attuned by Fate to cheerfulness,
That cast aside the gloomy shades of care,
And, dancing on, unchecked in their own gleetfulness,
Make Nature vocal with their songs of mirth.
                    The Merry Philosopher, 1699.

ALICE, finding herself once more the happy inmate of her peaceful dwelling, became again the light-hearted cheerful maiden, whose sunny smiles flung gladness over the hearts of the village swains, and whose step was so light on the festive green as scarce to rob the grassy blades of their moistening dew. Her mind, we say, rallied; but not so her body. The seeds of that cruel disorder Consumption, that flushed her cheeks with a hectic tint, rivalling the bright hues of the budding rose, were sown too deeply in the constitution to be easily eradicated. Day by day her father saw her fragile form wasting sensibly away, beneath the touch of the destroyer. Her chief delight was in rambling pensively among the green copses and leafy thickets that sprang up in the vicinity, and giving vent there to the outpourings of her sorrow-stricken soul, she passed the hours away in thoughtful sadness. With that pertinacious clinging to the object of her first love, which woman alone displays, she still cherished her early attachment for Barnwell, notwithstanding, from his long silence, he seemed, as she conjectured, to have forgotten her. From the occasional conversation she had with his mother, she learned that he had not written for many months past, and that she was entirely ignorant of his proceedings. Still she loved on in silence and in secret, and rejecting the many favourable offers that were made to her, preferred preserving her hand for him who had first gained her heart.

Amongst the many suitors who had fondly trusted to time to work a change in her affections, the most ardent and the most persevering was one Luke Martyn, the only son of a rich farmer in the neighbouring village of Yoxall. For a time he uttered his protestations in sighs alone, but by degrees he gained courage to address her in words. It is scarcely necessary to add, that he met with a firm and determined refusal; but rejection, instead of cooling the ardour of his love, only seemed to increase it. He grew more silent and reserved. Shunning the society of his companions, he sought, like her, the charm of solitude to allay his passion. With a mind far above the common level of his associates, he possessed a keener susceptibility to all the sorrows that environ man in his mundane career. He had expended the midnight oil in study. Snatching from books his chief solace, and with feelings deeply imbued with fanciful delineations of our olden poets, he had become a most enthusiastic admirer of their works. Living in an ideal world of his own creation, he was unfitted for encountering the harsh realities of life, and, as these burst upon him in all their native ruggedness, his heart yearned again for the tranquil seclusion of his own home, and turned with disgust from a world where spirits like his seldom find an abiding place.

By degrees, as Alice learnt his character, she admired him more. As the only kindred soul she knew, he became her companion. They now took their excursions together, and seemed to experience additional pleasure in each other's society. Alice was happy in finding one who could sympathize with her; and Luke was happy in the presence of the being whom he loved. One day, however, she missed him from his accustomed haunts. Expecting to find him in the course of her ramble, this circumstance caused her but little uneasiness, and she continued her walk alone. Day faded into twilight, and sunset flushed with its golden tints the tips of the distant forest; the woody glade rang with the gleesome music of heaven's choristers, and insects, dyed with all the gaudy colours of the rainbow, flitted by with their shining wings, humming, in unison, their vesper orisons. Night now began to steal on apace, embrowning the horizon with darker tints, and one by one appeared the stars—those silent monitors of man's unworthiness—to change the nature of the landscape. The moon uprose pale and silvery, flooding the prospect with its sea of light; and the gentle breeze, that had during the heat of the day scarcely ruffled the leaves of the oak or sycamore, now awoke with bolder tone the echoes of the fount. Alice was returning towards her own cottage, when she paused awhile in her path to gaze upon a scene of much rustic beauty. She was leaning over the parapet of a low wooden bridge, that spanned a meandering rivulet beneath, and had become wrapped in the contemplation of the prospect before her, when the sound of approaching footsteps aroused her from her reverie. Remembering the circumstances attending her previous abduction, she began to repent of her imprudence in remaining out alone at that hour, but her fears were soon set at rest by identifying, in the figure who now approached her on the bridge, the well-known person of Luke Martyn.

"Ah! Miss Alice," said he, as he approached, "I fancied it must have been you that I saw from the vale; few others can appreciate a scene of so much simple beauty."

"You are at least right in your first surmise," returned Alice; "but why tarries my companion behind, when I required his presence earlier?"

"Why, I have been packing up my little property for a journey I am about to take?"

"A journey?" faltered Alice.

"Yes, Miss, and I did not intend to bid you even good bye; but my heart was too full to allow me to leave you without saying whither I was going."

"Going, Luke!" repeated Alice, as if fearful of trusting to the evidence of her senses. "Whither?"

"To London, Miss."

"And what to do there?"

"Why, seek my fortune, like others have sought theirs before me. I have heard that he who has a willing arm and a steady mind need never want in London."

"But why form so important a resolution in such a sudden manner?"

"It is not sudden, Miss, if we call that sudden which is the effect of a momentary impulse. I have thought of it long and deliberately."

"And your reason?"

"Ah! that I must not reveal."

"Indeed!" cried Alice; "why not?"

"It would offend you like, or at least cause you uneasiness, which I would never cause willingly."

"You have already caused more by withholding it than you could have done by imparting it," rejoined Alice.

"Well, then, Miss, since you must know, *you* are the cause."

"I! Luke?"

"Yes! Miss Alice, you. I need not repeat that I have loved you—that I love you now, though all hope of gaining your affection in return has long since passed away. I found, whilst I was near you, that my passion increased, and though it cost me a hard struggle to make up my mind, that struggle was at last successful, and I determined to flee from the place that had procured me so much unhappiness. You seemed the only person with whom I could converse with pleasure, the only one who seemed to appreciate me as I vainly fancied I deserved to be appreciated; and it cannot then be wondered at that I should spend my happiest days in your company, but—shame on my manhood for allowing these tears to fall—this must now cease. I join the London waggon as it passes the end of

yonder lane. Farewell, Miss Travers, and may you occasionally think of the blighted hopes, and pardon the presumption, of poor Luke Martyn, the peasant!"

"I can scarcely reply to you," faltered Alice, "for the words seem to choke me. With you I lose my dearest friend; yes, *friend*, Luke, for that is all we can ever be to each other; but, ere we part, accept of this poor token of my esteem."

Luke kissed the relic with rapture, as he recognized a small gold locket containing a portion of her hair.

The shrill horn of the waggoner now reminded the traveller of the approach of the lumbering vehicle.

"Farewell! dear—Miss Alice, I should say—God bless you!" And blinded by tears Luke darted up the lane towards where the waggon was making its appearance.

"Stay, Luke; you have left a packet behind you!" exclaimed Alice, discovering a paper enclosure at her feet; but the retiring sound of the horses' bells told her that Luke was already far on the road towards his destination.

Finding he did not return, Alice, much moved by the recent event, stooped to gain possession of the letter. The light of the moon enabled her to peruse the superscription: it was directed to herself. Hastily tearing it open, she found some well-written lines declaratory of his unfortunate passion, in which he expressed a hope that the sight of them at intervals would restore him to her thoughts. A letter was also enclosed, written as if the writer had intended to depart without seeing her, but being merely a fuller exposition of the reasons for his departure, mentioned in the above conversation, we need not allude to it further. Alice placing these in her bosom, retraced her steps homeward, slowly and mournfully, meditating on the noble heart she had rejected; and with wishes for her own happiness, she blended prayers for his prosperity.

CHAPTER XXVI.

THE ROUNDHOUSE.

Here Vice and Crime do hold their nightly court,
And when good things of day are hushed in sleep,
Make noise and revel through the live-long night.
* * * * * * *
Whilst crime walks hand in hand with virtuous woe,
And shames its mild companion.
                    The Clerkenwell Gallants—1654.

THE Clerkenwell Roundhouse was a large, and, for the time, a commodious structure, being a circular stone building, with grated windows, and partitioned off into cells, for the better security of those whose inclinations or fears might lead them to plan an escape. It was adorned on the exterior with high wooden frontages, with a rudely-carved representation of a pair of fetters, wedged into the wood-work. A capacious portal, conducting the reluctant visitor to one of smaller dimensions, which led to the hall itself, was a prominent object from without, and was calculated to excite many misgivings as to the nature of the accommodations provided within. This hall which we have mentioned formed indeed the Roundhouse itself, the passages branching from it merely leading to the cells which have before attracted our notice. Hither, after the affray at the gambling-house, were Barnwell and his partner in the disturbance conducted. The demeanour of the latter had now subsided from the most frenzied excitement into the greatest apathy. The insanity of the moment having passed away, a state of moody sullenness succeeded, and he answered the question put to him by the official of the place in dogged monosyllables. As for our hero, he continued to rave and tear his hair with the fury of a maniac. The money that Mr. Thorogood had given him to pay to the stockbroker, had gone—to the last farthing. *One hundred and fifty pounds lost in one night!* The reflection was madness.

It is now time that we take a glance at the other characters who figured conspicuously in this scene. We have said that the hall into which Barnwell and his companion was conducted, was circular. We should have added, that a long row of low wooden benches was ranged round the apartment. On these there were many sleepers, some in the tattered garb of vagrancy, others bedecked in the more fashionable and costly costume of the fops of the day. Sleep that, like Death, levels alike both the peer and the commoner, had here huddled all together. From the lips of many came low, incoherent ravings, connected with the previous night's debauchery; others muttered snatches of the then popular ballads; but all wore, more or less, upon their faces that haggard look of mental and bodily depravity, that a long course of nocturnal excesses stamps with an indelible brand upon the countenances of its victims. In the centre, perched upon a high stool, emblematical perhaps of the dignity of the personage it supported, sat Michael Muzzle, or Muzzling Mike, as he was more usually called by those who knew him, with a pipe of considerable longitudinal dimensions in one hand, and a very much-befrothed pot of porter in the other. This was no other than the presiding official of the place whose duty it was to receive the prisoners that were conducted before him, and examine them, previous to their being brought the following morning before the magistrates. Around him were gathered the few watchmen who had been the means of capturing our hero; and with these Mike held a long and, as it proved, a very confidential conversation, dividing his immediate attention between the pipe on one side and the porter on the other.

"Pish! only a bobbery is it these gentlemen are after being brought up for?" exclaimed Mike, after a pause, "perhaps we can settle it in a pleasanter way, maybe, than fronting the beaks. I made sartin it was a cracking case at the least."

"I do not exactly, Sir, understand you," replied Barnwell.

"And how the divil should we be understood," pursued the first speaker, who insisted on the plural prerogative of royalty, "when we've not made ourselves understandable at all at all? Justice, you see, gentlemen, is a spalpeen that must be looked after, or there would be no governing the ragamuffin. Now, as the scale of nations depends upon the equilibrium of the moral forces rendered subservient to the proper maintenance and support of a well-regulated and highly polished-up society, it follows that a necessary due and proper respect should be paid to the statutes of the land, in contradistinction to the insubordinate recklessness of nocturnal debauchery, you have herein, and just now, sanguinarily and contumaciously exhibited."

"Ah; that's the *pint!*" remarked one of the watchmen.

"Silence!" cried the first speaker; "and let us proceed with our category. This being the case, young men, it also follows, that it would be advisable to say nothing at all about this squabble, and to bury the indiscretions that you have been cognizant of, in oblivion."

Mike, who kept this imposing narration ready for the use and edification of all new comers, now refreshed the channel of his oratory with a copious supply of malt from the pewter, and looked majestically round to convince himself of the effect it must have had.

"I am still at a loss to divine your meaning," responded our hero, perceiving that an answer was expected.

"Why, p'rhaps, the gen'l'man ull stand summat," suggested the elder of the two watchmen, deferentially as well as impatiently.

"Silence, thou earth-worshipper," interrupted the legislator of the Roundhouse, emitting from his lips an extra effusion of smoke; "is our words to be extracted from our mouth before it has reached our official lips? Annihilate the thought! Yes, gentlemen, if ye'd prefer going back to the open air, rather than being locked up here, I can accommodate you with the choice, on the reasonable terms of five guineas from the mint of her Most Gracious Majesty, Queen Anne."

"Alas!" cried Barnwell, with a sigh, as he reflected on his loss; "we have no money."

"No money!" echoed the other; "oh, the debauched rhapscalions, to annoy her Majesty's most quiet and peaceably disposed subjects! No money! Away with the noisy revellers to one of our darkest cells—these benches are too good for them. No money! Oh! horrible depravity."

And amidst the utterance of such remarks as these, were the two young gamblers conveyed away from the presence of the horrified law-expounder, and ushered into a cell that terminated one of the stone passages before mentioned.

The dungeon—for such it was—in which they now found themselves, was a damp, close place, to which a small grated window at the top of the east side alone answered the double purpose of admitting light and air. The noisome stench that greeted them on their entrance was alone sufficient to excite repugnance to their abode; but when they saw that a few shocks of straw formed their only couch for the night, or rather morning, for it had passed the midnight hour, their aversion increased.

There was, however, no alternative; so, throwing themselves down upon the hard floor, the two left to their own reflections, endeavoured to gain a few hours of repose.

The dead silence that prevailed, favoured, indeed, the inclinations of both. Barnwell was far from anxious to commence any conversation; his brain was on fire with the events of the evening, and his mind was too much torn by contending emotions to allow of his entering into any discussion respecting the conduct of the officious watchman. His companion, on the other hand, flung himself, on his entrance, down in one of the corners of the cell, and was soon wrapped in meditation.

"My poor mother," he cried, when he fancied Barnwell was asleep; "how have I deceived thee! This money, which you gave me, as all you possessed, to enable me to proceed to India, is gone—not a shilling left! How shall I dare to present myself again before you? Gone! Oh, damnable thought!"

Broken words and disjointed sentences, such as

these, marked the feelings that agitated this young man's breast, and called forth a response from Barnwell, who thinking of the kind and affectionate parent he had left behind, became equally impressed with a vivid sense of his own misconduct.

Morning, however, threw its slanting beams down through the narrow grating on the sleeping prisoners, and with it came Lance Locksley, the under ward-keeper, to conduct them before a magistrate. We shall pass over the scene that followed, and merely state in a few words that the interview between Barnwell and that functionary terminated 'in the latter consigning the former to jail until the necessary fine had been duly discharged.

There was now no alternative, but to candidly confess to his employer, Mr. Thorogood, the unfortunate position in which he was placed. It was the result of a hard struggle to decide upon this ; but decided upon it was. A letter was immediately dispatched to Cheapside, and shortly after the merchant himself made his appearance.

Without uttering one word of reprehension or reproach, the hind-hearted merchant payed the whole of the fine demanded, and, accompanied by Barnwell, returned to his own house. The result of the interview that then took place demands a separate chapter.

CHAPTER XXVII.

THE CHURCHYARD RENCONTRE.

What ! not believe in ghosts ? Oh ! monstrous mass
Of human incredulity ; egregious heap
Of unbelieving atoms. Why, these ghosts
Are constant visitors to some I know,
And play fantastic trick, and gambols droll
With many whom they favour with a call.
Sometimes they tap one, bailiff-like, on shoulder;
Or pat the head with patronising hand.
Sometimes they take the likeness of yourself,
And then you see straightway a double man,
Yourself the real, and your ghost the false.

                 Midnight Visits—1683.

" TEN pounds to one you don't !"
" Done !"
The wager was accepted.
Such was the result of a long discussion in the tap-room of the Queen's Head tavern, Islington, as a party who had been figuring as the principal personages in the conversation began to be putting on their cloaks and hats preparatory to their departure for the night.

The conversation had for some time turned upon the probability of supernatural revisitation, and, as it is always usual with this topic, the nature of the subject imparted some of its icy chilliness to the minds of the hearers, who, notwithstanding it was a summer night, shivered and shook, either with fear or cold, as much as if the corresponding month had been December instead of July.

The theme of the discourse was the arrival of an inhabitant of the other world in the quiet and secluded churchyard of St. Mary's, Islington, which being near the scene of action, and standing then alone in the midst of waste land, was thought a fit place to receive so unearthly a visitor. Amongst others who had boasted vauntingly of their courage was one Philip Manning, a young military officer, who having just returned from Flanders, with the glowing effects of Marlborough's victories still ring-

ing in his ears, Death knew for him no fears, and Superstition no terrors.

At the insinuations of his companion, relative to whether he dare encounter this same nocturnal perambulator, he only laughed, and when a laughter-loving disciple of Æsculapius, one Matt. Marvell, proposed the wager with which our present chapter opened, Phil. Manning accepted it, as readily as if its execution were the easiest thing in the world ; and the ghost an old companion, who had invited him to partake of a bottle of port, of a similar antiquity.

Such was the state of affairs, when Meggott and Clayton, unseen by each other, leaned over the shoulders of the other listeners, to observe and profit by the information now being given.

" My dear Philip, you surely will not go on an enterprise of so much danger, at such an hour, and on such a night," said the pouting Kate Woolston, daughter of the landlady of the Queen's Head, and between whom and Philip there was said, by the gossips of the neighbourhood, to be some little affection.

" And why shou'd I not go, Kate ?" tenderly inquired the young gallant. " Have I aught to fear as being more dangerous than a glance from that wicked pair of bright eyes of yours ?"

" Come ! come, Master Manning," cried Marvell, " to your task ; it is now twelve, and there is no time to lose."

" But the rain is pouring down in torrents, and a thunderstorm is near at hand," said Kate ; and as she spoke, the pattering of hail against the diamond-panes of the parlour window, with the rumbling of thunder in the distance, corroborated her assertion.

" No matter !" replied Philip ; " I will prove that my courage is not to be daunted by imaginary antagonists. One kiss, Kate, before I go, and that will be a sufficient charm against all witchcraft."

" That shall be your's, Philip," responded the blushing maiden, " if you wish it ; but here is that more likely to nerve your heart, and preserve you against the fury of the elements :" and as she spoke a bumper of brandy was filled by her trembling hand, and drank with a sweetener from the lips of her who filled it.

" And now, how am I to prove that I have been ?" cried Manning.

" By bringing one of the bones that you will find strewn over a new-made grave in the middle of the church-yard," replied Marvell.

" Agreed ! my hat and cloak."

Kate brought them both, accompanied by an ardent aspiration for her lover's safety.

" And now to the execution of my task. Farewell, Kate ! and rely on my speedy return."

And with that Manning departed.

Marvell determined to test the bravery of the officer ; and, remembering that he had a skeleton's dress in his possession, worn at a recent masquerade, soon after slipped away from his companions, to deter the other from completing his errand.

Nor was he the only one that was anxious to do so. Meggott seeing in this adventure an opportunity for plunder, and disguising himself in a similar manner, also exchanged within a few minutes the parlour in the Queen's Head for the less congenial, but, as he anticipated, the more profitable church-yard of St. Mary's.

Anxiously were the moments counted during Philip's absence by those who remained to await

the issue of the wager. The lightning increased in brilliancy with every flash, and the thunder rolled over their heads in a tone loud enough to resemble the simultaneous discharge of whole parks of artillery.

We must now turn to the churchyard. Marvell arrived there first; and carefully selecting the nearest path, ensconced himself behind a tombstone for his hiding-place, unconsciously selecting that opposite to where Meggott was secreted.

A third, covered with perspiration from the haste he had made in coming, was not far off. This was Clayton, who, on the same mission of plunder as Meggott, and unaware of his companion's proceedings, had provided himself with a watchman's great coat and lantern, availed himself also of the marble screen a neighbouring tomb-stone afforded him for watching the appearance of Manning.

The noise of the rain and the rumbling of the thunder, now no longer distant, prevented either of them from being aware of the presence fo the others in their immediate vicinity: and when Manning, who had proceeded by a circuitous route, and at a moderate pace, at length arrived, they were made sensible of his approach only by the sound of the French popular air that the officer was carelessly humming for his own gratification. It was now a fearful crisis. Meggott and Marvell, each uttering a loud groan, and rising simultaneously from behind their respective tombstones, were confronted together. A vivid flash of lightning, accompanied by a loud peal of thunder, showed both of them in their horrible and unnatural costume. Marvell, who, since his arrival there, had become strangely impressed with terror, now wanted not the promptings of his own conscience to betake himself to flight. Meggott, too, at first alarmed, perceiving at a glance, the cause of the other's fears, stalked at a most ghostlike slowness of speed after him; but stepping in his progress over a plank thrown across a grave newly dug, the plank tilted, and he became immersed up to his neck in an uncomfortable admixture of water, decayed bones, and moistened clay ; whilst Clayton, observing the scene from the situation where he was, had much difficulty in keeping his laughter from having an audible vent.

The disappearance of Meggott, however, only served to make Marvell run the faster ; and when he reached the parlour of the tavern he had so recently left, in his skeleton's dress rendered more fantastic by flight, and breathless with speed, his sudden appearance threw the whole of the visitors in a state of consternation, which his fear-excited visage was by no means calculated to abate.

Meggott in vain endeavoured to extricate himself from the grave into which he had so prematurely fallen ; and would doubtless have perished had it not have been for Clayton, who, seeing the position in which his companion in vice was placed, hurried to the spot, and assisted him in setting foot once more on firm earth. The adventure, however, proved more fatal than either of them anticipated at the time, for a party of the watch arriving, who had been alarmed by the noise, they secured the two burglars as they were escaping from the church-yard, and took them into custody. The next day underwent an examination before the city magistrate, and being identified as the two fugitives that were concerned in the Hampstead burglary, Meggott suffered a short time afterwards the extreme penalty of the law for the murder of Mrs. Tabitha Royster ; and Clayton, for the share he had in the robbery, was transported for life to one of our penal colonies.

One word more as to the remaining personages who have so suddenly figured in our pages, and we have done ; confining our pen for the future almost exclusively to the adventures of Barnwell, and his infamous companion. Philip Manning returned to the Queen's Arms with the trophy of victory in his hand, won the wager, and married the blushing heiress to the tavern, Kate Woolston, as the reward for his courage and constancy. Matt. Marvell, till the day of his death, unconscious of the trick that had been played upon him, became a fervent believer in the supernatural, and forswore wagers from that time forth, living an altered man, and dying a timid one. Manning, it yet remains for us to say, in process of time, resigned his martial costume for the tapster's jacket, and established the tavern as one of our best-conducted places of entertainment, beholding a group of little ones growing up about him that have handed down the name to the present possessors of the hostelry, even to the moment at which we write.

The chapter, reader, that thou hast just concluded, is not without a moral. Exert thy ingenuity in finding out wherein it lies.

CHAPTER XXVIII.

GOOD RESOLVES FRUSTRATED.

Behold this man, a compound of those things
That tend to soften or improve the heart !
Honour and goodness, probity and zeal :
Virtue, good temper, clemency and pride—
That honest pride that scorns a deed of vice ;
And all united in the breast of one
Who holds the station Fate ordained to him
With conscious meekness, and a firm belief
That death will only be an easy path
That brings him unto Heaven.
                         The London Merchant.

" And now, Barnwell, I trust you see too plainly the consequences of your departure from virtue to heedlessly repeat it. I once more take you into my confidence ; once more restore you to that position in my favour which you formerly held, and once more place implicit reliance on your probity ; see that it is not again abused."

" My kind, generous employer," responded Barnwell, " your reproaches would have hardened me in my vicious courses, but your advice, so touchingly given, and your generosity, so readily bestowed, has quite vanquished me. You shall learn to how great an extent you have been deceived in the youth you trusted, how undeserving I have been of your favours, and how, through me, you have been———"

" Hold !" interrupted the merchant ; " I will hear no more. You are a penitent, and that is all I require. I know how aptly youth will slide from right to wrong ; how readily they listen to the voice of the tempter ; but I require not you to tell me how you have fallen, how you have listened. It is enough for me to know you *have* done so ; and it suffices that you have given earnest of amendment.

" You will resume your office duties this morning ; let us to business, and remember,'' added he, in an impressive tone, " the past is forgotten."

" What a noble disposition have I wronged !" thought Barnwell to himself, as he hastened to the counting-house, determined to make amends for his former neglect by his present zeal and activity ; " what injury have I done to one who thus requites me for it ! Well ! well ! the time may come when I may show that I am not undeserving of his clemency ; let me hope, in the mean time, that that day is not far distant."

Such was the result of a long, but not unimportant, interview that took place between our hero and his employer. It exerted a most beneficial influence over the mind of the former, and was the means of reclaiming him from his vicious courses from a period that was only brief, because he wanted strength of mind to combat against the temptations by which he was assailed. But let us not anticipate.

For one month Barnwell's conduct was such as to convince Mr. Thorogood that his remonstrances were not without their beneficial effect. During this time he saw but little of Eleanor, for he could not help connecting her—though he scarcely knew why—as being in some way linked with his disgrace. Milwood had, in the interim, been far from idle in her vocation. Aided by rich presents from Sir William Brandreth, and the share of plunder which she obtained from Vavasour, her style of living was one scene of continued splendour and extravagance. The money which she so easily obtained took wing as speedily, and she became again constrained to seek some new method of replenishing her purse. It was then, and not till then, that she bestowed a thought upon the City Apprentice, and determined to call again upon his resources for the supply of her wants; she sought an interview with him, the result of which proved fatal to the peace of the unhappy youth. How this was brought about we shall now proceed to show.

It was towards the close of one afternoon, when Barnwell, fatigued by the duties of his office, was standing listlessly at the door, inhaling the fresh air that came floating past him, imbued with the smoke of the myriads of chimneys that the city contained, when, casting his eyes towards a female passenger that was hurrying towards him, he recognized in the features of the new-comer the countenance of Milwood.

But it was not that cheerful, blithesome face, that he had been accustomed to gaze upon. The cheeks had lost their roseate tints, the eyes were duller than they were wont to be, and appeared bedewed with tears. Sorrow seemed to have passed with a heavy hand over the features on which he had previously dwelt with so much rapture, and he could not be but deeply sensible of the change.

The heart of our hero failed to support him in the trial, and as she approached, his love returned towards her he had slighted with more than tenfold its former vigour. "Eleanor," cried he with emotion; "why do I see you here, and here thus altered?"

"Why, rather," returned Milwood, "are you thus changed? But I will not reproach you; if your heart is not your accuser, what I say would have but little effect. I see you have forgotten me; —have ceased to love me. For three long tedious months have I watched—anxiously watched—for your arrival: I need not say that I have watched in vain. But I came not here to tell you this; I am about returning to France, in what capacity I will not grieve you by naming. That it is a menial office I have undertaken, you who know my unfortunate resources must be well aware. But before I went—before I left England for ever—I determined to take one long and last farewell of him who had alleviated my sorrows, and shared my pleasures. It is for this purpose that I am here, it is for this purpose that I have once again sought to intrude myself on your notice. Farewell, and may you be happier—far happier—than her whose heart you have broken, whose earthly happiness you have destroyed."

"Eleanor, my dear Eleanor, we must not, cannot part thus. I love you as fondly and tenderly, nay, more fondly and tenderly than ever; cast me not then away from your thought, I beseech you."

This was exactly what Milwood desired. Her previous profession—that of the stage—had made her as accomplished an actress off the boards as she was on. Her power of simulating the different passions was perfect; and, aided by the knowledge she possessed of the frailty of human nature, there were few, as we have before had occasion to observe, who could withstand her attacks. When woman thus unites with those blandishments nature has bestowed upon her, the hypocritical instructions of art, dangerous indeed becomes her influence over those with whom she comes in contact.

"This is but fruitless converse, Mr. Barnwell," continued she; part we must; I cannot bear to meet as a friend the man I have looked upon as a lover. Once more, farewell!"

"Stay," said Barnwell, whose mind was swayed by two opposite impulses, love, and a conscious sense of duty to his employer; "stay but one moment."

In that moment, virtue had gained a temporary victory.

"It is better, perhaps, that we should part, Eleanor," resumed Barnwell, after a pause. "Your presence I feel, though know not why, to be dangerous to me. Absence perhaps may prove beneficial to both of us; but with me, at least, a recollection of those happy days we have spent in each other's society will always remain."

So ready an acquiescence to what she had said was more than Milwood had anticipated, and for the time somewhat disconcerted her; but that presence of mind, which seldom failed her, was soon regained.

"I did not expect you could have so readily banished me from your heart," said Milwood; "but it may be better that you can view my departure with apathy; even though such departure does hurry me from happiness to misery."

"How!"

"Yes! I must candidly confess that the very dress I wear—and which, as a present from you, I shall be loth to part with—even *this* must be sold to defray my passage to the Continent."

"No!" exclaimed Barnwell, with vehemence; "*that* it shall never be, whilst I can be the means of preventing it. Here, take this purse; it is somewhat weighty, and will more than pay the expenses of your journey. Ask me not how I came by it, but take it whilst I have the power to give it you."

"This is indeed kind of you, George; but, say—"

"Ask me no questions," returned Barnwell, confused; "but fly—haste away from this accursed spot. I hear my employer returning. No thanks I require—I *deserve* them not."

"Once more, then, I bid you farewell!" cried Milwood, as, hearing the approaching footsteps of Mr. Thorogood, she left the office.

"And now, welcome, happiness!" said Barnwell, as he resumed his occupation, "though it has been purchased at the expense of my own honesty."

CHAPTER XXIX.

THT PAGEANT.

Froth.—By the mass, here's a goodly show.
Tapster.—Aye, marry is there, Master Francis Froth;
And this is not the half on't. London pours
Its thousands out to gaze upon the scene,
And still there's much that will go unobserved.
Plays, masques and revels, pageantries and shows,
Processions, banner, music, and the aid
Of fire and water, wine and wassailing,
Are all combined, to celebrate the day
When our good King ascends the English throne.
                        A Trip to the Coronation—1598.

A WEEK had passed since the recital of the conversation recorded in the preceding chapter, and that week had been rendered memorable by two important events having occurred therein. We say important; not with immediate reference to the personages who have hitherto figured in our pages, but as far as regarded the change that at this time took place in the sovereignty of the country in which they lived. The "good Queen Anne," as she is emphatically called by her biographers, though for what earthly reason, save that servile adulation to royalty that royalty always exacts, we could never very distinctly conceive, had been gathered to the home of her fathers, and the Hanoverian George the First had been proclaimed in her stead. That hypocritical solemnity, the general mourning, having now passed away, preparations were made on a scale of unusual splendour for the coronation of the then reigning monarch. The conduit on Snow-hill—pulled down immediately afterwards—flowed with wine for three days. A fair took place in Hyde Park; and a public circus was erected in Smithfield, where equestrian entertainments were given gratuitously to the public. Montgolfier balloons, then attracting everybody's attention, rose from different parts of the metropolis, freighted with confectionary, and when at a certain height, discharged simultaneously showers of bon-bons and sweetmeats upon the heads of the admiring populace. The Strand and Fleet-street were thrown into one vast arcade, the road being carpeted all the way, and huge festoons of laurel and arches of flowers linked the opposite houses together down the whole line of route. Never—at least not in the recollection of the *then* oldest inhabitant—were such rejoicings ever known. Notwithstanding the heat of the summer, oxen were roasted whole at the corner of every street, and served out to whomsoever might apply for their portion; stalwart hogsheads of malt were emptied at every hour of the day by those whose thirst was greater than their taste, and who were willing to have that thirst gratified at the expense only of a severe squeeze; and, to crown all, Business threw away his staid garb and steady gait, to run riot in Enjoyment; and Pleasure, decked out in her gayest colours, waited only for solicitation to bestow her favours. It was, in short, one vast holiday. The lord and the lowly-born; the peer and the peasant; the artisan and his apprentice; the shopkeeper and his shopman, were on this day at least equal—for the same entertainments were open to all. Like the colours in a kaleidescope, the objects appeared under so many different phases, and were so diversified by their number and variety, that the eye roved about from one to another, still insatiate, still unsatisfied.

The old clock of St. Paul's had scarcely allowed its index of Time to point out the transit of noon, than a gay and noble procession was seen to make its way from the palace of St. James towards the east. The twelve sonorous strokes of the "iron tongue of time" died away upon the air, and tones of the most joyous music succeeded. The trumpet sounded its shrill clarion, and the flute its softer melodies, as if the air, transmuted by a new kind of alchemy, had thrown off its grosser particles, and had melted into music. But to these sounds, the rumbling of many carriages and the tramping of many feet were added. Horses richly caparisoned with cloths of gold came first, bearing on their backs the *noblesse* of the realm; then followed a long array of carriages drawn by cream-coloured steeds, and heralding the approach of the state carriage, in which the people saw their future monarch arrive soon after. Loud and long were the shouts that made the welkin ring as His Majesty and his mighty retinue passed beneath the antiquated portal of Temple Bar, and hats and caps were flung into the air with a reckless disregard of their ever again returning into the hands of their owners. Still—impeded not by the closely-wedged mass of living beings that lined the path—the cavalcade progressed onward amidst the ringing of bells, the discharge of cannon, and the shouts of the populace. The coronation was fixed upon to take place in St. Paul's Cathedral, and hither accordingly the crowd pressed, restrained from entering the churchyard only by the exertions of the regiments drawn out, in uniform, to preserve due order.

At length, the swelling of the mighty organ had rolled its last diapason away like the sound of distant thunder, and the ceremony was declared concluded. The procession returned back to the palace, and the populace back to the enjoyments provided for them. But what were the festivities by day compared with those which took place at night? Fireworks grouped into a hundred ingenious devices and pyrotechnical illusions illumined the horizon with a light, as brilliant almost as the light of day. St. James's Park was thrown open into one vast promenade, with its leafy avenues of trees actually *smothered* with brilliancy. Chinese lanterns hung at regular distances bedecked with flowers, and coloured lamps of every hue were suspended in tasteful variety from each yielding branch, that appeared bowed down by the lustrous weight it supported. The ornamental water—now in the centre of the enclosure, but then occupying a large space of uncultivated waste ground in the centre of the park,—was the arena of a mock sea-fight, in which the naval manœuvres of a fleet at sea were imitated to a nicety by small craft manned by wooden soldiers, and filled with combustibles, but whose motions were regulated by machinery at the side, invisible to the eye of the speculator. Chinese temples, Persian minarets, Turkish mosques, Arabian tents, and the characteristics of every nation, were ranged beneath one immense canopy, figuratively and allegorically signifying the wing of Britannia, overshadowing the whole; and in these were sold refreshments, each of a kind peculiarly appropriate to the country. All was riot and revelry. Banners were waving, music was playing, drums were beating, guns were firing, bells were pealing, and ever and anon were born onwards on the shoulder of the breeze deafening shouts of mirth and joyousness, with which wild songs of drunkenness and debauchery were at times commingled.

On these scenes gazed Barnwell, with feelings

that savoured more of astonishment rather than admiration, of curiosity rather than delight. He was alone; for though the merchant and his family had invited him to accompany them on their sightseeing expedition, he had lost them in the crowd, and he was now, as we have before said, alone. And what a horrid feeling is this loneliness in the midst of a mighty city; when, standing amidst thousands, we recognise not one, and seem a shipwrecked Selkirk on the sea of Mankind. This is really solitude; this it is to be alone in the great world, a cipher amongst millions of units, adding to their number, but not increasing their value. This did Barnwell feel to be his situation at that moment, and so did he think; but the reflection had scarcely escaped his lips, than some one plucked his sleeve, and, turning round, he beheld Milwood at his side.

"Come! 'come! my roystering apprentice," cried she; "alone and melancholy on a day like this! May I inquire, in the words of Benvolio—'Prithee, what sadness lengthens *Barnwell's* hours?'"

"To which I might make Romeo's answer," said Barnwell; "'not having that which having makes them short.' But why, Eleanor, do you still remain in England, when I fancied it was your intention to pass the remainder of your life in France?"

"I will tell the reason to you anon," replied Milwood, as a cloud of passing sorrow seemed for the moment to shadow her countenance; "but it is a sad tale, and fitted for more sombre scenes than this, where all around breathes of happiness, unalloyed by the thoughts of sorrow. Let it suffice, for the present gratification of your curiosity, to know that I have been compelled, by unavoidable circumstances, to apply your kind loan to a different purpose from that to which it was originally intended it should be applied. But come! a truce to sadness; I see you have not forgotten our joint studies of Shakspere; so let me ask you, is there no play to ease the anguish of a torturing hour, that you are thus moping it away in solitude."

Barnwell, dazzled by the high spirits, good humour, and gaiety of his companion, at once forgot all the strict resolutions that he had formed, and candidly confessed that he should be glad of a companion in the festivities of the night.

"Why, that's well said," replied Milwood; "and now I think on't, I have two tickets of admission for the Grand Masque of the law students in Gray's Inn; we will go thither, and join in the revelry of the night."

"With all my heart," responded our hero, with whom but little persuasion was required; and, accordingly, they went towards their new destination. Making their way through the dense crowd at Pall Mall, and turning up the Haymarket, to avoid the great mass of people who were assembled in Fleetstreet and the Strand to witness the illuminations, they wended their way from Holborn towards Gray's Inn, and soon after arrived in the noble Quadrangle, on the northern side of which stood the building they were in search of.

CHAPTER XXX.

THE REVEL.

Fazio—What mummery is this?   [querade,
Ribaldo—No mummery, my lord, but one vast masquerade,
An unframed picture of our motley world,
In which each plays a part that fate ne'er gave him,
But which his better interest has prompted.
Man thus assumes a mask to aid himself,
And cheats all others with the mockery.
                              Love in Masquerade—1714.

THE large Hall of Gray's Inn was indeed a striking object to interest the beholder. It was built of brick, in the style prevailing from the time of the eighth Henry to the first James. Projecting angular and mullioned windows, then illuminated with a vast blaze of light, produced a striking contrast to the sombre, embattled gables of the upper portion of the building, which was completed by a roof heavy enough to dislocate the walls, and a turret fashioned after a most nondescript style of architecture.

Entering the hall, a party of maskers or mummers met them at the door, and, after a mock ceremony of introduction, allowed them to pass to the interior. This, which was the last revel in which the students ever indulged, was conducted on a scale of the most unbounded magnificence. The Lord of Misrule, or Master of Merry Disports, as he was sometimes quaintly styled, sat on a high throne at the further end, surrounded by twenty others, apparelled in liveries of green and yellow, with ornaments of scarfs, ribbons and laces, profusely thrown over their other gaudy attire. Bells were suspended from each of the caps worn by the mummers, and being set in motion, jingled a strange melody, not unbefitting the occasion that brought them together.

These "revels" as they were called, being intended to represent in some degree the manners and customs of their predecessors, the greater portion of the students were clad in the monastic garb of friars, whilst others assumed the ragged dress of pilgrims and mendicants supplicating the visitors for alms; and the money thus obtained was spent in renewed attacks upon the huge flagons of sack that custom authorises should be drank upon such occasions.

Nor were the young frolicsome students the only ones who thus laid care and study on one side to welcome the approach of folly. The grave benchers and saturine barristers assembled in the hall with hearts equally intent on merriment, and threw away their black gowns for what they considered a more genial dress for the occasion.

"Now, then," cried the Lord of Misrule, with burlesque solemnity, "we conjure ye, by virtue of the high office which we hold, to fill your bumpers to the utmost, to open your eyes to the widest, and to shout till ye make the old walls of Alma Mater ring with a thousand echoes, whilst we give you, ye good men and true of Gray's Inn, and ye visitors therein assembled, the health of our most mighty and puissant monarch, George the First."

A volley of huzzas, intermixed with the jingling of bells and the clattering of the horn-cup on the tables, told how enthusiastically the toast was responded to.

"And now," continued the Master of these merry disports, preserving the same ludicrous gravity as before, " let your goblets again be filled, till the amorous liquor within kisses the silver brim without, and bathes the margin in its nectar ; let he who fails in the observance of our mandates dread our earth-annihilating vengeance, and shun the darts of our globe-illuminating eyes, whilst we call upon you to quaff off a bumper to—our noble selves !"

The expectations of all, raised by the bombastic fustian of the exordium to the greatest height, suffered now a slight depression. Mock murmurs of disapprobation and signs of insurrection succeeded.

" Now, by our halidome," exclaimed the monarch of fun, as if enraged at the manner in which his health had been received, " this is more than we can well bear. What, ho ! who waits there ?"

Two sturdy fathers in their monkish costume immediately obeyed the summons.

" Ye are good attendants, truly," pursued the speaker, " to obey me now ; why did ye not anticipate my full intent, not wait till it assumed by words a form more tangible. Away with the ringleader of the revolt to the scaffold—there off with his neck—"

" Oh, mercy !" cried several.

" None shall be granted; so, once more, off with his neck—"

" My lord !" shrieked others.

" Neck-*handkerchief !*" continued his High Mightiness, apparently enjoying the terror which he had occasioned.

" An' it so please your Highness," cried one of the servitors, kneeling before him, " a pilgrim hath been found kissing Miss Sarah Tartlet, our pantler's daughter."

" Ah ! is it so ? Oh, ho !" cried the monarch, " bring him before me instanter. An insult offered to Sally Tartlet is an insult offered to our royal person, and an insult offered to our royal person must be avenged without delay."

The unlucky culprit was arraigned, tried, and pleady guilty.

" Then, now for the sentence ;" pursued the Sovereign, " and from my wisdom, let all who hear me profit. Henceforth shall justice cast on one side her scales, and on the other tear off the envious bandage which poets and sculptors have tied over her eyes. England shall be a free and untaxed country, and sack shall be sold at twopence a quart. Pilgarlick here has had his swing ; and now we'll have ours. He shall experience two most dreadful deaths, and have a leap from the leafless tree without benefit of clergy. First shall he be drowned."

" Drowned !"

" Aye, marry, drowned ; as my distant relation Clarence was, in a butt of Malmsey, only we'll reverse the sentence ; and, instead of the man being in the malmsey, the malmsey shall be in the man."

A loud laugh followed this sally.

" And then he shall be hung !"

" Hung !" echoed a hundred voices, with tones expressive of astonishment.

" Aye—*out to dry.* Is not that a punishment truly great enough for him ? and now, my masters, let us away with the semblance of law, and cultivate an acquaintance with the Muses ; so broach me another cask, warder, and let us have one of your staves."

In scenes like these was the great humour of the scene (whether rightly or not we leave the reader to form his opinion) supposed to consist. The rest of the entertainments consisted of a masked ball, in the entertainments of which the noblest and fairest of the land thought it no discredit to participate. With the dancers Barnwell and Milwood mingled. The former, influenced by the blandishments of the latter, again resorted to intoxication as the means of depriving his mind of the powers of reflection. He again broke loose from the bonds of propriety, and, dashing anew into the dark abyss of dissipation, became lost to all sense of virtue, proper pride, and manly dignity.

Drink—that damning curse to the sons of Adam, has thus ever proved the nurse of crime. The love of intoxicating liquids at first, like a river narrow and scarcely large enough to be noticed at the source, is, by degrees, more and more dangerous, till, rushing on with increased force, it whirls the unhappy craft that trusts to it for guidance, into misery, and, overflowing its banks, leaves behind only a wide and melancholy waste of ruin and desolation.

CHAPTER XXXI.

THE PROGRESS OF VIRTUE.

Foresight.—Well ! by my troth I wish thee safely home :
Thou'rt a rare youth, and may arrive at eminence,
I trust thou wilt, for well dost thou deserve it.
   Allworth.—I thank thee for thy benison, kind sir,
Heaven make it prosper !   The Apprentice—1604.

THE winding of our narrative compels us now to return to Trueman, whom the reader may, perchance, recollect had arrived at Edinburgh, for the purpose of securing some papers necessary to further an extensive mercantile speculation in which his employer, Mr. Thorogood, was at that time engaged. In aid of this, he found the letters of introduction which Fuller had given him peculiarly serviceable. They gained him access to the first circles of society in the Scotch capital, and rendered his task much easier of accomplishment than it otherwise would have been, deprived of his unknown relative's assistance. Ignorant of his noble parentage, and believing himself to be only the poor widow's son, Trueman looked upon Clara, whom he still loved with all his former ardour, as a being far beyond him in birth, and regarded his ultimate union with her as chimera which it was his duty to dispel rather than encourage.

In this he was, to a certain extent, successful. He had so tutored his mind to obey the dictates of his reason, that he had taught himself, if not to overcome his love, at least to expect no fruition of his wishes. The object of his journey to the North being now gained, he set out on his return homeward, anxious again to behold the fair Clara, and learn whether any prospect of a union with Sir Robert Otway still existed. Leaving with infinite regret a city where he had been so welcomely received and so hospitably entertained, he once more crossed the borders ; and, ere five days had elapsed since his departure from Scotland, found himself within a few hours' journey from the metropolis. As he passed the Seven Bells at Hampstead, he could not repress an anxious desire to behold again Alice, who could, as he thought, furnish him with some particulars, which it might be his interest to know. Accordingly, reining in his steed, as he passed the rural hostelry, he entered ; but to his infinite surprise and disappointment, beheld the place of Alice supplied by a person whom he did not know, and had not previously seen. This was Cicely, who, after the violent death of her aunt, Mrs. Tabitha Royster, had taken possession of the tavern and the various appurtenances thereunto belonging. From her he learned that Alice had been accused of the murder and ultimately declared innocent; but, of Sir Robert Otway, beyond the knowledge that his schemes had been frustrated, he could obtain no information.

He was, accordingly, about to leave the house, when Cicely, informing him that there was a visitor upstairs who, seeing him enter, wished to have a few minutes' conversation with him, he retraced his steps, and returned to an apartment in the inn to which he desired the person to be shown.

He had not to wait long, ere Mr. Hugh Clinton —for he was the inquirer—made his appearance. Being suspended from the exercise of his magistratal functions, his demeanour was more deferential that when we last introduced him to the reader as signing the warrant for Alice's committal; and bowing humbly to the astonished traveller, he begged to know if he had the honour of addressing Mr. Trueman, of the firm of Thorogood and Company?

"I certainly have the honour of acting for Mr. Thorogood, and bearing the name of Trueman," said he, smiling at the ceremony of the self-introduction; "but, to what cause I am indebted for your visit, I have yet to learn."

"You shall soon know it, most honoured Sir," returned the other: "my name is Clinton, until recently holding the office of magistrate in this county, but now an humble limb of the law. I recognised you by the description given me, and have expected your arrival for some days."

Trueman bowed in acknowledgment of the compliment.

"Edmund Otway, the brother of the late Sir Robert, desired me to see you without delay."

"The late Sir Robert!" emphasised Trueman; "Is the Baronet then no longer alive?"

"Alas! no! sir," replied Clinton; "he was burnt to death in his mansion at Marylebone some time since."

"'Tis strange," meditated Trueman to himself, "that he should be thus punished for his vices. But who is this brother of his? I was ignorant of the Baronet having so near a relative."

"These despatches that I convey may perhaps explain," said Clinton; handing, as he spoke, a sealed envelope.

From these Trueman learned the particulars of Sir Robert's death, and the departure of Colonel Travers and Alice to Lichfield; with this was coupled a request that Trueman would hasten to London without delay, and an intimation that he might prepare himself for intelligence of a somewhat surprising nature. The letter was signed "Fuller, the late astrologer, now Edmund Otway, the Baronet's brother."

"And how did you come into possession of these?" inquired Trueman.

"Why, I have had the honour of being the legal adviser to the house of Otway for some time," replied Clinton, "and if I mistake not in that capacity, I shall be still able to serve you, most honoured sir. Mr. Otway gave this packet to me in London, with a strict injunction to await your arrival on this road."

"Then you must be fatigued with the delay. A glass of wine I trust would not be found objectionable?"

"Far from it;" at once replied the other; and in another moment a bottle of sherry made its appearance on the table, which was in due time succeeded by another.

"And, may I ask who is the inheritor of the Otway estates?" inquired Trueman; finding that under the influence of the wine his companion was becoming communicative.

"That is not yet exactly known," returned Clinton, leaning mysteriously across the table, as if anxious that what he said should not reach the ears of a chance listener.

"Is there any mystery in the affair?"

"Hum! no, not exactly. The estates are good however, and not encumbered. There are some broad lands and fine pastures, that will be valuable to the heir."

"And he is—"

"A young man, who has at present no idea of the good fortune in store for him; but who he is, or what he is, I have yet to learn."

"You were saying," continued Trueman, "that you had some further intelligence to communicate; does it bear reference to this?"

"Oh! dear no!—to yourself. You have had a narrow escape of being murdered, or, at least, robbed," said Clinton, "near St. Alban's."

"Indeed!" responded Trueman. "How?"

"You remember the old tavern where you slept near there?"

"Perfectly!"

"And encountering one whom you supposed to be an inhabitant of the world of spirits?"

"I do remember this indeed, for it made an impression on me which is not even now effaced; but how came you to be aware of this?"

"By the confession of a criminal, Mark Haydon, that passed through my hands, in which he states that knowing you had a considerable sum of money in your possession, he followed you to the inn, and aware of the existence of many subterraneous passages in the old mansion, he availed himself of one of these for the purpose of gaining access to your room."

"In which he succeeded. But why was I conducted so far from my apartment, when there he might have accomplished his errand?"

"The noise of footsteps," pursued Clinton, "alarmed him, and he was compelled to retreat; beckoning you, however, to follow him, which I believe you did."

"But his mysterious disappearance——"

"Was caused by a fear of discovery. The sliding pannel was still open in your room, and might—had any one have entered—led to detection. The attempt was to have been renewed on the following night, when it would doubtless have been successful, had not your hasty departure on the following morning thwarted the plan."

Trueman smiling with remembrance of the fears to which that visitation had given rise, now that the mystery was explained, gave way to an ebullition of laughter. So contrary are the emotions that may proceed from the same source!

It was now verging towards night-fall; and being anxious to reach London without delay, Trueman thanked Clinton for the attention he had displayed, and proffering a remuneration, which was, however, somewhat lothfully accepted, he threw himself on the back of his steed, and in another hour was at his employer's house. Mr. Thorogood welcomed his return most warmly; and Clara, if the heaving bosom and flushed cheek that his presence inspired might have been taken as criterions, did also not regret his arrival. Barnwell was not there to receive him, being, as usual, neglecting his business for the society of Milwood, and spending in reckless debauchery the money his employer had so laboriously earned. On presenting to Mr. Thorogood the papers which he had so anxiously wished to obtain, his gratitude knew no bounds, and he at once embraced Trueman as his friend and partner. Clara reading in her father's eyes the language of his heart, also thanked him for the means he had given them of maintaing in the City their former importance, and begging his acceptance of a gold chain, as a token of their regard, the blushing girl expressed a hope that as he wore it, it might recall her to his remembrance.

"And now," said Mr. Thorogood, "name what you demand for the services you have done me?"

Trueman hesitated. His heart told him what he would wish to say, but his lips refused it utterance.

"If none else can name the wished-for boon, be mine the task," exclaimed a voice near him.

Turning round, Trueman's eyes fell upon Edmund Fuller.

"Aye," continued the new-comer, "it is this—the hand of Clara, the merchant's daughter!"

"And willingly is it granted," replied Mr. Thorogood: "take her; and may she make you as excellent a wife as she has me a daughter!"

"How!" exclaimed the bewildered youth; "is it possible that so wealthy a merchant can think of wedding his child to one nearly if not quite penniless?"

"Virtue alone confers riches," said the merchant; "if, indeed you had nought else to recommend you, your worth would have been of itself sufficient to have interested me on your side, but you are even better endowed by Fortune. Yes! Trueman, I have heard from Mr. Edmund Otway here your whole history. I have known how you have smothered that passion in your breast which you thought would have been inimical to your employer's interest to openly avow. I have seen both you and Clara checking the purest impulses of Love, surrendering yourselves at once to the sterner dictates of duty; and thus have you reaped your reward. Take her—may you be happy; and now that I see you have somewhat recovered from your surprise, allow me to congratulate you on your accession to the Otway estates."

"Yes!" said Fuller, finding Trueman incapable, through astonishment at the new dignity that had fallen upon him, of returning an answer; "it is, indeed, as the merchant says. In you I behold the son of Sir Robert Otway—in me you behold your uncle."

Surprise, pleasure, and gratification was visible in the faces of all present.

CHAPTER XXXII.

THE BROKEN HEART.

Amidea.—I shall be married shortly.
Pisanio.—Aye! To whom?
Amidea.—To one whom you have all heard talk of,
Your fathers knew him well! one who will never
Give cause I should suspect him to forsake me!
A constant lover, one whose lips though cold
Distil chaste kisses: though our bridal bed
Be not adorned with roses, 'twill be green:
We shall have virgin laurel, cypress, yew,
To make us garlands: though no pine do burn,
Our nuptial shall have torches, and our chamber
Shall be hewn out of marble, where we'll sleep
Free from all care for ever. DEATH, my lord,
Shall be my husband.
                    Shirley's Traitor, 1633.

THE hours of Alice were now numbered. Day by day she grew worse, instead of better, and sleep, instead of alleviating her anguish, only brought her visions that racked her mind and refreshed not the body. Her father, as may be conjectured, saw the approaching demise of his daughter with the heartrending conviction that her recovery was now impossible, and as he beheld her sinking into the grave, with the impress of the Destroyer branded on her heart, the knowledge that she was fast departing whom he had fondly hoped would have been the solace of his old age, rived his mind in twain, and seemed likely to render him a fit companion to accompany her in a long dark journey she was about to undertake.

"And is there no Hope?" inquired Colonel Travers of the physician, as he left the apartment in which his patient was.

"I grieve to say it, Sir; none!" was the response; "she may linger a few days longer, but medicine has no more power over her."

"Poor girl!" ejaculated the sorrow-stricken parent; "with thee departs all that makes my life endurable. Thy poor mother is happily not alive to see thee perish, but thou—her very counterpart—whom Heaven apparently sent to modify my grief for her loss—thou to be taken away, when I require thy presence most, almost induces me to arraign the justice of the High One, and anticipate by violence my own dark doom."

"Take comfort, Sir," cried the physician, much moved by the grief of the Colonel; "rely on it, that wise Power that ordains all for the best will not desert you now. Your daughter may be spared by this a life of wretched misery. Better is it that she should bid adieu to the earth thus early than pass on it many years of care and sorrow."

"Thou sayest truly, Gardner, and I should not murmur at the fate that awaits her, but bear it all with resignation. I will so bear it, and by this show that I am not unmindful of the Scriptures' holy precepts. But, Heaven knows the task is a difficult one! I have seen, unmoved, on the field of battle the bullet whirl past me, untouched, and lay low my next comrade; I have looked on Death then with apathy; but now, to see her whom I loved so much, die without being able to make one effort to preserve her, tears my heart in pieces, and unnerves me more than all."

As this was said, tears flowed in torrents from his eyes, and he sank exhausted by grief and the violence of contending emotions into a chair beside him. The physician, knowing well that where sorrow becomes thus great, sympathy in another

would be useless, if not impertinent, withdrew from his presence; and left the heart-riven officer in the solitude of his sadness.

Alice, at her own wish, had been removed from her apartment above to the drawing-room, where, reposing on a couch at the open window, she might feel the fresh air of heaven kissing her pallid cheeks, and sun her eyes in the prospect which the raised casement revealed. It was truly a sight to cheer and soothe the mind of an invalid.

" Is not this, my father, a noble scene?" cried Alice with enthusiasm, as, reposing on one arm, she gazed with beaming eyes upon her weeping parent, who was bending over her.

" A scene, my child," responded he, " that I trust you will yet behold often repeated. Trust me," he continued, though the trembling accents in which he spoke displayed his consciousness of the vanity of his wishes, " thou wilt be happy still with me for many years to come."

" Nay, my dear father, not so," breathed the dying girl. This is the last sunset on which I shall ever gaze, and death presents to me no aspect of such terror, that I should fear to die."

The Colonel would have spoken, but tears choked his utterance."

" Nay, weep not, my father, you see I shed no tear. Nay, nay, weep not, or mine own tears will fall in spite of me. Remember me to poor Luke Martyn," pursued Alice, in a feebler tone, and should you, perchance, see George, tell him that I love him still, aye, even to death, though the vow he breathed upon his father's grave he causelessly has broken. Give him—" and here the words seemed to linger on her lips—" this ring; it will serve, perhaps, to remind him of me when I am no longer a sojourner upon earth, and with it say that my last prayer was for his happiness. And now good night, my father, my eyes grow heavy, and my pulse beats languidly. I would seek repose; blessed visions of happiness hover around me now. Once more good night, good night, dear father, Heaven bless you."

Overcome by his feelings, Colonel Travers

imprinted a fond parental kiss upon her feverish forehead; and seeing that Alice was disposed to slumber, averted his eyes from the couch, and gazed upon the beauteous prospect before him, that he might not disturb what he fondly trusted would be a refreshing and beneficial sleep.

The dew—those tears shed by Heaven over the face of the declining day—fell lightly on the earth, but not more lightly than the Colonel removed the veil that shrouded the features of Alice, to gaze upon his child. She was asleep. Her pale and intellectual countenance was rendered still more expressive by a partial smile that had died away upon her lips as she fell into slumber, and gave guerdon of the cheerful spirit that animated her soul. Her stillness—fit type of the approaching change—was at first unobserved by her father, save as that absence of motion that a deep sleep always brings with it; but finding her respirations growing less frequent, until at last they ceased altogether, he became agitated and bewildered. The features still assumed an appearance of placidity, though it was of that immovable kind that sculptors impart to their creations. But as the Colonel was wavering between hope and fear, Alice breathed.

It was no usual respiration. Such a sigh smote terror to his heart. It was prolonged and deep, seemingly borne down by the weight of a dying prayer to Heaven—and no wonder; for *with that sigh the soul of Alice had departed to another world.*

CHAPTER XXXIII.

THE PROPOSITION.

This is a sorry mode of spending time ;
We should be chary of our minutes here,
And, like a prudent husbandman, lay by
A thrifty portion for our use hereafter,
Not waste them in debauchery and vice.
Bah ! my heart aches to think on't.
                    A Mad World, My Masters—1681.

We should but fatigue and disgust the reader, were we to recount the many scenes of dissipation into which Barnwell—no longer in his noviciate of vice—now plunged. Let it suffice to say, that gambling and drinking formed his nightly occupation, and coming in contact with the very dregs of society, his manners were no longer those of the unsophisticated country youth, but had degenerated into the effrontery and ruffianism of the town brawler and the tavern bully. We purposely pass over the narration of such scenes of vicious folly, which would not tend to the interest or amusement of the reader, and come now to the most important event of Barnwell's career—that stamped an indelible stigma on his name, and added to his other titles of infamy that of MURDERER.

Summer had long since faded into Autumn, and Autumn had now nearly in its turn given way to Winter, when two figures might have been seen shadowed against the coloured blinds of Milwood's dwelling, apparently in deep and earnest conversation.

The two shadows were those of Milwood and Vavasour.

"Come," said Milwood, passing, as she spoke, a cup of wine towards her companion, "you don't drink! What ails thee, man? Thou art a goodly gallant truly to sit there and mope, when a woman is thy boon companion."

"I was thinking," returned Vavasour, "how we could most easily replenish our purses. The gaming table has been but an unprofitable field to me of late, and your extravagance has, I wot, scarcely left you richer than myself."

"So far you are correct; but my banker will be here, I expect, shortly, with a supply; and then "——

"Your banker!"

"Aye, the merchant's apprentice, Barnwell. It is near his wonted hour, and I told him he must not expect to see me in good humour unless he brought with him a few of his employer's gold pieces."

"Then I must depart. Since I plucked him at the City hell, he may not possibly have considered my presence as agreeable; so fair decoyer of human pigeons, I most humbly take my leave."

"Well, success go with you, and when you return you may expect to hear of my good fortune, till then farewell."

And throwing the folds of his roquelaire more gracefully around him, and depositing a military cap somewhat jauntily on his head, Vavasour departed.

"A vanity-stricken coxcomb!" muttered Milwood, as she watched him ambling down the street; "I to supply the outgoings of his purse, a likely thing, i'faith! but here comes Barnwell, with no empty hands, I'll warrant me."

"My dear George," exclaimed she, rising to meet him, "I have been anxiously awaiting your coming. It is cruel of you to make me wait so long in vain. But you look sad and downcast."

"I am vexed, much vexed, Eleanor," replied our hero; "my associate, Trueman, has returned, is married to my employer's daughter; whilst I—but let me not think of that—to morrow the account-books will be examined, my delinquencies will be known, and then a dreadful punishment awaits me."

"But is there no method of avoiding this crisis?"

"None! Flight will only corroborate my guilt, and, alas! without it I have no means of restoring to my employer's coffers that money of which I have robbed him; yes, *robbed!* though the word seems to stifle my utterance."

"But calm yourself, George, a mode may still be found."

"How?"

"You have an uncle."

"True; but I have written to him—suppressing, of course, the real cause of my pecuniary embarrassments, and he has refused to grant me any further loan, until I assign a pretext for asking it."

"But he is rich; you are poor. He is old, and will not live to enjoy the wealth he has created; you are young, and require its aid. Another year, and he will, most probably, cease to exist; surely there can be but little harm in depriving him of that year."

"I do not understand you," stammered Barnwell.

"Indeed! you used not to be so dull of comprehension. When happiness and riches are the stakes for which we play, we should not be too scrupulous as to the means by which we gain them."

"You would, then, persuade me to rob my uncle?"

"Nay, not rob; it is no robbery to take one's own. The riches of your uncle will be yours after his death; as I have said, he has not long to live, but your exigencies forbid you waiting for his decease. Where, then, is the arm of depriving him of those few months which would only be a burden to him, and hindrance to you."

"Eleanor!" cried Barnwell, vehemently; "you surely cannot mean that I should murder him? No! no! I have not heard aright; I have been dreaming; my brain is wandering, and conjuring up a hundred vivid fantasies. You surely cannot, do not, mean that I should murder. Faugh! the word chokes me."

"You are choice, methinks, in your names. I should style it, rather, a recipocal obligation. What pleasure can there be for an old man that he would live to enjoy?"

Milwood saw that she had a difficult game to play; but she had gone too far to recede. She knew that a desperate effort must be made, and that this was the time; so, changing, like an experienced politician, her tactics, she took the 'vantage ground of the question, and thus replied:—

"George! you, who have known me so long, and under such circumstances, should be the last to doubt my sincerity. What I have said, has been another proof (if any such were needed) of the fervent—the devoted love I bear you. In advising you, I have considered not my own feelings, but your welfare. I have been actuated, as Heaven is my witness, alone by the best and purest motives. I could not, George, bear to see you disgraced; to hear your name linked with infamy; and you, the only being I have ever loved, pointed at by the finger of scorn, as a mark for every gossip to carp and sneer at. Each word that spoke your shame would be a dagger to my heart. What, then, have I urged? That which appears the only method of rescuing yourself from disgrace. The deed is done, you replace the money: and who need know the way in which it was accomplished?"

"Oh, Eleanor! you madden me," cried Barnwell, furiously; "you have waked a demon in my breast that gnaws my vitals. Each word you utter sears my brain like fire. What! what shall I do?"

Milwood saw the advantage she had gained. Barnwell was wavering; and knowing that the stoutest oak will fall by renewed applications of the axe, she hesitated not to strike another blow. The blow was successful.

"George! I implore—I beseech you," cried she, dropping on her knees, and giving vent to a burst of tears, "not to allow this, the only opportunity you have of benefitting yourself, pass away without a struggle, at all events, to place yourself beyond the reach of unmerited exposure. For your own sake—for *mine*, comply with my request."

"Eleanor! my resolution is shaken. I am urged onward to the damning act by some inward impulse, that I know not how to account for. Yet, let us postpone it until another day, at least."

"And by that means render it useless," interrupted Milwood, who well knew that delay would but hinder the fulfilment of her wish, and give her victim's better principles an opportunity of again asserting their supremacy. "No, George, the blow must be struck this night, or never. To-morrow your defalcations will be made known—your past conduct will be manifest: it is now nightfall, and I shall expect your return in a few hours. In the meantime take this pistol; it will ensure a speedier death, and be the least likely to lead to discovery. You can use it without being observed; and life will be gone without the pang that usually accompanies its departure. I would be most merciful, you see, even in my gloomiest mood."

"Oh, torture!" ejaculated Barnwell, "my brain's on fire; my limbs refuse to do their office, my throat's parched, and———"

"Here," cried Milwood, pouring out, as she spoke, a tumbler-full of brandy, "take this—it will steady your nerves; and, mind, no wavering now—no act of irressolution, or we are lost—lost for ever!"

Barnwell drank the proffered draught at once; and, maddened by its potency, now, with eyes, that gleamed with fire, and features that seemed o'erspread with ashy paleness, seized the pistol, and, darting a look of inexpressible anguish at Milwood, rushed like a maniac from the house.

"Ha, ha, ha!" laughed Milwood, as she watched his receding form beneath the lamps, "whichever way you may choose to act now, fond, lovesick youth, your destruction and my welfare is certain. If the murder is committed, why I shall have the wealth; if not "—and here a sarcastic smile played on her lips—" thy doom is sure, and I am quit of thee, without further trouble. Either way, I am safe."

And, applying a glass of wine to her lips, she took up a book, which she had laid down previous to Vavasour's entrance, and continued its perusal, without betraying the slightest symptom of agitation. In such unenviable apathy we leave her, to follow the steps of our unfortunate hero, who was fast proceeding towards his uncle's residence at Camberwell.

CHAPTER XXXIV.

THE MURDER.

Between the acting of a dreadful thing,
And the first notion, all the interim is
A fearful fantasm, or hideous dream.
The genius and the mortal instruments
Are then in council, and the state of man,
Like to a little kingdom, suffers then
The nature of an insurrection.   Old Play.

WHEN Barnwell rushed from the apartment in which the scene narrated in the previous chapter took place, and found himself once more in the open air, his senses seemed for a time to have forsaken him. His wild demeanour, dishevelled air, and contorted features, the darkness of the night—for it *was* night—allowed to be passed unnoticed. For some days before, the weather had been exceedingly sultry. Not a breath of wind had fanned coolness into the atmosphere, and a stifling vapour had settled over London that, formed of the accumulated clouds of smoke that had risen beyond the houses, hung like a funeral pall over the site of our mighty city. Many were the conjectures to which this had given rise. Some—and these were the majority—foreboded a return of the great Plague; others, and these were the enthusiasts, predicted the near approach of the termination of the world; whilst some—and these were right in their surmises—foretold the inhabitants that an earthquake was not far distant.

This earthquake was the precursor of that which, twenty years afterwards, filled the churches with trembling and prayers," and sent millions into Hyde Park, and the fields thereunto adjacent, to listen to the ministry of Whitfield, and derive consolation from the discourses of his fellow-labourers in the theological vineyard.

The night previous to the one on which our hero departed on his murderous mission, a few faint shocks had been felt. First at Hammersmith, then a meagre hamlet, containing scarcely a dozen houses; afterwards in Fleet Street, to such an extent, that a few houses tottered from their foundations;

and, lastly, the vibration, apparently proceeding in a south-easterly direction, passed under the bed of the river, and spent its fury upon Rotherhithe, where, according to a chronicler of the period, "a fearful gaping of the earth took place, and swallowed up several low cottages on the marshy ground near the Thames." It was amidst scenes and rumours of this description that Barnwell passed; but he was too intent upon the accomplishment of his own mission to heed them more than slightly. Onwards he went over London Bridge, and down the road leading therefrom, with unabated speed, until he entered the precincts of Camberwell, and neither heeding the fury of the wind, the vivid flashes of the forked lightning, or the approaching sound of the thunder, pursued his way towards the Grove. Stepping on one side, to avoid the intrusive gaze of any unwelcome passenger who might be passing at that hour, he cast his eyes towards the building in which his uncle resided. The old clock of Camberwell church at that instant struck the hour of eleven, and as the sounds of the dying hour were borne away by the gale, a loud peal of thunder shook the heavens, followed by an instantaneous blaze of light, which for a moment illumined the whole hemisphere by its transitory splendour.

Barnwell was for the instant startled by the crash that seemed to tear heaven and earth asunder; but having recovered his self-possession, and, remembering that there was a private path that led to the back of the garden, he hastened towards this with a firmness of step that belied the trembling of his heart. Unfastening a small wicket, he entered a narrow gravel path, that led downwards to the house, dividing a steady avenue of tall poplars, that interlaced their branches so closely together as to shut out all light. Stealthily creeping, like a criminal, towards the open lawn that fronted the house, he beheld a taper glimmer from the opposite room, the windows of which being open, and in a level with the grass-plot, enabled him to obtain a full view of the interior. His uncle was reading, apparently some sacred volume, which ever and anon he would lay on one side, and, burying his face in his hands, busy himself in meditation.

"Oh, Heavens!" thought Barnwell, "I cannot—dare not, murder him thus, whilst so defenceless, and whilst so engaged! 'Tis worse than murder. I stiffen with horror at mine own impiety. What, if I resign my dreadful purpose, and fly this spot? But, whither could I go? *To-morrow!* and my employer's once friendly door will be closed against me, my name stained for ever with a damning crime, and I, an outcast. He now approached the window, but the utterance of a few words from the old man whom he was about to murder suspended his intent. Barnwell here moved aside the branches of the tree behind which he had been concealed, and again made an ineffectual attempt to pull the trigger of the pistol. Startled by the sound, the old man exclaimed in a tremulous voice, as he looked towards the spot:—

"Ha! a robber!"

"Nay, then," cried Barnwell, "there is no resource left," and discharging the pistol as his aged uncle approached, the bullet leaped to his heart; and the heavy groan and fall that ensued, told the marksman how well the aim had been taken.

*   *   *   *

A quarter of an hour had elapsed since what we have above narrated had taken place. Scarcely had the winged messenger Death reached its abiding place in his uncle's heart, ere Barnwell had flown to give him succour. But this, together with accompanying repentance, had arrived too late. Recognizing at a glance the form of his destroyer, the old man wept with sorrow at the discovery; and whilst Barnwell sought to assuage the blood, that flowed in copious torrents from his wound, his last breath was spent in beseeching Heaven to pardon his murderer.

CHAPTER XXXV.

THE BETRAYER.

Oh, who can tell the damning fears of guilt !
How conscience-stricken the whole heart gives way
To fearful phantoms and chimeras dire ;
Sees in each face a reader of its own,
And finds in every breeze that rustles by
An echo of its crime.

The Murderer's Last Crime.—1734.

ANXIOUSLY were the moments counted by Milwood during the absence of Barnwell on his mission of crime. Swift as the lightning thoughts flew across her mind, each raising fears of ultimate discovery and disappointment; and, as each came, visions of torture flitted athwart her eyes,. and damped the pleasure that she anticipated in the contemplation of the event.

"Surely," she soliloquised, "he could not have missed the deed—the plate, too, must be his. What, then, if he implicates me in his guilt? Psha! What care I! he cannot prove it. My course, then, is safe. But should he—Fie! away with all my fears; he comes, the babbling weapon in his hand too. The foolish youth! to bear with him the witness of his crimes. No matter; his booty must be mine. Now, to make free his entrance."

And, unbarring the bolt that secured the door below, Barnwell was admitted, with his hands flushed with blood, and his features blanched by terror.

"Now, then," cried Milwood, "Quick! quick, you are pursued! No! Why, then, this haste, and frightened form?"

"Look *there!*" exclaimed Barnwell, his eyes darting fire from their sockets, and his whole demeanour becoming that of a maniac, "see you there! mark how those eyes glare on me; thinkest thou I could be cool or calm, when those follow me wherever I may go? Hide me, oh! hide me from their scorching gaze."

"Psha!" cried Milwood; "the effects of your heated imagination—no more—come, quick! the money—you have got the keys, of course—he had them doubtless about his person."

"What! thinkest thou I could rob as well as murder? No!" pursued Barnwell. "I saw the bleeding corpse of him I loved lay stretched before my feet—life's tide was ebbing fast—he blessed me —I—the *murderer*—blessed me with his parting breath; and whilst I there leaned over him, prayed forgiveness for the deed. Oh! horror! even the bare remembrance of the act curdles my blood, and makes each nerve shake like an aspen leaf, the sport of every wind."

"Then you have brought me no gold, after all," returned Milwood, in a tone that betrayed much disappointment and vexation. "None!" responded Barnwell; I could not dare to tempt Heaven's vengeance with the commission of another crime."

"Fool! Madman! Dolt! Idiot!" energetically exclaimed Milwood;" and do you think that I am to be your shield to save you from the consequences of a crime like this? That I am to screen you from the results of such an unprofitable murder?"

"Eleanor!" cried Barnwell, "do *you* speak this? Are these the same lips that advised—nay, urged me on to the commission of an act which Heaven forbids, and my nature abhors? Such language is unkind—unlike the being that I loved."

"Nay, no more foolery of love now. 'Tis truly time to speak in tender accents, when your hands are bathed in your uncle's blood—when your soul is stained with your kinsman's murder."

"Milwood, I beseech you to tear not my heart thus. It was you who first taught me what crime was—you who showed me how to rob—you who plunged me into every vice—until that led to murder; and it comes not well from you, who taught me all, to upbraid me now the deed is done!"

"Tush! boy, I cannot save you, even if I would: for see—here come the officers of justice. And screen you from their vengeance I cannot."

Barnwell, apparently dumb-founded by the apathy which Milwood evinced, threw himself into a chair, and resignedly awaited the event.

The persons who had attracted Milwood's notice, now pressing forwards, burst open the door of her dwelling, and rushed up-stairs towards her room. Milwood prepared to meet them with composure, and, suspecting the errand on which they had come, determined to be beforehand with them, in the confession of the act.

"There is the murderer you seek," cried she; "away with him to the punishment which he so richly deserves."

"Murderer!" exclaimed an old gentleman who had led the rest. "Now, Heaven forbid that that should be another crime now added to the list of those I have, alas, just heard of; how, say you, Barnwell, my once trusty confidant and clerk?"

Barnwell, at the sound of the well-known voice, had raised his head; but almost doubting the evidence of his senses, he could not persuade himself that the appearance of his employer was not a delusion.

"My kind master, Mr. Thorogood!" at length exclaimed the youth; "*You* here to witness my disgrace—and Trueman, too! Nay, this is cruel—the hardest task of all."

"Barnwell," continued his employer, "finding you had been absent from your home all night, we came here, upon the advice of one Captain Vavasour, to seek you."

Here Milwood gave a convulsive start, as she muttered to herself the name of "Vavasour!"

"And, learning from him," pursued the merchant, "what line of conduct you had lately followed, hastened hitherto to caution you against the arts of such a woman as the one I now find you with. Another crime than that which I came to tax you, and to pardon, I thought could not be yours. Nay, turn your head not now, but tell me—this rumour of a murder—of which you heard her speak—say 'tis false, and I will bless you. False! aye, as the lips from which the odious falsehood came."

Barnwell would have spoken, but tears and the force of conflicting feelings, for a while choked his utterance.

"The lady you have been so kind in complimenting," cried Milwood, with a sarcastic smile playing on her features, "thanks you for the language you have used, but yet regrets that she cannot verify it. That a murder, and a most barbarous one too, has been committed, all London will soon testify—that the person murdered is your apprentice's uncle at Camberwell, I have good evidence to prove, whilst that HE is the murderer he will not, I think, himself dare to deny."

Barnwell looked at Milwood with astonishment; but she heeded not his glances; and if she shrunk beneath them, the feeling was at all events concealed from those present.

"I strove," continued she "to prevail upon him, by every means that I could think of, to abandon his fiendish purpose, but in vain. He seemed like a madman bent on its commission; and crying, 'Money that must be mine,' rushed from this room last night, and I saw him not until he returned this morning, pale and bloody, as you now see him, to beg me to shield him from the consequences of the damning crime he had committed."

"It cannot be," cried Trueman. "Well do I know my friend whom you malign; and know that he's incapable of such an act as this. Speak, George; refute the base calumniator."

"Alas!" sobbed Barnwell, "it is too true. I am guilty, and I am ready to expiate my crime. Lead me to my fate."

"Unhappy youth!" exclaimed Mr. Thorogood. "I came here with a generous intent, which you have thwarted. My object was to save you, not to punish."

"I triumph, then, at last," exultingly cried Milwood. "I—a woman—one of that sex that ye, the boasted 'lords' of the creation, have styled the *weaker* sex; and yet I triumph! This is my work —mine—ha, ha, ha! mine."

"And dearly you will rue it, Madam," replied an officer of Newgate, who had accompanied the merchant thither. "Here is a warrant, upon which I commit you for robbing a gentleman in the Poultry, about May last, and for which you would then have been taken, had it not have been for the protection of the young man whom you have now ruined."

Milwood, with a scornful glance at the official, sullenly asked to see the document, when, finding it correct, she yielded herself to the custody of the officer, and, in company with the rest, proceeded to Newgate.

CHAPTER XXXVI.

THE PRISON—THE SENTENCE.

This is no woman, master jailor,
But some vile fiend in woman's guise,
I'll warrant me.
*   *   *   *   *   *   *
Poor youth, I pity him,
Aye, from the very bottom of my heart.
                    The Maid's Revenge, by Shirley.

A FEW weeks had elapsed since the events narrated in the last chapter, during which Barnwell and Milwood had been tried and found guilty. However lenient the judges might have been disposed to have been, the crime was one which would not admit of any clemency being shown; and accordingly our hero was sentenced to undergo the last penalty of the law, in obedience to the social precept, that blood demandeth blood.

Incarcerated in a cell, from which the light of day was almost entirely excluded, his meditations were of the most depressing and gloomy kind. Now he thought of the kind relative whom he had murdered; and the bleeding corse seemed still before his eyes. Anon his fancy wandered to the place of his birth, and he thought of the broken-hearted Alice, and his mother, whom he judged it prudent to keep in ignorance of his unhappy fate, lest the sudden shock might kill her. It was now winter; and as he recalled the bright hopes and fond anticipations with which his journey to London had that time twelvemonth been accompanied, his heart sunk within him, and his whole frame shook with horror at the contemplation of the destiny which was soon to be his. In conformity with the prison regulations of that day—afterwards much improved by the exertions of the philanthropic Howard—all clothing, save a meagre garment, which was scarcely sufficient to cover the body, was denied him; and he suffered as much from the bodily effects of cold, as from the burning fever that was raging in his brain. A pitcher of water had been placed on a stool at his bedside, but it served not to quench his burning thirst; and as the few faint rays of light streamed through the iron bars, on to the miserable straw couch on which he lay, they lit up a countenance where misery and despair seemed to have done their worst.

Mr. Thorogood and Trueman had often visited him in his cell; but their consolation afforded him but little relief. It seemed to stab his heart afresh to speak of former times; and this in their topics of conversation was therefore studiously avoided. From them he obtained a full insight into Milwood's true character. He drew at once the difference between the golden idol he had worshipped, and the earthly figure that was hid beneath.

As for Milwood, beyond a temporary regret that she should have so far committed herself as to hazard, as she had done, her imprisonment and consequent transportation for life, which was what the court awarded her, she experienced none of the rigours of the law that Barnwell did, and consequently her reflections were not of so gloomy a nature. Her chief consolation was derived from the triumph of woman's deceit over man's sincerity. Her object had been accomplished, and she cared not for more. At her last interview with Barnwell, he had upbraided her for the heartless hypocrisy with which she had acted towards him, and taxed her with having ungenerously connived to plunder him. This she denied, alleging that the deceit she had used was for his benefit, and maintained alone to ensure his happiness; as she knew that her real indifference towards him becoming known, would have, perhaps, a serious effect upon him. Vavasour—to whose jealousy of Barnwell the merchant was indebted for his timely discovery—Milwood affected to view with the most thorough contempt. His cheateries and frauds were, however, not suffered to go unpunished; for, upon information given by Milwood, the affair at the City Hell was made known, and, upon being tried, he was sentenced to the pillory for having practised illegal games of chance. Thus did she plan revenge for all who had thwarted her in her career, and in all was she instigated by one all-powerful, one ruling passion—that passion was the Love of Vengeance.

CHAPTER XXXVII.

THE INTERVIEW.

Stay thy rash hand, I pray thee, impious man,
Nor dare rush into thy Creator's presence
With crimes like thine, unhallowed and unpardoned.
Think what it is to die, and be a blank—
A blot upon the human page of life.
Without a mother's sigh to waft thee home,
Or friend to smoothe thy pillow into ease.
Thou canst not—dare not die.
        Drahcnalb, the Death-Doomed. 1754.

WHEN the essence of immortality—that ethereal spirit of whose nature or abiding place we know nought, but of the possession of which we feel certain—was first breathed into a mortal form, it was intended, doubtless, as a heavenly companion to accompany us through the hills and dales of life's pilgrimage, whilst the body remained on earth, and to ensure us that kind of purely intellectual happiness hereafter which would constitute an existence of the most perfect bliss that the mind of man is capable of imagining. Rashly, then, to stop the flow of that vital current, or hurry that spirit prematurely into another state of being, must be an act which is fraught with the most direful injury to our future happiness, and which, may perhaps bring with it—for reason and analogy both teach us so to suppose—the *annihilation of the soul* itself. Surely then suicide must stand foremost in the list of crimes which man's frail nature is capable of committing. Murder may be followed by the just death of the murderer, but suicide, *the only crime on earth without a punishment*, must meet with a more dreadful retribution hereafter.

So thought Barnwell. In consequence of the inflamed and dangerous state of a wound, which he had given himself by means of a rusty nail found by him in the cell and ground to a sharp point, the justices had awarded him a brief respite from his sentence till the surgeon pronounced him in a fit state to undergo his doom. The interim was therefore one of intense agony and torture. During his waking moments his past life appeared in all its formidable reality and hideousness present to his view, and when he slept—if his feverish repose be worthy of being called sleep—fearful dreams flitted athwart his couch, making night even more terrible to him than day.

But as he now slept, a brighter and fairer vision passed before his gaze. His fancy flew back to the period of his youth, when Alice, the fond companion of his childhood, used to watch over him as he slept, and bend her beauteous face in sympathy o'er his.

He was in an alcove, where the clematis and the fragrant woodbine interlaced the trellis-work with their clinging tendrils. The day had been a warm and sunny one—one of those genial days of summer to be met with alone in our much-injured climate, where a clear blue and cloudless sky is the canopy spread by heaven above, and a green verdant plain tufted by small flowers is the carpet that Nature spreads for us below. He saw Alice in all her youth and beauty at his side, and begging him not to break his vow. His hat and stick carelessly flung on the green sward, and his handkerchief was placed on a bench beneath, to serve as a pillow for his arm. Happy! happy youth. Well would it have been if the vision had continued; but at the moment that he was on the eve of responding to the earnest protestation of Alice he awoke, in time only to perceive the real nature of the insubstantial vision. And to what reality did he awake! to a cold, loathsome dungeon, dark and dreary, with but a few faint rays of light—fit emblems of his own hopes—streaming into his cell. He saw how justly his abandonment of Alice had been visited on his head; he had, indeed, broken the oath—the sacred tie—that he had made at his father's tomb, and terribly, most terribly, had he been requited.

He was engaged in reflections such as these, when the gaoler arriving, broke in upon his meditations, by announcing to the unhappy youth that a female prisoner, named Eleanor Milwood, having permission from the Governor to see him, was desirous of obtaining an interview.

This was a trial for Barnwell which he was not prepared to undergo. His love, however, for Milwood—for even now he had some—induced him to accede to her proposal. In a few moments afterwards, therefore, the gaoler retired, and, soon after, re-appeared with a woman, who, bursting from the entrance towards our hero, bathed his hand with kisses.

The gaoler retired.

"You have been ill, I hear," cried Milwood, with a tone of sympathy; "so ill as to render your life uncertain. I could not refrain from seeing you, George, even though the inclination upon your part might be the reverse."

"This is kind of you, Eleanor," responded Barnwell, pressing her hand in his—*very* kind. I scarce could have expected it—I will not upbraid you now."

"Alas!" exclaimed Eleanor, "your voice, too, is feeble! your pulse beats languidly, and your hands are feverish. Say what I can do to render you more happy?"

"By telling me," urged Barnwell, with great earnestness, "your motives in urging me on to the commission of these crimes."

"You shall know all, dear George, but not now; I will place a packet in your hands this evening which shall reveal all—aye, every action of my past life; but, indeed! indeed! I am not to blame. It was the deceit and hypocrisy employed at first by your sex that made me practise it in mine."

"I have, then," said Barnwell, dejectedly, "loved a visionary form; whilst the reality was far different."

"That is partly true," responded she; "but whilst imagination creates and embellishes an object by flights of fancy, it receives, as in this instance, no lustre from it. Love is more delighted with that which it bestows, than with that which it finds; and whilst woman bows down to its mandate, man, proud man, revels, in the superiority of his nature, and, like Pygmalion, bows only before his own creation."

"But how," inquired he, "hast thou attained this mastery over our sex, seeing, Eleanor, that you acknowledge their supremacy?"

"That is one of the first studies of our sex," returned Milwood. "It is necessary for our existence to study profoundly the mind of men; not the mind of man in general, but the minds of those men who are around us; those to whom we are subjected, whether by law or by opinion. It is necessary that we learn to penetrate their very sentiments, and the means that we employ to this end are their conversation, actions, looks, and gestures. Man may philosophise better than woman on the human heart, but she will read better than they the hearts of men."

"Unfortunate and sensitive beings!" cried Barnwell; "you expose yourselves with unguarded bosoms to combat with man armed in triple mail. But you, Eleanor, if you had remained under the noble safeguard of virtue, you would have found laws ready to protect you; there your destiny would have met with an invincible support, and you might have been still happy."

"Alas!" replied Milwood, "you know not what you say. We are those who, most susceptible, are the most cruelly punished for any error that we may perchance make. Love is the history of a woman's life—in man it is only an episode. In the one it is a drama—in the other a scene. Reputation, honour, esteem—all depend upon a woman's virtuous conduct; whilst with man the laws of morality seem, in the opinion of the world, to be suspended in their intercourse with women. They may have received services from a woman, and instances of devotion, that would bind indissolubly two friends together, and attach eternal dishonour to him who should the first forget them; but with woman they may free themselves from every tie of gratitude, and attribute all to love, as though that sentiment which is an additional gift could diminish the value of the others.

As Milwood uttered the above speech her form dilated into a majestic consciousness of her own truth-telling powers, and she seemed like one of the ancient Pythonesses of old, delivering the oracles in words of fire. Rhetoric of Nature's teaching hung upon her lips—she was eloquent from the nature of the subject; and as each sentence rolled into audible existence, the enthusiasm and animation that lent fresh blood to the cheek, and renewed lustre to the eye, told how nearly the cause of her sex lay near her heart. And how truly indeed she had spoken, we leave it to the reader to decide.

———

CHAPTER XXXVIII.

THE PACKET.

Life is a current fraught with many windings,
That now will meander calmly on its course
Through moss-gemm'd dells and sunny passages,
And then will burst into a gloomier path,
And mock the rugged rocks with its loud voice.
Just so will life proceed from grave to gay,
From happiness to sorrow, joy to care,
Till Death's wild briers choke the passage up,
And bar its onward progress.
                        The Ladder of Life—1774.

THE intervening hours spent by Barnwell after the departure of Milwood, were passed in deep and earnest reflection. He saw that her mind had been fashioned in a noble mould, but that circumstances had injured the impression. Desirous, therefore, of learning what had influenced her to adopt her present course of life, he anxiously awaited the arrival of the promised packet that was to reveal this to him. Long he was not kept in suspense. Ere night had come, the looked-for communication was placed in his hands, and it was with an eager eye and a beating heart that he broke the seal. On doing so, he read the following narrative, which we have given here at full length, though glanced at before, in order that it may serve as a beacon for others to see and avoid the dangerous shoals and quicksands by which their voyage of existence is environed. In it will be found the true nature of that mighty under-current that so powerfully sways our real motives, and as the history of a life which may, perchance, find its parallel at the present day, we break the seal, and present our readers with the contents of

THE PACKET.

You asked me, George, for a recital of the motives that induced me to incite you on to the commission of those crimes at the very recollection of which your noble heart must shudder. By so doing, the history of my past life becomes so interwoven with that which relates to you, that the narrative would be incomplete without it; and, therefore, if I commence at an earlier period of my existence than might perhaps at first seem in unison with an account of my present state, it is given not so much from a motive to interest you, as to extenuate myself. You, indeed, know me not, if you fancy that I was always as you now have seen me —selfish, arrogant, and deceptive. No! once I was all that virtue could desire, that purity could wish for; but let me not anticipate. I have a dreadful task before me; *that* must be accomplished.

I have often mentioned to you that I claimed France for the place of my birth; and, nursed in that sunny clime where the passions thrive and flourish in all their native wildness, it is scarcely to be wondered at that I should be equally as sensitive to the passion of Love as my countrywomen are acknowledged to be. The spot where I was ushered into this chequered world was a small but exquisitely compact cottage, situated at the conflux of the Rhone and a smaller river, which discharged their crystal streams at the base of the verdant mountain that sheltered us from the bleak winds of the north.

It was a beauteous spot : so beauteous, as to make me, even now, happier for gazing on it, though the image is but fashioned by my fanciful imagination. Our cot was shelved on a projecting ledge of this mountain that I was speaking of, and commanded an ample prospect over the country upon every side; whilst small farm-houses, peeping from behind the groves of maple and acacia trees in which they were embosomed, sent up wreaths of white smoke into the air, as a sign that the habitation of man had been fixed in a region which might have been created for the abode of angels. I will not dwell upon a description of this spot, though it is one that causes my heart to gush forth in rapture as I recall this Paradise to my mind; but, you may imagine that such a scene as this was not lost upon a wild, enthusiastic creature such as I was then.

My father I had never known—he had died before I had come into existence; but my mother I well remember: she was a kind, warm-hearted parent, with an affection for me that seemed to unite in its intensity a mother's love for her first-born with the conjugal devotion that had characterised her attachment to her late husband. To her I was indebted for my early education; and though my infancy was the scene of many an impetuous burst of passion, it cannot be said that it was owing to the want of admonition from my parent; for if words that carried reproaches with them could have had an effect upon a child, I should have been the meekest and quietest of my age. But, haply it was not so. It is true that my mother's lips were foremost in checking my wilfulness and obstinacy, but her actions contradicted her; and I therefore cared but little for the verbal reprimands I received. The fact was, that I was spoiled; and having thus early my own way, a path was opened me then that afterwards disclosed a road of danger and peril. I would linger on a recollection of these early scenes of my girlhood with redoubled pleasure, since a recital of what followed becomes so painful by the contrast; but I have voluntarily pledged myself to the performance of a duty. And this duty must be performed.

I had reached, then, my sixteenth year, when the event occurred that I am going to relate. You must imagine me young and (as they told me) beautiful; susceptible to every tender emotion, and yet ignorant of the full force of Love. I had been the envy of all the fair peasants of the neighbourhood, and the one sought for by all the males. Such a circumstance, then, produced vanity and love of approbation. I felt myself superior in intellect to those by whom I was surrounded, and sought to improve the difference. I was from a child fond of showy and costly attire, and in this did my mother encourage me, little thinking that she was cherishing such a serpent in my bosom. This inordinate love of dress increased from day to day; and by the time that I had thought fit to arrogate to myself the title of a woman, it had reached its full extent. Here was laid the foundation of my pride

One night, as the festival of La Rosiere, when the *paysannes* of the province assemble on the plain to celebrate by moonlight the anniversary of the *Fete of the Flowers*, I had become more than usually wrapped up in the contemplation of myself. I was the observed amongst the observers; and the homage that was paid me served only to fan the flame of vanity that burned within my breast.

The companions of my youth I treated with a cold

disdainful air, that, by mortifying them, increased my own consequence; but there was one—whom I cannot now think of without emotion—that experienced a very different treatment at my hands. This was a young officer, by name Ernest Clairmont, whose manly form and ingenuous countenance immediately attracted my notice. I had then not learned to disguise my real sentiments; and the admiration that had been awakened in my breast, soon found an echo in his own. He stepped forward; asked me to dance; I consented. He spoke to me, and the full, rich tones of his voice fell like music upon my ear. He talked to me of love, and protested unchanging constancy. I heard the words, and was undecided how to act. We had wandered a short distance from the rest, and he repeated the question. I could not say nay to his entreaties; my heart would not let me; but I asked for time to consider of his proposal. He renewed his vows of ardent affection, and we returned to the dancers. He told me had just returned from the military academy at Fontainbleau, and that he was *en route* for Lyons, his native city; but, that I might consider of what he had spoken, he would hire apartments in a cottage adjoining our own. He did so, and the months that followed I look back upon as the brightest spots in my existence. Ernest became my constant companion; we wandered on in solitude, save that the chamois would occasionally bound across our path, and that the nimble marmoset and squirrel would steal upon our privacy.

Our time was mostly occupied by study. Ernest had been in England for many years, and he learned me the language of the country. Succeeding practise has made me a greater proficient in it than in my own; but of that anon. He was my tutor, and never did tutor find a more docile pupil than Clairmont did in me. I loved him for his kindness towards me first, and then a new sentiment impelled me to love him more. This was the interdiction which my mother placed on our interviews. She told me he was inconstant, and I laughed at her fears; a *roué*, and I reproached her. We quarrelled it was our first quarrel, and I felt its full force. Returning to my room, I burst into tears; but it was not that I regretted having given cause for our rencontre; I rather rejoiced in it; but I cried with indignation at hearing him whom I so loved spoken of so vilely. I flew to meet Ernest that night—my attachment inflamed by obstinacy. We met; he earnestly urged me to elope with him—I hesitated; he recalled my mother's threats—I consented. A post-chaise bore us that very evening towards Paris.

The morning's dawn saw us in the capital of France. We chose for our residence a fashionable street in the Fauxbourg St. Antonie. Every luxury that the season could furnish, or money procure, was ours; but still I was not happy. My disobedience at first made me wretched; I thought of the home that I had left behind me; of the mother who was watching for my return in vain; and, as I thought of these things, tears rolled in torrents down my cheeks, and I became, for some time, insensible to the caresses of Ernest. Months rolled away, and the affection of Clairmont began visibly to abate. For a time, however, he concealed his decreasing love, and I was fain to believe the excuses that he made to palliate his conduct. He went out early, and returned home late, and I could see by his care-worn visage, and wildness of demeanour, that those hours which he spent away from home, were passed in evil company. I had thus but little of his society, and my temper and disposition became changed as well. I grew restless and discontented, he morose and sullen; I prayed him to reveal the causes of his misery—he refused; but that night he returned home worse than ever, and, as I fancied at the time, infuriated with wine. Words arose between us, and a severe quarrel was the consequence. The next morning he left me as usual, and I was determined to watch him. As I was on the eve of departing, the servant brought me intelligence that a lady, fashionably attired, was below, and wished to see me. I desired her to be admitted; when, judge of my astonishment when I tell you that I beheld in the person of my visitor—*my mother!*

For awhile I was almost paralysed with surprise; but her kind accents and soothing tones in some measure revived me. She urged me to return; told me that she had spent many anxious weeks in tracing out the place of my residence, but that she had only that day, by accident, been able to succeed. I heard her with calmness, and replied with firmness. I told her that my pride forbad me to retreat; that though I was, as she surmised and as I had good reason to believe, linked to a most notorious gambler, it was my duty to love that gambler; and that therefore I could not leave him. She asked me if I was happy. I could not reply by words; but the same emotion that prevented me from pronouncing two syllables of such a blissful meaning caused me to give vent to my feelings in tears. I fell upon her neck; and, thanking her for the interest she took in my welfare, affirmed my resolution, at the same time, of remaining with him I dared not call, in her hearing, by any other name than husband.

With a sad heart and sorrowful countenance my kind parent withdrew, to call again in the evening, when I might have had more time to consider of her proposal. As she left the house, it seemed as if the last link of the chain of happiness had been severed.

I pressed my hands to my fevered brow—I found them scalded with hot burning tears. Thinking that perchance the fresh air might contribute to revive me, I resumed my original determination, and was once more resolved to discover the cause of Ernest's unhappiness. The task was a difficult one, for the streets of Paris were by me comparatively untrodden; and as for the *locale* of the gambling-houses, I knew them not. Happy would it have been for me if that ignorance had continued!

It was now near nightfall, and the Boulevards and Les Champs Elysées were beginning to attract their usual concourse of idlers. I was far from being able to be a participator in the revelries of the night, being only an unwelcome spectator of them; and therefore, that I might avoid them better, I took the advantage of a small obscure street, that led down towards the Seine and the Pont-Neuf, for the purpose of returning to my own residence—for I began to despair of finding Clairmont. I had got about half-way down the street, when, hearing the sound of voices in dispute, I stopped and listened. The house was a dingy-looking mansion, where the bricks were trembling out at the sides, in defiance of the iron stays that were made to support it; and the windows, dusty and uncleaned, boasted a few yards of tattered muslin, through which a scanty supply of flickering candles were attempting to display their brightness. Being still summer, the windows were thrown open to catch the breeze as it rustled by, and the voices of course were heard much plainer than if the windows had been closed. Amongst them, I could distinguish, with terrible distinctness, the voice of Ernest. He was disputing. The words 'cheat,' 'knave,' and 'liar!' were given and exchanged. The clanging of swords succeeded; and, impelled by a fear for the safety of my lover, I rushed up the tottering staircase into the room above. I saw a *rouge et noir* table in the centre, with the ill-gotten gold of the victims scattered over the floor. Around it were standing the master of the house, his croupier, (known to you as Vavasour), a few other bystanders, and Ernest. The cause of dispute was the money that had been lost by him; and now he stood, with his drawn sword, defying them to bar his egress. A few violent lunges and passes were exchanged between Clairmont and the proprietor of the den, when my arrival fortunately prevented a blow, that Ernest would have received, from taking effect. He turned round, and beheld me at his side, when the reward that I got for my anxiety was only a volley of abusive epithets, and at last a blow! That blow was never forgiven. I returned home—he followed. He called me a traitress: and told me that I was mean enough to be a spy upon his actions. I retorted: reproached him with having so soon forgotten his vows of love to me. He laughed; and owned that they were only assumed at the time to serve his own vile purposes. Of what followed I can but give a very faint description. I fainted; and in such a swoon did I remain all night. When I awoke, I found myself alone. Ernest was gone! Whither, he gave me no clue to ascertain; nor have I ever seen him since. Vavasour called upon me the following day, to proffer me his love. *His* love! Ha, ha! As if such a creature knew the meaning of the passion in its true purity! But I took care to conceal my mortification and resentment, and accepted his offer, of accompanying me to London with something like a show of gratitude; but it was only that one grand object might be fulfilled. It was accomplished, and I at length succeeded. That object was revenge! I rushed that night from my room into the church of St. Ursule, and swore upon the sacred altar of the Saints that I would revenge myself upon the whole sex for the injuries I had received from one. From that time I made man my constant study. I wormed myself into his confidence and sought to gain his love; and in this I was always successful. Dissimulation and duplicity were my handmaids, and faithfully did they serve me. I strove night and day in my new employment, and with each I gained an increase of hypocrisy. My conscience I stifled altogether, that its remonstrances might not check me in the path that I was pursuing. That I might be even more accomplished in my art than seemed at first possible, I sought and gained an introduction to the Stage, knowing that the power of acting would give me a greater influence over my real passions, and, cloaking them beneath a more specious garb, would supply me with a more copious language in which to clothe my ideas, and enable me at the same time to deliver those ideas with greater force. In this I succeeded to a miracle. The first person on whom I tried my powers of blandishment was Oswell. He was an actor, and, therefore, perhaps he seemed more difficult to encounter; but I fed his vanity, and conquered. He was married, and the victory was greater. I desolated his domestic peace, and my triumph was complete.

Such was the way in which I sought to wreak my revenge. Many a shrewd politician, a wise philosopher, and noble Baronet have listened to the voice of the tempter, and fell. I have brought the proudest of them to my feet, and laughed within myself as I did so. A woman has done this, and has gloried in it—for even now, George, I regret not what I have done, if I except that portion of my career that relates to you. Of that do I sincerely repent. Had you not have known me, you might have been happy. Your virtues deserve a better fate, and I would that that fate were yours; but, so far as I am interested in the result, you will bear with you my sincere acknowledgments of the kindness—albeit the mistaken kindness—which you have shown me, and that in your last orisons to heaven, you will not forget that there is one whose remaining portion of life is embittered by a recollection of the injuries she has inflicted undeservedly upon you, is now her earnest prayer. Think, George, that she who has penned these few lines, is more sinned against than sinning, and that, though the world will speak harshly of her when gone, her motives were just when living. She has been deceived, and she deceives; wronged, and she wrongs. But for you, she would have looked back upon her past life without regret; but for her, you would have lived on, happy in bestowing happiness, without reproach. Then now, Barnwell, I have to take my farewell. We shall never see each other again on earth; elsewhere we cannot meet, for the recording angel who has noticed your guilt, will blot out the entry, when your temptations are remembered. For me, I shall suffer as perhaps I deserve to suffer. An outcast from society, life presents nothing more for me to live for. For you, conscious of the natural rectitude of your own heart, Death can present no terrors. Then, like two travellers whose fate impels them to take different roads, we separate. Farewell! and that you may forgive her who has wrought all your present

woe, as you hope yourself to be forgiven, is the last request of the unhappy

HELENE ST. VICTOIRE,
(otherwise Milwood.)
Newgate, December 11, 1724.

The above packet, which had evidently not been written without a struggle, was not read by Barnwell without emotion. He perused its contents with eagerness—he concluded it with regret.

"Here," said he, aloud, as he placed the communication in his vest, "is an instance of how greatly the finest feelings of humanity can be perverted. Here is a noble mind overthrown by the very means that should have ensured its triumph! The vase is now shivered into atoms; but the flowers, dead and faded, are still redolent of their former fragrance."

Nor was he wrong in his supposition. The heart of Milwood had suffered great alteration; but its innate nobleness was not changed. There was still remaining the shadow of its former greatness; and, conscious of that, she felt that repentance was most due to him on whose head the vials of her wrath had been most injuriously poured. True woman, even to the last! Her many faults were rather of the head, than of the heart.

CHAPTER XL.

THE EXECUTION.

The fatal tree is ready for the youth
Whose deeds have hurried him unto his grave.
The executioner is at his post,
And ready to receive his victim.
Peace to his ashes! The Force of Fate—1674.

IN the heart of the metropolis, in close contact with a thronged and busy thoroughfare, stands a building, of which—if the stalwart masses of stone that compose the structure could speak—many a sad and heart-rending tale would be related. Its purpose is the incarceration of criminals—its name is NEWGATE. The most indifferent spectator of the horrid front of this human sepulchre—this stone cemetery of the living—cannot gaze upon it without emotion. as he reflects upon the many hopes and hearts that lie entombed within. Even now its sad and sombre appearance must strike terror into the heart of the beholder; but, when compared with the horrible dungeon that occupied its place at the period of our narrative, the present Newgate is a palace, its gloomiest cell a Paradise. Such have been the changes effected by time!

This was then the place in which our hero was confined. The disorder that had visited others had not left him unscathed.

The time allowed him as a respite had expired, and the following morning he was condemned to die that death which the law of his country had awarded as the punishment for murder.

The interval was passed in solemn meditation and earnest prayer. He resigned himself to his fate, hoping that his faults would be considered as not having emanated from a naturally vicious disposition, but from the force of that temptation to which, since the days of Eve, frail man has been subjected. The greater part of the night was occupied in writing a long, conciliatory letter to his mother, in which he explained the cause of his guilt, and the repentance that had followed. He begged her to overlook his many transgressions, and still acknowledge him as her son; whilst, though he prepared her for the intelligence, he kept the manner of his approaching death a secret from her till it could be kept no longer.

To his former employer also he addressed a few parting words conveyed by letter. He confessed the embezzlement of which he had been guilty, and in a tone of the most sincere contrition sought forgiveness for his crimes. He thanked him for the many kindnesses he had received, and wished that he had been more deserving of them; concluding his epistle with a hope that his fate would serve as a warning for all youths not to trust themselves within the power of temptation, lest they should heedlessly fall victims to it as he had done.

These letters had scarcely been finished, ere the gaoler in attendance entered, accompanied by a person whom Barnwell had no difficulty in recognising at once as his friend Trueman.

The interview was an affecting one. The two who had met together in happier moments could not now be restrained from exhibiting their emotions. Manhood melted into tears; even the sternest heart would have softened at the sight, and it was some time before either could find words to express the violence of their feelings.

Before they did so, a pause—fraught with eloquence from the nature of its very silence—had succeeded.

" I came not to reproach you, Barnwell," cried Trueman; " but, as I thought, to bring you comfort. Alas! I was deceived; for none have I to offer."

" Indeed, my friend," responded Barnwell, " for such I still must style thee, although my crimes have made me undeserving of thy friendship—to see thee is alone a pleasure, though a melancholy one, I must confess. My sense of guilt indeed you cannot know; 'tis what the good and innocent like you cannot conceive; but what I am—and what I have been—should render me an outcast from your sight."

" Nay, not so," said Trueman, in reply; " these are the genuine signs of repentance; the only preparatory—only certain way to everlasting joy. It is for this the faithful minister prepares himself by meditation, devotes himself to prayer, and daily dies that he may live for ever. For this he turns the sacred volume o'er, and spends his life in painful search of truth. The love of riches, and the love of power, he looks upon with just contempt and detestation. He only counts the souls he wins, and makes his highest fame the good he does mankind."

" 'Tis wonderful that words of thine should thus act like a charm to banish all despair; but so it is with these, my friend. Truth, hand in hand with mercy, flow in every sentence, attended with a force and energy divine. I hope, in doubt—yet trembling, I rejoice. I feel my griefs increase—yet, still, my fears give way. Joy and gratitude supply more tears than the horror and anguish of despair had done before."

In conversation such as this, did the night wear away into morning, and when Trueman, with tearful eyes and aching heart, left the cell, the dawn that had already appeared in the eastern horizon seemed as the herald of a beauteous day.

The recent excitement which Barnwell had undergone, caused his wound to break out afresh; and,

faint from the loss of blood, and want of sleep, Death already seemed to have marked him for his own. A further respite was now impossible; that morning was to be his last day of existence.

*　　*　　*　　*　　*

The gray light of a winter's morning was streaming over the blackened chimnies and time-worn housetops of the metropolis, when a busy crowd were collected round the open quadrangle, ready to behold the last offices of the law carried into execution upon the unfortunate victim of mistaken energies, who was now about to expiate, by a dreadful death, the crime he had committed.

The execution, as was customary at this time, was arranged to take place at Tyburn, and hundreds of spectators of the scene were already gathered at the doors of Newgate, ready to behold the melancholy cavalcade proceed on its way down the road.

The bell of St. Sepulchre's had scarcely boomed the matin hour of five, ere the loud noise caused by the unbolting of the heavily barred doors awakened the populace from their lethargy. A general cry was raised that the object of their anxious inquiries was at last amongst them; and looking over the sea of heads, that seemed swayed, like a mighty current, to and fro, the eye discerned a low cart, used by the civic functionaries for that purpose alone, filled by many persons, each of whom had some important part to play in the drama of Death now about to be performed.

Foremost appeared Messrs. Wheeler and Charlton, the sheriffs, who, in their robes of office, were stationed nearest to the horses; then came the Rev. Mr. Colton, the Chaplain of Newgate, whose melancholy duty it was to pour the last exhortation of repentance into the ear of the dying man, and teach him to look up to Heaven for that mercy which his fellow men, in conformance with the law, had denied him whilst on earth; next him was Mr. Woolmer, the Governor of Newgate, whose duty it was to see that the ceremony was conducted in proper form; but by far the most interesting object in the scene was Barnwell, who, with pallid countenance and down-cast eyes, stood erect amongst those around him, his wrists and arms manacled, and legs constrained by strong iron shackles; but his youthful figure still graceful and unbending, and his deportment such as to call forth many a tear, or excite many a word of pity from the myriad-lipped throng who had assembled to witness his death.

A little delay elapsed before all the necessary preliminaries could be arranged, but at last the mighty cavalcade began to move. First a troop of prancing dragoons sallied forth to clear the way; next came a detachment of foot soldiers to keep off the pressure of the mob; following them appeared the vehicle itself drawn by two horses, and which bore the criminal and the functionaries of Justice towards the fatal tree of Tyburn; then another regiment of foot soldiers; and, lastly, came the populace—a huge mob, rending the air with shouts and—though thus early—tokens of drunken revelry, that contrasted strangely with the melancholy catastrophe they had come forth to witness.

Onward they went over Holborn Hill, and down the street from whence it takes its name. The half-drawn curtains and open casements, through which the inhabitants of those houses they passed on the road were endeavouring to gaze upon the procession as it rumbled by, betokened the interest the death of one so young had created in their breasts. The entrance of a flock of cattle into town for awhile stopped their progress; and taking advantage of the pause which ensued, Barnwell turned round to gaze upon the assembled throng. A mass of human faces met his view, none of which he recognised; but extending his vision upwards, he fancied that he saw in the projecting balcony of a house opposite to Fetter Lane the persons of his late employer and Trueman. As his eye rested upon them, their faces were averted, as if to check the feelings to which a recognition under such circumstances would have given rise; but their features were so undelibly stamped upon his recollection, that he could not, he thought, be mistaken, in the supposition that those were familiar to him.

The obstruction having been removed, the cavalcade passed on, and as our hero turned back to gaze upon the road they had taken, he beheld a hand waving a kind adieu in the distance, and a handkerchief, undulated by the passing breeze, bidding him a silent "farewell," that was afterwards raised to the eyes of its owner, to dry the tears which the circumstance above narrated had caused to flow in torrents.

Strange is it that the links of memory should be so mysteriously connected. That act reminded him of his departure on *that very day twelvemonth* from Lichfield, when Alice had taken similar means to give him a parting recognition. The revulsion of his feelings when he contrasted his then ambitious hopes with the present melancholy termination of them, was more than he could bear; and, sinking on to a rough oaken settle that had been provided for his accommodation, he buried his face in his hands, and resigned himself to his fate, in that worst kind of apathy that is the offspring of despair.

They now neared St. Giles's Round-house, and his heart died within him, as he reflected that each step brought him so much nearer to his end. The draught that, pursuant to custom, was proffered him from the "St. Giles's Bowl," as the last refreshment which the criminal was to taste on earth, he took mechanically; but the draught moistened not his parched lips, nor quenched the burning fever that was raging within. He turned from it with a sigh, for it seemed like the voice of some prophet, warning him that his hour had arrived.

They had now entered the Oxford Road. Hedges were bounding the thoroughfare on each side, and ever and anon some tall tree, shorn of its garniture, would extend its gaunt and naked boughs into the air, as if to emblem the life of him who was passing beneath, whose leaves of hope and happiness had died off, one by one, till a decayed and withered trunk was alone remaining.

Another stage of their journey had been passed over, and they at last reached TYBURN. The fatal implements of death were visible in all their hideous reality before him. The triple tree, which knew no change of seasons, which grew not green with Spring, nor yellow with Autumn, was there waiting to receive its victim. The mob gathered like carrion around the spot. There was not an eye unmoistened by a tear; not a heart but that beat responsive to the emotions which swelled the heart of Barnwell. The scaffold was ascended; the cap drawn over the face of the criminal, and, with abated breath and eager gaze, the preparations were watched. Another moment, and the drop had fallen, leaving the warm, yet lifeless, body, swinging to and fro in the air. In that moment, a loud piercing shriek ran through the crowd, and a woman fell senseless at the feet of the bystanders.

A mother had beheld the execution of her son!

CHAPTER XLI.

THE FATAL LEAP.

Oh! who can tell the pangs that rend in twain
A mother's heart, when she beholds that form
To which she's given life and manly vigour,
Stiff in the cold embrace of marble Death?
A mother's love, the purest and the best
That mortals know on earth.
                    The Child of Crime —1723

A CROWD immediately gathered themselves round the unhappy woman. Restoratives were applied, but in vain; and a surgeon that attempted to open an artery, found that the blood—so great had been the shock—had stagnated in her veins. It seemed as if the principle of life had been so imparted from the parent to the child, as to cause the existence of the one to depend upon the other. They had both died at the same moment.

Mrs. Rachel Barnwell—for it was indeed that unhappy woman—had come to town in the hope of learning the cause of her son's not writing. The lumbering waggon had, at her own request, set her down on that spot, from which she intended to cross the Hanover Fields into the City. The immense mass of human beings, however, who had assembled there, detained her, a most unwilling spectator, on the road, and she was constrained for a few minutes to remain. In that interval, the circumstance we have narrated in the previous chapter took place, and the souls of mother and son were both launched on the wide ocean of eternity together.

Thus perished George Barnwell, the victim of his own passions. Had he possessed more firmness and greater control over himself, he would have been a noble and worthy member of the society in which he moved. He had talents which, if rightly applied, would have won for him a high station amongst his fellow creatures; and impulses, which, if rightly directed, would have been to him a beacon that would have pointed out with unerring light, the road to joy and happiness: as it was, the first served only to accelerate his downfall, the last only to mislead him. The moralist points him out as a warning for youth to avoid the temptations that beset him on his path, and the historian relates his melancholy history as that of one whose virtues and vices were so intimately commingled, that it is difficult to discover where the one terminated, or, the other began. In both lights his fate may not be without a lesson. His sun was bright when it rose, and clouded when it set—it is in the power of youth to continue its brightness to the last.

The body after hanging the usual time was consigned, in conformity with the laws of the land, to a grave within the precincts of the prison to which he had been committed. His deceased parent was removed in a hearse to her native place, where, followed by the sympathising mourners of the neighbourhood, who had evinced much respect to her when alive, she was buried in privacy and in quiet.

We must now return to Milwood, against whom Barnwell having refused to give that evidence which would have subjected her to a more condign punishment, but one charge—that of robbery—remained. On this, there being no witnesses forthcoming, she was acquitted, and once more let forth to prey upon society at large. But whether her energies failed her, or that her spirit was really broken, her success was not, as formerly, commensurate with her endeavours. Since her recent incarceration, her health had suffered much, and her beauty with it had undergone sad mutations. Those by whom she had been formerly welcomed, now shunned her. One by one her acquaintances dropped off, and with them vanished her resources. Poverty stared her in the face. She struggled up for some time against her adverse fate, but the increasing difficulties by which she was surrounded, at last overwhelmed her. Sinking under the privations she had undergone, her once noble heart, bowed down by suffering, and her spirit quenched by disappointment, she fell lower and lower in the scale of degradation, until at last the streets became her only home, the cold, stony pavement her only pillow.

It was one black cold night in the depth of winter, when the roads were baked by frost, and the hard, icy surface of the pavement rang back a shrill echo to the unsteady footfal of the casual passenger, that Milwood felt the horrors of her situation to have arrived at a crisis. The heavens were obscured by masses of black clouds that, impelled by a cutting easterly wind, drove huge drops of rain with vehemence on to the earth, and drenched the traveller to the skin. The wind roared in fitful gusts; and the sound, blended with the loud pattering of the rain, fell harshly upon the ear of Milwood. It was such a night as to induce even the well-attired passenger to gird his cloak more closely round him, but for the poor and ill-clad—God help them—it was indeed a night of fearful suffering.

Amongst the latter, there could have been none who felt the severity of the weather more intensely than Milwood. She had passed the two previous nights in the street without food and without sleep, yet suffering severely from the effects of the deprivation of both. Her dress was of the thinnest texture, being the faded remains of one she had worn in her better days, and the warmth of this was scarcely increased by an old black shawl, which, having found some days previously, she had pinned tight round her neck. As she shivered beneath some sheltering door-way, to avoid " the pelting pitiless storm," few would have recognised in the emaciated vagrant before them, the once gay and beauteous Milwood. Her features were wan and pale, her eyes burning fearfully in their fallen sockets, like two livid coals, and her sunken cheeks and weakened frame, told a tale of misery that, if expressed in words, would have wrung sympathy from the heart of a miser.

Beg, she could not—she *would* not. Her mind revolted at such abasement; but by what other means was she to live? All those who had shared her prosperity passed her with a deaf ear turned to her complaints, or contented themselves by honouring her with a nod in the shape of a silent recognition. It was evident she was despised, contemned, LOATHED. Oh, it was a horrible thought! Her past conduct rose in vivid semblance before her. She thought of Barnwell, whom she had injured; of Clairmont who had injured her. She thought of this, and she would have given worlds had the faculty of memory not

remained to torture her with a Pandemonium upon earth.

The sullen reprimand of a watchman forced her from her lurking-place. The rain was still beating down into her face, but the copiousness of its drops were outrivalled by her tears. She hurried onwards through the back-streets and narrow lanes of the city, for what purpose she knew not; but the rapid motion seemed to divert her attention, and give her relief.

It was late; but, from the houses of the more opulent around her, were bursting upon the breeze the jocund sounds of riot and revelry, wine and wassailing. The flickering red light that danced uncouthly on the close-drawn blinds, told of many a blazing fire that was burning bravely within. She turned to the cheerless aspect before her, and shuddered at the contrast.

From the ample kitchens below, rose the savoury steam of baked meats and skilfully fabricated dainties, each hot from the huge oven that flanked the spacious fire-place. How joyfully would she have accepted of the very refuse that was now being thrown to the dog, and have blessed the hand that gave it. She thought of the money she had heedlessly squandered away on a single feast, and again did Milwood shudder at the change.

Still the storm ceased not; she grew faint and languid. Her weakened limbs refused to support her; her head grew dizzy, and she sank on to the step of a door-way, in the last stage of exhaustion. Pressing her cold, clammy hands to her burning brow, she again sought relief in tears. But they came not as before, at her bidding. It seemed as if the very fountain of her sorrow had ceased to flow. Her eye-balls ached with gazing; but they were moistened by no tear. She would gladly have wept, but could not. Her body, too, was growing, with the transit of every moment, more and more enfeebled. She had not tasted food for nearly three days, and a period of apathy and loathing succeeded, which is the natural consequence of the deprivation of sustenance. It was a terrible death to die—that of starvation; and to die that death, too, in the midst of plenty—for, at the very house by which she was sitting, a few bricks, cemented by mortar, were all that separated her from a sumptuous banquet, at which the first merchants in the city were presiding. This rendered death, then, still more terrible. To feel the veins one by one ceasing to ebb or flow; to perceive the pulsations of the heart lessen by degrees, and grow less and less frequent; to know that a season of protracted suffering is yet to be borne, and that, at last, the body, worn and exhausted, is to crumble into dust, almost ere life departs—oh! this was, indeed, agony beyond the power of endurance.

Suddenly a new and daring thought flashed across her brain. She would not die of HUNGER at least —any death were preferable to that, and she seemed, unwittingly, to have adopted the means by which she could release herself from her sufferings.

The place in which she was now seated was situated at the very extremity of Lower Thames Street. Before her extended the arches of old London Bridge. The roaring sound of the waters rushing over the dangerous fall that then existed, and which the increasing loudness of the wind was not able to deaden, seemed to her like cheerful music, changing her gloom into a mood of joyousness.

She rose and hastily hurried down the long flight of stone steps that led to the water-side. The river appeared a black mass at her feet, and the waves dashed in reckless fury over the pebbled beach; but they daunted not the heart of Milwood. She cast a furtive glance around, to see if any casual wanderer was present to give her unwelcome rescue; but all was still, save the torrent that reared its white crest of foam against the time-worn arches, and dashed against the sides. For a moment she hesitated, and *but* one moment. The spirit of Barnwell seemed to beckon her onwards, and the voices of her many victims rang in her ears, and urged her to meet her fate. Throwing her arms wildly above her head, she plunged in, and the loud plash which succeeded revealed the force with which that plunge was made. A few ripples rose to the surface; but the body came not with them, and bruised and battered by contact with the massive stone-work of the arches, the form of Milwood was dashed through the stream that forced its impetuous way beneath the bridge, and at last sank on the opposite side, never to rise again.

A crushed bonnet and shawl picked up by a waterman on the shore of Rotherhithe, was all that remained to tell the fate of the unhappy and mis-guided MILWOOD.

CHAPTER XLII.

THE REWARD OF VIRTUE.

Last scene of all that ends this strange eventful history.
                                         Shakspere.

THE nuptials of Clara and Trueman, which had been postponed in consequence of the unfortunate fate of Barnwell, were now at last arranged to take place; and such merrymaking as this caused, was never heard of before amongst the good citizens of the old London.

It was one fine sunny morning in May, when the birds were twittering a welcome and congratu-lation from every bough, and the clear blue sky was spreading a boundless canopy overhead, that a carriage, built in the true antiquated style, and with the horses decorated with ribands and true lovers' knots, was seen to draw up before the door of Mr. Thorogood's residence, and wait there in all due and proper solemnity. Immediately afterwards several other carriages, all taking their example from the first, rumbled over the pebbled stones of Cheapside, in the same direction, and, forming a long line at the worthy merchant's door, gave war-rant that an affair of some very great importance to those people concerned was on the eve of taking place.

Nor were these who so imagined disappointed in the least, as the event proved; for, in the course of half an hour, several blue coats and black satin unwhisperables were seen to make their appearance from the house, each with a human being inside, which said human being, if one might judge by the air of satisfaction that, settling on their features, curled their lips into roguish smiles, were on very good terms with all the world, themselves included.

Immediately succeeding these, there came a troop of bridesmaids, all heralded by the sound of brocaded satin rustling along the passages, each dressed in white, and looking as amiable and tempt-ing, as the most philanthropic of Epicureans possibly could have desired. Then, the gentlemen whispered peculiarly soft nothings into the ears of the fair bridesmaids, whereat, much giggling and laughter ensued, and the little preparatory cere-mony concluded by the ladies and gentlemen getting, after a very primitive example, two by two into the carriage, and there remaining in exceeding close proximity.

But, last of all came Trueman—for though he succeeded to the Otway estates, we shall continue to call him by that name, which is most familiar to our readers—with Clara, his beauteous bride, hanging on his arm. Never were a pair more equitably matched. Her slight and fragile figure, rounded off into a form of the most exquisite pro-portion, seemed to rest upon his for support, and the crimson flush that suffused her spotless neck and features, was but the tribute she paid to her own maidenly decorum and his worthiness. Behind came the good old merchant himself, his eyes be-dewed with tears, and his aged brow furrowed by care, that had notched also its impress on the heart. He saw that the hope of his old age was now destined to twine round another tree; but he saw also that it was better that it should be thus, and the old man was content.

The line of carriages at last began to move. At first they went but slowly; but, as the houses were changed for hedge-rows, and the chimnies for flowers, the horses merged into a canter, and bore the joyous group gallantly along. The road led up a winding steep, at the summit of which was a small church—evidently the church of the village. Here the carriages stopped—for the ascent was almost too great for the horses to overcome—so the parties engaged rambled on foot up to the top of the hill, and then what a delicious prospect opened to their gaze.

Beyond, blended in the distance with the blue sky that rested on its margin, appeared the sea, its ample bosom spread out as far as the eye could reach, and with its surface studded here and there by a few white sails. Beneath them shelved the chalky cliffs, for which that coast is famous, and rock and valley, lighthouse and beacon, mingled in the prospect on either side. The country in which they were was Sussex, and the little village of Woodcliffe was situated in the very prettiest part it. Here the nuptials had been arranged to have been solemnised; for it was in close proximity with this place that Mr. Thorogood had bought and furnished a pretty little villa adapted to the wants of the new married pair, and where they might spend their honeymoon undisturbed.

But, however, it was not the prospect; but the marriage they came to see about; so, reminding them of this, Mr. Thorogood led them to the church, with its antique porch, and crooked spire peering above the creeping ivy that surrounded it, and finding the clergyman in his cannonicals already there assembled, the ceremony was com-menced without any further delay.

We shall pass over, as ingenious chroniclers are apt to do, all the particulars connected with the event which are unnecessary to be recorded in our pages. How Mr. Thorogood shed tears when he gave the bride away, and how she blushed when she answered with a trembling "yes" to the clergy-man's inquiry as to whether she would take True-man to be her wedded husband, and we shall likewise omit mentioning the circumstance of Trueman joyfully ejaculating the same monosyllable when he was asked whether he would take Clara to be his wedded wife.

The ceremony being concluded, the whole party returned to the carriages, in which they were driven to the villa, where a repast of more than ordinary splendour and delicacy awaited their arrival.

And when they got there, they found that the villa was most admirably chosen, and most deliciously situated, that the air was remarkably provocative of a good appetite, and that the viands and refreshments set before them to gratify that appetite were unquestionably excellent.

As for Mr. Thorogood, he determined to give up all the idea of returning to that busy world in which, by active industry and careful probity, his fortune had been made. A quiet residence he had long wanted, and this he had at last found. His daughter tended him as fondly and as affectionately as ever, and her love, though now divided between Trueman and her father, seemed to increase in intensity, from the very circumstance of its being carried into two seperate and distinct channels.

With Trueman, Clara would wander forth at eve along the sea-shore; when silvered by the young moon, the gentle ripples would break in wavelets of light at their feet, and murmur music of sunnier lands, as they danced joyously onwards. It was then that Trueman would recal the story of their early loves, and point out to Clara how their duty and constancy had been rewarded; and as he pressed her yielding waist closer to his own, he repeated those vows of love, and again swore eternal attachment to her.

Their evenings were thus usually past in rambling through the beautiful scenery of the neighbourhood, or if the weather deprived them of out-door recreation, Clara supplied the vacuum with music. Towards the close of one sultry afternoon in July, when Clara had been engaged in extracting the most delicious harmony from her harp, that stood at hand, the near approach of horses' feet startled them from a reverie into which they had fallen, and their surprise was not diminished, when the servant, announcing that a gentleman was below who wished to speak with Mr. Trueman, Edmund Otway, otherwise Fuller, the astrologer entered the room.

His reception was of the warmest description. Trueman was delighted to renew his acquaintance with his uncle, whose generosity and disinterested conduct had long before won his heart, and begged of him to honour his habitation with a prolonged stay, a request in which Clara and her father most earnestly joined.

Fuller, however, with many apologies, declined the invitation. He had come, he said, from a wish to see his nephew comfortably settled, before he returned to the Continent, whither a vessel was now ready to convey him. He had determined, he said, to pass the remainder of his life in study, and for that purpose he resigned to Trueman all the remaining lands to which he was entitled; and stating that his stipend, derived from the produce of a small estate in France, was more than sufficient to supply his wants, he declined all other aid.

Necessity compelling him to depart with the sunset of that night, Fuller took a hasty farewell of his grateful relative, and those by whom he was surrounded; and shortly afterwards the distant sound of horses' feet was heard rattling over the stony road that led through a wood, down to the sea-shore.

Mr. Thorogood and Trueman watched the receding figure as far as the eye would permit his progress to be traced; and then night coming on, breathed as they returned to the table, a fervent prayer for his safety and convoy across the Channel.

Many letters did they afterwards receive from him, all expressive of the happiness his present secluded home afforded him; and it was many years afterwards that a letter, sealed with black, reached Trueman, from the housekeeper, telling him that his uncle had died, according to his own prediction, on the anniversary of his birthday, and that his last request was, that the funeral should be rigidly private, and that the manuscripts which fell into his nephew's hands should be burned without being read.

All these injunctions were strictly complied with, and the inclinations of Trueman tending little towards astrological knowledge, the destruction of the manuscripts, which were chiefly of that nature, was complied with without a pang.

Years passed away, and at a green old age, surrounded by those whose happiness constituted his, died Mr. Thorogood. He died as the mellow fruit, worn by age and bursting with its own ripeness, falls—without a struggle. His death peopled Heaven with one more good spirit, and left the earth with one good man the less.

In process of time—for Trueman still kept up his intercourse with the great city—the once humble apprentice to the Cheapside merchant, became Lord Mayor, and well did he fill the civic chair. Justice and clemency were blended in all his acts and mandates, and long after youth had passed from him, and manhood had almost merged into age, he was pointed out by the parents to their sons as a worthy model for their imitation.

To Clara, his youngest daughter, who in figure and features as well as in name was the very counterpart of her mother, he would often relate the story of his life, and never did the name of Barnwell escape his lips but it was accompanied with a sigh.

He would show her how the unfortunate youth yielded to temptations which he ought to have overcome; and from that he deduced a moral that warned her to beware of the FIRST STEP in vice—the rest would soon follow. He pointed out the fatality of depending on riches for a title to happiness; the sunshine, said Trueman, lies in the heart, not in the circumstances by which that heart is surrounded, and this he proved from the life and death of his unhappy father, Sir Robert Otway. Milwood, he added, was one of those instances of perverted talents that Nature is too apt to furnish us with. Where we would admire we must abhor; what we would praise we must despise. Barnwell was the victim of his own follies; Milwood the victim of her own passions. The one was too apt to let his impulses run away with him; the other too often checked her purest emotions. The history of both is not without a parallel. In all ages, and in all countries, there have been, and will be, those who will realize too closely the career of Milwood; and, unfortunately, too often do we behold in the ruined prospects of some youth lured by pleasure from the paths of virtue, the semblance of Barnwell.

Let the examples of both be remembered, that the reader may find that he has not spent his time unprofitably, nor the writer occupied his in vain.

THE END.